Nadene LeCheminant

THE
GATES
OF
EDEN

Cottage Street Books
Salem, Oregon

Published 2019. First edition.
Copyright © 2018 by Nadene LeCheminant

ISBN 978-0-9600215-0-5 (paperback)
ISBN 978-0-9600215-1-2 (ebook)
Library of Congress Control Number 2018914146
Printed in the United States of America

Editor: Jane Parnell
Book Jacket: Jennifer Quinlan, Historical Fiction Book Covers
Cover Photo (boots): © Nicola Hanney
Cover Photo (background): © Bashkatov

Cottage Street Books
Salem, Oregon

BOOK CLUB QUESTIONS INCLUDED

For historical images and more information about the book, visit www.NadeneLeCheminant.com.

THIS IS A WORK of fiction inspired by the life of my great-great-grandmother, who converted to the Mormon Church and journeyed from England to the Utah Territory in 1856, pulling a two-wheeled handcart over the Rocky Mountains. Shortly after she arrived, the girl became the polygamous wife of a man almost four decades her senior.

Although my ancestor's story provided my initial inspiration, the primary characters in *The Gates of Eden* are wholly imaginary. The public characters, however, are real; they are directly quoted or abide by generally known facts about their lives and personalities. The novel is based on historical events that took place in Utah during a three-year period beginning in 1856.

The sources for chapter quotations are provided at the end of the book.

PART ONE

Hunger

1

... WE NOW INVITE you to a feast of fat things, to a land that will supply all your wants with reasonable labor; therefore let all who can procure a bit of bread, and one garment on their back ... doubt no longer, but come next year to the place of gathering ...

—"Seventh General Epistle of the Presidency of the Church of Jesus Christ of Latter-day Saints," *The Latter-day Saints' Millennial Star*

Liverpool, England, 1855

At first the neighbors just threw insults, but eventually someone landed an egg on their door, even though eggs were dear that winter.

And it wasn't just the neighbors. Josephine Bell's own brothers hurled taunts as well. Edward, raised a gentleman, forgot his gentlemanly manners and shoved the Bible in their faces, flipping through the pages so roughly he almost tore the family history.

"What do you want with the Mormons?" Edward implored, his voice caught between pleading and fury.

"Edward, our family record! You'll rip the page," his mother Elizabeth remonstrated. "Take care, son. And your father would not be pleased to hear you raising your voice to your mother and sister."

Caught off guard at the mention of his recently deceased father, Edward looked sheepish for a moment, but he soon bore down again. "Your preposterous new religion—*that* is what's ripping our family apart. I would rather see you join any church but that one." He pushed the Bible in their faces again. "This is God's word! Not that rot you got from the missionaries."

"It's fine for you to speak about God's word!" his sister Josephine retorted. "When you and your chums tip the bottle every Saturday night until you can't stand straight."

"Joe Smith was a blackguard," her brother William said earnestly, pushing his spectacles up the bridge of his nose. "I hear the Mormon prophet kept thirty wives, one for each night of the month." He blushed at his own words, obviously not used to speaking so coarsely in front of his mother and sister.

"That will be quite enough," Elizabeth told her sons.

An angry frown crept over Josephine's face. The girl had heard the rumors on the street, but she knew it was best to ignore them. She was decided: The Mormon missionaries were promising a land of plenty across the ocean, and how else was she to change her fate?

And her fate? That was the problem.

Last year Josephine and her mother had started their career at the Dorsett & Company Woolen Mill in the picker room, whose dank stone walls gave the feeling of being entombed alive. The place was so dimly lit it strained their eyes. Some days they ripped buttons from used clothing, recycling dresses and trousers; other days they picked twigs and burrs and even dung from sheep's fleece until their fingers were raw.

After three weeks, mother and daughter had been moved upstairs to join the weavers. A long bank of windows let in streams of light when it wasn't raining outside, but the unheated room was almost as cold as the picker room, and the floor vibrated noisily as shuttles slammed yarn into long rolls of cloth.

Mr. Griggs, a boss with a scowl etched into his forehead, had made it clear when he moved them to the looms. "If you make a mistake, it comes out of your pay. If you lose an arm on your shift and can't do your work properly, you'll be let go, nothing to be done for it."

Josephine tried to concentrate on keeping her arms intact, but her mind was often elsewhere. During the tedious hours from dawn to dusk, she gave herself over to visions of warm scones with clotted cream. Ten hours a day, six days a week, dreaming of beefsteak pie and waiting for the few shillings that were placed ceremoniously in her and Momma's hands each Saturday night. The amount was not enough for them to buy butter more than once every fortnight. And although Josephine stuck wool in her ears to dull the clatter of looms, she still left each day with the cacophony ringing in her eardrums and the noise on the streets outside strangely muffled.

Leaving the mill should have offered freedom, but the walk home was no better. First, the butcher's shop, with its row of rabbit haunches and sausages hanging in the window, and then the confectioner's, its platters of meringues and marzipan making the girl aware of the empty ache in her stomach. The singsong cries of costermongers were so piercing they drowned out the horse hooves on the cobblestones. "Oysters! Sheep's trotters!"

Always—more food! Even the sour stench of night soil on the streets was overpowered by the sweet fragrance of roasting chestnuts.

In the past, Josephine had assigned names to emotions. Sad, happy, impatient, amused. In the last year she had become familiar with another emotion, one strong enough to keep her awake at night: the desperation of hunger.

Each night on the walk home she lifted her skirt over fresh droppings of manure and stole sideways glances at the painted prostitutes huddled near the steps of Saint Nicholas Church. They plied their trade, keeping hunger at bay; their eyes fastened on every male stranger with a mixture of hope and dread. Josephine would pull her cloak tight against the clammy fog and hurry past street urchins selling matches and newspapers. Lads hobbling on crutches; a girl with no arms. Josephine knew they had sacrificed limbs to a machine, making cloth for people who lived in other parts of the great city, or even across the seas. She would look straight ahead, trying to ignore their pleas.

As if I had something to give them, she thought.

In the slums of Liverpool, Josephine was discovering, it seemed to be every person for themselves.

When she and her mother had first broken the news of their decision to be baptized, Edward's face had flushed an angry crimson, and even the normally placid William squinted through his eyeglasses in disbelief. In part, Josephine thought her brothers simply seemed embarrassed. In recent weeks the girl had heard their friends laughing at them.

"Will your ma and little sister be taking a dip in the river?" Edward's oldest friend asked, rubbing his hands with pretended glee, while another friend raised a mug in the doorway of the Stag Ale House and jeered, "Here's to Joe Smith and his gold plates!"

Josephine had heard the Mormon missionaries preach about the golden plates Joseph Smith had dug from the hillside near his home in New York State. The plates were inscribed with stories of bloody battles between ancient American Indian tribes, and they had been collected into scriptures called *The Book of Mormon*. To tell the truth, Josephine herself was a bit uneasy about the origins of the book, but that didn't dampen her resolve.

When one of Edward's friends teased, "Hell, I reckon Will and Ed could go to Utah and get themselves a whole passel of wives," all Josephine heard was the tantalizing word: *Utah*. A land of abundance, the missionaries said, where manna and blessings flowed down from heaven, where no one went hungry.

Now Elizabeth beseeched her sons. "I wish you would allow us the respect to determine our own future." And then, faltering, "Perhaps the missionaries can answer your doubts." She seemed to have lost her characteristic poise in the face of their fierce disparagement.

"Doubts? Well yes, let's talk about doubts," Edward said, his voice high with emotion. His sister was startled; she had never heard him talk back to Momma.

"I don't *doubt* Joe Smith's golden book came from a runaway imagination," said Edward, clenching his fists. "I don't *doubt* he's a charlatan. And I don't doubt this foolishness will lead you to misery."

"Edward, you're the one who's making a mistake," Josephine said, more sharply than she had intended. "Momma and I are going to a better life. There's nothing here for any of us. Surely you can see that."

At that, the younger brother William shrugged and seemed to give up the argument. He still seemed dumbfounded by the family's sudden poverty. A year ago, when their fate had abruptly changed, he and Edward had started at the Dorsett & Company Woolen Mill alongside their mother and sister. One week in, William left for a position at the docks and Edward stormed out in disgust. After a drunken spree that lasted a fortnight, Edward went on to a greengrocer on a backstreet near Albert Dock, and after that disappointment, worked as a compositor at a book press on Cooper Street. Now he was talking of landing a position as a pressman, although no offer had been forthcoming. In the meantime, his chums bought him cheap beer and he wore his gentleman's frock coat and cashmere trousers with care, lest the cloth wear thin before he could afford another set.

Josephine's older sister had taken a different approach. Meaghan seemed torn between sincere curiosity about her sister's new beliefs, fear of where they might lead, and the suspicion her sister had been taken for a fool.

Crusted egg, the same egg thrown by the neighbor, was still on the door when Meaghan visited, and she lugged a pail of water and helped Josephine scrub the wooden panel.

"It's a shame no one's taught them better manners," Meaghan said crossly, in solidarity with her sister. "Not to mention the foolishness of wasting an egg." She took another swipe at the dried yolk.

And then: "Josie?" Meaghan cautiously asked, "Do you think ..." She concentrated on the last streak of egg white.

Josephine bit her lip, and her sister left her sentence hanging. Instead, Meaghan brightly asked, "Are you going to ask me in for tea?" She poured the cleaning water onto the cobblestones, dropped her dirty rag in the pail, and took her sister's arm. "I bet you have some leftover champagne hidden in that pantry of yours."

Of course, there was no champagne, and no pantry either, only a single half-empty shelf, but Josephine set out two slices of bread, a meager pat of butter, and the teapot with the broken spout.

"Scones, dear," Josephine said with perfectly instilled etiquette. "Your favorite." And, "Would you like a glass of champagne with that? This vintage is particularly agreeable." She poured a cup of weak tea and offered the single chair to her sister and sat on the narrow bed—the one where she and Momma slept.

"If only the tea really was champagne!" said Meaghan, taking a sip. She waited a moment before asking again, "Josie? ... Do you think you should slow your decision to get baptized? It's not been very long, and perhaps you've rushed things."

Josephine nervously straightened the folds of her skirt.

"Reverend Phillips preaches as much truth as the Mormon missionaries," Meaghan said. "And I don't see anything in King James that makes mention of American Indians."

"They are Nephites and Lamanites," Josephine clarified, feeling a bit self-conscious. "The two tribes in the *Book of Mormon*." She spread a thin dab of butter, keeping her eyes on the bread. If she looked at her sister, tears would spill over. "I've stayed up nights over this. But I'm—"

I'm hungry, that's what, Josephine thought.

"I can't do this anymore," she said dully. "Bread and potatoes and bread and potatoes, and not enough of them at that. That miserable woolen mill. This flat." She cast her hand around the room. Walls etched with water stains and grime hardened by decades of neglect. A single nail holding their few items of clothing. The window broken, the room drafty. In the alley outside, sewage and heaps of garbage gave off a sickening stench.

"The Mormons offer a new life," Josephine said. "Surely God would want that for me. And I believe in their gospel."

And then she broke the news she had dreaded sharing. "Meaghan? I'm going to go to America. Momma too."

"America!" Meaghan clutched her heart. "Josie. Oh, Josie. You never said anything about that."

"Have some more tea," said Josephine, offering a thin smile and trying to distract her sister.

"I don't want more tea! Josie, what's this about America?"

"The missionaries say in the Utah Territory life will be different—better. With enough to eat. A lot of the Saints are going. The ship leaves—" Josephine swallowed hard. "It leaves in April."

"April! But that's only—oh, Josie." Meaghan knotted her hands. "I understand, I do, but the thought—" Her words tumbled out. "You're leaving? How do you know you'll be safe? And Momma too. And America is so far away. Will we ever see each other again?"

That was Josephine's worst fear, the one that gnawed at her in the middle of the night, but she bravely said, "I think God has opened a door. Don't you see? *Please* see. I think Momma's looking for an open door too. For both of us."

"But you have no money! How will you pay for passage?"

Josephine repeated what she had heard from the missionaries. President Brigham Young, a Vermont carpenter who had taken Joseph Smith's place after the prophet was murdered, was offering loans through his Perpetual Emigrating Fund, loans that would enable the Saints to take passage to the Utah Territory.

"President Young said not to wait, the Church will provide loans," Josephine said.

What she neglected to tell Meaghan was this: Their loan would only go so far; she and Momma would go on foot across the North American continent, pulling a handcart.

The morning of their baptism, Josephine's brothers came to block the door as they tried to leave their flat. Edward spread his arms across the threshold, shouting, "If you let them dunk you in that river, that's the last you'll see of me."

Josephine could smell his beery breath. She pushed angrily past her brother. "Then that's that. We don't need you."

To Josephine's shock, Edward wiped his hands as if he were freeing himself from both of them, and walked out. William pushed up his glasses and looked helplessly at his older brother—he had never been strong-willed and had relied on his brother for cues about how to proceed through life. "I guess it's goodbye then," William said. He tipped his hat, as if politeness could make up for callousness, and with a last timorous glance at Elizabeth, followed his brother.

The November weather was raw, and a squall threatened. Josephine sucked in her breath, looking at the River Mersey. White-caps flashed and the current looked too swift for baptism. Josephine looked at her mother for reassurance, but Momma was wearing a forced smile and didn't seem to notice the scene. Elizabeth hadn't said a word on the long walk there, ever since Edward had stormed out and William had crept out behind him.

"If you're not born of the water and the spirit, you can't enter into the celestial kingdom," said Brother Woodcock, standing at the side of the river. "Baptism is a sign to our Heavenly Father that you have chosen to do his will."

The missionary guided Josephine down the muddy slope, but at the water's edge she stopped mid-step. "I can't." She panicked, stumbled backward. Meaghan was right! This was happening too fast. But Brother Woodcock seemed to anticipate her apprehension, and calmly guided her one step at a time into the current, assuring the girl her sins would be washed away. Her skirt swirled and floated and she pushed it down. He dipped her into the thick brown water, its current tainted with the night soil of Liverpool, and pushed her shoulders beneath the surface. Josephine lost her balance and grabbed his hands. Without thinking, she opened her mouth and drew in a mouthful of icy water. She came up sputtering.

And then it was her mother's turn. Still wearing a rigid smile, Elizabeth waded into the river.

What sins does Momma have? Josephine wondered. *What does she need to wash away?*

The girl couldn't think of a single flaw. Not even an inconsequential one. She winced, thinking of the way she and Meaghan had made a habit of poking fun at Momma's insistence on manners and proper deportment. Now, while Josephine shivered with cold, Brother Woodcock immersed her gentle, gracious mother in the current.

Meaghan had shown up unexpectedly and was watching silently from beneath a willow tree on the bank. She tapped one heel nervously and clenched her hands. As Momma emerged from the water, Josephine noticed that she avoided her older daughter's eyes. When Josephine looked again, Meaghan was gone.

The walk home seemed longer than the walk there. They bent into the wind, which bit at their drenched bodies, and once they arrived the flat was not much warmer than the air outside. Josephine hung her cloak on the nail, scrubbed her hands over the bowl of cold water. She changed into her gingham, pulled two potatoes from the shelf, and took up the knife.

She and Momma were hungry and tired and half frozen, but they had been born of the water and the spirit, and now, Josephine knew, the Promised Land was theirs for the journey.

2

UPON A FIRST introduction to a lady or gentleman, make a slight but gracious inclination of the head and body. ... It is ill-bred to shake hands. If you meet a lady for the second or subsequent times, the hand may be extended in addition to the inclination of the head ... Bow with slow and measured dignity; never hastily. ... Cultivate a soft tone of voice and a courteous mode of expression. It is better to say too little than too much ... modesty of speech, as well as manner, is highly ornamental in a woman.

—*True Politeness: A Hand-Book of Etiquette for Ladies*, written "By An American Lady"

It hadn't always been this way, but once the downfall was underway, its trajectory was swift and damning.

The Bell family hadn't been rich, but they weren't poor either. They didn't live on an alley that smelled like a sewer. Instead, they lived on Middleton Street in a tidy row of red brick houses, most of them belonging to merchants. In front, a cast-iron railing protected Elizabeth's pocket-sized rose garden, and inside, wine-red *fleur-de-lis* wallpaper adorned the parlor, serviceable ornamental rugs covered the floors, and generous windows invited light into the tall-ceilinged rooms.

Papa's establishment, the Bell Apparel Co., also had provided the wherewithal for a series of tutors for Josephine and Meaghan, and in the mornings one could hear the two sisters recite their lessons. English history, grammar, arithmetic, French, and at Momma's insistence, the English poets.

Josephine and Meaghan were quick at their lessons but slow at the needlework that followed. Momma said needlework was "part and parcel of being a lady," and so needlework it was—a dreadful hour of pricked fingers and ineffective protests as they embroidered peacocks and pansies onto samplers, which Elizabeth proudly hung on the stairway walls.

In spite of their mother's best intentions, the sisters shared a decided lack of patience not only with needlework but with the entire edifice of etiquette that dictated the lives of well-bred young ladies. The horsehair petticoats and whalebone corsets were fit to strangle one, they complained—but only to each other—and the afternoon calls on other well-bred young ladies were tedious, the talk plodding along from one dull topic to the next, mostly concerned with inquiring about the other one's health, and the health of their family, including, of course, aunts, uncles, the dear cousins, and anyone who had of late spent a night under the family roof.

Indeed, since childhood the sisters had preferred each other's company. Now Josephine was sixteen and Meaghan two years older, but many people mistook them for twins. They shared fair skin, inquisitive copper-green eyes, and rich cinnamon-colored hair, and they were so small in stature they looked younger than their years.

"God help my daughters!" Papa laughed when he saw them trying to tame their unruly locks into ringlets. "Even their hair is rebellious."

Momma never found out about the worst—and most delicious—improprieties. The afternoons they flung off their shoes and stockings and pulled their skirts and petticoats up to their knees and took turns in the swing that hung from the cherry tree. Down there in the meadow where the road dead-ended, they would swoop through the air, out over the stream, and sing parlor songs in falsetto voices.

Or this: the evenings they impersonated Papa's supper guests. There they would sit, idly perusing *Ladies' Cabinet* magazines while the downstairs parlor voices rose higher and higher, until the windiness of the bewhiskered, half-sauced men was too much to resist.

"Indeed." Meaghan would stroke her imaginary beard and lower her voice. "I do consider his politics more than a bit rash where the poor are concerned. The poor, old chap, are deserving of their wretched condition."

"Poppycock!" Josephine would huff, drawing herself up to her full height—which, admittedly, was not very tall.

"Ah, but surely you must give me this point. They create their own sad stew of a life—"

"One without meat, I dare say," Josephine interrupted gravely.

"—And then complain when they have to eat it." Looking aside, as if at a servant, Meaghan said, "Ah, there, another glass of port, yes … I say, where did you get this stuff?"

At that, the sisters would laugh at their clever bravado with such gaiety Momma would come to the foot of the stairs. "Jose-*phine*! *Mea*-ghan!" she would call. "To bed. Now. And if you don't comport yourselves like ladies you will never attract a suitor."

In the mornings the sisters took turns sitting on the dainty chair in front of the mirrored dresser, brushing out tangles that had accumulated during the night.

"Jose-*phine*! *Mea*-ghan! Comport yourselves." Josephine cheekily imitated Momma's voice.

"I haven't slept a wink worrying about not attracting a suitor," Meaghan mocked, shaking out her curls over her shoulders.

But one morning Josephine slyly noted, "You may have already attracted one. I notice Harold Bradford has been eying you."

"He has not!" Meaghan stopped pinching her cheeks, forgetting about the blush she was going for. "He has?"

"On Sunday. In church." Charlotte, their droll little lapdog, came toddling into the room, her fur dragging along the floor, and Josephine reached out to stroke her neck. "He stared at you just as Reverend Phillips talked about who can find a virtuous woman," Josephine said, before solemnly intoning the Bible verse in a cadence very much like the reverend's. "She layeth her hands to the spindle."

"I don't want to lay my hands on the spindle! Why is it always more handiwork?" Meaghan threw up her hands, but then cautiously asked again, "He really has? Harold Bradford—I mean? Looking at me?"

Josephine ignored her question. She twirled a finger coquettishly through a ringlet and said, "Reverend Phillips also preached against being courted by boys from Devonshire."

"Now you're teasing!"

Josephine gave a last pat to Charlotte's fluffy fur and wrapped a bow around her own disorderly tresses. "He said they're overeager for an embrace."

"Josie!"

"Shh! Or Momma will be calling up the stairs!"

The two sisters couldn't have presented a more stark contrast to their mother, whose delicate side ringlets and chignon graced a long, white neck. Momma didn't move awkwardly in her voluminous bell-shaped skirts, as some women did; they only made her appear more gracious. Sometimes at night Josephine would catch her parents dancing in the parlor, Papa laughing and whirling his wife around the room, Momma, not realizing she was spied upon, allowing her skirt to fly through the air.

In the mornings Papa—his mutton-chop sideburns freshly washed and his tight-fitting waistcoat pressed to perfection—didn't give himself over to his breakfast eggs and hot roll until Elizabeth appeared at his side. Momma's rich black hair was held back with two silver combs—a gift from her husband—and she gave off the faint scent of lavender water. Once she sat beside him and began to sip her tea, Papa put down his newspaper and picked up his fork; all was right with the world. And in an orderly fashion, as soon as the tall clock chimed nine o'clock, he perched his top hat on his head and picked up his walking stick and strode four blocks to the Bell Apparel Co.

Any outsider would have guessed Robert Bell had provided comfortably for his wife Elizabeth, his two older sons, and his two daughters. But before he was even out of his thirties, his family discovered otherwise.

One ordinary morning Papa's young shop assistant ran to the house, calling, "Mistress Bell! Mistress Bell! It's Mr. Bell. Come quick!" Josephine saw a flurry of petticoats rustle by as her mother rushed down the stairs and out the front gate, forgetting her shawl in her haste, and the girl followed, running down the street like a commoner.

As they entered the shop, the boy pointed to Papa, lying motionless on the floor. "Mr. Bell took a spell as we was sorting ties," the assistant reported. "He said something about a pain. Wrapped about his chest, it was. Then he was a goner."

After her husband's heart attack, the bills gradually mounted and Elizabeth began to discover the extent of Robert Bell's indebtedness. His shop—indeed, their entire lifestyle—had been kept afloat by loans, and now the creditors were calling. The Bell Apparel Co. and its contents were sold to a man named Harris, and Elizabeth was forced to sell off the family possessions one by one. She sold the dining table, the chairs, the velvet chaise. Josephine watched in shame and panic as strangers carted off her bedstead. Momma sold Papa's gold watch, his waistcoats and top hat and walking stick; indeed, it seemed to Josephine that all traces of her father were disappearing. Before Elizabeth's year of bereavement was even properly underway, she traded her black crepe mourning dress to stave off hunger. Finally, at the end, stripped of standing but still retaining her customary dignity, she put the house itself up for sale.

Her two grown sons, Edward and William, offered as much help as they could, but they were struggling with their own impending poverty. Work was even scarcer than in years past, and prices more exorbitant, and the two sons couldn't rescue their mother and sisters from downfall, especially since Edward—Josephine noted sourly— was likely to lose any spare change that came his way down at the Stag Ale House.

In spite of her own lack of spare change, Josephine was determined to hang on to one last remnant of her former life, and her mother indulged her. The green satin slippers offset her copper-green eyes and were a gift from Momma, and the girl had worn them at her sixteenth birthday party in their home on Middleton Street. They were almost too small now, but when Josephine looked at them she felt a thin trace of hope about a future—*any* future—that didn't include hunger and daily desperation.

Just before they lost the house, Josephine lost her roommate. Harold Bradford had advanced from eying Meaghan in church to calling on her.

"Do you like him?" Meaghan asked one night, with a bit of an anxious expression. Josephine had been more than a little muted in her enthusiasm.

"I'll allow he's agreeable to the eye," Josephine said carefully, remembering Harold's broad, intelligent forehead and easy grin. She didn't meet her sister's eyes as she stroked Charlotte's ear. A buyer had been located for the lapdog. Was everything of value about to be lost? Even her sister? Even her dog?

But Meaghan plunged on, oblivious to her sister's pain. "When he calls he says, 'How's my fair lambkin today?'"

Josephine began to laugh, forgetting her trepidation. "He calls you a piece of mutton?"

"Josie!" Meaghan exclaimed. She lowered her voice and whispered conspiratorially, "He gave me a kiss. Under the cherry tree down in the meadow ... Actually, two." She absentmindedly caressed the dog's neck, her thoughts obviously still under the tree with Harold.

"What was it like?" Josephine asked, more curious than she let on.

"Nice ..."

"Do you think he'll propose?"

"I suppose if he wants to keep kissing me!" Meaghan laughed.

"Does he know you're without means?"

"He doesn't have much himself, although I imagine he will someday. He speaks like a book. And his uncle managed to secure him a clerking position with Lloyds Bank. He'll start after the first of the year. I imagine things will be tight for some time, but some-day we may have a better lot."

In spite of Harold's eagerness at courting, Meaghan seemed as star-tled as Josephine when the inevitable finally happened. One Sunday afternoon Harold leaped off the horse-drawn bus in front of their home, stood in the stripped-down parlor, and asked Momma for Meaghan's hand.

The courtship and wedding happened too fast for Josephine. The week that the last of the furniture was being carted off, she stood in the first row of Saint Nicholas Church with her mother and William as Edward escorted her sister down the aisle. Afterward, Josephine came home to a place so empty she could hear her voice echo off the walls.

"Momma, the house feels so forlorn." She was thinking—first Papa, and then Edward and William, who had moved out a fort-night ago. And now Meaghan.

"I know. I am sorry." Elizabeth drew her daughter to her breast and cupped her chin, lifting it. "Josie?"

Something in Momma's voice made the girl nervous. She stiff-ened, waiting.

"I have had an offer on the house. I am to sign the contract tomorrow. The proceeds should be enough to cover the last of our debts."

Josephine looked at her mother wordlessly, her eyes filling with tears. Finally she managed a weak, "Momma, can't we just stay here?" She turned her head away and stared at the vacant walls, whose paintings, just the week before, had been toted away picture by picture. And then, although she well knew the reason, "Why do we need to go?"

"I wish I had more to offer you, Josie. It will not be this way forever. I promise." Elizabeth gazed around the empty room as if she, too, had lost her bearings. She ran her hands across her neck. Those hands, her daughter knew, had seen scrub brushes and the inside of kitchen pots, but all Josephine could remember at that moment was how often Momma's hands had been employed arranging hydrangea blooms for the parlor and penning invitations in dainty script for afternoon teas. They were white and pretty and unlined.

"But where will we live?" Josephine asked.

She soon found out. Her mother seemed ashamed as she led the girl down to Fishermans Lane, near the wharf. She turned into a close-walled alley, where ancient stone walls gave off the stink of centuries of crowded humanity. Rats skittered here and there as Momma led the way up a set of dark steps and scraped open the door.

Josephine stared at their new home: a dismal flat furnished with one chair, a battered table, and a lumpy bed—too narrow for one, almost impossible for two. She remembered the etiquette instilled since youth: Assume polite self-possession no matter what the conditions.

And this: A cheerful appearance shows good judgment and proper taste. In conversation, never touch upon the causes of one's affliction.

She looked at Momma. Her mother, she knew, could pull it off.

One week later, Josephine and Elizabeth began their shifts at the Dorsett & Company Woolen Mill, where the rules from the *Hand-Book of Etiquette for Ladies* flew out the window. In the sunless picker room, no one cared a wit if they bowed with "slow and measured dignity" upon first meeting. Amidst the deafening clatter of looms, it would have been madness to "cultivate a soft tone of voice."

3

AND WHEN YE shall receive these things, I would exhort you that ye would ask God, the eternal Father, in the name of Christ, if these things are not true; and if ye shall ask with a sincere heart, with real intent, having faith in Christ, he will manifest the truth of it unto you ...

—*The Book of Mormon: An Account Written by the Hand of Mormon, Upon Plates Taken from the Plates of Nephi*, written by the Prophet Joseph Smith

At first her new life felt like a dream, one that would end, that should end. But as the calendar trudged forward, Josephine knew there was no going back.

Slushing home from work through the narrow lanes, her fingers chilled and her unwashed hair fringed with fog droplets, the girl thought—for the thousandth time—of her former home. She re-created the supper table with its glorious centerpieces. Hare soup in a rich broth, smoked herring. Applesauce and succulent roast pork. Papa would offer the first slice to Momma, who would smile at his loving intentions before passing it on to her children. On Sundays, the main course was followed by mince pie or almond pudding, and for company—trifle. Back then, Josephine had been oblivious to how dear each morsel was.

Each night after Josephine and her mother arrived at their flat, the girl would enact her usual ritual. She would rub her hands together for warmth, thinking all the while of the furnace that had heated their home on Middleton Street, and she would strike a match to the burned-down candle, remembering the lanterns that had cast a golden glow about the walls.

And she would try not to complain. That would mean, she knew, acting more like Momma, who seemed to be putting a braver face on things than she herself could manage. Even though their change in circumstances was just as difficult for her mother, Josephine couldn't remember Momma complaining even once about the monotony of bread and tea, or the woolen mill, with its stink of lanolin. Some nights the laments spilled forth before Josephine could stop them, and then she would chastise herself and make promises.

Tomorrow I won't go on about plum pudding. Or teacakes with fresh strawberries.

But she would break the promises, almost every day. Momma was patient most days, but sometimes she would wince tiredly and remonstrate, "Oh Josie. We have talked about this before. There is nothing to be done for it, child. No amount of wishing will bring back your father, or our house. Or our supper table."

One night as Josephine and her mother rounded the corner onto Fishermans Lane, they saw two street preachers on upturned crates in front of the Cork and Barrel public house. They were surrounded on all sides by a ragtag crowd.

"Take yourselves back to America!" one man shouted, while another grumbled, "Ach, who set you up to speak for God?"

As the preachers tried to make their voices heard above the fracas, Josephine noticed they had a strange accent, with vowels that stood up a little too stridently. "We bring you glad tidings, for God has revealed his truth in these latter days. He has spoken through the mouth of his prophet—Joseph Smith!"

Josephine forgot the sour pit in her stomach as she studied the crowd. The faces were thin. Jackets were missing buttons and didn't look thick enough to keep out the cold.

The shorter preacher coughed timorously, covering his mouth as if he were thinking twice about continuing, but the lanky one gallantly pushed on with a speech that sounded as if he had delivered it more than a few times. He held aloft a book of scripture and proclaimed, "This sacred volume—*this*—contains God's own handwriting! From the pen of the prophet."

"Your prophet's probably just like the rest of the preachers," a ruddy-cheeked woman guffawed. "Promises. And then what? He ain't got nothing for the likes of us!" She was joined by a man with ripped trousers who yelled, "We can't eat holy books for supper!"

"Ah, but that is the very thing." The preacher waved the book. "Here, *here* is comfort and cheer for the downtrodden."

"Momma, who's Joseph Smith?" Josephine asked, flexing one foot and then the other, her toes cramped by narrow button boots.

But Elizabeth's reply was drowned out by the missionary. "God has called you to gather to a land of plenty where he is building up his kingdom. There, he will bestow upon his people a feast of the fat of the land."

Josephine could hear a fiddler just inside the door of the pub, scraping out "Sally My Dear" for all he was worth. Against the raspy backdrop, the Mormon missionaries beseeched the crowd. They called their listeners to repentance and spoke of damnation, yes, but they lingered most persuasively on the topic of the Lord's mercy for the poor, painting a vision of a far-away place where no one went hungry.

Around her, the tide slowly began to turn. Josephine heard a man beside her whisper with wonder in his voice, "Why, 'tis the old gospel come to Earth again!" And then another person, and another—even those who had taunted the loudest—grew quiet and began to listen with curious expressions.

Evening after evening the preachers stood there on their crates, and Josephine and her mother took to lingering.

"Most of them look like they came from the poorhouse," the girl observed as she looked at the bedraggled crowd. "And they don't seem to have much learning."

"They may be paupers," Elizabeth said, "but I will remind you that we are no better."

The promises of the Mormon missionaries—Josephine couldn't help it—followed her home. Each evening she boiled water and peeled potatoes, and when they sat down for supper in the thin candlelight she sized up their lot: a pot of weak tea and two half-spoiled potatoes on an otherwise bare table. The bare table—that was the problem, as was the single shelf that served as a pantry. It, too, was empty.

Like Josephine, who had walked away from Middleton Street with her green satin slippers, Elizabeth had managed to save one beloved possession—a book of poems by William Wordsworth. Each evening after supper mother and daughter attempted to retain some small semblance of their former lives; they read. One would sit on the chair, the other on the bed, and they took turns with "The Tables Turned" and "The World Is Too Much With Us." They recited "Ode on Intimations of Immortality" and "It is a Beauteous Evening, Calm and Free." The factory whistle would blow at dawn, they knew, but for a few moments, Mr. Wordsworth bequeathed a tenuous sense of normalcy.

Sometimes, as Momma read, Josephine's mind wandered, re-membering the words of the missionaries. "A land of plenty. The blessings of this Earth."

We are certainly ripe for some blessings, the girl thought.

When the reading had ended for the night, she crawled onto the pallet and pulled the thin covering over her shoulders.

I wonder what would be asked of me in return.

After a month of listening to the Mormon missionaries on their make-shift pulpits in front of the Cork and Barrel, Josephine and Elizabeth attended their first Sabbath meeting.

Men took off caps at the door and bowed their heads as they stepped over the threshold. Women, smelling of wet knit shawls and boiled cabbage, held children's hands as they squeezed into the rows. Most of the children had the stunted look of poverty, and their faces were sallow, like those of their parents.

Morning light streamed through the tall windows and Josephine could hear rain drip in the alley outside as she watched the missionaries, Brother Jennson and Brother Woodcock, offer sermons and prepare the sacrament. When it was passed around the room, she slowly sucked the piece of bread, and swallowed a sip of wine, imagining a pastoral vineyard far away from the city, even though Brother Woodcock told the congregation they should be imagining the atonement of Christ.

The following Sunday, and the one after that, and then in a regular pattern, she and her mother walked the two miles to the place of worship, a dilapidated building constructed in the 1700s and neglected in the 1800s. The slate roof was crumbling and the plaster ceiling was water-stained, but the rented room was clean and tidy.

The Mormons were decidedly less formal than the stiff-backed congregants Josephine had known at her old parish. Before their change in circumstances, she and her family had attended Saint Nicholas, where they occupied a sturdy oak pew under a ceiling so high it seemed to be aiming for God himself. Each Sunday the girl listened to the peal of bells, breathed in Anglican incense, and sang the ancient hymns. But since their loss of economic status, Josephine and her mother had stopped attending the Church of England parish, even though Reverend Phillips assured them they were still welcome.

"There's no disgrace in coming on hard times," the reverend said. That wasn't true, Josephine thought resentfully. There was plenty of disgrace. She guessed her mother felt it too, although Momma's composure seemed implacable, her feelings hidden beneath layers of good manners.

Josephine was pragmatic enough to realize it was best to lay aside former expectations and try to accept her lot, changed as it was. And she couldn't help but notice that when she and Momma arrived at the Mormon meetings, the church sisters—for they called themselves "sisters"—welcomed them with genuine affection. The two were fussed over. After each service, Josephine and her mother conversed with converts near a table set with the best refreshments the missionaries could procure, and the girl forgot her want.

For the first time since Papa died, the first time since Momma sold their house, the first time since Meaghan married and moved to the outskirts of Liverpool, Josephine began to feel a sense of balance. Many Saints were painfully thin, and many were stooped from hard labor, and sometimes Josephine felt guilty; she was embarrassed to be associated with such a rough class of people. But still, she had to admit that the Sabbath meetings felt like coming home. One morning each week, Josephine forgot the misery of standing in place ten hours a day, assaulted by the thunder of looms pounding out cloth.

"Josie, child, what do you think?" Elizabeth asked after they arrived home one Sunday. Her mother put on the potatoes to boil while Josephine set out two plates and bread.

"About the Mormons?" Josephine asked, knowing full well what Momma meant. Her mother's question was one she had asked herself dozens of times. And every time, her heart warred with her mind, for the stories the missionaries told were preposterous.

Brother Jennson was the meeker of the two, but he was animated by conviction as he told the congregation he had known Joseph Smith. "His eyes burned a fire into me," he said. Josephine couldn't imagine a fire in Brother Jennson; he seemed far too courteous and cautious. His legs were too short for his round little body, with one even shorter than the other, giving him a lopsided walk as he approached the pulpit. His nose was the most prominent feature of his face and his hair was thinning in patches, but his expression was one of charity.

The Prophet Joseph was tall, Brother Jennson said, and like himself, limped. The chip in Joseph's front tooth made for a slight whistle when he talked. And his talk! This was what gave Josephine pause, for the missionary said the Mormon prophet had not only offered sermons but had pronounced prophecies and recounted visions of angels. Joseph even said he had seen Heavenly Father and his Son, and that an angel had revealed a holy book to him, one inscribed on gold plates. The Latter-day Saints—Joseph's people— had not been allowed to view the plates; they were too sacred. At God's behest, the prophet had hidden them away in a cave.

Brother Jennson gave Josephine and Elizabeth a copy of this *Book of Mormon*, and politely but fervently urged them to read its pages and then kneel before God and make their wants known, asking to know the truth of its message. And so each night mother and daughter shut out the sound of the ongoing quarrel in the downstairs flat as they read the saga of an ancient Hebrew prophet who built a boat and sailed west across the Atlantic Ocean, from the Old World to the New. Out of his loins came two tribes.

They read about the Nephites, the tribe that followed God's commandments, and the Lamanites, who fell away into wickedness. For their iniquities, God cursed the Lamanites with a dark skin. Descendants of that tribe were known as Indians, Brother Jennson said, and they were even now attacking American pioneers as they made their way west to new settlements in California and the fertile valleys of Oregon, or to the Utah Territory, where the Mormon president and prophet, Brigham Young, had established God's kingdom on Earth.

The missionary said a mob of Illinois ruffians had murdered the Prophet Joseph in the upstairs room of a jailhouse, where he was being held for ordering the destruction of a newspaper printing press; the newspaper had slandered the Saints.

But Joseph's prophecies and revelations had already taken root. His band of followers had grown from his family and neighbors to the surrounding region, and then outward in ever-widening circles. And now, here they were—Brother Jennson and Brother Woodcock—in Liverpool, having carried Joseph's message all the way across the ocean to Fishermans Lane.

"I don't know what to think, Momma," Josephine said. "I'm still trying to work it out."

That night after her mother fell asleep, Josephine climbed noiselessly from the bed they shared, knelt below the window, and hoped—*listened*—for God's voice. She yearned for the missionaries' promised "burning in the bosom," the sensation that would confirm the truth of their creed.

"Dear God," she whispered. "I'm praying about the Mormons." She had never said more than a quick "Our Father who art in heaven" recitation before bedtime. This kind of assumed intimacy was new, but she was counting on the Latter-day Saint God to be more approachable than the formal God described by Reverend Phillips.

"The missionaries said you talk to everyone, not just prophets. Or grown men." She bit her lip, wondering how to proceed. "They say you'll send a burning feeling to let us know if this is true."

Josephine shifted the position of her knees on the hard wooden floor, and froze for a moment as her mother stirred in her sleep. Outside the window, silver-blue light from a full moon mingled with fog, and inside, a sliver of that light stretched across the cracked-plaster walls as if searching for something.

"I think I want it to be true. I want to give myself over to something with more ... *promise*."

Josephine thought of the mountain valley far away in America where, according to the missionaries, the Lord was gathering his people. She contemplated an earthly kingdom of God, one where mothers purchased eggs and sausages for the breakfast table, where no street children reached out dirty hands for a farthing.

Can such a place exist?

And the heavenly kingdom. The missionaries had spoken of that place too, far above the soot-stained sky of Liverpool—the celestial kingdom where God and his angels resided, the place where those who hungered for the Lord would be fed eternally.

Josephine gazed out the window, up into the sky. "My papa died," she confided. "We lived on Middleton Street. Me, my sister Meaghan. Momma and Papa, and Edward and William—they're my brothers.

"And now ..." She faltered. What could she say about her life now? Her knees ached.

"Perhaps—" Her whisper trailed off.

Perhaps what?

Could this Mormon God offer some kind of grace, or at least consolation? Josephine heard the bells of Saint Nicholas, and then, the drunken men weaving in the street below.

"In the Sabbath meetings, I feel peace," she said. "I look around the room at the faces and I see hope."

Although she wasn't certain, the girl guessed that faith might be a fragile thing, at least when it was new. But hope—hope was strong; it was unquenchable. In church meetings the Saints bore testimony of the truth of the gospel, and Josephine heard the yearning behind every word. She heard the longing behind their tears, for it was her own longing. In that room, where the missionaries passed the bread and wine while morning light streamed like heaven through the tall windows, the world beyond seemed to disappear. A calm descended, an orderliness within herself.

Is it true?

Josephine didn't feel the promised burning in the bosom. But as the night wore on, and then, as the sky began to grow light, the girl felt a hush settle over her, and then an excited anticipation. Soon, she knew, the night soil men would head home to their sleep. Factory whistles would pierce the air, and fathers and mothers and children would rush to the dirty, noisy mills. Peddlers would harness their donkeys to broken-down carts. Painted women would walk the streets and half-starved urchins would take up their place in doorways, their hands outstretched. The world would go on in its callous, predictable way, with the hungry in that accursed year of 1855 growing hungrier.

But she—Josephine—would be free.

The girl thought of the Mormon message, with its invitation to a heaven on Earth, and she knew: She would say *Yes.*

4

THE PEOPLE ARE very different in this country [England] to what the Americans are. They say it cannot be possible that men should leave their homes and come so far, unless they were truly the servants of the Lord; they do not seem to understand argument; simple testimony is enough for them ... Almost without exception it is the poor that receive the Gospel.

—Excerpt from a letter written by English missionary Brigham Young to Joseph Smith. (Young later would be ordained president and prophet of the Mormon Church.)

But before the deliverance, came the want, more want than Josephine had ever known. The girl and her mother passed up tea and potatoes and began subsisting chiefly on bread in order to save a small portion of their wages each week. They stashed shillings in a jar pushed under the bed, and in late winter, emptied the jar and gave their all to the missionaries. The coins weren't nearly enough, but the church loan would make up the remainder—the ticket for passage across the ocean, and the handcart they would pull across the prairies and mountains to the Salt Lake Valley. Josephine could tell her mother was worried about borrowing money, especially after being ruined by Papa's debt, but Momma kept repeating, as if to persuade herself of the fact, "When it is time to repay, we will find a way."

Walking to the mill each morning, Josephine counted the number of days before their departure. Fifty more days listening to the deafening hammer of looms. Forty more days of lint clogging her lungs. Thirty more days hearing children cry out against the whip that came down when their pace slackened. Twenty more days arriving home with the stink of lanolin on her dress. With ten days to go, she and Momma packed a crude wooden crate they had managed to secure, although in truth, there wasn't much to pack; their belongings had been reduced to almost nothing.

The morning of their departure, they woke well before dawn and lugged their crate down the stairs. They arrived at the wharf two hours early, but Albert Dock was already swarming with early risers. Boys hawked newspapers, their shrill voices advertising the latest murder. Fishmongers were rolling out barrels of gutted haddock, black-skinned Negroes were unloading tea and tobacco, and greengrocers were already barking, "Penny a lot, fine russets!" The girl had never seen so many people in one place.

"Josie, stay close by or you are apt to get lost," said Elizabeth, picking her way over oyster shells that littered the ground. The girl dodged pickpockets and held her mother's elbow.

Cargo vessels sailed into the harbor and fishing boats lifted anchor to sail out, and then, suddenly, Josephine saw the sight that made her breath catch in her throat.

Our ship!

Its great hulk lay broadside to the wharf. Tattooed sailors climbed the rigging and hauled water casks aboard, and a long line of men, sagging under their loads, carried bedding and sacks of rice and flour up the gangplank. Elderly women carried bread loaves and cabbages, and mothers pulled toddlers along by the hand. Josephine recognized many of them from the Mormon meeting, and she saw the missionaries helping carry their bundles. She was momentarily ashamed of their poverty, ashamed she belonged to these people. But then the scream of a factory whistle pierced her thoughts. Elation rose—it wasn't summoning her!

Her jubilation was cut short when she spotted Meaghan and her husband standing at the edge of the dock, her sister's face searching the crowd.

"Meaghan!" Josephine cried, waving her bonnet. "Over here!"

Her sister plunged into the crowd, abandoning her husband and almost tripping as she ran toward Josephine. She caught her sister and held her tight.

"You can still change your mind," said Meaghan, her eyes moist. "Please change your mind. Please! Don't go."

"I've already bought my ticket. And who will go with Momma if I stay here?" Josephine asked, but in truth, she was beginning to feel dizzy. The thought of leaving Meaghan and her home, pitiful as it was, made her feel as if a stone was pressing against her chest.

What if our ship capsizes at sea? How will I pull a handcart over mountains?

What if I never see Meaghan again?

"And besides," Josephine prattled on, trying for the familiar humor she shared with her sister—and attempting to calm rising panic—"I hear we'll each have our own steward on board. And there will be steam heat in our private cabin. Who can pass that up?"

But the joke fell flat. Meaghan's shoulders collapsed. There had been no persuading her sister to stay. Now, standing at the wharf, Meaghan pulled a present from beneath her cloak and pressed it into her sister's arms. "It's a goodbye gift then," she said.

Josephine stared at the hand-stitched quilt, dumbfounded. It was small, and looked as if her sister had run out of time halfway through the job—but still, Josephine calculated the cost. Meaghan *hated* needlework. How many dreadfully dull hours had it taken to sew the patches together?

"To keep you warm," Meaghan said.

The quilt was all blues and greens—the color of the English countryside. In its corner Josephine saw, in neat, tiny stitches, the words: Remember Me.

Josephine thought, *What is the cost of faith?*

Meaghan clung to Momma, and then clung even more fiercely to Josephine. And then the sisters stood without words, gripping each other's hands, tears sliding down their cheeks, until the ship bell tolled.

Josephine broke away and helped Momma carry the crate up the gangway, through the salty mist. She watched sailors unfurl the tall sails, watched the canvas flutter in the breeze. She stood unsteadily as the grand ship rocked beneath her feet. The girl felt an air of unreality. She clutched her quilt and searched the crowd for her sister's small, heart-shaped face, but it was lost.

PART TWO

The Gathering

5

THE GALLANT SHIP IS UNDER WAY

The gallant ship is under way,
To bear me off to sea,
And yonder float the streamers gay,
That say she waits for me.
I go devoted to his cause,
And to his will resign'd;
His presence will supply the loss
Of all I leave behind.
And now the vessel's side we've made;
The sails their bosoms swell:
Thy beauties in the distance fade—
My native land farewell.

—Hymn from *A Collection of Sacred Hymns for the Church of the Latter Day Saints*, words written by William Phelps

April 8, 1856

Dearest Meaghan—

Yesterday the ship lifted anchor & pulled away from Merry Olde England! At first it was difficult to stand for the rolling about on the waters.

The Ship Captain assures us the passengers will be Well Fed— Smoked hering & fresh rolls with sweet cream. It goes without saying that all our rooms are private & the steerage is well lighted—you would wish you had come!

Actually, as you may have sermised, there are no fresh rolls, & the steerage is anything but well lit—Always my poor luck. Alas, I guess it is good the below deck is so dark, as it provides more privacy for the ladies as they dress for morning prayer!

Now every where upon the deck people of all ages are penning letters to loved ones left behind. As I write these lines, I wonder what you are doing this moment—Are you missing me as I miss you?

I must admit that when I first came to the wharf & contemplated the Ocean that would soon roll between us—I almost lost courage and turned back. It is hard to imagine the Utah Teritory for I have only seen it in a print the misionaries showed us—But I am thankful & glad to leave behind the squalor and stink of Fishermans Lane & the weary work of the mill. The door to hope has opened & I have walked through.

Here, the Sea stretches out forever & there is a feeling of adventure unlike I have ever known. Perhaps that is what Heaven is like—the openness, the invitation onward.

I feel releived, dear sister, to think of how your own prospects have improved. I am certain Harold will show his resourcefullness at the bank. For now, please know I will think of you every day & pray our goodbye will not be forever—

With Longing & Affection,
Your Josie

PS   I will mail this letter when we arrive in New York city.

Just before the gangplank lifted, several people changed their minds, shouldering their way through the crowd and back to the dock. But after the doubters had disembarked, and with an exuberant cheer from the Latter-day Saints, the anchor was lifted and the great ship began to move.

Josephine felt as if her own anchor had been pulled up too; she was strangely unmoored. Whitecaps beat against the ship's hull as the wharf slowly receded, until all she could see was the last of the smokestacks belching grime into the soggy English sky, and then, just a dim outline of the shore. She wondered if she would ever see her homeland again, and wondered, once again, what her new home would be like. Zion, the missionaries called it.

Roiling emerald-gray waves surged up and crashed down, making it difficult to stand upright. The wind pulled at her braid and tangled strands of hair. Her stomach lurched, but she was not certain if the sensation came from the roll of the ocean—or fear. Or excitement.

She hugged Meaghan's quilt about her shoulders. Embroidered on its border was a strip of cheerful bluebells, flowers that spread in dense springtime carpets under shady oaks—a familiar scene in the English countryside. She wondered, would there be bluebells in the Salt Lake Valley? Perhaps blossoming on the shore of the strange salty lake? She had heard that rains weren't abundant in the Utah Territory and that the land was dry, but having never seen a desert, the scene was difficult to imagine.

The children didn't seem to be bothered by the cold. They ran and tumbled about the deck like a band of monkeys, stretching their thin arms wide like wings and imitating the bark of the seagulls that followed the ship. They clustered at the railing, squealing in glee and calling to the dolphins that leaped through the waves.

"Ahoy, mateys!"

Although Josephine vaguely recalled that a soft voice and modesty of speech are a lady's best adornments, she rambunctiously joined in. "Ahoy!" she cried, waving to the dolphins.

"Josie," her mother gently chided, "it is best to leave the yelling to the children."

Just then a tall, broad-shouldered man, leaning lightly on a duck's head cane, limped toward the children, "God-ay, mates, what's all this balderdash then?" His mock frown couldn't conceal his amusement. "Ya, lads, there'll be no leaning over the railing. The ocean might snatch you unawares."

The man's cheeks were ruddy and his bushy eyebrows were blacker than his beard, which was threaded with silver. Although he looked as if he had tried for a neat, trim beard, Josephine noticed that his hair, like her own, seemed to have mutinied against the comb.

The man turned to the crowd, doffed his cap, and offered a good-natured bow. "*Velkommen!*" he called with a stiff Danish accent. "I have been called to be your ship president, but there's no need for formalities; you can call me Brother Larsen. Brother Hans Larsen, and pleased to meet you." His barrel-chested voice rang out above the fussing children, and at a commanding six feet two, he could be seen even by those farther back.

Brother Larsen announced the shipboard schedule in a ceremonious manner, as if he were offering a sermon of great import. "Five o'clock! All to make their beds! Men to retire to the deck while the ladies dress." Josephine's shawl began to flap in the breeze. She wondered how much privacy would be provided for dressing.

"Six o'clock! Each to clean their assigned portion of the ship. And throw the refuse overboard."

Hans Larsen's double row of brass buttons gave him an official air, and to the men in poor-fitting sack coats and women in well-used bonnets, he must have looked the part of a regular ship captain.

"Seven!" he proclaimed. "Assemble for prayer, after which the sisters will prepare breakfast.

"The bugle will call you to prayer meeting each evening on the deck, weather permitting. All will be in their berths ready for retirement at eight o'clock, children bedded down and lanterns out.

"Right then." The ship president surveyed the crowd with a kindly smile. "We come from many places, we each bring our different ways, but we are one family in the Lord's eyes." As an afterthought, he nodded at a group of restive young men and added, "Lads, be vigilant against nay-saying and grumbling."

Indeed, Josephine had already heard a few of those very naysayers. Some had gone below and were complaining about the cramped quarters and the chamber pots—just a series of buckets placed here and there.

Now the rest of the Saints clambered down to the steerage and surveyed the dimly lit space: a close ceiling, no windows, bunks stacked one on top of another and sardined in from bow to stern. There was barely enough room in each berth to sit up. Josephine guessed that many of the passengers were used to living in cramped, dark holes, but still, she noticed their faces fall.

One of the young malcontents muttered, "What in hell. It's darker than a mine shaft in here."

He was immediately countered by a church sister who said, "And we can take our fill of light up on the deck," and a one-armed man who bravely offered, "It's a wee bit crowded now. But our flats in Great Salt Lake City will be as grand as the rich."

And then the crowd surged forward, and Josephine and her mother were swept along in the mass of people. Women tried to keep track of children, men hoisted luggage, and everyone rushed to claim an empty berth.

"Five to a berth!" Hans Larsen called. "Married couples will sleep in the middle. Women and girls are to sleep in the stern. Men and boys in the bow."

"I see they've put us at a safe distance from the men," Josephine said mischievously. She already had decided: Humor would be the best strategy to choke down fear.

"Josie," said her mother as they placed their crate on a thin straw mattress in an empty berth, "we are not in the picker room or on the streets, where young ladies have abandoned all manners. I will ask you to act like a lady in spite of the circumstances."

"And of course, our steerage is first class," joked Josephine, choosing to ignore her mother's request for decorum.

"Yes, that is certain." Elizabeth smiled and shook her head. Her reminders frequently ran headlong into her young daughter's cheekiness, and she often seemed to give up.

But although Josephine laughingly disparaged conditions on board, and although she felt an unsettled panic, she also knew that this—all of it—was a temporary obstacle on the way to the Promised Land.

She suddenly spotted a small girl, almost underfoot, who seemed adrift in the crush of people. Her cheeks were damp and her sobs came out like hiccups.

"Hush now," Josephine said. She leaned down and reached for the child's hand. "What's your name? And why are you crying?"

"My mum," the child said in a tiny voice. She rubbed her eyes with tight fists. "I lost her."

"Ah, this is not a good place to lose a mum now, is it. But she's here. Somewhere. Shall we look?" The child gazed up bashfully and nodded.

"What's your name?" Josephine asked as she smoothed the girl's limp hair and scanned the aisles.

The child placed her sticky fingers in Josephine's hand. "Rebecca."

"Rebecca. That's a lovely name." Josephine noticed that her elf-like face was scattered with faded pox scars. "I think I see your mum! Right up there."

Josephine had caught sight of a woman wearing an alarmed expression, standing on her toes searching the crowd. She nudged Rebecca forward.

When the woman spotted her daughter, her shoulders collapsed with relief. "I thought I had lost the child," she said, taking Rebecca's hand. She seemed disoriented, her bonnet askew and her hands clutching her bundle a bit too tightly.

"Sit here with us," Elizabeth kindly offered the woman. "Do you have a berth? We have—well, not plenty of room." She smiled at Rebecca. "But certainly room enough for such a pretty girl and her mother."

"Ta. If you've room," the woman said. "We don't want to cause trouble. This is kind of you." She had fine blond hair like her daughter, and like Rebecca, she was missing several teeth. Her bony shoulders looked like broken angel wings.

"My name's Sister Ashdown." She hesitated, cupping her hands over a swollen belly. Her unborn child looked as if it were clamoring to come out. "Sister Lydia Ashdown. And this is Rebecca." She wiped her child's nose with a handkerchief. "Her father stayed behind, as he's not a believer. The girl's having a bit of an ordeal over it."

"Yes, and I know about the unbelievers," Elizabeth said. She looked past the woman. "I have three of my own."

Meaghan.

Josephine's heart ricocheted back to their goodbye at the wharf. She felt as if she had been abandoned, even though she was the one who had done the leaving. Now, with each swell of water, they grew farther apart.

As Josephine ate her first meal aboard ship, she pretended to mock horror. She wiped her mouth with an imaginary napkin and told her mother, "This tea, I must say, tastes like—dare I guess—salt?" She smoothed the folds of her skirt with exaggerated politeness and curled her fingers delicately around the handle of her tin cup. "Where is the steward? I really must speak to him."

"Child, I sometimes wonder how you came to be mine," said Elizabeth, laughing.

Josephine joked about the hardtack and salty tea that came with the price of their ticket, but truth be told, Josephine was elated; boiled beef was on the menu as well, and she hadn't had a slice of beef since leaving Middleton Street.

When the midday meal had concluded, almost every soul seemed to light upon the same idea. They rummaged in their bundles for quill pens and scraps of paper, and ascended to the sublime freedom of the main deck. There, they crouched on benches or on the dirty floorboards and turned their faces upward toward the sun. Using knees or *Book of Mormons* as slates, they began to write letters home.

One woman stared at her paper, weeping soundlessly, and Josephine wondered whether her letter would be kindly received. She had heard that many family members, just like Edward and William, had stopped speaking to the converts, and she guessed it was unlikely many would meet again.

Josephine dipped her quill into borrowed ink, tamped down the corners of the paper—the breeze had caught them—and began, *Dearest Meaghan …*

She imagined confiding the newly revised rules of etiquette: A lady should not oftentimes be seen in public. An exception may be made if one is sleeping berth to berth with five hundred Latter-day Saints. One should make polite inquiries about family members, but only if one is certain the inquiry will not create distress or lead to weeping; tears are unbecoming in a lady. At all times, assume an air of delicacy. An exception may be made in the unlikely event that one is undressing in front of hundreds of strangers or, as the case may be, squatting over a bucket to conduct one's most private affairs.

After supper, after a sermon on deck, after prayers, the Saints began descending en masse to the steerage. Josephine watched, but something kept her feet from moving. She knew Momma would be worried, she knew the shipboard rules, but she delayed going below. Instead, she stood silently at the side railing. A few sailors scrambled up the rigging and a small circle of earnest-looking church brethren conversed near the starboard. Otherwise, she was alone, and the solitude—so rare—was dear.

The girl watched the wind whip the broad sails. She ignored Brother Larsen's admonition and leaned out over the railing as far as she could, until the ends of her shawl billowed in the wind. Earlier, the setting sun had lit the edges of the clouds—gold, and then pale lavender. Now the dark sea was turbulent, swelling and falling, its waves slapping against the bulwark.

Perhaps I should be afraid, Josephine thought. But she wasn't.

The briny spray hit her face. She closed her eyes and felt the vast ocean move beneath her feet. This was a freedom she couldn't have imagined. She felt as if she could *breathe*, more expansively than she had breathed for a long time. Her lungs filled with air—*this* air—salty, windy, wet.

Hardtack sat heavy in her stomach. And even though the voyage had just begun, beef stored in the hold already gave off a rancid smell. The salty tea sloshed about in her belly, making her queasy. And there would be five weeks of the same—six or seven if the winds didn't cooperate. The chamber pots were always full, and the reek was already thick enough to make one's eyes water. Passengers were stacked on top of passengers, two bunks high, separated by aisles almost too narrow for passage. She and Momma would share their berth with three strangers, and that berth would provide the only space they could occupy on the lower deck.

And her sister wasn't here.

But as Josephine stood there, mesmerized by the waves, she gave herself over to some ancient tidal rhythm. The ship crested toward heaven and then fell toward the deep, echoing her emotions.

Cresting. She was eager. Falling. She was frightened. Cresting. She was free. Falling. She was heartbroken. There was no solid ground.

And yet.

… There was. She remembered going down into the River Mersey with the missionaries. When they had immersed her, the river was so cold it stung, but memories of the chill had receded. All she remembered now was the feeling of newness that had enveloped her afterward—after the dreary walk home, after changing into dry clothes, after a cup of tea. There was a sense of … what was it?

Purity. It was purity.

The girl felt the immensity of the ocean and sky. She held tight to the railing as droplets of water baptized her again and again.

Father in Heaven, she prayed, *bless this ship. Bless all of us. Please take us home.*

6

I, UNCOMMERCIAL TRAVELLER for the firm of Human Interest Brothers, had come aboard this Emigrant Ship to see what Eight hundred Latter-day Saints were like … Indeed, I think it would be difficult to find Eight hundred people together anywhere else, and find so much beauty and so much strength and capacity for work among them.

… It is surprising to me that these people are all so cheery, and make so little of the immense distance before them … By what successful means, a special aptitude for organisation had been infused into these people, I am, of course, unable to report. But I know that, even now, there was no disorder, hurry, or difficulty. … There were many worn faces bearing traces of patient poverty and hard work, and there was great steadiness of purpose and much undemonstrative self-respect among this class. …

What is in store for the poor people on the shores of the Great Salt Lake, what happy delusions they are labouring under now, on what miserable blindness their eyes may be opened then, I do not pretend to say. But I went on board their ship to bear testimony against them if they deserved it, as I fully believed they would; to my great astonishment they did not deserve it.

—*Bound for the Great Salt Lake, The Uncommercial Traveller*, written by Charles Dickens

April 18, 1856

Dearest Meaghan—

    Well, we are still Right Side Up! & we have not drowned, all though the fact some times surprises me—

    Several nights ago, after we retired, a furius gale struck. Some said the Devil himself had seized the ship—it rocked so wildly, throwing trunks & bundles & even people about. Waves heaved over the sides of the ship & the Ocean roared & we all waited in darkness & the terror of a watery grave. From every berth I heard fervent prayers asking forgiveness for sins & uttering farewells to loved ones

    The waters are calm now, all though some joke that we are blown back & forth so often that many days we go backwards more than forwards—But I trust we are still headed onward to the Promised Land & that we shall arrive in safety & good cheer. Brother Larsen blessed our ship before we sailed—& all though some ships out from England have foundered on the rocks, we are carrying through. Now I am longing to feel the Earth under my feet again.

    I wish I could receive a long letter from you with news of Home—I am anxious to hear word. Do you hear from Edward & William? Please tell them we are well contented & healthy

Missing You Dearly,
Your Josie

If Josephine thought she had left work shifts behind, she was mistaken. But this time, work brought a deep satisfaction. Rather than shaping cloth, she was shaping children. Each morning after the breakfast pots were scrubbed, she climbed the hatchway to the main deck, where she immediately was surrounded by children. The screech of textile looms had been replaced by their laughs and shouts.

    "Miss, listen to me, I got the answer!"

"A, B, C, *D!*"

"Apple, boy, cat, *dog!*"

Hans Larsen had asked permission of Elizabeth first, stopping her as she and Josephine strolled the length of the deck.

"I presume your daughter is as talented as yourself, Ma'am," he said to Elizabeth, tipping his cap and grinning. "I hear she's received a proper education, and I'd like to call her to be a schoolmistress while we take passage to New York. The good Lord knows we must take proper care of the youngsters in our charge."

"Call me Elizabeth." Momma smiled in return. "And you are right. My daughter has had a proper education. She has been tutored in grammar and arithmetic and French. Although I am quite certain we will not need French!"

Josephine thought she detected pride in her mother's voice. The pride went both ways, she thought, as she looked at her mother. Momma somehow managed to look elegant, her blouse clean and hair neatly combed, even though many of the women on board had lost any fastidiousness they once might have had about their appearance. Their dresses were rumpled and their hair tousled when they took off their bonnets.

"Ah, right you are about the French! Quite, quite," Brother Larsen said heartily. "I'm hoping for a lass who can teach the children who speak Welsh, and Danish—my native tongue, and a fine one. The little urchins will need a proper dose of English if they're to live in America. And they would benefit by learning sums, too."

"Yes. Well, as for your proposition, you will have to ask the lass yourself. She is a bit stubborn, and who knows, she may refuse your request." Elizabeth laughed and tilted her head toward her daughter—a little too flirtatiously, Josephine thought, frowning.

But when the good president gripped the duck's head handle of his cane, turned to Josephine, and bowed with mock solemnity, he won over the girl as quickly as he seemed to have charmed her mother.

He turned his grin back to Elizabeth. "Proper good, then. I'm sure Josephine will do just fine. Especially as she is your daughter.

"But Momma, I've never taught before," Josephine said that night as she pushed loose straw back into their pallet. "Where do I even start?"

"You could begin with the alphabet," her mother replied, before suddenly losing her composure and clenching her stomach. The surface of the ocean had been almost glass-like for several days, the waters calm, and Momma's seasickness had subsided, but in the last hour, the waves had grown rough.

The rocking of the ship didn't affect Josephine, although so many others were sick that she sometimes felt nauseated all the same; the stench of vomit hung thick in the air below deck. Her mother, on the other hand, had suffered from seasickness since the second day. She often struggled to keep down the hardtack and salt pork, and sometimes went hungry by choice.

Elizabeth lay back weakly on the mattress, but her queasiness didn't stop her from joining her daughter in trying to recall the arithmetic games and alphabet rhymes of childhood.

By the following morning, the new schoolmistress wasn't confident, but she wasn't terrified either as she fumbled through a roughly outlined lesson in front of three rows of children, attempting to be heard over the flapping canvas sails. The children were delighted with the attention—Josephine guessed that few had received much schooling, or attention for that matter—and they seemed eager to please. But the little scamps also were inventive in their search for mischief. After lunch Josephine found them in the company of several indulgent sailors, imitating a rude sea shanty.

What will we do with a drunken sailor?
What will we do with a drunken sailor?
What will we do with a drunken sailor?
Early in the morning!

Josephine's first impulse was to join the children, but she quickly caught herself.

"Children! Henry! *Peter!* That song is not fitting—for children or for Latter-day Saints." And then, more firmly, "Come away from the ropes. All of you. I'll teach you one of our own songs."

She struggled, trying to recall by heart the lyrics of a single Mormon hymn, but at least one child had complete faith in her abilities. Rebecca, the daughter of Sister Lydia Ashdown, sidled next to Josephine and tried to wrap her short arms around Josephine's skirt, at the knees.

"Yes, miss—Sister Josie," the small girl said earnestly. "I want to learn the Ladder-day Saint songs. I don't got the words down. But Mum says you can learn us most anything."

In the afternoons, after school, Josephine would join the sisters as they sat on the deck knitting shawls and darning socks, or stitching the handcart covers they would need for their trek across the North American continent. Mothers kept their eyes on their younger children as they talked of grown children—those who mocked the church—left behind. The women mourned parents and siblings they feared they would never see again. They fretted about damp dresses; things never seemed to dry out in spite of all the clothing ropes strung across aisles. They wondered about the construction of the handcarts and talked both eagerly and fearfully about the mountains they had seen only in sketches from a trail guide. They planned their new homes in the Salt Lake Valley.

Listening, Josephine began to hope—began to plan—for her own home. Calico curtains at the windows. A flock of chickens in the yard. Apple trees, and corn stalks standing in neat rows. A stream running nearby. She would plant bluebells; she would create an English meadow. She and Momma had little now, but the missionaries had promised a life of abundance. When they arrived, would homes be provided? She knew building a home would be far beyond their skills, but perhaps someone could help. They would find work; they would pay for the labor. She imagined cooking fine meals at the hearth, perhaps not right at first, but after they were settled in. Roast beef surrounded by carrots and turnips. Fresh milk! Perhaps some strawberries and cream for dessert.

Often, by midafternoon, languor had set in and the women worked in companionable silence, their hands busy with needles and thread and yarn, but Josephine would grow restless. Once she caught herself listlessly humming "What will we do with a drunken sailor?" She looked around in panic, dropping a stitch.

Did anyone hear?

But she needn't have worried, for a few of the sisters had already started singing, "Come, Come, Ye Saints." If Meaghan were here, she would have laughed at the "drunken sailor" slip-up, but Josephine, intent for once on propriety, simply picked up her knitting needles and joined in.

The evenings were Josephine's favorite times. After supper the ship bell would ring, and everyone who was not down with dysentery or seasickness ascended to the deck. Prayer meetings were held every night.

The church elders—men who had been ordained to God's holy priesthood—passed around hymn books, with songs dedicated to sacrifice and the last days and the kingdom in the mountains of Zion.

After the hymns Brother Larsen would preach. "Trust in the Good Shepherd," the ship president said. He lifted his hand toward the billowing sails and pronounced, "We have set our sails for the reward of everlasting life. The Lord will direct our course." The familiar words, spoken each night in his resonant timbre, made Josephine feel safe, and as she watched mothers suckle infants under shawls and toddlers nestle against big sisters, she felt as if she was part of an extended family.

Sometimes Hans Larsen gave them gentle reminders. "Ya, and there have been reports of disorderliness." The president would lean on his duck's head cane and finger the scruff of his beard. "And some have been cross at shortages of food. We will not reach the goal unless we pull together as one. I would remind you to show Christian charity in all your dealings. When we arrive, there will be blessings enough for all to partake."

Josephine took comfort in Brother Larsen's words, but his first counselor, Elder Ernst Clough, was another matter. Elder Clough made the girl nervous. He had the narrow, sloping shoulders of a woman, but his back was as straight as the ship's mast. His talk was straight, too. He could be counted on to mention the destroying angel laying waste to apostates and blasphemers. As he talked, the girl concentrated, not on his words, but on the Adam's apple protruding from his neck, bobbing up and down.

"Our pilgrimage is but a refiner's fire." *Up.* "Our journey will separate the faithful from the infidels!" *Up.* "We will be sorely tried." Elder Clough seemed to take pleasure in the fact of their being sorely tried, but assured them, as if to put their hearts at rest, "Our trials will be short, and our reward eternal."

After the preaching, men and women bore testimony of the truth of the gospel and thanked God for their deliverance from the Babylon that was Europe, although many admitted to missing their native homeland. As the nights passed, some Saints spoke in tongues. They usually began with the admission of sin, and then proclaimed the joys of repentance, and finally, Josephine would hear the nonsensical phrases pour forth.

Lala-iglala-id! Igla-no-do-dod! Nohi-kidit-laga. They clapped their hands and spoke with such energetic abandon that some slumped forward, spent, after the gift departed.

"Our Prophet Joseph Smith tells us this is the pure language of Adam," Elder Clough explained.

The first night she heard the pure language of Adam, Josephine's brows came together in a perplexed frown, and she sent her mother a questioning glance. Elizabeth looked uncomfortable but was saved from having to respond, for Brother Larsen broke in, as if eager to move on.

"Ah. The spirit of our Heavenly Father has been poured out upon us this evening. Right, then. I reckon the good Lord won't look askance now if we tap our toes a bit."

And with that, the hymn books were gathered up and the Saints turned to merriment. Young people performed skits and men sang feisty ballads and a newly formed band, dubbed Bound for Zion, played high-spirited polkas. Between tunes, Josephine sometimes caught her pupils singing, "What will we do with a drunken sailor?" and collapsing into each other's arms, giggling. The oldest Saints were the first to tire, and then the mothers and fathers, but young people urged the musicians to keep playing.

Last, each night, came the fiddler. Gavin Sayers was from Wales, and he couldn't walk without a crutch. The first time Josephine saw him, his scuffling gait reminded her of the crabs she had seen at the wharf the morning they left Liverpool. Gavin limped to the center of the circle and laid his crutch on the deck. He had a full head of red hair and a boyish face scattered with freckles, and he wore old trousers like all the men and boys. His suspenders, also red, hung so loose they couldn't have held up anything; they were for show.

But when Gavin put his bow to the fiddle and struck up "Weevily Wheat," the music exploded, as did the crowd. Gut strings snapped and flew about, people clapped, and everyone except Ernst Clough caught their second wind and began to dance, reveling in freedom and the good, clean salt air. Children squealed and spun in dizzy circles, and Brother Larsen kicked his good leg as high as the young men.

Josephine grabbed her skirt and whirled so fast she almost lost her footing. And all the while, she watched Gavin's arms, bare to the elbows, as he gyrated in the lantern light. She saw the way his neck cradled his fiddle. She looked at his crutch lying on the ground and wondered how someone who is crippled might earn a living for his family, and then, as his fiddle rasped into the next song, twirled until her skirt flew in a wide circle.

"Alas, 'tis a pity that fiddler's too young for the likes of me," Sister Peart Maisey confided cheekily. Josephine felt her face grow hot.

The first morning on board, Sister Maisey had bustled up the aisle looking for a berth, and Elizabeth had invited her to join them. Now they were five—Josephine, Momma, Sister Lydia Ashdown and her daughter Rebecca, and Sister Maisey.

As the song wound into an abandoned frenzy, several young couples slipped into the shadows. Josephine slowed her steps and followed them with her gaze. One young man and woman leaned against the railing, bending into each other. She felt a strange confusion rise in her chest, one of giddiness and heat, and she suddenly thought of Meaghan and Harold Baker.

Elder Clough also noticed the couples, and strode after them, his jaw jutting forward so far it seemed his shoulders were running to catch up. Josephine soon saw the young lovers emerge from the darkness, one girl rubbing her hand across her mouth, and her beau, straightening his hair and setting his cap back on his head in an embarrassed manner. Josephine quickly looked away.

Josephine saw Elder Clough crack his knuckles, and then he spat out the words. "Lusting! Right in our midst. Where is the shame?"

"Mercy, but that man goes on about lusting," Peart Maisey said cheerfully. "I could go for some meself, but I reckon that ain't in the gospel plan."

Sleep was often slow to come to Josephine. The lines for the bucket toilets, with their whispered conversations and fretful children, stretched through the aisles, and after her return from the toilet she shivered as she crawled into the bunk; her clothes always felt clammy. Rebecca nestled next to Sister Ashdown, sleeping with her thumb in her mouth. She mumbled in her dreams, sometimes scratching the fleas that crawled through her hair. Rebecca wasn't the only one making noise. People coughed all night, and Josephine could hear the croak of vomiting. The closed-in feeling of hundreds of bodies in such a tight, below-water space made the girl uneasy.

Sometimes, long after the lanterns were extinguished, she heard muffled grunts and high-pitched sighs coming from the married section. She strained her ears, tensing her body and holding her breath to listen. Were those the sounds Meaghan and her husband made in the night? Josephine remembered Elder Clough's words and felt guilty at the strange pulling in her loins. Suddenly she had the irrational fear that her mother, asleep beside her, could read her thoughts.

What does it mean to lust?

She heard panting. A soft groan.

The girl tried to stop herself from wondering, *Would Gavin Sayers make that sound?*

There was so much she didn't know.

"Good gracious, but we's packed in like a load of sheep, ain't we," said Sister Maisey one night as she glanced around the tween-deck. "Well, 't'aint nothing to be done for it now, is it. We left Queen Victoria's pastures long ago—and now we's committed."

The buxom woman had a throaty alto voice that reminded Josephine of a bad concert she had once heard, and Sister Maisey's all-purpose remedy for every difficulty, including claustrophobia, was a "spot of tea." Each night the good sister trundled back with her cup of weak tea and tugged her trunk from under her bunk, wheezing with exertion. She placed her cup on top of the trunk with exacting care, attempting to make sure the movement of the ship didn't jostle its precious contents. She had just sprinkled her tea with a "pinch of sweet" and taken a sip when Josephine felt swells, larger than she ever had felt before.

"For the love of angels!" Sister Maisey exclaimed, as hot tea splattered down her expansive bosom. She clutched her cup and nervously patted down her frowzy bangs.

Earlier that day Josephine had watched dark purple thunderheads pile up on the horizon. The ship had sailed on, straight toward them. Now she heard the wind gather intensity. Deckhands yelled to each other as they battened down hatches, and then the ship began to roll wildly, sparking whimpers from the smaller children. Josephine and her mother frantically struggled to lash down their crate as the vessel lurched up and crashed down on great cliffs of water and the low keening of the headwinds ascended to a roar. The girl heard the creak of timber and what sounded like waves crashing over the bulwark.

"Lord have mercy!" Peart Maisey cried, and Brother Larsen

shouted, "Steady on, steady on!" People began to pray with fervor. "Lord, we have given our all to you. Protect us from sinking into the deep!" Some begged aloud for repentance as kettles and tinned goods rattled forward and slid backward.

Josephine clung to the post of her bunk as passengers were hurled from side to side against the wooden partitions. In a wild confusion, sacks of potatoes, barrels of herring, casks of salted cabbages—all were tossed about like playthings. Josephine heard people stumbling, some still trying to reach their bunks.

"Momma! Are there really sharks?" Josephine shuddered at the thought of sinking into the black sea.

When the lanterns were extinguished, the steerage went dark and the travelers grew silent; all Josephine could hear was the monstrous waves, the crack of thunder, and the howling wind. She clenched the post of the bunk post until her hands hurt. She didn't know if the vessel was floating—or sinking.

The storm continued for what seemed like an eternity, the thunder deafening, the immigrants hushed. Josephine was exhausted. Once the hatches were closed, foul air permeated the steerage until Josephine felt she could hardly breathe. As the ship tossed wildly about, chamber pot buckets spilled, and so did the contents of people's stomachs, until the floor was a slimy mess.

Peart Maisey was the first to break the silence. "Afore this's over, I fear we's all headed for the bottom of the sea."

Sister Lydia Ashdown, sitting next to her on the lower bunk, said, "Have faith in the Lord." Her voice was so soft in the darkness that Josephine could hardly hear it. "He'll rebuke the sea."

"But when?" Sister Maisey said, sounding worried. "He's surely taking his time on the rebuking. I fear the ship'll toss herself wrong side up while the good Lord tarries on his throne."

For a moment, Josephine forgot the storm and laughed out loud, but her mother said, as if to calm herself as well as the others, "The Lord will protect us. I am certain of it."

"This is right question'ble protection he offers," Sister Maisey countered.

Rebecca began to whimper. "Mum, Mum. Can we go home? I want to go home."

Josephine heard other children snuffling, and longed to be top-side under a sunny sky, innocently teaching her students the English words for *food, sleep, sea. Mama, papa, prophet.*

At seven o'clock the next morning, the winds calmed and the ocean grew eerily still. Once the captain gave word, passengers slowly emerged from the lower reaches of the ship, looking dazed, gulping fresh air.

"Glory 'pon glory, we's ain't drowned!" Sister Maisey fluttered happily, her pendulous breasts jouncing above her voluminous skirt. "And now, 'magine, not 'nough of a breeze to blow out a candle."

Rebecca tried out the new phrase. "Glory 'pon glory! Glory 'pon glory!" She danced around her mother and pulled at her skirt, showing off her cleverness, but she was ignored. Lydia's hands set-tled protectively across the top of her swelling stomach.

"Josie," Elizabeth said, "help me go down and scrub the floors before someone slips."

"Momma," Josephine sulked, "why do we always have to be the responsible ones?"

But Josephine was saved by Brother Larsen, who decreed that the women would stay up on deck for a sermon, while the men would go below and scrub the floorboards. Only one man—the white-whiskered Brother Hubbard—was excused; his leg had been injured when a cask fell. As no physician was on board, Hans Larsen prescribed bed rest for him. And no dancing.

"I ain't firm on how many more days the good Lord'll give me for dancing," Brother Hubbard protested. "I don't intend to waste them in bed."

"Ya, and you'll probably live to see another day." Brother Larsen chuckled. "You rest up, and I reckon the ladies will still be here after your leg mends." He tipped his cap to the sisters.

Han Larsen's voice echoed the bass undertow of the ocean as he reassured his flock, "We are pilgrims at sea, and like all pilgrims, we must pass through tribulation. But the Lord has rebuked the raging waters, like the days of old. God directs our ship. All will be well."

But all was not well. One infant, coughing, could change everything.

7

THE LORD TAKES many away, even in infancy, that they may escape the envy of man, and the sorrows and evils of this present world; they were too pure, too lovely, to live on earth; therefore, if rightly considered, instead of mourning we have reason to rejoice …

—Excerpt from a funeral sermon by Joseph Smith for two-year-old Marian Lyon

May 12, 1856

Dearest Meaghan—

How are you?—I dearly wish I could hear news from home.

We are well here all though Momma has come down with the Seasickness. As she brushed out her hair yesterday I noticed for the first time how frail she looks. She thinks of you & Edward & William almost constantly, fearing she shall never see her children again. But her mind is set—She is fixed on getting to Zion. There is no turning back she says

Some times it seems that everything has happened in such haste— just yesterday we passed the misionaries on the street & now here we are drifting in the middle of an endless Ocean. I look out as far as I can see—there is nothing but Sea & Sky. Some times a great loneliness comes upon me. I remember you & me sitting together with our needle work—As much as I dreaded the irksome pastime, now I would give anything for an afternoon of cross stitch with you. But I know God has called me on this voyage. It is difficult now, but a land of abundance awaits at journey's end—

Have you seen Edward & William? Do they ask about us? Please tell them that we are healthy & happy—All is well.
   I miss you terribly

     With All My Love,
     Josie

PS I neglected to tell you in my last letter—I have been called to teach the children on board. The work is a joy. I teach sums, and many children who don't speak English are learning the language so they can make their way in America.

After the storm, the ship captain tallied up the losses. A corner of the mainsail had torn, he said. Standing at the bow, his bull neck red with sun, he informed them that his second mate was washed overboard and lost at sea, but these misfortunes are bound to happen as the sea is not always a kind mistress. The good news, the captain said, was that the ship was moving along at twelve knots, and skies were clear.

That night the Saints rose, one by one, and poured forth testimonies and thanksgiving. As the ship glided along, its sails spread full to the wind, they pledged a renewal of faith. They repented of their sins.

Brother Hans Larsen came last, offering his glad tidings. "Last night the Good Shepherd softened the hearts of our captain and five of the crew. They have asked for baptism. They will leave the ship when we reach New York City, and go right on through with us. All the way to the Salt Lake Valley."

"Ya, and one of the sea men's a carpenter and can help us before we even begin our trek," Hans Larsen said. "He's promised to help build our handcarts when we reach Iowa City."

Josephine leaned toward her mother and whispered, "Momma,

are the handcarts not built yet?"

"I do not know, child," her mother said. "But I am sure everything will soon be put in proper order."

Sister Lydia Ashdown's labor pains began in the middle of the night. Josephine, lying in the top bunk, rolled over and listened to the suppressed moans coming from below. They soon turned to muffled screams. In the dim lantern light, the girl saw a midwife hurry to their berth. Alarmed at the noises, Josephine was relieved when the woman assigned her a job.

"Bring a basin with hot water. Be quick!"

By the time she returned, the midwife was already spreading Lydia's legs and comforting her, saying *Breathe, breathe*. Josephine held up a blanket to shield Sister Ashdown from the curious stares of children in nearby berths and watched, horrified, as a red, slippery head emerged from the woman's private parts. She felt faint, and then frightened, suddenly all too aware of her coming womanhood.

Will I have to endure that pain someday?

The midwife caught the infant, swung it upside down, and slapped its bottom. A piercing wail filled the steerage. At that moment Josephine felt a pulling at her knees. Rebecca had crept underfoot and was clinging to her skirt.

"Sister Josie, miss, is my mum going to die?"

"Oh no, 'Becca!" Josephine took a deep breath to settle herself and said, "You have a new baby sister. You're the older sister now and you must set an example."

Upon hearing Josephine's words, Rebecca puffed out her chest with pride. The exhausted mother cradled the little body in her arms and stroked the silky hair. She smiled tenderly at the newborn, which had opened its eyes and was sucking eagerly at a breast.

"Her name will be Joy," Sister Ashdown announced.

"We take joy in the calming of the storm," Brother Larsen prayed the next morning. "We take joy in the gospel message. Most of all, O Father in Heaven, we take joy in this newborn, who has come from your heavenly home to join us on our journey. Her name is most fitting."

But by Saturday, the baby's name mocked the mother.

Typhus and dysentery had been making their way through the ship. Josephine, embarrassed, tried not to watch as women nervously waited in line for the buckets, attempting to hold back diarrhea. Others shook with chills or burned with fever. Some muttered and rolled back and forth in agony. On warm days, the sick were brought up into the fresh air and sunshine in hopes of reviving their bodies and spirits. The baby Joy was carried up, too, but the ocean air and her mother's milk were not enough to save her.

Josephine knew the moment the baby died because she could hear Sister Ashdown begin to keen—long, almost silent sobs, interrupted by the staggered intake of breath, weeping that sounded like drowning.

"Mum! Mum! What's wrong, Mum?" Rebecca pulled at Lydia's skirt. She squirmed for a place on her mother's lap, but that lap was taken by a lifeless baby.

Josephine reached for Rebecca. "'Becca, your mum needs you to be a grown-up girl now. Do you understand? You must be very quiet. Your mum is tired."

The ship's carpenter constructed a small coffin of rough planks and placed stones in the bottom. Josephine watched him bore holes in the sides—to make it sink faster, he said. But when the ship bell solemnly rang and the Saints stood around the coffin and Brother Larsen commended the infant's soul to God, when the body was lowered into the sea, it didn't sink quickly. Josephine watched as the small box bobbed about, only slowly disappearing beneath the waves. The setting sun had fired the ocean as red as blood, and then the air turned clammy and dark.

As thick fog began to settle about the sails, Josephine suddenly realized how exposed she was, how exposed they all were. Just a floating community of hungry souls rocking on a vast sea.

We aren't alone, she told herself frantically, trying to convince herself of the fact. *We are on our way to the Promised Land!*

God is protecting us, even though I don't always understand his ways.

Her thoughts were echoed by Brother Larsen. "We can't comprehend the mysteries of our Father in Heaven," he told them, but his normally ebullient voice sounded flat. He faltered, rubbing his beard. He leaned hard on his cane.

"Our mortal existence is uncertain. Why is it that this babe was taken from us?" He paused and looked upward, as if asking God himself that very question. His expression was that of a kindly father, but the Mormon leader suddenly looked older. Perhaps he was remembering his own daughter. Josephine had heard that his only child had died of cholera last year, followed by his wife. They had been planning to make the journey with him but hadn't gotten farther than the local graveyard.

In the awkward silence that followed, the first counselor stepped forward. "The only difference between the old and the young dying is that one is freed sooner from this corrupt world," Elder Clough declared. "This babe has been delivered from the clutches of Babylon."

Sister Ashdown clenched the hand of Rebecca, now her only child.

"We sail with the God of deliverance and power," Ernest Clough trumpeted, his Adam's apple bulging with all its might. "He is our captain. He will protect those who are righteous, whether they abide on Earth or—like this babe—in heaven."

Elizabeth didn't attend the funeral, nor did she see the little coffin drift away in the waters. The constant motion of the ship had heightened her seasickness, and like many others, she was lying in her berth, a pail nearby. Josephine wondered if there was more to it. The girl often caught her mother at the ship railing, staring into the distance, always in the direction of England. Josephine would go and stand alongside, and the two would gaze silently at the eastern horizon.

One night they watched a river of stars in the heavens, and saw the moon rise, lighting the sea until it sparkled like a field of diamonds.

So much beauty and so much sorrow, all at the same time, Josephine thought.

"I wonder what Meaghan and the boys are doing tonight," said Momma, her voice high and bright, but her daughter caught her wiping the corner of her eye with her shawl. And then, in the same sunny tone, "I am guessing Meaghan will be having a baby of her own sometime soon." Elizabeth's forced good spirits gave the impression she was contemplating baking up a batch of tea cookies to celebrate the arrival of a grandchild.

Josephine couldn't even pretend at cheerfulness. "I imagine so," she said dully, taking off her bonnet and feeling the breeze rake her hair. She had brought Meaghan's hand-stitched quilt—its delicate border of bluebells—to the deck, and she hugged it about her shoulders, as if its neat cloth squares would bring back her sister.

Heavenly Father, I have put my life in your hands. Please ...

The girl imagined large comforting hands—*God's* hands—reaching out to her, but her thoughts were interrupted by her mother, bent at the railing, trying to hold back retching.

And then neither said anything more, for it seemed there was nothing to be said.

Sister Ashdown's infant had been the first to die. The baby Joy was followed by an elderly widow, and then a Welsh shepherd boy and a blind blacksmith from Lancashire. Two girls, ages six and nine, were followed by their mother, already weak and missing a hand from an accident in a cotton mill. The ship's carpenter ran out of wooden planks after the seventh death, and so the bodies simply were slipped over the side of the ship. They floated away like debris on the ocean. With each passing, the shipboard community grew quiet, perhaps contemplating their own—or their children's—narrow escape from a grave in the sea. With each death, Brother Larsen offered comfort, and the survivors clung hungrily to his words.

One morning, after seven weeks at sea, the first mate climbed to the crow's nest, searched the horizon, and shouted, "Land! I spot land!"

Josephine joined in the exuberant cries around her and rushed to the top deck so quickly she tripped on the hem of her skirt and skinned her knee.

"Where?" she cried, squinting into the distance. White beads of foam drifted on the surface of the water and wet spray rose into the chilly air, but the girl didn't feel the bite of the cold. "Where?"

Some passengers stumbled down the stairs into the hold, frantically searching for bundles and boxes to take ashore, but most people crowded eagerly onto the deck, searching for a glimpse of America.

At first, the North American continent looked like little more than an illusion, a mere suggestion of fierce hope, indistinguishable in the distance from the sea. But Josephine slowly saw that the emerging mass was unlike the blue-on-blue blur of water and sky. It had edges. She began to make out a faint strip of land. She closed her eyes and clasped her hands and drew in lungfuls of strong, fishy air. Soon she saw the tall masts of outgoing ships, and gradually, coming into view, the waterfront buildings and church spires and rooftops of New York City. The shore grew closer with each gentle lap.

Some knelt, and some began to sing hymns. They cried, "America, America!" as the gulls swooped and screamed overhead.

"We are mooring in Zion's harbor!" Brother Larsen exclaimed, but his voice was drowned out by a shipful of Mormons. Elder Clough tried for pious decorum but even he couldn't hide his elation, throwing his cap in the air so high it sailed away.

That afternoon a health inspector came aboard to examine the ship's log for details about deaths at sea—eighteen in number—and to scan the crowd for signs of cholera, typhoid fever, or smallpox. He flinched and covered his nose as he stepped on board, and Josephine, standing near him, suddenly felt self-conscious. She wondered if she smelled, if they all smelled, after a month and a half drenched in filth and sweat, surrounded by pungent toilet buckets. There was so little water that washing one's face and hands and feet had been difficult, if not impossible, and the flea-ridden bed pallets had been brought to the deck only twice for airing.

The health official scrutinized first one person and then another, noting those who appeared to carry infectious diseases. And then the ship put down its heavy anchor at Castle Garden, the fortress-like immigrant receiving center. There in the harbor, officials quarantined the sickliest passengers and herded them onto a boat headed for the hospital, separating weeping families.

Josephine was jostled into the colossal rotunda, where hundreds of newcomers from around the world waited to be more closely examined. She had never seen such a huge crowd.

She caught sight of Gavin Sayers in another line, his red hair falling over his forehead as he leaned on his crutch. He looked more commonplace without his fiddle. The animation was gone and his limp was more pronounced. Around him, people sat on trunks yawning, and some slept stretched out on the filthy floor while their children played about their feet. Mothers nursed infants and crooned lullabies while they gazed upward in wonder at the cavernous ceiling. One of the sisters tended to old Brother Hubbard's broken leg, unwrapping and re-wrapping the dirty strip of cloth. Gavin seemed detached from the scene, although Josephine noticed that his gaze followed anyone who walked by with sausage or apples from the vendor stands.

Hunger was settling insistently into the hollow of her own stomach, and the line had wound its way down to the last few immigrants by the time she and her berth companions reached the inspector.

Sister Maisey puffed forward triumphantly on her small feet, as if she had just won a race rather than placed last. The busty woman beamed at the official and praised the *magnificent* city of New York—at least what she could see of it so far—and the *first-class* treatment by the ship captain and his crew—although she noted for the record that the second mate had washed overboard—and she even praised the inspector himself, before he cut her off. Elizabeth stepped forward next, her hair pulled into a graceful chignon, looking as if she hadn't spent the last seven weeks retching over a bucket. Josephine followed, offering a hopeful curtsy.

"Your destination?" the official asked, as he carefully examined each of them.

"We's headed to the Promised Land!" proclaimed Sister Maisey, who failed to elaborate exactly where that was.

"The Utah Territory, sir," Elizabeth said, in a refined accent.

"Aye, the Utah Ter'tory, quite right! Oh my," Sister Maisey echoed, as she patted her frowsy bangs into place.

The inspector's eyes settled on Lydia Ashdown, who stooped rather than stood. She looked past him, her face pale and indifferent. Josephine balled her fists as she watched Rebecca trail along behind. Lately, the little girl had seemed almost an afterthought to her mother.

The inspector's long pause seemed to imply that Sister Ashdown's health status was troubling. He hesitated, tapped his documents with a precise air, and finally cleared his throat and said, "You'll do," and waved them breezily through the gate.

8

ANOTHER LARGE BATCH of Mormons passed through our city yesterday morning. They numbered between four and five hundred and comprised men, women and children—some of the women carrying babes in their arms. One man was limping along on a wooden leg, and we noticed two or three old men and women who seemed fitter for tottering over the grave, than for taking the weary pilgrimage to Utah.

—*Davenport Daily Gazette*

May 26, 1856

Dearest Meaghan—

We are in America! Even though I am on a foreign shore I wept for joy upon seeing land. When we sailed into the harbour we beheld great majestic ships with towering masts coming & going & and lined along the peirs.

We landed at an imigrant center they call Castle Garden, all though I did not see a castle or a garden any where. When my feet finally touched land it was a curious sensation—the ship had finally ceased its unending too & fro, & now the World itself felt as if it were swaying. Even though it is dreadfully cold here I thank God for our safe arrival over the perilus Seas!

Some of the Saints were taken for sick quarantine, & several of the sisters are ill with the pox—they draped a veil o'er their face to hide the scabs.

The First Counseler—Elder Cloe—says New York is a wicked & abomnible city—and some of its inhabitants have been terribly unkind—but I still wish we could remain here a few more days. Shops of every kind line the streets—entire shops selling just bonnets, or just gloves, or only petticoats & chemises & corsets! And the streets themselves—they are a mad confusion! Hundreds of hogs run up & down in search of scraps—& there are carriages & horse carts & wagons all vying for the same place in the road and ending up in a helpless tangle—& imigrants who speak in Old World accents, & you should see—women wearing Bloomers! They are like pantaloons & said to be from Arabia.

We are sorting ourselves out & Elder Cloe is making arrangements for our railway passage to the Iowa Teritory—where we will begin our hand cart journey.

I hope all is well with you. My thoughts dwell on you more than I can say. If you see Edward & William, please tell them that Momma & me are well contented, God is with us in this new land & we are safe in his care—

With Love & Affection,
Your Josie

PS   I am mailing this before we board the train tomorrow, & will (eagerly!) look for your return letter. It is best to send it to Fort Kerney, Nebraska Teritory, on the Oregon Trail—where I hope it reaches me. Please write

Castle Garden, the immigrant receiving center, had once been a grand performance hall, but now its stifling air was heavy with the smell of unwashed humans and rancid cheese and herring gone bad. The Saints were to sleep on the gallery floors, but night was a long ways off, and Brother Larsen decided fresh air would do them all good. Soon they were making their way from the harbor, braving the chilly breezes of spring.

But they had no sooner reached Broadway than a crowd of Gothamites began forming, eager for a first-hand look at Mormons, as if the Latter-day Saints might be more curious than the albinos and midgets and giants of P.T. Barnum up the street. The locals eagerly counted each man's wives with lewd curiosity and seemed disappointed to find only one apiece.

One leered at Josephine and called, "You going to Utah to be one of Brigham's girls?" while another guffawed, "She's a proper bit of frock, but I suspicion he's already got more'n he can handle."

Josephine drew her shawl across her breasts and looked straight ahead, trying to make herself even smaller than she already was. Her lip quivered and she tried not to tear up—she didn't want to give them that—but Sister Peart Maisey seemed to take the man's words, directed at Josephine, as her own personal affront, one that shouldn't go unanswered.

Drawing up her chest with such indignant righteousness she seemed about to burst out of her corset, Sister Maisey boasted, "Pshaw! I'll tell you die'reckly, so you can run home and tell it to your other rib. I's got four husbands meself, and so what!"

And to herself, "Fie on that bit of rusty guts. He ain't smart 'nough to see a hole in a bucket."

Josephine forgot she had been trying not to cry; now she tried not to laugh. Suddenly she remembered—Elder Clough! She looked about nervously, hoping Ernst Clough hadn't heard Sister Maisey's indelicate talk. But the first counselor was occupied near the front of the procession, advising the Saints to ignore the scrutiny of the blasphemers and march straight ahead as befits Jehovah's soldiers.

"Look neither to the right nor to the left," he called out, motioning them along the walkway. "These vulgar blackguards consider us peculiar? I say, God considers them more so, and rightly."

Josephine walked on, trying to mask her consternation. Why did these horrid rumors follow them halfway around the world? The church brethren she was acquainted with could barely support one wife, and it was certain most were too honorable to contemplate taking another.

Aside from Sister Maisey, who couldn't be trusted with simple propriety, the Mormons stolidly ignored the taunts, and the locals soon tired of their amusement and drifted away. In spite of the rude reception, Josephine couldn't help but be mystified and enchanted by the city. The scale of everything seemed larger and more prosperous than anything she ever had seen. She felt almost dizzy as she peered up at the top stories of ornate cast-iron buildings. She gaped at the horse-drawn buses, which rushed up and down crowded streets so rapidly it was a wonder how riders got on and off, and why no one was crushed. Behind plate-glass fronts, dressmakers' showrooms jostled for space with cafés and woolen goods emporiums and milliners' shops.

As Josephine walked under a "Fine Silks" sign, she heard Elder Clough pronounce New York City the great Babylon. "Its enticements are nothing but idolatry," he warned as he herded his flock along the streets of Gotham.

The girl, dressed in her faded apple-green gingham, stared longingly at the enticements, lingering especially on the ladies' boutiques, where petticoats were embroidered with butterflies and dresses were ribboned with black velvet.

"Satan cannot seduce us unless we give our consent," Ernst Clough barked. He lifted his arms as if to shield the sisters from the sights of the place. "The Almighty will crush this abominable city under his foot!"

"I say, the Lord must wear a frightful shoe size," Peart Maisey joked good-naturedly as she gazed at the lofty buildings. She seemed as delighted by the sights as Josephine.

Although Elder Clough was of the opinion that the Saints couldn't leave fast enough, Brother Larsen was more pragmatic in his approach.

"Some will need to stay on here," Hans Larsen said. Many had ventured forth with more faith than farthings—God bless them— and would need to work a season as shipbuilders or street pavers or laundresses before they could continue their journey west.

"They will be in our prayers as we depart," he said.

Josephine's mother had tied their last few coins in a handkerchief. The amount was just enough for the railway passage to Iowa City and supplies for the trek, but looking around, Josephine almost wished they were out of money too, so she could stay a while and take in all the enticements.

The next morning, as she and her mother waited at the Rock Island depot, she quickly decided the train might be its own adventure. She was standing on the wooden platform with the others when she heard a piercing steam whistle and the clang of a bell, and then the rails began to vibrate as a monstrous black locomotive came roaring into the depot. With a screech of its brakes, the great beast rumbled to a stop and sat panting loud, rhythmic gasps.

Billows of black smoke rose into the frigid air as the engineer dumped ashes overboard, and then the conductor pulled a watch from his vest pocket and called, "All aboard!" Josephine felt as if she were entering another world as she climbed the steep steps to the railway car. They were really on their way! She looked out the windows and her heart started beating fast.

We'll see the country!

She remembered the Sunday drives with Papa—meadows and oak groves and tumble-down castles—and she wondered what America would look like. She doubted there would be another city to compare with New York.

But Elder Clough, who had arranged railway passage for the Saints, guided them past the long bank of windows, into the next rail car, and then the next, and several more after that, until at last the girl found herself in a drafty car with windows so grimy she could barely catch a glimpse of the view outside.

Josephine was seized with claustrophobia. She thought she could smell fear in those around her, and felt an unexpected wave of compassion for these people—*her* people. But on the heels of sympathy came shame. Her people had teeth that were rotting and work-roughened hands, red as lobster claws. Even their finest cloth-ing, which they wore for the journey, was pitifully worn. How had the Mormons become her family? They could have been a horde of sheep being hauled to market.

With a jolt, the floor started to move and the train chugged forward, its string of cars clattering along behind, slowly picking up speed on the uneven track bed.

"Momma?" she asked nervously. "Do you—do you think this is safe?" She tried not to think of the train accidents in the news: head-on collisions, boiler explosions, wheels running right off the tracks.

"I am sure Brother Larsen is watching for our safety."

"But Brother Larsen's not the engineer."

Momma smiled. "No, Brother Larsen is a lot of things, but he is not the engineer."

The first hour was like all the hours that followed—the clack of wheels, the rocking from side to side—through Albany, and then Buffalo, through Cleveland and then on to Chicago, until the girl lost track of time. At larger cities, the train would roll into a depot with a refreshment saloon and the conductor would call, "Fifteen minutes for breakfast!" And then it would be two bits for a piece of pie, which Josephine and her mother split.

Nights were the most difficult, as the train hurtled onward, its whistle shrieking. Babies cried until it seemed they would wear out their little lungs; the noise made it impossible to sleep. Josephine crouched against the side of the railway car, closing her eyes and waiting—*waiting*—to reach Iowa City.

The second afternoon Rebecca nuzzled her head into her moth-er's skirt and soon Josephine heard soft sobs coming from its folds. The girl's cheeks were smeared with dirt and her pale hair was tinged gray with the drifting cinders of the locomotive.

"Mum," Rebecca sniffled. "I don't want to ride a train no more. I want my pa."

"We will be there soon, child," said Elizabeth, laying her hand on the girl's head.

Although Josephine felt almost as young and vulnerable as Rebecca, she mustered up her courage and said, "'Becca, this is an adventure. Don't you want to go to Zion? The other children are going."

"But when are we going *home*?"

"This will be our new home," said Josephine, hoping it was true.

During the numbing miles, her thoughts drifted back to her former home—on Middleton Street. And like Rebecca, she couldn't stop thinking about her own father. Strolling through the park, his hat perched jauntily on his head, she and Meaghan's hands tucked in his arms. The way he would chuckle and *humph* at their jokes, or tease them about their unruly hair. The way he pulled toffee from his vest pocket and dangled it in front of their faces as if they were still five years old. She felt longing, but she felt something else too, something that stung.

How could you have done this to us?

The girl pushed down her anger at Papa, at the way he had piled up debt unbeknownst to his family. After each wave of anger, she pushed down the emotion that followed.

Guilt.

But she didn't stop with reviewing the sins of her father; she had her own misdeeds to think about. Josephine remembered how she and Meaghan, in fun, had impersonated Papa's supper guests, with all their talk about poverty. The consensus in the parlor was that the poor—the shiftless, slovenly poor—are deserving of their fate. How could she and her sister, sitting there in their ruffles and lace, have been so naive? How could she have thought hunger and destitution a joking matter?

When the train laid over in Chicago, the weary travelers gathered at the edge of the depot, waiting for instructions.

"God-ay everyone! Hallo?" Hans Larsen shouted. "Can you hear me in the back? Ya? ... Proper good, then. The railway company has offered to let us sleep in their warehouse. If you have bedding, bring it with you."

He was interrupted by several strangers. "Well, well," one drawled, leaning against a post and spitting a wad of tobacco. "It's another band of polygamists. I suppose you're all going to Utah to serve as worker bees in Brigham's hive."

A flush crept up Josephine's face, and she noticed other sisters looking down with embarrassed expressions. They appeared as confused as she felt, but she was comforted by Brother Larsen's demeanor. He didn't appear nervous or ill at ease. He simply advised the women to quicken their step, and later he appointed brethren to stand guard in shifts.

The last thing Josephine heard before she fell asleep was a downpour on the roof, as if the clouds had conspired to dump their refuse on the Saints. The rain was so loud and the girl slept so soundly that she didn't know the mob beat on the warehouse walls with clubs until Elder Clough reported it later.

"They are serpents in the devil's own image," he said, but Brother Larsen said the men were simply God's children gone astray.

In the morning Josephine asked uneasily, "Momma, why do people keep calling us polygamists?"

She remembered the jeers in New York and the rumors she had heard in Liverpool, and her brothers' taunts about Joseph Smith's wives. Even Reverend Phillips had gently suggested they steer clear of the Mormons. He and his fellow ministers had come across anti-Mormon tracts that alleged the missionaries were gathering virgins to transport to Utah.

"That sounds a bit far-fetched," Reverend Phillips admitted, "but something isn't quite right. Why are they so anxious to gather everyone to Utah? What's wrong with worshiping here? The Church of England has been doing just that for three hundred years."

Now Josephine asked herself the same question. Is it so important to seclude ourselves from the world? Of course, if we are treated like this everywhere we go, she thought, choosing a home in a remote wilderness would make sense.

As her mother took off her nightcap and brushed out her long braid, Josephine asked again. "Why do people call us polygamists?"

Elizabeth pulled roughly at her tresses, in a manner unlike her usual self. She didn't reply to her daughter's question until she had finished winding her hair into a chignon. "The devil has their tongue," she finally said, with a tartness that was also unlike her.

Elizabeth retained her genteel comportment, but when the Mormons boarded the train again, Josephine noticed that her mother held back until everyone else had climbed aboard, and for a moment the girl wondered if Momma would board at all.

And perhaps she wouldn't have, had she known, for now the Saints were loaded into empty cattle cars, heading out from the stockyards. The cars smelled of longhorns, and although the excrement had been swept out, the stink remained.

The train rattled on, more than two hundred miles, until it ran out of track. When the conductor announced they were pulling into Iowa City, Josephine knew she should have felt grateful, but a sick stomach had claimed her back in Illinois.

"Look at this bunch," said Peart Maisey as she clambered down from the rail car. "Poor as Job's turkeys." She wobbled a bit, as if her knees were disoriented by the lack of motion. "Ah well. 'Tain't nothing to be done for it, is it, so we may as well make the best of our lot."

Josephine's clothes stank of cattle, and when Gavin Sayers limped by on his crutch, she turned the other direction in embarrassment, even though she was certain his clothing was just as sour. Her crate seemed twice as heavy as it had leaving Liverpool; Gavin's trunk was carried by one of the brethren.

Sister Lydia Ashdown's frail shoulders sloped forward as if she was spent, but she had a determined look in her eyes. Suddenly, right there in front of the depot, the woman clasped her hands and began to sing "The Spirit of God Like a Fire Is Burning." Josephine stared. The tune sounded more like a disturbance than a hymn. The girl didn't join in, nor did any of the others. The song died away before the second verse.

9

ON THEIR ARRIVAL on the frontier they were informed that Brother BRIGHAM had received a revelation from God, directing that in order to try their faith and thus test who among them were worthy the honors of the faithful, they should journey to Salt Lake in hand-cart trains!

—*The New-York Times*

June 8, 1856

Dearest Meaghan—

Well, we finally arrived in Iowa City just over a week ago—& tomorrow at day break we begin our walk! Brother Larsen delivered our hand cart today & it is as sturdy as any covered wagon. Momma & me practiced pulling the cross bar. It is not so heavy! We shall make good work of it—

Brother Hans Larsen continues as our President. Our party consists of English, Swedes, Danish, & Welsh—& how he presides over such a babble of tongues I can not fathom. It must have dismayed him that not one of the men had ever seen—nor yoked!—an ox team in his life.

Momma & me are each allowed 17 lbs. of personal effects—our only belongings now. I am taking an extra dress—the gray wool, for warmth—& 3 pairs of stockings—Also, my green satin slippers, which Momma considers purely impractical. You see, I am still a thorn in her ever patient side! We will also haul our bedding, skillet & dishes, water, & some provisions. My bedding is your dear quilt, with its gay flowers to remind me of Home.

Tomorrow we will rise early & then, we are on our way to the Promised Land! All is right with the world, it has been a trying journey thus far, but we have been assured of blessings at journey's end. I have put my trust in the Lord—He is our hope & guidance

My only sorrow is that you are not here. As it is, I think of you every day & pray for you—

With Love & Affection,
Josie

PS   I will mail this letter when we reach Fort Kerney, & dearly hope a letter from you is waiting there. It is distressing to be so far apart, & not know how your dear ones are.

The party had arrived in Iowa City long past dark and started out on foot in the rain. By the time they reached the campsite, Josephine's skirt was heavy with the weight of water. It was after midnight before she crawled into a crowded tent.

At dawn the girl pulled open the flap and discovered they were surrounded by a muddy tent city that extended as far as she could see. The acrid odor of fresh manure filled the air, and she saw hundreds of women crouched over campfires, boiling coffee and frying salt bacon. The smells made her stomach ache with hunger.

This chaotic campground at Iowa City was what Peart Maisey called "the flurryment," and what the brethren were calling the jumping-off place. To Josephine, it seemed she and Momma had jumped off long ago—back when they first lugged their crate up the gangplank of the ship.

The Saints were rounded up and divided into companies, and Josephine noticed her mother's face light up when she learned Brother Larsen would be president of their company. Feeling uneasy, and a bit uncharitable, the girl mentally counted up the months since Papa had died.

"We'll still not be needing any formalities as far as titles," President Hans Larsen told his group of more than three hundred people. "You can call me Brother Larsen."

Women and girls were given instructions and demonstrations: This here is how you dig a fire pit and start a campfire. Here's how you cook johnnycakes, guard against burning them. You'll be expected to take a turn at milking, you'll need to make soap, and if you haven't already, you'll need to sew a handcart cover. London manners don't count for much here, hem your skirt up two inches so you can walk over boulders and mud. And get accustomed to conducting your private matters with little privacy. Darkness and your long skirts are the best cover, although one side of the trail will be reserved for you.

The handcarts, Josephine soon learned, were not finished. Many had not even been started. She heard the feverish sound of hammers and saws from the time she woke until late into the night.

"Mercy, that noise is loud enough to wake the snakes," exclaimed Sister Maisey as they stood in the shallows of the stream one afternoon, washing their arms and feet.

"Then we shall hope the hammering is soon finished and the snakes remain asleep," said Elizabeth, laughing.

Rebecca asked, "What're snakes?" while her mother looked around fearfully and fretted, "The missionaries in Liverpool never said anything about snakes."

"'Twas one of their stories touched on the matter, I recolleck," said Peart brightly as she soaped her arms. "A snake with a prop'sition—to a certain lass name of Eve."

Lydia's face puckered with anger. "Sister, your blasphemy is not pleasing to the Lord."

Josephine ignored the conversation. She checked the horizon, and seeing no men about, lifted her skirt to her knees. She studied the water for any unusual slithering movements, held her breath, and waded one step deeper, digging her toe into the oozing mud.

"Josie, take care," Elizabeth said. "We have been warned about quicksand."

"Creeps!" Josephine suddenly shouted, as she felt a tickle against her calves. She hopped up and down frantically, holding her skirt high, and sloshed through the muck to the shore, strands of sedge wrapping themselves about her legs at every step. "A snake!"

Rebecca tumbled toward the shore so fast she tripped over a log and fell into the mud. "Eeeyow!" She wiped the front of her dress with both hands. "What are snakes?" she asked again, as if she were trying to decide just how distressed to be.

Her mother decided for her. "You will not go near the water again, Rebecca! Do you hear?" Sister Ashdown shuddered, grabbing the girl's hand and thrashing up the bank.

"But how will I wash the mud off?" the child asked.

Josephine looked down shakily and saw marsh grasses wrapped around her legs. She sighed and looked up meekly. "I'll allow the snake might have just been a weed."

Sister Maisey wobbled up the bank and suddenly began to laugh, splashing droplets with every bounce of her breasts. "For the love of angels! A weed, the lass says."

Josephine, still befuddled, looked back at the sedge, waving innocently near the water's edge, and then she dropped her wet skirt and began to laugh too.

Rebecca, her face a question mark, giggled uncertainly. "Sister Josie, miss. Do snakes live in the water?"

"That's right, 'Becca," Josephine said in mock seriousness. "Snakes live in the water. They look very much like weeds."

"I'll not have you teasing her," said Lydia, uncharacteristically cross. "She's only a child. And she needs to understand the perils we face."

"Aye, we must know our snakes. True, true," Sister Maisey agreed affably.

"We should return to camp," Elizabeth said. "Our supper will not cook itself."

"Rebecca, child, you can share my plate," Peart said. "We'll put butter on the bacon, we will."

"Butter?" Rebecca clapped her hands with excitement.

"Oh dear," Peart backtracked. "'Tis just an es'pression, love."

"Grass snakes! The first danger of the trip!" Josephine said playfully, as she walked alongside her mother back to camp.

Even the boys had been set to work, cutting trees and carving spokes for the two-wheeled handcarts. Fashioned of Iowa hickory and oak, the boxes on wheels measured three feet across and four feet long and looked a bit like the spindly carts of street sweepers. The sides were eight inches high and each one had a crossbar for pulling. Josephine overheard Brother Larsen ask about metal rims for the wheels. He was told there were none; Brigham Young had decreed they were not needed.

"Each cart may need to hold near five hundred pounds," Hans Larsen explained, a bit sheepishly, Josephine thought. He looked with concern at Gavin Sayers and old Brother Hubbard, still nursing his lame leg. The president's eyes finally rested on Sister Abigail, an elderly widow wheezing up phlegm.

"There will be no turning around once we leave Iowa City," he said pointedly, but gently.

"The Lord will carry me through," Sister Abigail said.

Brother Hubbard declared, "I'll lean on him as well."

"And I'm needed for the fiddle," Gavin said.

"Right. We'll trust in the Lord then," Brother Larsen conceded.

He told them they would haul most of their provisions, and said to take care; before they plunk down their money, they best smell the salt pork to see if it's rancid and check the flour for worms. "The merchants of this place will take all your money if you're fool enough to give it to them. They're eager with tales of pioneers who starved along the way for lack of provisions. You'll only need what's on the list, and the old chaps can find some other fools to prey upon."

"Momma, really?" asked Josephine as she knelt that night over the fire pit, arranging kindling. "Everything we'll need for four months? We'll pull it?"

"That is what we are told, child," Elizabeth said. "But Brother Larsen said the supply wagons will carry some of our food. And we will have Peart and Lydia to help with our cart." She smiled at the two women.

Lydia looked worried, but she lifted her chin and said, "The Lord will do my pulling for me."

"This handcart plan looks a bit daft if you ask me. But then, none's asked my 'pinion now, has they," said Sister Maisey, as she made her first attempt at balancing the cooking tripod over the fire pit. It toppled into the ashes. She tried again; it toppled again, this time flattening the stack of kindling. She looked at the tripod in consternation and gave a disheartened nod of her head.

"Ah well, I may not need to learn this partic'lar skill after all," she said. "I have me doubts that me old drumsticks can push this load of knick-knacks over the mountains anyhows."

"How big are mountains?" Rebecca asked.

"They're like English hills, only bigger," said Lydia, taking the child's hand.

"Do we pull the carts or push them?" Josephine asked.

"I believe they said both," her mother said. "Push from behind and pull from the crossbar in front."

Josephine and Elizabeth bargained—nearly begged—for flour and lard and slabs of pork. Standing in front of the bulbous-nosed merchant, the girl eyed the dried peaches and apples with longing, and tried to content herself with the basics. She hoisted a sack of flour to their campsite, discovering with dismay how heavy it felt.

Hans Larsen had given the command: Each person would be allowed only seventeen pounds of personal effects. Up until two days before departure, Sister Maisey was still struggling with the rule. Each day, as women churned butter and made cakes of soap and sewed rice bags, Peart Maisey was useless. She stood in front of her sad little pile of possessions and wrung her hands. It was the first time Josephine had seen her truly distressed. The woman lugged her belongings again and again to the brass scale, where one side would tilt sharply up and the other side swing down. Then she would carry her things back to the tent, blinking back tears, and plop down on a stump.

"Lord in his mercy, how can I leave me rose china cups behind?" she asked plaintively. Her voice cracked. "I don't give meself airs over it, but 'tis the only fancy thing I's ever owned."

Her pile was finally whittled down, with only a *Book of Mormon* and the china left. Sister Maisey would have to choose one or the other, and she looked as if she were weighing the two items on a momentous scale within her mind—these pounds warring with those.

"I know what the brethren would counsel," said Peart, kneading the folds of her apron with her plump hands. "And I don't want to start off me journey on the wrong foot with the Lord. But surely it's only so much a soul can be asked to give up."

"I'm sure you're right," said Josephine as she pressed the plunger into the butter churn. "God doesn't ask more than we can give."

"Aye, but that's the rub, 'ain't it? I *can* give them up," said Sister Maisey, clutching a cup. "And I reckon the prophet's words are more 'portant than tea in a proper English teacup."

Her shoulders sagged as she reached for the *Book of Mormon* and set it atop her possessions. She picked up the delicate cups and saucers, and Josephine watched her set them in the mud near one of the hand-dug latrines, where someone else could adopt them, or wish they could.

A small exodus had begun within days of their arrival. Josephine heard that laborers in Iowa City were scarce, and townspeople were offering high wages to those who would delay their journey. Women could earn their board and five dollars a week for sewing or washing, and men with skilled trades could earn as much as ten dollars a day. Some men sat up late, poring over maps by lantern light; they walked around the handcarts looking apprehensive and then decided out loud that perhaps they would cross next summer, with a wagon and team, and maybe a cow or two.

But that wasn't all. Upon seeing the soggy confusion of the camp and the unfinished state of the handcarts, some converts simply melted away. Josephine heard of women who grew fainthearted at the thought of their children walking across the continent. One girl, she was told, began a courtship with a local rancher and was already dreaming of marriage, and another ran off with an adventurer who had been lured by mercantile opportunities in San Francisco. The rumor also was circulating that some single and widowed sisters had grown apprehensive about tales of polygamy and had taken their luggage, and children if they had any, and offered themselves to local families for domestic work.

One evening two young men passed Josephine's tent saying, "Bloody hell if they'll have me pushing one of them carts in front of all them people in wagon trains."

"We're not bloody pack animals," the other agreed.

Elder Clough overheard the two and castigated them for their cursing, but left his worst condemnation for the deserters. "The doubters have consigned themselves to hell," he warned. As if in response to the apostates, he painted an inscription on the side of his handcart: The Righteous Will Prevail.

But Hans Larsen took a gentler tone, urging the backsliders and faithful alike. "If we stay true, the blessings of God will rain down upon our heads. Ya, like manna from heaven."

Josephine sometimes wondered if the deserters made her mother nervous, but Elizabeth seemed composed, and determined. The girl tried to take her cue from her mother, and from Brother Larsen, who offered continual comfort and cheer.

When she had listened to two strangers on a street corner in front of the Cork and Barrel, she hadn't envisioned all this. She sometimes wondered whether her physical strength, and her faith, was sufficient. No pioneers had crossed the country with handcarts before. They were the first.

As the carpenters finished each handcart, the president himself would pull it to its new owners, lay his hands on the side panel, and offer a blessing. When he hauled their new cart up the hill one afternoon and parked it in front of their tent, Josephine forgot her apprehension. This handcart was theirs! And so new it smelled of resin. She ran her hand along the wooden rim of a wheel and lifted the heavy crossbar and tried to pull. The empty cart, caught in a rut, barely budged. But when Momma joined her, the wheels rolled forward, and the girl felt a surge of strength.

She thought of the Promised Land that lay ahead. When the missionaries talked of a land of milk and honey, did they mean *milk* and *honey*? She could almost taste the sweetness. She thought of the mysterious inland ocean, the Great Salt Lake. And the air! The air, the missionaries had said, was not like Liverpool. It had a crystalline quality, so pure you could almost see heaven.

Now the day had arrived. Josephine lay awake listening for the four o'clock bugle. She heard her mother's delicate breathing and heard the oxen mill restlessly. Hundreds of immigrants, huddled in tents, lay sleeping—or perhaps lying awake like her. She thought she could sense a restless tension.

She sat up eagerly when the bugle sounded; the company was to start an hour after sunrise. "Sakes alive, but that bugler's got a set of bellows, don't he," Sister Maisey said good-humoredly as she tugged on her shoes and patted down her bangs. "If he blows any harder he'll strangle the poor instrument."

"He *is* still new to the job," Elizabeth said.

"Ah, and I credit him for the brave attempt. It's better'n I could do in a lifetime of trying."

In fact, it didn't matter that the good brother couldn't hold a pitch. His reveille was lost amidst a melee of braying mules and bawling heifers. But the company's early start didn't happen. The sun was high in the sky and the cool mist had evaporated into buggy humidity before breakfast was put away, tents were folded, carts were packed, and the oxen were yoked.

Brother Larsen called for his company to kneel in a circle. He lifted his palms upward. "Father in Heaven, bless us, your people, as we follow your call to gather to Zion," the president intoned. "We've already come a long way. Have mercy, O Lord, and give us the strength to walk and not be weary."

Josephine thought of the two men who had arrived in camp just the day before. They had turned back from their quest for the Oregon Territory after three weeks on the trail. "I'd take hell over the Nebraska Territory," one said. "The dust cakes your nose and you cough till your chest wants to explode. The damned river ferry sank and a stampede of buffalo drove off twenty of our best cattle." Now they were heading the opposite direction—east—to try their luck in Ohio.

But somewhere between the taunts about polygamy and Brother Larsen's blessing of their handcart, Josephine had put aside any newly formed cracks in her belief. She had committed, to this people and to this God, and in her decision, she felt a kind of freedom, an abandonment to doing something extraordinary, something outside the polite constraints of her upbringing. God had called her, and here she was on this sultry June afternoon, answering the call.

Silence settled over the band of immigrants as they gazed westward, facing thirteen hundred miles of unknown territory. They were composed of more women than men, and more children than either.

Josephine had heard the prairie was seemingly endless, but its waves of tall grasses beckoned. They swayed in the wind, looking a bit like the waves of the ocean they had just crossed. Purple clouds hung low in the distance and a storm had started to gust, making the sea of green come to life.

She heard the cries of *Gee up!* and the crack of whips, and the oxen heaved forward with the creaking supply wagons. Younger children, roped to the back of handcarts as protection from Indians, began to skip and shout *Gee up, gee up*, and older children, drafted as herders, called after cows.

"Aye-oh, it's cheerio to this camp then, 'ain't it," Peart Maisey said jovially as she panted into place at the side of the handcart; Elizabeth had told her not to worry about pulling just yet.

"Hurrah! Hurrah for Zion!" the brethren whooped.

Gavin paused on his crutch, gathering strength, and Brother Hubbard limped into line. In the confusion, oxen strained different directions and she heard Brother Larsen shout, "Steady, old chaps!"

"'Becca, come on now!" Josephine called. "We're going to our new home."

The boxy carts nearly bumped into each other as they were pulled into single-file position. Pots and kettles clanged, a rooster crowed. Josephine adjusted her gawky sunbonnet, and she and her mother lifted the crossbar and bent their backs into the load. She felt exhilaration rise in her breast, and then panic, and then exhilaration again, as she strained to pull their handcart into the long line.

Elizabeth said, "Well, it is the Promised Land then. Let us go in peace."

Since the death of her infant, Sister Ashdown had seemed a bit too fragile for the journey, but she was always good for a hymn about Zion. She raised her voice with "High on the Mountain Top" and the company, more than three hundred strong, joined in.

I'm a pioneer!

The girl lifted her head into the rising wind, and began the long walk west.

10

THE HANDCART SONG

Ye saints who dwell on Europe's shore
Prepare yourselves for many more,
To leave behind your native land,
For sure God's judgments are at hand.

These lands that boast of liberty
You ne'er again will wish to see
When you from Europe make a start
To cross the plains with your handcart.
And then with music and with song
How cheerfully we'll march along
And thank the day we made a start
To cross the plains in our handcart.
For some must push and some must pull
As we go marching up the hill;
So merrily on our way we go
Until we reach the Valley-o.

—Excerpt from a beloved Mormon folksong sung by the handcart
pioneers, written by John Daniel Thompson McAllister

June 13, 1856

Dearest Meaghan—

    We are in the Wilderness! Several days ago we left Iowa City—& now here we are—a long string of hand carts bumping our way across this rolling grass land. It seems to stretch on forever.

    There is beauty here of which I have never known—meadow larks cheer us on our way & gay flowers beckon on every side. I can scarcely remember the cramped alleys of Fishermans Lane as we traverse this vast land. Some times the wind blows like a fury & there is even lightening— When it thunders the booming voice of the sky sounds like God himself speaking. At night the stars hang over head as if from his ceiling. I know the stars that shine on me also shine on you & so we are not so far apart after all.

    Each night we have a gay old time around the camp fire. A boy named Gavin Sayers plays his fiddle & there is even dancing. Pres. Brigham Young says dancing is of God & not the Devil—That there is more dancing in Heaven than in Hell—

    I know you did not accept the message of the misionaries & I know it is only a romantic dream but I often envision you here before the fire with us

    How are Edward & William? Tell them we are blessed in our faith—It is our Father in Heaven who leads us as we make our way across this unknown land—here the sweet love of the Lord is poured out upon us. These are the Latter Days, when the crooked things shall be made straight & the gathering has commenced. We go forth with songs of thanks giving & joy!

    Momma says she will write a separate letter. The night bugle has blown & she says it is best I go to bed now as morning will not wait for sleepy heads.

    I think of you always & pray for your Immortal Soul—May we meet again at the feet of our dear Savior.

                                  Your Affectionate Sister,
                                    Josie

PS A trader came to our camp and promised to deliver my letter. I hope it finds it's way to you in Merry Olde England! We are hurrying to arrive before the fall, ahead of the cold

Pioneers heading west in great lumbering wagon trains had their fun at the expense of the handcart Saints, who pulled their loads like beasts of burden.

"Maybe we should unhitch our oxen and let the Mormons do the job!"

Josephine was proud of her handcart, but even so, at first the sound was embarrassing. The wheels groaned and screeched with each rotation, as if complaining about the weight. That was not the only embarrassment. By late afternoon, her bladder pressed against her until she ached for release, but the treeless prairie offered no privacy. She finally was forced to squat, ashamed, behind two women who held up their skirts as a curtain. While she stooped, chiggers took bites of her ankles, leaving red, itchy welts.

Sweat ran down her back and gathered under her armpits, staining her dress. Accustomed to the cool mist of England, her bonnet became unbearably hot, and the unforgiving sun somehow seemed to find a way under its hood. Josephine's pale skin, which had been locked away from the sun in the woolen mill, soon turned the color of the dirt track.

The handcart pioneers had joined a long line of farm wagons and high-topped prairie schooners stretching clear to the horizon. Most of them belonged to Gentiles—the term Mormons used to describe people who didn't share their faith. Hundreds of cattle moved alongside, trampling grass and stirring up clouds of dust.

Her mother pulled the crossbar and Josephine pushed the cart from behind, and then they reversed positions; she pulled while Elizabeth pushed. Blisters formed on her hands, and after supper she took her mother's sewing needle and pierced the skin. As they packed up in the morning, she tied handkerchiefs around her hands, but they soon were raw, leaving blood stains on the crossbar. Blisters appeared on her feet. Her back throbbed with pain, and when Hans Larsen called a halt for the night, she found it difficult to stand erect.

But she was comforted by Brother Larsen, who told them, "You are the chosen people. The angels are walking with us." He encouraged those who were old or pregnant or frail, and sometimes took babies from women's hips and carried them. "When you are tired, the Lord will comfort you and encircle you in the arms of mercy."

It was true. Josephine felt God's mercy. With each step, she was heading toward redemption—on Earth and in heaven. Every mile of the Oregon Trail had its challenges, but they were light, for the girl already had grown to love the wilderness of grass, so different from the narrow streets and sodden alleyways of Liverpool. The rolling prairie seemed to expand before her as she walked—her footsteps in rhythm with the metallic *clank clank* of cowbells—and she felt newborn freedom.

There was the fear, real enough, of heading into the unknown, and the fear of leaving the familiar behind, but there was promise too. All of life's possibilities seemed to beckon. She didn't know how to express it to Meaghan, she hardly even knew how to think about it—these feelings of hope and grief and happiness and longing, all at the same time, like nostalgia for both the past and the future, and a sense of being fully alive in the present.

She tilted her bonnet back and watched flock after flock of geese fly overhead in large V-shapes, listening to their throaty honks high against the sky.

"Josie, you will bring out the freckles if you keep pushing that bonnet back," Elizabeth said.

"But Momma, how can I see the birds?"

"I know it seems as if we will never see civilization again, but you still need to remember that you are a young lady. You will want to attract a beau."

"But I can wear my bonnet properly when we get to the valley. And then I'll turn properly unfreckled again, just as you wish."

Josephine sent a teasing glance back at her mother, but when she saw her face, creased with weariness, and her back, bowed over the cart, she quickly complied, pushing her bonnet back into place and tightening it about her neck.

When the party stopped in an oak grove for the noon rest, Josephine roamed among the prairie roses and wild geraniums with Rebecca as if she, too, were a small girl, and they gathered cheerful sunflowers in a bucket.

"Miss Josie, where're we going, again?" Rebecca absentmindedly reached down to scratch a mosquito bite on her ankle.

"Utah."

"My mum says we're going to Zion. And you say we're going to Utah."

"They're the same place, 'Becca. That's where the Saints live."

"How come they live there, 'stead of at home?"

"That is their home," Josephine said. "And soon it will be our home." They stopped to study a bee purring in a black-eyed Susan.

"Will there be horses there?"

"Yes."

"I like horses." Rebecca sucked at the gap between her front teeth. "You know that one ox? His name is Tup. I saw a man call Tup a little devil. How come he did that?"

"He probably wanted him to mind his manners." Josephine bent down to examine a patch of wild strawberries.

"Buv-ver Larsen gives Tup sugar. Then Tup goes like this." She buried her tongue in her hands, wriggled it back and forth, and called out, "Slurp slurp slurp!"

"You're silly!" Josephine laughed and stuck a prairie rose in Rebecca's thin hair.

"Can we pick a strawberry? I never tasted them afore." Rebecca reached up and carefully fingered the petals of the flower behind her ear. "How far's Utah?"

"You can pick strawberries. If we walk and walk, and then walk a piece more, we'll get to Utah. In the mountains."

"How did they find Utah? If it's up in the mountains?"

"President Young had a revelation. When he came to the valley, he said it was the right place."

"I heard a rel-levation," Rebecca said, stumbling over the big word. "In church. Buv-ver Larsen said Prophet Joseph got a rel-levation. But now I can't 'member what it was." She stuck her thumb in her mouth as if it were a piece of taffy.

"He saw God and brought forth a book. The book was his revelation."

"Hmm. I don't know how to read books. Mum says that's for learned people." As she leaned down again to scratch her bite, the rose fell from her hair. "Ooh! I lost my flower," she laughed. "I like holding your hand, Miss Josie."

In the afternoons, thunderheads often piled up overhead. Clouds hung lower and lower over the prairie until rain began to spill in long slanted streams down the violet sky.

"Aye, and the good Lord always sends a storm to let us know he's still up there," Sister Peart Maisey would say. She would duck against the downpour and pull the sides of her bonnet close about her chin and throw a jest upward as if addressing the Almighty himself—"Can we not have 'nother sort of sign now and again?" Peart couldn't kindle a fire in the best of times, let alone when the wood was wet, and pushing her frumpy frame forward ten miles a day was hard enough without rain pounding down her back.

But even as the road turned into a mass of heavy gumbo that stuck in bucket-sized clumps to Josephine's feet, even as mud clogged the wheels of the handcart, the girl felt an odd exhilaration. She would turn her head upward, feeling the sloppy drops roll down her cheeks.

The creak of the wheels, with their wooden singsong, had ceased to embarrass the girl. Indeed, the rhythm often lulled her into a drowsy state. Life was reduced to a state of slow simplicity, just this hypnotic scraping noise, this putting one foot in front of the other thousands of times each day. Across Iowa Territory, into Nebraska—

the grass was sometimes taller than the girl's shoulders. At the Platte River, the Gentiles took to the south side and the Mormons claimed the north, and at night Josephine could see campfires on both sides of the river flicker in the dark. She felt wonder at everything—the smell of clouds, the *chirrup* of crickets, the way mist rose out of the bottomlands and the heavy humidity settled into green twilight. She was tired, often too tired for talking, but she was content.

Not everyone had such an easy time of it. In spite of the relentless sun, Lydia's skin turned sallow. Her bony shoulders sagged above the hollow breasts that were a constant reminder of her lost child. She had been exhausted before they even started out, and she hadn't hemmed her skirt as instructed. Now it dragged through the mud.

Physically, Sister Maisey was faring no better. In fact, worse. "I wish I was a barrel of bacon," she said as she wheezed along. "That way they'd let me ride in the supply wagon."

"Tup could pull you!" Rebecca shouted gleefully. The girl had been tied to the back of the handcart so she wouldn't wander off, but there was no danger of that. She seemed to like mingling with Josephine and the three women and kept up a constant stream of chatter until the afternoon, when she fell quiet. Then she became so weary she tripped over her toes and asked, as if she hadn't heard the answer a hundred times, "Why do we have to walk so far?" And hopefully, to Josephine, "Miss Josie, can you carry me?"

"I'm sorry, 'Becca. I need to pull the cart." Josephine answered the same way each time, never impatient, even though she had answered the question again and again.

"In all my born days, I's never been so wearied," Sister Maisey said, fanning her neck. "This walk makes a body long for the grave. At least if I was in the ground pushing up daisies I could rest." She hadn't been asked yet to take a place at the crossbar; it was obvious her help would be no help at all.

One day they spotted two fur traders headed east, their wagon kicking up dust. The traders wore greasy coats fashioned from animal skins, and a colorful sign on the side of their wagon announced:

BEAR & WILDCAT SKINS!

Sister Maisey watched them with a wistful expression. "I's half a mind to ask 'em for a ride."

She wouldn't be the first to long for a return to civilization. Several of the brethren already had joined small wagon trains headed back to the States, driven by pioneers abandoning hopeless mining claims and the Gold Rush bust in California.

Josephine watched Sister Maisey stolidly put one foot in front of the other. How would she ever drag herself thirteen hundred miles across the plains and up over the Rocky Mountains? When Brother Larsen called a halt for the night and the pioneers pulled their hand-carts into a circle as protection from wolves and cattle thieves and Indians—none of which had been spotted yet—Sister Maisey was always the first to buckle her knees and sink to the ground in relief.

Once Josephine and Elizabeth had unpacked the supper supplies, Peart finally began to flutter about, unrumpling her skirt and looking busy. She was the designated water hauler because the task of cooking was still beyond her. She would locate the bucket with great ceremony and noise, as if she wanted it to be known that she, too, was doing her bit, and trudge away to the river. Brother Larsen joked that the waters of the Platte were too thick to drink and too thin to farm, but drink it they did, after Peart lugged her hard-won prize back to the campfire, skimmed off the drowned gnats, and let the mud settle. She always asked hopefully, "Here's enough then, is it?"

Her standby—tea—was replaced by coffee. Only the flavor of coffee could disguise the water, which tasted so foul that sometimes even the cattle turned their heads away before they reluctantly seemed to realize that Platte River gruel was all that would be offered.

But Peart Maisey got stronger as the days passed, and her native cheer resurfaced. She stopped talking about hanging up the fiddle and plodded along as steady as old Tup. Each day she roused out of bed at the first note of the bugle. "Aye, the Lord's given us a new-made day," she said, battling a comb through her hair. "Another op'tunity to get on his good side." She pulled up her voluminous skirt to wedge small feet into stiff shoes and chuckled, "But I's a mind to talk with him 'bout eating dust every step. Achh."

Sister Maisey did manage to refrain from complaining about the dust, but she couldn't hold herself back from lamenting the raw bacon, which was their fare when the wood was too wet to spark a fire. One night Sister Maisey stood at the damp fire pit, putting her weight on one foot and then the other, eager for supper. She hadn't mastered the skill of starting a fire, it was true, but she finally put forth her contribution.

"Rightio!" she called cheerfully, as if just thinking of a jolly fine idea. "'Tis no good to fiddle-faddle about with this biz'niss." And with that, she bustled to the handcart and pulled out a tin. "I held this back for a 'mergency. And I reckon this here's one." She opened the tin and sprinkled black powder over the wet twigs. The blaze leaped up so quickly her skirt almost caught fire.

"Gunpowder!" Peart announced proudly. "A peddler sold it to me at Albert Dock. To fight Indians."

"Sister Maisey!" Josephine sputtered. She didn't know whether to be horrified or delighted, and realized she felt a little of both.

"Fire!" Rebecca cried, delighted, flapping her hands like a bird.

"Why, Sister Peart Maisey! You do surprise me," said Elizabeth, laughing. "You know, of course, we cannot be using this method every night. Perhaps never again."

"Like I said," Peart chimed, "only for 'mergencies."

When the flames calmed down, Lydia hung the kettle precariously over the fire. The week before, her exhaustion had made her so careless the kettle had tipped, spilling stew into the ashes.

"Let me help you," said Josephine, reaching to balance the kettle. Sister Ashdown *needed* help. Sometimes, in her distraction, she didn't notice the dirt she kneaded into the bread dough, or she allowed the crust to burn while the loaf inside remained doughy. Or she didn't notice when Rebecca limped from a rock in her shoe.

Josephine often thought of Meaghan as she walked, remembering her face as the ship pulled out from the Liverpool wharf. She tried to recall snatches of conversation, the scenes that made up their childhood. How they would take refuge up in their room from Edward's teasing. How they dressed their dolls for afternoon tea. Meaghan's doll, Tess, and Josephine's doll, Lizzie, had china heads with rosy cheeks and petal lips. The sisters had enacted the ritual so many times Josephine almost remembered the conversations word for word, and what she couldn't remember, she made up.

The dolls at the supper table, Tess ladling the steaming broth of hare soup for Lizzie, in imitation of Momma's proper etiquette.

"How come Tess always gets to be mistress of the house?" Josephine asked.

"She's older—well, *I'm* older."

"But I've not yet had a turn to preside over the table."

"Tomorrow it can be your turn," Meaghan informed her in a big-sisterly way.

The dolls sipped their broth contentedly with dainty motions.

And then, "My dear, you really must have another serving of soup," Meaghan said.

"How kind of you, but I must resist. I have my waist to think of, you know." They giggled.

"Then it's on to the mutton and mint sauce."

"How properly delightful!"

The miniature dishes were arranged on the miniature table, which had been carved by Papa during a lull in his business, when he wasn't needed as often at the shop. His business had picked up before he had time to carve matching chairs.

"I am distressed that I cannot offer a chair," Meaghan said.

"That is quite all right, my dear. We do the best our circumstances allow, don't we."

And so they regretfully were forced to stand through the hare soup and mutton and mince pie. But their china smiles were untroubled throughout the entire meal. Life was good.

One morning Josephine's reverie was interrupted by thunder. She looked at the sky—not a cloud. A moment later she felt the ground shake under her feet and saw what looked like a hundred buffalo stampeding their way, hoofs pounding the earth, trampling everything in their wake. A volley of shots exploded, and she saw bursts of smoke flare from the ends of rifles, but most of the brethren were poor shots and Brother Toon was the only one to make his mark.

As the men skinned the shaggy creature and cut off portions for each family, Josephine tried to ignore the glazed-over eyes in its mammoth head, and what she imagined was an expression of innocent surprise.

As she sliced the meat, she felt a choking sensation in her throat; the great beast, once running wild, was now cubed and frying in the skillet.

And yet. Her stomach was empty. She had been hungry all day. The grease sizzled and popped in the skillet, making her nauseous with guilt and famished at the same time.

"We have not had fresh meat for a long time," said Elizabeth, watching her daughter's face. "This is what God has offered. You have a tender heart, Josie, but your heart is more bountiful than your circumstances. Be thankful for this gift."

Along with the others, Josephine ate everything on her plate, even a slice of tongue, and she boiled the bones for broth.

The buffalo left another gift as well. Trees had long since given out, and the women gathered dried buffalo dung in their aprons to serve as kindling. Josephine noticed that Momma, who had displayed a reserved dignity as she descended in station—from her home on Middleton Street to the flat off Fishermans Lane, from arranging roses in the parlor to picking apart rags in a wretched factory, from traveling by carriage to suffering the indignities of a crowded ship and filthy rail car and absurd wheelbarrow—simply couldn't bring herself to touch the droppings. Elizabeth looked away when her daughter brought an apronful of dung to the campfire and smiled wanly when the stew was served, but Josephine noticed she still ate her share.

Each night as lavender dusk settled over the prairie, mist rose from the river, and the Platte, miles wide in places, took on the sheen of the setting sun. As shadows deepened and campfires were lit, Josephine smelled the musky fragrance of burning wood and smiled at the spring peepers, giving out their tiny, insistent chirp as if the world depended on it.

"The mist at night makes me think of England—of the country-side," Josephine told her mother.

"Perhaps it is best not to think too much of home," Elizabeth said.

"But you do ..." Josephine ventured, surprised at her own directness. The girl often studied her mother, trying to guess her emotions. And although Josephine reveled in the freedom of the trail, although she had fallen in love with the loamy beauty of the grasslands, even though she knew she was headed for the Promised Land, sometimes the longing for home swept over her like an ocean wave. There was this life here, and that life there, and almost nothing to tie them together—except memories.

"I try not to. It is hard enough al—" Elizabeth caught herself. She paused, as if deciding whether to go on. "There is already enough sorrow."

Josephine watched her mother out of the side of her eyes while she pretended to study the stars. Her mother was hard to read, inscrutably composed even after they had fallen so far, as if circumstances still demanded graciousness of her. Even though she was on a trek where women stooped at the side of the road to empty their bowels, she seemed determined to carry herself with proper deportment.

"I know you say not to think overmuch of our old life, but I miss Papa," Josephine said.

As the girl walked each day, she sometimes tried to recall every small detail about her father, and other times tried not to think of him at all. It was always the same old wound, seemingly scabbed over and yet so easily scratched raw again—longing for his presence, anger at his leaving them impoverished. She remembered the way he greeted her when he arrived home, 'How's my little girl, then?'"

Josephine was hopeful. She believed. The trail beckoned, and abundance waited. And yet sometimes, when she was most exhausted, her spirit grew exhausted too, and the balance shifted.

"Do you think he would have come with us?" she asked. "If he were alive? Do you think he would have been baptized?"

Her mother was quiet.

"Do you think we would have come if we hadn't lost our home?" Josephine remembered the supper table, laden with delicacies. The apple tarts. The almond pudding. Poached eggs and broiled haddock. "If we weren't hungry?"

"Child, you are a precocious one. Even more so than Meaghan. You ask too many questions." Elizabeth twisted her wedding ring. "It is probably best not to dwell upon things that will never be."

And with that, her mother turned away.

11

AN IMMIGRATION of four thousand persons was passed on the Plains by Elder Richards' party. ... All were in good health, first-rate spirits, and the parties looked forward to their arrival at Salt Lake with the pleasurable anticipations of people going home. ... the "hand-cart" portion of the companies were having the best time—a fact which will gladden the heart of brother Brigham. Hand-cart travel over the Plains is one of his great hobbies.

—"Very Late from Utah," *The Latter-day Saints' Millennial Star*

July 21, 1856

Dearest Meaghan—

I received your letters at long last! An entire packet at Fort Kerney! It was good to hear your news of Harold's promotion & that you will sometime be moving to a home of your own. I am happy for you, dear sister. I have a dream of my own home too—one for Momma & me—surrounded by tall trees & a brook.

I am glad to hear that William has found a job as a Clerk & pray that Edward will be able to move up at the press.

You will never guess—We have entered Indian Country! Mother and I saw wigwams with mountain men & Indian women married & living together! Nothing on this journey surprises me any longer—It is as if all the rules of civilization have been left behind.

How strange the Indians are—They go about with paint on their faces & wear ear rings like women & feathers in their hair—which is shaved save for a strip along the top. Momma would probably not like me to make note of it, but I saw some of them naked from the waist up! I was thankful they left us with our scalp! They only wanted to trade fish.

But we would rather have elk, as there is all the good fishing we want in the river. Sister Maysey said the fish are so thick here she could stick a knitting needle in & spear 3 fish on her first try. (Actually, she couldn't! She is not very useful at anything!)

The Oregon Trail has the most beautiful scenery I have ever witnessed. I wish you could be here to see it—I even wish you could smell it! At night the scent of sagebrush fires fill the air—& the perfume of the cedar trees reminds me of the spice jars in our old kitchen.

I must close now. I send my love and prayers

With Affection & Love,
Josie

PS When we reach Fort Laramy I will send this letter with a trader headed East. Perhaps there will be another letter from you—I am hoping—

Each night, Josephine felt her face grow warm as Gavin Sayers picked up his fiddle and spun into a hoedown. She wondered if people could see her watching him with such rapt attention. He played his instrument with abandon, almost as if he were dancing. The only part of his body that didn't move was his lame leg. She hoped, when she passed him in the evenings, that her armpits didn't smell too badly of sweat.

The fiddling began after supper. After the sisters washed dishes and mended torn clothing and darned a sock or two, after the men greased axles and pitched tents, after the brethren preached and the Saints prayed, everyone put aside their weariness and worries. They sang and danced.

As Josephine watched Gavin, she tried to remember what Meaghan had said about kissing. How had she phrased it?

"Nice."

Josephine wondered what "nice" meant. How did it feel when someone's lips touched your own? It was hard to keep her thoughts corralled, even during sermons.

"There has been some dissension in our community," Brother Larsen said one Sabbath morning. "I know the way is difficult, but it is made more difficult by backbiting and murmuring."

Where would he put his hands? On my back? My neck?

The girl reached up and touched the side of her neck.

Around my waist?

"Don't be over-quick to find fault with another." Hans Larsen paused to stroke his beard thoughtfully, while some of the Saints looked at their feet as if chagrined by his words.

He lays his fiddle down. Draws me close. We stand so close I can feel his heartbeat!

"Our Father in Heaven asks that we love one another as he has loved us."

Is that a sin?

After the sermons, the Saints were invited to bear witness to the truth of the gospel. Gavin never bore his testimony. He sat toward the back, whittling penny dolls and whistles for children.

Josephine noticed that Momma had never borne witness in the meetings either, but one night the girl contemplated her own offering.

Would Gavin think better of her?

I can't bear my testimony just to have the attention of a fiddler!

People stood, one after another, offering gratitude to the Lord, affirming their faith. "I know beyond doubt that the gospel is true," they said. Logs shifted in the bonfire, sending up sparks. Josephine could hear the soft low of oxen as they bedded down for the night. Suddenly she found herself rising.

What am I doing?

She fidgeted with the cuff of her sleeve. She could feel the eyes of the congregation on her. "I know ..."

What do I know—for certain?

Coyotes barked and a camp dog growled. Above, the great silence waited, deep and dark, lit with thousands of stars. It was too late to sit back down.

And then, she felt it. A curious, almost giddy sensation began low in her belly and moved up her spine.

Is this the burning? The one the missionaries promised?

She felt utterly alive. She saw the circle of pioneers as if for the first time, their faces lit by the bonfire. And above the fire, the constellations—the Big Dipper, the Little Dipper, the Lion—fires in the sky. Her heart hammered against her chest.

"I know we are led by God." She was suddenly nervous. She dug at a hangnail.

"I know that these are the last days, when Christ shall come again. That we must take the Holy Spirit for our guide ... that we are being gathered up for salvation."

And what else?

She tried to remember what the others said. She glanced at Gavin. He had stopped whittling. He was looking at her, and his gaze made her bashful.

"I say this in the name of our Heavenly Father. Amen." She sat down abruptly.

After the evening bugle called, as Josephine crawled under her quilt in the tent, she felt grown up. She could smell the fragrance of smoke on her clothes. She smiled in the darkness, thinking of the burning. Thinking of Gavin's gaze.

Josephine wasn't the only one looking at another person. Hans Larsen began coming by to say hello to her mother, sometimes offering to take a turn at pulling the cart. Elizabeth was easily the most beautiful woman in camp, with her lustrous black hair and swanlike neck. Even her apron was always clean, as if she weren't walking hundreds of miles. In the middle of the wilderness, her elegance held; she still called salt a "condiment," and when Josephine and Rebecca gathered flowers, Elizabeth created a centerpiece, almost as if they were sitting at a proper dining table rather than in the dirt. Alongside her mother, Josephine felt gawky.

She watched uneasily as the two bantered, her mother's dulcimer voice interweaving with Brother Larsen's rich bass. For the first time, the man looked a bit hesitant, almost shy. As Josephine washed clothes in the river, as she fried johnnycakes or gathered currants or filled her apron with buffalo droppings, she fretted, thinking of Papa, thinking of the absurdity and outrageousness of the two of them—her mother and the company president. Openly flirting! How could her mother be so shameless? Her husband not even two years dead. And the passing of Hans Larsen's wife even more recent. Her mother had dropped the "Brother Larsen" and was now calling him "Hans." When he walked out with her mother in the evening, Josephine squatted by the fire. She felt … what? Alone? But her mother was there every day, pulling the handcart alongside her daughter, so "alone" wasn't the right emotion. The girl thought of the Salt Lake Valley. What would happen then?

The country became drier, and Josephine's lips chapped and split. Her face was caked with dust, and she swallowed it when she walked. The oxen plodded along with their tongues hanging out, panting heavily. Sometimes, at the noon rest, the girl would take buckets of water and let Tup and the other oxen gulp as much as they could hold. She washed the dust off their noses with her handkerchief, talking to them softly all the while.

The road became rutted, and then began rising and falling— the first hills. As the party coaxed their carts over half-buried boulders, axles ached with the load and sometimes broke. The weather lurched between chilly nights and scorching afternoons, and arid winds attacked the carts, splintering the wood. Men rubbed bacon grease on the axles, but wheels still wore down. Nights and rest days often were given over to repairs.

Brother Larsen offered daily prayers—for the Saints, for the oxen, for the handcarts. He entreated God to hold their little carts together until they arrived in the valley.

They had entered bluff country, with its yucca and prickly pear, its screech owls and snakes. Curious clay cliffs and tawny, flat-topped hills were covered with juniper and split by ravines. Sister Ashdown thought the chalky hills, with their bands of ochre and cream, looked forlorn enough to make one weep, but Josephine thought they looked romantic, especially the spire the pioneers called Chimney Rock. She could see the eroded, solitary monument for miles in the distance, and on their approach, she saw hawks soar about its flanks.

Each day Josephine studied Gavin from a distance. She studied the way sweat made his shirt cling to his chest as he limped along, the way his pants hung lazily over his rail-like legs. Sometimes he seemed to be in pain, but he also seemed bored by the grinding monotony, and she overheard him telling his friends, "I almost hope the Indians will attack." They all agreed, with no small amount of bravado, that the diversion would provide much-needed entertainment.

But they seemed almost as surprised as everyone else when a party of Pawnees approached the company. Sister Maisey nervously fanned her face with one hand and Rebecca was so unnerved she couldn't even cry; she stood frozen. Josephine shrank in terror, crouching behind the handcart. But even in her fright, the naked chests of some of the Indians startled her, and drew her in. She peeked around the edge of the cart, staring at the muscled, brown bodies, and then looked away, holding her breath. She hoped her mother hadn't noticed. In spite of her fear, it was soon obvious they had come in friendship, hoping for a trade.

"Swap. Swap," they said, holding out freshly caught fish. "Shirt. Swap."

Josephine stood up slowly. Sister Maisey stopped fanning. She smiled broadly at the Pawnees, who stood there in their earrings and necklaces and feathers, and said under her breath, "They's fixed up in their Sunday best, they is. Just for the likes of us."

The girl tried to connect the tales she had heard about Lamanites with the men standing there, holding their fish. Somehow they didn't seem as depraved as the scriptures made them out to be.

"The *Book of Mormon* tells us these creatures are the original Lamanites," Elder Ernst Clough said that night in his sermon. "They are a fallen race, and the Almighty God has cursed them with a dark skin."

When Hans Larsen next came to pull their cart, Josephine asked, "Are the Pawnees wicked then?"

"No more wicked than anyone else, I suppose." He picked up the crossbar with a smile at Elizabeth.

"But some of the Indians have attacked the wagon trains."

"Right you are, lassie. But they were here first. I reckon we've been dining on their buffalo a bit overmuch."

Older children scampered ahead, looking for buffalo skulls along the trail. The skulls, bleached a dirty white, had frightened them at first, but now they were becoming used to the sight. The party soon saw the first alkali mud flats. The parching wind blew the white dust into swirls, and it stung their skin and eyes. Josephine tried to blink away the pain, but tears only seemed to inflame the burning.

"An ox that drinks alkali water can be dead the same day," the president warned, and the men yelled at the poor beasts and even beat them, trying to steer them away from the brackish water, but water had grown too scarce and their thirst was too great.

Tup was the first to go down. Several men poured hot lard and vinegar down his throat; they anointed his head with oil and blessed him, rebuking his sickness, but by evening he was dead.

"Tup isn't moving," Rebecca said. Transfixed by horror, she stared at the huge carcass, its horns splayed out toward heaven.

"Come away from the body," said Sister Ashdown, tugging Rebecca's shoulder.

"But why doesn't Tup move?" the child asked, blinking back tears, her voice rising.

"God has taken Tup to his bosom," Lydia said. The woman looked exhausted. Her face was pinched and her hair seemed as if it had grayed since their journey began.

"Where is God's bosom?"

"His bosom's up in the sky, love," Sister Maisey said. "That Tup will be content there, he will. There's grass aplenty."

"But I want Tup here! Not in the sky." Rebecca's voice took on an edge of hysteria.

"You'll be with Tup someday," Josephine comforted.

"I w-want to be with him n-now!" The child sobbed, realizing the enormity of her loss.

Elizabeth gathered the little girl in her arms. "There, there," she hushed.

But Elizabeth wasn't around to comfort her own daughter as she wept that night. Josephine buried her face in her sister's quilt, confused at her tears for a dead ox. Or perhaps her tears were for her father, or the thought of losing her mother, who was out walking with Hans Larsen that very moment.

After that, almost every day Josephine saw dead cattle by the side of the road, victims of alkali water. Sometimes the party even camped near the bloated carcasses. Many bodies had dried to racks of bones, covered with matted hide, but they still gave off a stink. A mountain man, headed east with furs, told them, "You can smell your way to Utah."

As the party approached Fort Laramie, in the Wyoming Territory, Josephine began to realize the first leg of the journey had been the easy part. Now the Rocky Mountains stood between the pioneers and the Salt Lake Valley. According to traders at the fort, this was the point of no return.

"Take courage," Brother Larsen exhorted. People were strung out along the plain, the weakest dragging along well behind the main company. Each day the president walked back and forth along the length of the ragged procession, encouraging the Saints with every mile. "The Lord has chosen us in these last days to receive his gospel. If we keep the faith, we will view the land he has promised us. He will open the floodgates of heaven."

As Josephine came in sight of Laramie Peak, far more massive than the tame hills of her homeland, she saw a veil of clouds hanging low against its purple flanks. The snow on its summit shimmered with the gold of the setting sun. She couldn't take her eyes from the isolated mountains that lay ahead, feeling the invitation and warning of their fierce beauty.

The girl walked past the carcasses. She walked even though her boots were shredding. She walked past the point of no return. On the other side of these mountains, she knew, some kind of heaven waited.

12

THE QUESTION RESOLVES itself into this—are the Saints willing to sacrifice the little they may have, except the most necessary articles of clothing to wear on their journey, and haul their own provisions across the plains[?] ... some of the faint hearted will feel that the mill of "Mormonism" grinds rather hard. We would inform the latter, that there is no particular use for them in Utah. Probably if they went there they would soon find that the climate did not agree with them, and they would want to try the more congenial air of California, or some other portion of the devil's dominions.

—"The General Epistle," *The Latter-day Saints' Millennial Star*

August 9, 1856

Dearest Meaghan—

How are you, dear sister?

I am writing this letter in the tent by candle light & I hope the candle lasts to the last sentence! I asked one of the Sisters for a piece of candle—we have run short again.

We are in the Desert. Sister Maysey jokes that sand has become our main condiment for supper, & I think she is right at that! The Oregon Trail is a hard task master, but the mountains are sublimely beautiful—tall & dressed with snow—telling of God's glory. Brother Larsen encourages us to gird up our loins as we cross this wild land— that the blessings of peace & plenty are ahead if we keep our eyes toward Heaven. I do wish the Plenty he speaks of would come sooner rather than later!

Each time someone opens the tent flap the candle blows out—& so I will say goodnight. I think of you every day as I walk, often remembering past memories from our childhood, & miss you more with every passing month. I will pray for you, as I hope you will for me—

Please give my love to Edward & William. I am sorry we parted on such discordant terms. Most of all, I miss you, & pray for you each day—

With Longing & Affection,
Your Josie

PS   You can send letters to Salt Lake. No one seems to know where, perhaps just address them to Handcart Party, Care Of Pres. Hans Larsen, Great Salt Lake City, Utah Teritory

As the Saints wound their way up the bleak, barren swell of South Pass in the Rocky Mountains, heading toward the backbone of the continent, Josephine broke up the monotony with thoughts of Gavin Sayers.

Walking in the moonlight … or sitting by the campfire after the others are asleep …

My dearest. You have captured my heart.

He talks in a hoarse whisper and places his hand on her cheek. He runs his fingers tenderly along her neck. His fingers—they feel soft as goose down.

Oh Gavin, how I have longed to hear those words.

Would they be sitting down, by the fire? Or standing, behind a supply wagon?

Standing, she decides. *He pulls her close and gazes into her eyes—a long look that says everything.*

"Momma?"

Elizabeth, bent into their load, stopped to remove a rock from her shoe, and looked back at her daughter with an expectant smile.

"Is it a sin to think of someone?"

"Who are you thinking of?"

"Just someone …" Josephine waited while Momma shook the rock loose. "The fiddler."

"Gavin?" Her mother's voice rose in surprise, but she quickly recovered. "Of course it is not a sin." Elizabeth gave her daughter a penetrating look. "How are you thinking of him?"

Josephine felt a slight constriction in her chest. Her face felt warm.

Her mother offered the rote caution: "A young lady must guard her virtue above all else." And then, "Has he been looking at you?"

"No," Josephine admitted disconsolately.

"But you are looking at him."

Josephine was embarrassed. She was a little sorry she had broached the subject, although it was exhilarating to hear her mother say Gavin's name out loud, as if saying the name somehow made the relationship real.

"Josie, we all begin our lives as young women by looking at young men. I looked at your father just the same. It is what you do with the looking, where it leads."

"Oh! It has led nowhere!"

Her mother was silent as they picked their way over a gully. "Your father kissed me. Before we were wed." Elizabeth seemed lost in nostalgia, and then seemed to remember the direction of the conversation. "But you must go slowly. If he looks at you, it is natural. But take care. Don't give yourself over fully to his embrace. A man will not want a rose whose petals have already been plucked."

"Momma! There has been no plucking!"

"I know. So you said. But he may press you in time. God forbids—certain activities before one goes to the altar."

Josephine thought of the mysterious moans in the night. "But what is a sin—exactly?"

"That is hard to say."

"Harold Baker kissed Meaghan before they married." Josephine immediately felt guilty for breaking a confidence.

But Elizabeth didn't seem surprised. "Their courtship was fairly short, as you recall, and you are younger, Josie. And his leg. Have you thought of that?"

"Momma, we cannot hold a limp against him!"

"You must think of the larger matter. How will he support you without the use of a leg?"

"He still has one good leg. And his limp doesn't hurt his fiddling any."

"There's more to earning a living than fiddling. We are in need now. But after we arrive there will be opportunities for a young man to support his wife, if they are able-bodied. You don't want to be in need after you marry."

Josephine paused. "He hasn't even looked at me yet," she confessed morosely.

But he has! Hasn't he?

She remembered his gaze when she bore her testimony. The firelight hadn't reached the back row where he sat whittling. Perhaps she only had imagined it.

Sage began to replace buffalo dung as kindling and the grassy fragrance of the prairie had long since given way to the strong, certain scents of pinyon and cedar. The sharp clarity of flaming sunsets replaced muted evening mist. The rickety carts bumped over boulders and ruts as the road climbed higher. Much of the time they got mired in sand, and the loads seemed to grow heavier with each passing day. Elder Ernst Clough seemed frustrated with the constant breakdowns, which slowed their progress.

"When an axle breaks," he said, "it is because God has seen a stain on a man's heart. The axle is but a representation of a man's own wheel come loose from Jehovah's plan."

Sister Maisey lifted her skirt over a boulder. "Pshaw! I've half a mind to take a hammer to that old bean's axle. Then we'll see how fast his cart strays from the path."

"I am sure he means no harm," Elizabeth said, but she wiped

the sweat from her forehead with an impatient gesture and let out her breath slowly, as if she, too, had taken her fill of Elder Clough's preaching. The man reminded Josephine of the sheepdogs that roamed English pastures, vigilantly biting at the heels of the herds.

Even pioneers making the trek in farm wagons were feeling the weight of their loads as their mule and oxen teams struggled uphill. Belongings once thought necessary were now cast out along the trail: boxes of books, bedsteads, rocking chairs. Josephine saw cast iron stoves and guns and mattresses, broken open, their goose feathers scattered. Barrels of bacon that had been purchased at a dear price in Iowa City lay abandoned.

Josephine joked that all she needed to do when her dress was dirty was find a clean one at the side of the trail. "And we should have just waited to buy," Josephine dryly told her mother. "We could have picked up bacon for nothing."

"Aye, and I wish we could find us a proper bite of black pudding," Sister Maisey said. "But I reckon none's foolish enough to throw that del'cacy away."

Rebecca squealed as she chased after lizards, but by afternoon she was spent, and during the night she whimpered and shivered next to Josephine in the cold tent. The child's mother sometimes drifted off into a world inhabited only by herself and her God, and in Lydia's absence, Rebecca had adopted "Miss Josie." The little girl stayed close by Josephine's side.

"I'm tired," she said, stumbling. "How many more miles?"

"I'm not sure, 'Becca. But we're getting closer every day." Josephine steadied the cart as they descended a ravine.

"How many more days?" The child's face was flushed with heat.

That was the question Josephine herself had been wondering. "I'm sure it won't be long."

Rebecca pulled her fingers along some rabbitbrush. "Elder Clough says Jesus is coming. That these are the ladder-days. Will we get there afore Jesus comes?"

"That's a good question. But I'm not sure when Jesus is coming."

Feeling rebellious, Josephine added, "And I'm pretty sure Elder Clough doesn't know either."

Rebecca seemed to ponder that pronouncement, and said dubiously, "He seems to know everything." She stopped to examine a dead grasshopper, and then asked, "Will Jesus come to Utah too?"

Josephine laughed. "Yes, 'Becca, I suspect he'll come right to the shores of the Great Salt Lake."

"Maybe he'll *walk* on the Great Salt Lake!" Rebecca said excitedly, clapping her hands. Her train of thought suddenly changed, and her elfin face took on an earnest expression. "Sister Josie, does Big-ham Young like children?"

"I think so!" Josephine gave Rebecca a curious look. "Why do you ask?"

"My mum says he is my new pa. Father for all the Mormons. Does that mean I won't have my old pa no more?"

"No. It just means you'll have two fathers."

"Hmm." Rebecca seemed to be mulling it over. She walked a while in silence, and then reached for Josephine's skirt. "My mum is sad."

"Why do you say that?" Josephine asked, but she already knew. As she paused to wipe her face with her kerchief, she remembered Sister Ashdown's lost baby.

"She cries at night. So that means she's sad?"

"Sometimes people just have to cry. To get all the sadness out." Josephine's fingers curled around Rebecca's hand.

"She cries out the sadness?" the child asked.

"Yes, we all do sometimes."

"So then after she cries, it goes away?"

"Well, sometimes. Sometimes it's still there." Josephine's feet, jammed against the toes of her button boots, ached.

"Sometimes I cry. I cry when I think of Pa. Even though I have Big-ham Young."

"I do too, 'Becca." Josephine dropped the child's hand and took off her bonnet and ran her hands through her hair. She thought of Tup and the graves along the trail, and Meaghan, so far away.

"Sometimes I feel like crying too."

Rebecca wasn't the only one who was tired. As the mountain road grew steeper, the Saints pressed their full weight into the crossbars, or pushed so hard from behind the old ones lost their footing. The wheels, thrown together in Iowa City without metal rims, often split, and the flimsy carts, constructed with green timber, groaned over boulders; Josephine worried their cart would break apart.

Women stopped long enough to give birth, sometimes behind a thicket of scrub oak or a stand of pines. They rode in one of the supply wagons for half a day, and then were forced to walk as someone even weaker took their place. The smallest children walked on their spindly legs, all the while begging to ride. The sick fell behind and arrived long after dark, straining their handcarts along the ruts.

The oxen were exhausted, too. During the noon hour they were turned out to graze, but sometimes they were even more tired than hungry. They lay in the sand and panted, and wouldn't stand again until the teamsters cracked the whip. On days when the whip didn't suffice, the brethren anointed them with sacred oil and commanded them in the name of God to rise.

The party pushed on, sometimes twenty miles a day, sometimes without water, sometimes with water so gritty the sand seemed to grind against the teeth. They sang hymns and marching songs to ward off tedium and fatigue, but Josephine's tongue often felt too swollen to sing, and the notes seemed to stick in her parched throat.

Even Elizabeth lost some of her equilibrium. Her gait slowed, and new creases appeared on her forehead and around her mouth. Her hands, once delicate, were calloused and rough, and her face, once clear as porcelain, was now weathered. Her shawl caught on branches and grew more tattered with the miles.

But Sister Ashdown was doing even worse. Her gaunt body seemed to be driven on only by numb determination, and she confided in an airy voice that she had stopped pulling the cart long ago.

"But it still goes forward. The angels are pulling it."

Josephine caught her mother's glance; the pulling and pushing, when Lydia dropped off, was done by the two of them, and although Sister Maisey had been willing enough to take a turn, she had only been in the way. As it was, most days she had trouble putting one stout leg in front of the other.

"I would walk barefoot to Zion if needs be and never count it as trial," Sister Ashdown said. Josephine glanced at the woman's shoes and wondered if she soon would have the opportunity to prove her claim. "My life is dear only as it is dear to my Savior."

"And was I to walk bare-feet to Zion, I would count every step as trib'lation," Sister Maisey said companionably. Her complaints never sounded quite like complaints, even during the worst times; rather, they seemed like she was passing the time of day in the best way she knew how. But the soles of her boots were growing thin too, and the soles of her feet bruised as the rocks became more jagged.

Lydia seemed not to have heard Peart. "When the Lord calls his sheep at the last days, I want to be there," she said. Josephine thought she detected a quiver in Sister Ashdown's voice. "I'm fixing to be on the side of those gathered up in the second coming."

"Aye, 'tis good to be on the right side," Sister Maisey agreed. "Me, I's always had the trouble to be on the wrong side of things. Me pa—God bless the miners—went to his eternity box with the black lung—rest his soul. I was barely four, and me ma all run out of hope. She gave me to the poor house, and I grew up beggared as an alley rat."

"We all grew up beggared," said Sister Ashdown, as if not to be outdone.

"Right at that. That's why we all picked up our belongings with the trouble to im'grate," Peart said amiably, as she gallantly wheezed uphill. "'Twas nothing for us in the old country but misery. Me, I's walking thirteen hundred miles for the fat of the ram on my plate at the other end. I ain't had a cut of mutton in ages."

Josephine laughed. "I could use a little fat of the ram right now," she said. Someone at the head of the line spotted a rattlesnake, and she tensed at the sound of a hoe smashing against rocks.

"When I get to Zion the brethren will bestow God's ordinances on me," Lydia said. "I'll be sealed to Mr. Ashdown for all eternity."

Josephine remembered the teachings of Joseph Smith. We are eternal beings, the prophet said, and we shall be together with our loved ones in the hereafter. Families can be sealed together in the temple of the Lord—the temple the Saints were building even now in Great Salt Lake City.

"No disrespect, sister, but that is one ord'nance I shall skip," Peart said. "Me husband was at the dram shop tipping the bottle every night of the week. I's well to be rid of him."

Josephine was surprised. Sister Maisey had never mentioned a husband. The girl thought of her own family. Would she see Meaghan and Edward and William in the next life even though they hadn't been sealed together as a family? For that matter, she wondered, would she see them again in this life? The girl remembered her last visit to Papa's grave, just before she left her homeland. She and Momma had been too poor to leave flowers, so they laid a few dandelions near the marker.

Each night the tightly drawn circle of handcarts closed out wolves and cattle rustlers and Indians, and closed in the oxen and milk cows and horses. The circle also closed in the Saints. There was no escape from the crush of people—the constant wail of infants, the sounds of joking and laughing and arguing and love-making. Each campfire was too close to the next, and darkness didn't bring privacy.

One night Josephine overheard Brother Toon, the best hunter in the company, shout at Sister Toon, "I've had enough of your cursed religion! This handcart business is madness."

Josephine watched as Sister Toon begged. She reminded him of the children. She wept. She knelt down and clung to his knees. "Don't leave me! Don't leave me alone with the children. I can't take them on by myself."

His voice dropped a pitch. "I came because you wouldn't have it any other way. Now look where you and your damned prophet have got us."

Sister Toon suddenly seemed to remember where she was, and

said in a pained voice, "Jacob, everyone can hear you."

"That, I don't care about," he said, saddling his horse. "I'll never see these people again."

"Jacob, the missionaries said we'll trod the path to hell if we don't go to Zion. Do you want that for our children?"

"There's no path to hell but this one. How could we have brought our children into this wasteland? I have never understood this church of yours, and every day it gets a little harder to figure."

With that, Brother Toon picked up his rifle and pack and headed out into the darkness. Josephine wasn't sure if he was headed west, toward California and Oregon, or back to the farms and cities of the east. She knew few people turned back after Fort Laramie.

Although Sister Toon continued to weep, Josephine guessed her husband would never return. Elder Clough, who had hurried over too late to intervene, said it was just as well; doubters would pay the penalty on judgment day.

When Josephine went to the river to wash up, Sister Toon was there, an odd look on her face, her eyes glazed over. She took off her bonnet and pushed her hands through straggly hair. "I never should have come," she said, as if Josephine were a confidant, and an adult. Her voice trembled. "I have lost everything. Everything. For what? This?" She looked down at the dirty water. "But my children. I had to bring them out of Babylon."

Josephine searched for an adequate reply, but no words came. She looked at the water swirling past, remembering a recent conversation with her mother. It had been a twenty-mile day, with the sickest collapsing at the side of the trail, and the party had passed more graves than usual, and dug one themselves. When they broke for the night, Josephine had gone out to gather sage kindling and sensed someone walking behind her. When she turned she saw her mother. Elizabeth came and put her hand on the small of her daughter's back.

"Josie, I am sorry I—" Momma looked out at the desolate stretch of rolling hills. "I did not know it would be so … All of this." She weakly waved her hand at the scene and then fell silent.

The girl had rarely seen her mother at a loss for words, and she felt something shift inside—a stirring of fear.

But her mother was quick to regain her composure. "Just remember I am here for you, child," she said kindly.

Sister Ashdown had been growing more withdrawn each day, retreating into her own world, but when Josephine mentioned Sister Toon's words, she came to life.

"What! Did she expect perfection?" Lydia exclaimed, dropping a greased skillet in her agitation. "Did she expect the roses to bloom beneath her feet and the birds to sing all the way to Utah? We are God's chosen people. He sends trials to test us." She grabbed the skillet from the ashes. "If Sister Toon wants to consign herself to the devil's furnace with her naysaying, that is her agency and I'll leave her to it."

"Aye, and I wish I had just a wee bit of that furnace right now to warm me hands," Peart said. She was darning the heel of a stocking and her hands were red with the cold.

"Do you think your salvation is a matter for joking?" Lydia turned on Sister Maisey, her voice turning shrill.

"Aye, and I's sorry, that I am," Sister Maisey said. "I don't mean to trifle with salvation. It's just that me hands are partic'lar cold. Is there wrong in saying so?"

The next morning Josephine watched, surprised but not surprised—nothing shocked her much these days—as Sister Toon and her children joined three wagons headed east. They belonged to three families fleeing Zion at a fast clip. Sister Toon's departure, and the sight of the Mormon deserters, left a pall over the company, as if each individual was weighing their own conviction. Josephine sensed the world tilting a bit, edging slightly out of control. She gripped the crossbar so tightly a splinter of wood worked its way into her palm. Her throat felt tight. But the valley lay ahead, and she was going there, and so she did what she was accustomed to doing. She placed one foot in front of the other.

She marched on with the others.

13

I WILL SAY that it is all right not to provide wagons for infirm persons to accompany the handcarts for it would encourage infirmity or rather laziness which is quite as bad.

—Excerpt from a letter written by President Brigham Young to Apostle John Taylor

August 24, 1856

Dearest Meaghan—
 This journey is wearing on me.
 We pass many graves each day. The first was shocking but I am growing accustomed to the gruesome sights, with their wood markers or some times just a pile of stones.
 Thankfully, only a few are from our party—all though we have many who are ill, mostly with mountain fever. The supply wagons haul a few of them but most struggle along on foot as there are not enough wagons for the sick and dying—and the scouts say we can not slack our pace or we will be trapped in winter snows to come. I will be releived when we have finally arrived & can tend to the sick properly.
 Some times as we walk I give myself o'er to the happy memories of Youth—& then I despare, having given up on the thought that I shall ever see Home Sweet Home again. Each mile only takes me farther from you—first an Ocean & now a lonely Wilderness. But I have cast my lot with the Saints.
 When I am at my lowest ebb, I wrap myself in your quilt & am

comforted. It is dirty & torn (I am sorry to confess!) but it makes me feel
you are not so far away

My thoughts are with you. Please pray for me.

All My Love,
Josie

Brother and Sister Toon weren't the only ones grumbling. Misunderstandings flared into arguments, and some arguments were even laced with profanity.

"Brothers and sisters, I have heard the discord among you," Brother Larsen said, but he didn't say it in an angry way. Rather, he seemed downhearted. "Heavenly Father calls us to dwell together in harmony. We have embraced one gospel. Let us be one people in our practice of it."

Elder Ernst Clough followed up the next night. He was a small man, but his tone was forceful, perhaps to match the weather. Black clouds festered in the west and gusts of wind whipped the folds of Josephine's dress.

"The spirit of Satan is in our midst, and it is the profaners and quarrelers who have brought it," he said.

Josephine studied the Adam's apple on Elder Clough's neck. Had it grown larger?

The girl closed her eyes and imagined she was far away … standing on an English hillside with Gavin.

I ask forgiveness if I presume your favor. But I must reveal my true feelings. What can I do to win your heart?

He tucks her cloak about her shoulders. Or perhaps it's his jacket? Yes—his jacket.

Oh my dearest, you already have my heart. My fate is your fate!

The grassy smell of spring … soft rain. She is wearing violet. No—green. Meaghan says green brings out the highlights in her eyes.

Let me shield you from the rain!

Gavin pulls the hood of her cloak over her hair—which is pulled into delicate side ringlets. The stones of a long-deserted castle are scattered about. He takes her hand, leads her behind the ruins of a turret. He can no longer restrain himself. He embraces her!

"I've heard too many of you complain," Ernst Clough continued, his voice rising as the wind picked up. 'It is hard, the road is too steep,' you say. What! Did you expect salvation would be so cheap?

"And yes," he cried, "we have our differences. Did you expect that miners and sod turners and factory men would all pull on their boots the same way? There are those among us who would sow discord over the differences, and they know who they are. They think to bring evil on the church, but they only bring evil on themselves."

Josephine saw people fidget and look at the ground. Some coughed. People obey Elder Clough out of fear, she thought, and Brother Larsen out of love.

One night she had seen Ernst Clough walking the perimeter of the camp, outside the enclosure, although he had warned others not to do the same. He cracked his knuckles and hunched into himself, and his lips moved as if he were explaining something to himself. He rubbed his sleeve against his eyes. Was Elder Clough crying? The girl had heard a few whispers; the man had been brought up by a constable, one who knew how to use a cane for purposes other than walking.

Now the elder exclaimed, "Well, let the backsliders moan and wail. The rest of us are going to Zion. We are going to claim our crown."

Peart Maisey was having none of it. For once, she seemed truly angry. "That old bean prattles on as if he's on pers'nal terms with the Almighty hisself. He imagines hisself the biggest lizard on the rock, he does."

"You are the very one he is talking about! The one bringing evil on herself," Lydia hissed, just as Josephine felt the first pricks of hail sting her cheeks.

"Fie! I shan't be humble-pied for that man," Peart said tartly.

That night the storm battered their tents until their blankets were drenched and water created small gullies in the trail to the latrine. Josephine imagined Elder Clough would have something to say about that too. Something about God's wrath at their faithlessness. They had given their all, she thought, but it wasn't enough for Ernst Clough.

On the western side of South Pass, the company entered a vast desert, its distances enormous and empty, its red soil broken by sandy washes. Clumps of Indian paintbrush dotted the sides of the road and rabbits leaped out from behind sagebrush, which grew as tall as Josephine's shoulders. Many mornings the girl had to scrape ice off the water bucket. Her hands burned with the cold.

Illness seemed to spread from handcart to handcart. What with the wet wood and exhaustion, sometimes the Saints skipped supper entirely and crawled into their tents still wearing their damp clothing; in the morning, another person had come down with mountain fever or typhoid or some unnamed malady simply called "trail sickness." Josephine looked with pity at the sick. She didn't know which was worse—being forced to rise again and walk through the pain, or being forced to squat by the side of the trail, huddled over a stream of diarrhea. Some boys pointed and giggled at what they called the "backdoor trot," but the sight wasn't amusing to anyone else, especially their mothers. The brethren blessed each victim, beseeching God for mercy. For those with the dreaded cholera, the prayers sometimes didn't take. Someone could sit down to breakfast with a nagging hint of lethargy, and be dead by supper.

After a half-dozen deaths, Josephine became numb. Death claimed the oldest and youngest first, and with each passing, the ritual would begin again. The prayer circle. The tears. Brother Larsen consigning the poor soul to God's mercy.

"Are they sleeping?" Rebecca asked Josephine.

"It's a kind of sleep."

"Sometimes I long for my own celestial rest," admitted Lydia, who seemed to career between piousness and hopelessness. As the days passed and her body grew frailer, her enthusiasm for walking to Zion seemed to diminish, but not her enthusiasm for her heavenly crown, whose appeal became brighter by the mile. "If I could, I would lay down my cares and rest until the morning of the resurrection," she said, sounding detached.

Josephine forgot herself and sputtered, "You have a daughter! A child!"

"Josie," Elizabeth said gently. "Remember your manners."

Lydia turned on Josephine. Her outbursts were becoming more common. "Do you think I don't know that? And my daughter seems to prefer you. So why should I care whether I leave her in the wilderness? She'll tag along with you, just like a mindless puppy."

At first, each grave was marked by a crude headboard, with a name, dates to mark the birth and death, and words of endearment. As time went on and the wood ran out and the deaths multiplied, graves often were marked simply by piles of stones. Sometimes the brethren buried the bodies right on the trail, and then pushed carts back and forth over the mound, packing the earth and sealing off the smell of human flesh from wolves. But Josephine could still hear them gather at night, and once she saw them sniffing and clawing at a fresh grave. The wolves followed the pioneers, their kills already made for them, and they often left the bones disinterred for all to see.

Almost everything, every day, tested their faith.

Why? Josephine often wondered. *Why is God asking this of us?*

Grief mounted and some grew more discontented and contentious, but the girl noticed something else too. A new tenderness was growing among many in the group, a kindness that broke through self-interest and the boundaries of class and language. Men offered their coats to children who shivered at the fire. Women, already short on flour for their own families, baked bread for the sick. They brought stews. They ripped strips of cloth from their petticoats to wrap the bodies of dead infants and sacrificed pieces of blankets to wrap the adults. At first, until they could no longer spare them, men volunteered boards from handcart panels for coffins. And after the burials, families took in orphans, sharing their meager supplies.

For many, the trials also seemed to bind them more closely to their Maker. The testimonies, borne at night around the fire, grew more fervent, as if the Saints were trying to make sense of their sacrifices. They seemed to seek deeper comfort not only from each other but from God.

Rebecca appeared bewildered—by everything. Her mother's vague distance and sudden temper. Bodies lying on the sand while men dug shallow trenches. The howling of wolves. She huddled against Josephine at night, as if she could find protection there, and sometimes cried out with nightmares, waking everyone in the tent.

One afternoon she came upon a rag doll with a homespun dress, propped against a wooden marker that said simply, "Rest in peace, sweet girl. Thy travels are over." Josephine guessed the grave was fresh, because the doll wasn't yet bleached by the sun. Rebecca approached the grave cautiously, a wistful expression on her face. Her only toy, so far in life, had been a blue marble found in an alley.

She hesitated before she asked, "Can I have that doll?"

"Yes, I think we can find room for it in the cart." Josephine quickly added, "For the times when you can't carry it."

"Did it belong to a little girl?"

"I think it did."

"Did the little girl die?"

"Yes, the little girl died."

"If I take her doll, will I die too?"

"No, you won't die, lambkin. I think that little girl would be quite happy if you took care of her doll for her."

"She won't be back?"

"No, she won't be back." Josephine picked up the doll and cradled it in Rebecca's arms.

14

COME, COME YE SAINTS

Come, come, ye Saints, no toil nor labor fear;
But with joy wend your way.
Though hard to you this journey may appear,
Grace shall be as your day.
And should we die before our journey's through,
Happy day! All is well!
We then are free from toil and sorrow, too;
With the just we shall dwell!
… All is well! All is well!

—Excerpt from what is known as the anthem of the Mormon pioneers, words by William Clayton, set to the music of a traditional English song

September 11, 1856

Dearest Meaghan—

Every day I reread your letters I picked up at Fort Kerney. All over again, each time I read the words—I rejoice to hear that all is well with you & Harold—& I am comforted to hear your words of encouragement for our journey. You can not have any idea how dear they are to me.

All though it's September the weather has turned warm again. We will soon reach Echo Kanyon. It is said to have the most dangerous river crossings so far. This journey is not for the faint of heart. Many

of our animals have given out & the company is worn down. We still pass numerous graves each day, & we some times bury our own—which causes unbearable grief for families. Momma & me continue well, but we are tired & eager to arrive. Brother Hans Larsen says we are nearing the Valley—which makes me want to weep with happiness & releif.

When we set sail Momma talked often of you & Edward and William. Now she is strangely silent on the subject—I think the topic has grown too painful to bear discussion.

I wish I could see you. What we would have to talk about! So much has happened in both of our lives.

I will send this letter when we arrive at Great Salt Lake City. (Arrive! What a sweet word!) May God hold you in his tender mercy, & may our parting not be forever. I pray for you every day & ask you— please—to pray for us in turn.

Yours with Longing & Affection,
Josie

I miss you so—please don't forget me.

They had crossed rivers. It seemed like a hundred times. They crisscrossed the Platte all across the Nebraska Territory, Saints and oxen lurching through the sandy shallows. Josephine had laid her boots and stockings in the cart, tied up her skirt, and taken Rebecca's hand, and then they splashed through grassy bottoms, their feet oozing into mud, their skirts dragging against their calves.

Long before they reached the Sweetwater, that gentle oasis that meandered through bluff country, they had fought their way across the treacherous North Platte. On the banks Josephine and her mother dipped rags in tar and smeared the sticky, black muck between the slats of the cart, caulking them to hold out the water before they began their assault on the river. Oxen flinched as they slipped down the banks, and people waded up to their waists. Wheels got lodged against boulders and carts tipped precariously. Hans Larsen allowed Gavin to put his crutch aside and ride in the supply wagon, while Josephine slipped on mossy stones and fell against tree branches and rocks, bruising her legs up to her thighs. Sister Ashdown was, as always, the last one over. She stood blankly at the edge of the river as if confused about which direction to go, and had to be persuaded to step into the current.

But there was no river like the angry torrent that rushed through Echo Canyon in the Utah Territory. It wasn't only the raging waters; it was the canyon itself. The river had clawed its way deep into the Earth, chiseling a narrow chasm through almost vertical cliffs—in some places the walls were within a pistol shot of each other—and immense boulders had rolled down the slopes, creating a chaotic path forward. The narrow ledge along the canyon wall tilted downward toward the river, and as the handcart wheels ground over rocks, Josephine feared they would slip to their deaths.

And then the crossing. Even Elizabeth seemed to lose her equanimity as she stood staring, transfixed, at the river.

"May God in his mercy preserve us," prayed Brother Larsen.

The men wrestled carts into the current. They called out warnings of hidden boulders, their shouts bouncing off the rock faces of the odd echo chamber. Oxen panicked and turned back midway. A milk cow was swept downstream. Carts overturned, and a Welsh immigrant nearly drowned as he carried an elderly widow on his back.

Midway across, Josephine floundered. Water rose above her chest and her feet were swept out from under her. She grabbed for a hold on anything in her path—a branch, a log, a horse—as she was swept downstream. Twice she went under, water filling her lungs until she felt they would explode.

When at last she reached the other shore, she ran along the riverbank, hugging herself and blowing into her hands while she frantically searched the river for her mother and Rebecca. She was flooded with relief when she saw them finally emerge. One of the brethren had risked his life carrying the child across. Now Elizabeth and Rebecca stood, drenched and shaking, coughing up water. Her mother's lips had turned blue.

The party was headed toward camp and a hot fire when the first flakes of snow drifted down through the icy air. They swirled in a tentative manner, and then grew heavier, covering the floor of the canyon. Josephine's clothes didn't dry out, and that night she was colder than she had ever been in her life. But she wasn't worried about herself; instead, she watched her mother shiver uncontrollably.

Soon after they started the next morning Elizabeth said, "Josie? Perhaps we could stop here for a while."

"I'll tarry with you too, then," said Sister Maisey, taking her shawl and wrapping it around Elizabeth's shoulders. She eased down onto the damp earth.

Some time passed before Momma felt strong enough to begin walking again. Peart, in a show of bravery, had her first go at pulling the handcart. She grasped the crossbar and teetered forward, heaving with all her might. Her face grew red. The cart moved only a foot. But she was determined. She let out her breath slowly and with a sharp intake of air strained forward again. Josephine joined her, and together they pulled and pushed the cart over the uneven roadbed.

"I'll do my bit, I will," said Peart, giving the girl a hopeful smile.

By afternoon Elizabeth was kneeling at the side of the road gagging up half-digested johnnycakes and running a high fever. Josephine frantically wet rags and pressed them against her mother's forehead.

"Robert," Elizabeth murmured. "Robert. Is that you?" Tremors racked her body. "Robert? I am in the parlor."

"Papa isn't here," Josephine started to explain, but she was shushed by Sister Maisey.

"Aye, and Robert's here, love," Peart said. "He's 'splaining how he's daft o're you."

"Robert, my head hurts so. I am not myself. Will you lie down beside me?" Elizabeth's teeth began to chatter.

"Aye, and he's laying abed with you. Right by your side." Peart clambered awkwardly to her knees and settled her stumpy body onto a patch of melting snow. She wrapped her arm around Elizabeth.

"Sister Maisey," Josephine whispered. "What's happening to Momma?"

"Your mum just has a touch of confu'sun. That's all."

Half an hour later they heard the clatter of horse hooves along the road and looked up to see Brother Larsen.

"Momma's sick!" Josephine cried.

"I heard." Brother Larsen quickly dismounted and knelt by Elizabeth's side. "Elizabeth? Can you hear me?" He cradled her in his arms and said, "I'll take her to the supply wagon. Do you have another blanket?"

Josephine ran for Meaghan's quilt. As she wrapped it about her mother, Elizabeth's body suddenly seemed very small. Brother Larsen gently lifted her into the saddle, and Josephine watched helplessly as he ferried her up the trail.

All that day, and the days that followed, they moved forward, Elizabeth in the supply wagon and Josephine and Sister Maisey coaxing the cart along. At times even Lydia, seeming to sense the desperate nature of the situation, began to pull her weight.

The party stoically crossed and re-crossed the river, making their way through the canyon. Sandstone columns, the color of burnt earth, stood like sentinels along the sides. The valley widened into a rolling expanse of sagebrush, and knobby hills on each side gradually lifted into mountains, with yellow aspen growing high on the rugged cliffs and spruce hugging the northern slopes. Bunchgrass lined the road and dust tornadoes swirled across their path.

Josephine dodged grasshoppers with bulging eyes and stiffened when she saw a rattlesnake coiled in the sun. Their cart often slipped backward, scraping for a toehold against flat boulders. Sister Maisey's walk became more of a dragging motion, and Josephine stumbled along in a dazed state, a sense of foreboding in her gut.

Momma got sicker by the day. An ugly red rash covered her

wrists and ankles, and then spread to her arms and legs. Again and again, she called for her husband. Again and again, she asked to climb down from the supply wagon so she could squat by the side of the road, where she let forth a stream of brown diarrhea. She once would have been horrified at such a public display of bodily functions. Now she seemed long past the point of shame.

The valley seemed to go on forever, and Josephine was relieved when they approached the top of a long slope. At last, she would be able to get a sense of the land and know how much farther they had to go. She knew they were in the final stretch of their journey. If they could only arrive soon, she could find a proper doctor.

As the girl came over the rise, she stopped. She gaped, speechless. She felt dizzy.

"Lord have mercy," Peart whispered.

Elizabeth, stiff with pain, fumbled her way to the front of the supply wagon, and Josephine watched her mother survey the scene ahead. For a long time, she stood. Her mouth opened, but no words came out.

And then Momma fell to her knees and wept.

The Saints had walked twelve hundred godforsaken miles, pulling carts loaded with all their belongings in the world, digging graves all the way across the desert. Now they were so close—almost there—only to discover that the most harrowing part of the trek lay ahead. In the blue distance, the jagged granite peaks of the Wasatch Mountains cut like teeth into the sky, and in the crevices, snow glared as if daring them to cross. Josephine's eyes traveled across the horizon. She saw no pass. The mountain range appeared impenetrable. Even the Rocky Mountains had demanded less of them; South Pass was simply an open saddle with a gradual ascent.

"We are walking over *that?*" she asked Brother Larsen, but for once, he had no answer. He just stood there in his torn jacket, as dumbstruck as the rest of them.

Josephine sat down alongside her mother, placing her arm around Elizabeth's thin waist. Momma suddenly looked like an old woman.

But within the hour the Saints did what they always did in the face of exhaustion and devastation; they picked up their crossbars and moved on, the churn of their wheels taunting fate.

"Aye, it's agony piled on agony," Sister Maisey said. For once, she gave a nod to the Lord. "Only the Good Shepherd hisself can deliver us." She turned to Josephine. "But don't you be worrying none, lass. He's watching o'er your mum, he is."

The party straggled in a broken line, three here, five there, into Mormon Flat, and pitched tents. A brook gurgled by the campsite; moss streamed gently in the current. Small birds fluttered in the willows and an owl hooted, but Josephine heard and saw nothing of the beauty.

Sister Maisey squatted over the fire pit, desperately trying to kindle her first fire. The clang of pots echoed through the camp. Dogs barked and cows bawled. Life was going on, just as it always had.

And yet it wasn't.

Her mother was shaky and had trouble walking. Josephine helped her into the tent, arranged a blanket for her. She shut the flap and lit a candle, hoping it wouldn't burn out quickly. And then she studied her mother's face. Momma was pale, almost gray. Josephine crawled next to her mother; she lay down and held her and tucked Meaghan's dirty quilt about her shoulders. Josephine felt her blood thrum in her ears. Her eyes stung. She stroked her mother's hand.

"Momma. Momma?"

She realized she had never told her mother how much she loved her. She combed her mother's unwashed hair with her fingers.

I love you I love you I love you.

"Robert?" her mother said. "Robert."

"*I'm* here! Your daughter. I'm here."

Her mother's breathing became labored. She opened her eyes and looked at Josephine as if recognizing her for the first time.

"Josie."

"Momma?"

"Meaghan will take care of you," Elizabeth whispered, her voice hoarse. She swallowed with effort. "She always was a good sister to you."

"Meaghan isn't here," Josephine said, terrified. "I'm the only one here." She felt like a small child.

"She will take care of you," her mother said, as if she hadn't heard Josephine.

"Momma! No! We'll be there soon."

"I am so tired, Josie. I want to rest."

Please God please God please.

Josephine listened to her mother's breath. This couldn't be happening.

I have given up everything! Everything for you. Please God please. Don't take Momma.

Her mother choked, trying to capture air. Her lungs took on a queer rattle. At the last, her chest stopped rising and falling, and her body grew still. Her grimace, frozen in agony, softened into a serene expression. Josephine frantically clutched her hand.

"Breathe! Momma. Breathe!"

But her mother was gone.

Elizabeth's hand grew heavy and strangely cold, and her body grew rigid. Josephine lay by her side until morning reveille. When Sister Maisey brought porridge, Josephine almost flung the bowl back at her. She felt a retching panic, as if she were drowning, and ran out of the tent, where she bent over and vomited up the sour taste of fear.

Brother Larsen himself dug the grave. His eyes were rimmed in red, and he didn't speak. Josephine cried at him the entire time.

"No! We have to take Momma with us! We're almost there. We can't leave her here all by herself."

He ignored her, digging four feet down—deeper than any grave they had dug before—before he hoisted himself out. But it wasn't deep enough for Josephine. She climbed in, crazed, and began scraping the dirt walls with a cooking spoon. The melancholy gray sky began to drip, and then ran in rivulets over her shoulders. She didn't notice.

Brother Larsen climbed back into the trench and knelt beside her. "Josie," he said. His voice trailed off. And then he joined her, using rough motions to dig the hole deeper.

Tired and hurried, the Saints had long since abandoned the extravagance of formal grave markers, but Brother Larsen walked up and down the hillside searching for the right shape of wood; Elizabeth would be properly honored. The women wrapped the body in Meaghan's quilt, its gay border of bluebells looking more out of place than ever.

Rain pelted the men as they lowered the body into the grave. They brushed clods of red mud on top of Elizabeth's chest, on top of her stomach and face. They piled on stones. Josephine rocked back and forth on a downturned bucket, sobbing. She felt as if stones were being stacked on her own chest.

The men pushed and pulled a handcart back and forth across the grave, packing down the soil to discourage wolves. They heaped brush on top and tried to light a fire to hide the scent of flesh, but the wood was too wet to ignite. Josephine hugged her mother's book of Wordsworth tight against her breast as Brother Larsen pounded the crude headboard into the ground.

ELIZABETH BELL

1821-1856

There was none dearer

They gathered in a circle and Josephine shut her ears against the tirade of empty phrases, the meaningless jumble of platitudes: Sister Bell died with her face toward Zion. She was a loving mother, a stalwart pioneer. May God in his mercy bless Sister Bell's daughter.

They sang "Come, Come Ye Saints," quietly at first, and then with a kind of fierce fervor, as if each person was clutching at hope. "And should we die before our journey's through, happy day! All is well! We then are free from toil and sorrow, too."

Josephine felt lightheaded as she heard the mocking claim, "All is well! All is well!"

The company waited half a day, and then the emigrants rolled out. Winter was approaching and they couldn't delay the march over the mountains. Josephine crouched by the grave, refusing to move. Once she left, there would be no visiting the site, no placing flowers at the headboard. Her mother would be alone in the wilderness.

It was Sister Maisey, in a clumsy, well-meaning way, who convinced her to come.

"Aye, and I'll just sit down awhile by you. If you's not coming, I ain't neither."

Josephine stared straight ahead.

"I know you's angry, child. And broke down. I'd be too. But your mum wouldn't want you tarrying here, just by yourself. She aims for you to go to the Promised Land."

Sister Maisey hoisted her thick frame upward and held out her hand. Josephine debated a moment and finally—defeated—took it. As she walked alongside Peart Maisey, catching up with the party, the girl looked back again and again, until they were out of sight.

"The good Lord giveth," the woman muttered, more to herself than to Josephine. "And the good Lord taketh. And sometimes the old bloke takes more than he gives."

That night the baying of wolves prickled Josephine's skin. When she finally fell asleep, she saw them circling the grave, the pups whining with excitement. She saw them paw the ground.

The girl woke with a start, remembering where she was. Here in this cold tent, far from home, winter on the way. She wondered if the wolves had already unearthed what they had buried.

She remembered Brigham Young's promise, "The Lord will provide. You shall come in safety."

But he didn't.

And they hadn't.

15

FAMILIES MIGHT START … with cows, hand-carts, wheel-bar-rows, with little flour, and no unnecessaries, and come to this place quicker, and with less fatigue than by following the heavy trains with their cumbrous herds, which they are obliged to drive miles to feed. Do you not like this method of travelling? Do you think salvation costs too much? If so, it is not worth having.

—"Sixth General Epistle of the Presidency of the Church of Jesus Christ of Latter-day Saints," *Deseret News*

September 25, 1856

Dear Meaghan—
    Momma died. We buried her at Mormon Flat. I miss you & Edward & William more than I can say—

Josie

—We reach the Valley tomorrow

A crust of snow glinted along the ridgeline, and in the distance, a bowl of jagged peaks leaned toward dark thunderheads. Willows sheltered in ravines, and aspens stood in groves on the slopes. Their leaves quivered like thousands of yellow butterflies, wings flickering in the sunlight and making a quiet clapping sound; their white trunks were etched with black markings. Dark green conifers ascended the mountainsides until they gave way to talus slopes, and the talus slopes rose until they disappeared among rock spires.

Summer was ending and the wind bit her cheeks, but Josephine was still sweating. The road grew steeper and then steeper yet again, and she watched the Saints—the old, the feeble, the pregnant, the children—pulling for all they were worth. Many women carried a baby on one hip, and carts were weighed down with the sick.

Just after the party stopped at dusk, Josephine came across a wounded chickadee at the side of the trail. She cupped the trembling bird in her hands and wandered into the trees, where she knelt on a cushion of fir needles. She caressed the soft down of its breast and ran her finger along the wing feathers, whispering all the while, "There, there. You'll be all right. Just rest." She made a bed of decayed leaves and gently laid down the bird. "You'll be all right." She stroked its back, but her touch and words of comfort did nothing to prolong the tiny creature's life. When it died, grief—and then guilt—pierced her like a hot wound.

Suddenly she saw Rebecca approach. All morning the little girl had trudged uphill, dumb with exhaustion but only rarely asking to rest. Despite that, Josephine's face tightened. The child had tagged along like a shadow, every step, for hundreds of miles. Couldn't Josephine have a single moment to herself?

Rebecca asked, "It's dead?"

Josephine didn't answer. She was surprised at her own anger. The child had identified the problem, exactly.

"Your mum died too," the little girl observed solemnly, as if she were still trying to comprehend the idea. She reached for a fold of Josephine's skirt. "Will you cry out your sadness now, Miss Josie?"

"No, Rebecca!" Josephine snapped. She jerked leaves over

the chickadee's body and shoved a stick into the loam—a sorry headboard for a sorry grave. "I will never cry enough to cry out my sadness. What do you think! You think you can just cry, and God brings back your momma? And your sister? And your papa? You think I want to be here, in the middle of this wretched desert by myself?"

Rebecca stiffened and fell back. Sister Maisey heard the commotion and hurried forward. She awkwardly patted the top of the child's head, and then Josephine's shoulder. "Aye, and you're not alone, Josie."

"Are you telling me what to think? I have never been more alone!"

Sister Maisey hesitantly ventured, as if she were afraid of starting an argument, "Aye, the Lord's with you, he is. And the brethren and sisters. They's with you too."

"These are not my brothers! Sister Ashdown is not my sister! You are not my sister. My sister and brothers are God knows how many miles away. And the Almighty is not with me." She pronounced "Almighty" with disdain. "I followed him all the way here, and look! He abandoned me." Her voice broke. "Joseph Smith preaches a fancy sermon about families in the next world. Where are our families in this world?"

Suddenly everything seemed so utterly useless. Josephine pulled more leaves onto the grave, until the mound grew a foot high. Would that be enough to keep out the wolves? She rolled a large rock on top of the leaves. It was futile, she knew.

We're born. We live. We die. And for what?

And what choices do we really have?

The girl remembered the woolen mill. She and Momma arrived before the sky grew light and emerged only after darkness had set in again. She remembered the pimply faced boy who lunged at the factory boss, screaming with fury and helplessness. He had been whipped for falling behind, and after his outburst, was whipped again and thrown into the alley, and now where was his daily pittance coming from? Had he joined the hordes of other stray humans begging for a bite to eat?

She remembered standing at Albert Dock watching the pathetic line of Mormons haul their wilted cabbages and sacks of rotted potatoes up the gangplank, their faces glowing with excitement about the miraculous possibilities ahead. She had been ashamed to join such a rabble of paupers, but then she, too, had walked up the plank, her stomach empty, trusting her fate to a backwoods prophet with a golden bible. What else could she do?

Once, on a day when a woman had buried two sons in the same grave, Sister Maisey had said, "The poor souls pulling these handcarts ha'nt much druthers. Meself included." She shrugged. "Fate's already picked our lot for us."

Josephine remembered bearing her testimony, and the lightning that spread through her body as she repeated the words she had heard others say. "I know we are led by God."

Are we?

What's the worth of a momentary burning sensation, one moment—probably imagined—in all the stretch of one's life? How can it count for anything, she wondered. What's the worth of belief if it brings only anguish?

Supper was awkward. Rebecca concentrated on the ground as she ate, and she ate very little. After Josephine washed the plates she approached the child.

"I'm sorry, 'Becca." Josephine's foot began to twitch. Shame had been added to guilt and grief. "I'm sorry."

The child said nothing, just sucked at the gap between her front teeth.

Josephine couldn't bring herself to look at Peart's face as she said, "I'm sorry, Sister Maisey."

"Aye, and I know you's sorry, lass." The woman hoisted the bucket and poured a cup of water. "Josie, no dearer mum e'er walked the Earth." She set the cup in front of Josephine, balancing it carefully on a log. "I admit I talk back to the Lord on a reg'lar basis, but in diff'cult circumstances, he's the one to set store by."

"How come he's not helping us? How do you know he's

even there?"

"Most times you don't. But you go forward anyhows, hoping things'll all work out. That you'll find a bit of cheer again. If 'er helps, love, think of your mum on a journey. Just as you are. You'll meet up yonder."

There was no fiddling that night. The party was too exhausted. Just after the prayer circle, Gavin Sayers limped to Josephine's side. His useful foot didn't look quite as useful as it once had; it had swollen so much he had been forced to cut the toe from his boot.

"I lost my own mother," he said. His boyish face looked bashful, and Josephine suddenly realized how young he seemed. "To the pox. I played at her funeral even though I was only twelve." He shoved his hands in his pockets.

Josephine knew she should say, "I'm sorry." She had waited half a year—across the Atlantic, the prairie, the Rocky Mountains, the desert—for a word from Gavin. And now he offered the eagerly sought-after gift, but she was deaf to its invitation. Looking at him standing there with his patched trousers and frayed yellow neckerchief, she couldn't remember why he had seemed so dashing. Josephine turned away, leaving him leaning on his crutch.

Morning brought another death. Ernst Clough, he who had castigated those who fell ill, accusing them of insufficient faith, now lay at the door of his tent, his Adam's apple still making a spectacle of itself in spite of his demise. He had told his flock he would rather die on the way to Zion than live in the godless land they had left. And so he had—died, that is—with a little encouragement from mountain fever.

Just several days earlier he had counseled that those who mourn for Sister Elizabeth Bell should rejoice. "For she has gone ahead to wait for the morn of the resurrection, and will rise in perfect attainment of celestial glory."

"That man is daft. Rejoice. Merciful Lord!" Sister Maisey had muttered. Lately, she had taken up a running commentary with herself.

Peart was not the only one angered by Elder Clough's words. Someone called, "And what of your own wife? Left behind in England! I hear she's a non-believer. Will she be cast down too? The devil's furnace, eh?"

"You've no business talking about my wife," said Ernst Clough, tight-lipped. "She will reap as she sows and there is naught I can do about it."

Now Peart looked at Elder Clough's body, stretched out on the ground, and she was silent, for once. She shook her shoulders as if making sure she herself was still alive, and then said to Josephine, "'Well, 'tis no good to tarry then. Breakfast it is. I'll get up the fixings."

Her corn porridge burned in the skillet, of course. Josephine hunched on a log and numbly swallowed each bite.

After breakfast the brethren dug a shallow trench, and Hans Larsen's words at the impromptu funeral constituted the shortest sermon the girl had ever heard.

"Our brother, Elder Ernst Clough, has passed from our midst. He will be remembered as a man devoted to his Heavenly Father. And to his chosen people. Right then, I would say more, but it behooves us to roll out before the day grows even later." It was as if Elder Clough's death had been an inconvenience rather than a tragedy.

As they pulled their handcarts into line, Peart exclaimed, "I can't help be relieved that one's gone to his end."

"He has not gone to his *end*," Lydia clarified. "He's gone to his Maker."

"I reckon his Maker had a second think after that partic'lar elder was made."

Josephine's head ached from the altitude. She heard the murmur of conversations and the bellowing of milk cows, but she heard nothing from Rebecca. The child hadn't spoken since Josephine's outburst.

Brother Larsen came by half a dozen times each day, offering to help pull. "We must bind up our broken hearts," he told Josephine, looking as if he himself had some binding to do.

He still made his rounds of the campfires and encouraged the Saints. Most were growing weaker by the day. His kindness seemed as if it had grown even deeper, but his sermons were pale, lifeless things. A light seemed to have gone out of his eyes. Sometimes, after the prayer circle, Josephine saw him slip out alone to walk the perimeter of the camp, and she noticed he volunteered many nights for guard duty. Perhaps he needed the solitude, she thought. She wished for her own solitude; everyone and everything crowded unbearably close.

They wound higher and higher, their carts creaking, up into the craggy mountains. The blood-colored leaves of mountain maple seared the hillsides, and were broken up by stands of brooding dark-blue spruce. Josephine could smell soil and decaying leaves and snow.

Now that her mother wasn't around to offer gentle reminders about how the harsh sun could mar a young lady's beauty, Josephine took off her bonnet. It didn't really matter anymore. Her braid fell loose and the unruly curls tangled about her shoulders.

They were nearing the summit of Big Mountain, where they would get their first glimpse of the Salt Lake Valley. The strong ones helped the weak ones, taking the hands of the sick and the lame. Men lifted tired children into the wobbly handcarts and pulled them up the steep incline, and they pulled the carts of older Saints. Now that the end of the journey was near, the party could spare the time, and they slowed their pace to accommodate women who carried unborn babies in their swollen bellies.

Late that afternoon the party rounded the crest of the mountain. The day had been still, but at the summit the wind gusted, cooling the sweat on Josephine's face. She stood with the others and gazed down, relieved and nervous, hopeful and afraid. A luminous cloud billowed high in the sky, and from it, streams of light swept downward like heavenly rays. Towering mountains fell away on both sides, and ahead, she could see a vast plain with a cerulean lake on the far horizon. Deep canyons stretched ahead of her, all the way down to the valley floor.

And what of Brother Brigham's desert kingdom? The girl couldn't see a thing. The settlement was hidden in the dusky blue shadow of the foothills.

PART THREE

Desert Kingdom

16

BREAD.

Set a sponge at night of a pound of flour, a little salt, if your yeast should not be salt enough, a gill of yeast, and water enough to make a thick batter. In the morning stir in as much flour as will form a dough, knead it well, and if the weather is cold set it in a warm place to rise. When it is light grease your pans, mold out the dough in loaves, put them in pans, and as soon as they rise again bake them.

—*The National Cook Book: By a Lady of Philadelphia, a Practical Housewife*, written by Hannah Mary Bouvier Peterson

Cedar City, Utah Territory, 1856

Emmanuel's birthday present was hidden in a coffin out in his father's carpentry workshop. Heber Dodd had constructed the coffin for Bishop Severn's senior wife, but Sister Severn was taking her time dying, and so Brother Dodd was left with an empty pine box, perfectly sized to hide a rifle for his oldest son.

Emmanuel's birthday fell on Thanksgiving, but that year in Utah grasshoppers got to the crops before the Saints did, and so there was little food left for a proper holiday feast. Brother Dodd and his wife Alberta deliberated for weeks; in the end, she slaughtered the family pig for the occasion. The side dishes were humble—corn, gravy, and a thin spread of lard on bread—but the centerpiece of boiled ham glowed like a pink jewel. For an hour before the meal, it sat on the table while the children finished their chores. Every time they stepped into the cabin, they couldn't keep their eyes off it.

From the oldest to the youngest, they had scrubbed their faces and dressed in their Sunday best, but Josephine's best was frozen solid. She had gathered the family's clothing from the line and stacked the trousers and dresses like stiff griddle cakes before bringing them inside, and now there was nothing to be done for it; her gray wool dress hadn't thawed in time. Her frock would have to do, even though it was too cold for gingham and the hem was frayed. Thirteen hundred miles had taken their toll.

But no matter. The fire kept a cheerful blaze, warming the girl from the outside in. The children had placed tallow candles along the mantle and on the table. In the soft glow, Josephine looked at the circle of faces gathered around the ham, whose name, until recently, was Patsy. Even as Brother Dodd said the prayer, each child clasped their fork, as if the *Amen* and first bite couldn't come soon enough.

"Mother?" Heber Dodd said, handing the first portion to his wife. Her real name was Alberta, but the church sisters called her Bertie. Heber called her "Mother." After birthing eight children, it was an accurate description, but the term at first startled Josephine, who was used to hearing Papa call Momma "my darling."

Nevertheless, she knew Brother Dodd loved his wife. Alberta Dodd may not have looked like much—her ankles were thick and her gray eyes looked as if they had faded over time to match the ashes she scraped from the fireplace—but Josephine noticed how her husband took her elbow when they walked home from church. They spoke in quiet, deferential tones, each conversation preceded by his clearing of the throat.

At the supper table, he never missed an opportunity to praise his wife's industry. He noted aloud that she rarely slept past the first crow of the rooster, and she was the last to retire at night, knitting and sewing right up until prayers, and then some. Unlike some children in the settlement, his own children never went missing buttons on their jackets, and his muslin shirts were bleached so white in the sun they seemed to take on its shine; at ward frolics, his wife's pie crusts were always the flakiest. She even helped scythe hay when the boys couldn't keep up.

"She's strong as an ox," Brother Dodd said.

He admired Bertie's thrift; in the midst of famine, she had somehow managed to stretch the contents of the root cellar for months. And although calls for her midwife skills interrupted his sleep on a regular basis, he was proud of her vocation. "Mother has delivered every baby in Cedar City," he bragged.

But most of all, he commended his wife for her testimony of the restored gospel. They had joined the church back in Missouri, and she had been stalwart ever since. When she stayed up later than usual on Saturday nights, finishing chores ahead of time to make sure no labor took place on the Sabbath, or when she bore testimony in church, the family patriarch reckoned aloud that she would reap more than her share of God's blessings.

Bertie Dodd's children loved her too. The first thing Josephine noticed when she stepped across the threshold back in October was a sampler over the fireplace: GOD BLESS OUR MOTHER. The words were embroidered in an elaborate script and bordered with hearts and angels; the two older girls, Sarah and Agnes, had each taken a turn with the needle. Unlike Josephine and Meaghan, Sister Dodd's daughters took to handiwork with the patience of Job.

Her eldest son, Emmanuel, brought his mother flowers when he came in from the fields, and the gangly fifteen-year-old noticed small things. When the wood stack for his mother's fireplace grew low, he was the first one out the door with the ax, and when he saw she needed water for the laundry or the family's Saturday night baths, he hauled bucketfuls from the irrigation ditch.

At first Alberta Dodd had seemed a bit imposing to Josephine, with her straight posture and sober demeanor, but the orderliness of Bertie's household was like a salve to the girl's chaotic emotions. Sister Dodd was as dependable as the sunrise. Each morning she rose before the rest of the household and stoked the fire and set the kettle on, and as soon as the breakfast dishes were set to dry, she began the tedious round of chores she had left off the night before. On Saturdays, the air was filled with the yeasty fragrance of rising dough, and the woman cleaned the two rooms and upstairs loft as if the Lord himself were coming for Sabbath dinner.

Not only was Alberta Dodd orderly, but she was kind. When Josephine arrived, the girl felt as if she had not breathed properly since she left Momma at Mormon Flat, and was unaccountably moved to tears when the good sister welcomed her "home." The older woman stopped kneading bread and set out a cup of tea for the girl, something no one had done since Josephine's last visit with Meaghan.

"I reckon you're worn out," Bertie said, wiping her hands on her starched apron. "I'll not ask you to start in on chores until you have properly rested, and I'm sure you'll need to be thinking about your school lessons soon."

"I was a school teacher on board the ship, and I suppose those lessons will do as good as any," said Josephine, remembering the frustration of lessons endlessly interrupted by the noise of flapping sails and rounds of sickness among her pupils. Now she had been called by the brethren to teach children in the small outpost.

"Most likely, the school session will only be for the winter," Sister Dodd said. "In spring the children will be needed for planting, and they'll work the harvest in the fall." She dusted her breadboard with more flour and put her shoulders into kneading the loaves. "We've not had a school teacher here before now."

Bertie apologized for the humble accommodations. "You'll sleep here," she said, gesturing with her floury hand to the puncheon floor in front of the hearth. "With Sarah and Agnes. I'm sorry, but this is the best setup we can do."

Josephine knew her stay with them was only temporary, as befits a community school teacher. She would soon go on to the next family, and all the houses would likely be humble. Before the year was out she would probably be familiar with the hard floor of a number of cabins.

Nevertheless, after sleeping on the ground for more than four months, the straw pallet felt soft as a feather bed, and even though the fire died down each night, her place by the hearth was still the warmest in the cabin. The boys slept in the loft among strings of dried onions and bags of cornmeal, and Brother and Sister Dodd slept on the only bed, in the adjoining room, the three youngest children on the floor beside them. Feed sacks had been sewn together and hung across the doorway, but the thin divider didn't mask their discussions of the price they would get for their wool or the receipts from Heber Dodd's carpentry workshop or whether they could trade Bertie's rich yellow butter this spring for a good used saddle; at her age, riding to outlying cabins without a proper saddle was becoming dangerous, and the babies wouldn't always wait for the farm wagon to bounce over the rutted roads. Bertie's midwifery skills brought a steady stream of bartered goods into the household, for what was more constant than pregnancy?

Sister Dodd herself looked as if she were built for having babies. Her hips were overly broad, so much so that her husband seemed diminished in her presence. Even Heber's hands were small. Josephine thought them hardly adequate for constructing the bedsteads and fireplace mantels and tables that helped the family get by. But Brother Dodd was tall, and he was agile in spite of his fifty-three years. Josephine thought he sometimes seemed uncertain of himself, but Sister Dodd seemed to guess his wishes and to accommodate herself to them before he even asked.

Even though the grasshopper plague had brought famine and suppers were meager and the children complained of never getting enough, Josephine sometimes slipped a corner of bread into her apron pocket. She would lie awake in the dark after Sarah and Agnes had fallen asleep, sucking at it, letting it soften on her tongue until it had no taste. She was always furtive, hoping no one would notice. What would the family think of a school teacher who stole bread from children, and right off the table? And yet she couldn't seem to help herself. She wasn't sure if it was plain hunger or something deeper.

Sister Dodd kept Webster's dictionary and the *Book of Mormon* on the mantle, but Josephine didn't keep Momma's Wordsworth poems there. She hid the book in the folds of an empty flour sack during the day, and at night she slipped the book under her blanket and held it against her breast. She remembered the rhythms, remembered how she and Momma had comforted each other with poetry back in the damp flat in Liverpool. They had read the lines so often the girl knew many by heart. Now the book's pages were warped from river crossings, and a section had fallen out after the binding came loose at the Sweetwater. The girl had left her mother behind, but Mr. Wordsworth followed her all the way to Cedar City.

She sucked her bread and held her book and tried to remember the exact lilt of her mother's voice, the way each sentence rose in a slight question mark, as if she were inviting the other to speak.

Josephine heard a child cough and listened to Brother Dodd snore in the other room.

How do you remember a voice?

She thought if she recited the poems often enough, the familiar cadence of Momma's voice would come to her, and so she talked to herself when she was gathering kindling for the fire, following faint deer traces on the rise behind the cabin.

"Turn wheresoe'er I may, by night or day, the things which I have seen I now can see no more."

She recited stanzas when she set out corn husks for the cows and whispered to the chickens as she scattered scraps and collected stray feathers for pillows.

"Where is it now, the glory and the dream?"

The cows and chickens were housed in the barn, and out past the barn was the corral, where Heber kept his two horses. Jake was small, and the color of mud. Easily agitated, the horse spooked at the sight of a rabbit and fidgeted nervously when the boys brought hay, keeping his distance and switching his tail until they left. Jake seemed flightier than the mules the girl had seen on the trail west. The other horse, Flicker, was the gentlest creature she had ever known.

Like her, Flicker seemed a bit misplaced in his own life, always looking around the corral as if surprised to be there. He was taller at the withers than Josephine, and in most horses, stature adds to graceful lines, but in Flicker's case, height only made him appear more awkward. The girl couldn't help but notice his crooked hind legs and protruding hips; she had heard Brother Dodd call him the "ugliest piece of horseflesh" he'd ever seen, and a poor plow horse at that, but whenever she passed the corral, Flicker turned his big ungainly head her direction and gave a hopeful whinny. When she walked closer, he pawed the ground in greeting. Josephine knew what the horse meant to the family. He was simply an animal bought on the cheap to hitch to the front of the wagon or strap behind the plow—nothing more.

One afternoon she took a deep breath and asked Brother Dodd if she could care for the horses. He paused from his work for a long moment, looking at her with a penetrating expression, as if seeing her for the first time. He tossed another handful of straw into the fresh cow droppings, mixing a batch of daub to chink holes in the cabin walls.

"You're too small," he finally said. "The horses are a job for the boys. If you want to help with something outdoors, you can help chink or do more hoeing."

Her protest slipped out before Josephine caught herself. "But the boys are small too, even Emmanuel!"

A wire of tension tightened across Heber's forehead. He looked tired as he stooped there over the tub, his neck red from too much sun. "You've already got more work than you can handle in the house. You need to help Mother." He gestured at his wife, who was gathering clothes from the line. "And there's teaching your school classes too."

The girl felt her stubbornness rise. She wasn't sure why it suddenly had become important to care for the horses, but she knew that aside from Emmanuel, who answered every request with polite acquiescence, the boys openly detested the chore.

"Perhaps I could just pitch some hay on my way home from school. It wouldn't take much time."

Heber sighed and wiped his hands. "What do you think, Mother?" He looked dubiously at his wife, but although Bertie usually deferred to his wishes, this time she took a different tack.

"Oh, let's let the girl feed the horses if she wants to. Heaven knows the boys don't like doing it." Josephine thought she detected a look of pity.

At that, Heber gave in. The next morning, Josephine was out before the sun warmed the rim of the crimson cliffs, before Brother Dodd could change his mind—forking flakes of hay into the manger. The air was cold, and the feed heavier than she had expected. She breathed in the musty, horsey smell and put down the pitchfork to listen to the gurgle of the irrigation ditch and the *whoo-whoo* of an owl, its call floating across the fields.

"Hello Flicker," she said. He cocked his ears and looked at her sideways.

She heard Jake snort from the other side of the corral as she stood on an empty crate, tentatively caressing the white streak that ran down Flicker's forehead. His coat was oddly coarse. The horse nickered softly, following her with his dark eyes. They were framed with the most delicate lashes.

Someone needs me.

"Hello horse." She scratched his ears and combed his mane with her fingers. "Do you want to hear a poem?"

You can say things to a horse, she thought.

"We will grieve not, rather find strength in what remains behind," she told him, running her hand over his cowlick. "In the soothing thoughts that spring out of human suffering, in the faith that looks through death."

Flicker looked at her with moist eyes and blew out softly, as if he understood the poet's meaning, although Josephine wasn't sure if she herself did.

"Be brave," she told him. She took a brush to his matted coat, combing out dirt that looked like it had accumulated for months, perhaps years. Tears started down her cheeks.

"Don't cry, don't cry," she told Flicker. She leaned her head against his withers and put her arms around his dusty neck and hung on.

Bishop Severn's wife died the day after Thanksgiving, and Brother Dodd's coffin—which had hidden the .54 caliber birthday present—was hauled to the Severn home. Emmanuel's new rifle was almost as tall as he was, and looked heavy, but the boy hoisted it across his shoulder and went out hunting almost every day. The girls started on a Lazy Daisy quilt and Bertie finished two rag rugs. Josephine began each morning emptying chamber pots; she swept dirt out of the cabin before walking to the drafty schoolhouse, where she started in on the alphabet. She hadn't yet mastered the art of corralling boys who preferred the outdoors.

Sometimes when she walked home from school, taking the shortcut along the dry creek bed, she surveyed the grim little settlement and thought she had arrived at the end of the Earth. But Flicker waited to greet her, standing at the fence whinnying as if his happiness depended on her. Perhaps it wasn't the end of the Earth after all.

17

THINK NOT WHEN YOU GATHER TO ZION

Think not when you gather to Zion,
Your troubles and trials are through,
That nothing but comfort and pleasure
Are waiting in Zion for you:
No, no, 'tis designed as a furnace,
All substance, all textures to try,
To burn all the "wood, hay, and stubble,"
The gold from the dross purify.

—Excerpt from a hymn written by Eliza Roxcy Snow, president of the Mormon women's Relief Society, poet, and plural wife of Joseph Smith and Brigham Young

October 28, 1856

Dearest Meaghan—

I am sorry for not writing sooner. I am at last settled in one place but somehow I can not write letters as I used to—I cannot seem to collect my thoughts

But all though I have not taken up my pen until this evening, you have never been far from my thoughts. I received your letter in Great Salt Lake City & was elated to hear your news! You will make a good Mother—better than me. Momma used to say I am even more impatient than you. I imagine Harold is overjoyed—He will be a Father, (I will be an Aunt!) To think just last year we evesdropped through the door when he came to ask Momma for your hand, & now you are an old married lady! I can only imagine the delight of gathering things together for the arrival of your little one—

As for me, we reached the Valley in September. I waited for directions after the welcome sermon—Everything was confusion, to say the least, with 300 people to sort out. At last I hear that I am to go to Cedar City to take up residence. One of the Saints carried me & Sister Maysey in his farm wagon—I sat in the back with a load of tools for the new iron ore operation near here.

I have been called as a school teacher. For now, I am staying in the home of Brother Heber Dodd & his wife Sister Alberta Dodd.

Evenings & Saturdays are given over to waging war against dust & dirt, & endless rounds of weeding, scrubbing laundry, boiling beans, baking bread, knitting socks, feed the pig, tend to the sheep, & a 100 other tasks. I even chop wood & cut hay. My chores include what we would call mens chores in the Old Country. Sister Dodd is also a midwife & so is often gone—leaving me with the children at any unexpected hour.

Somehow I manage to also teach 4 days of school each week. The stove there is not nearly hot enough to keep the little ones warm & it is a trial for them.

I think of Momma almost constantly, asking myself again & again—Was there some thing I could have done to save her? I am tormented by memories. But I must look to the Lord for my strength & comfort—& I must be content with my lot. Although food is in short supply, it is more than the bread & potatos that were my daily fare in Liverpool, & Brother & Sister Dodd are good Saints & kind to me—as are their children.

Well, I guess this has not been a very cheerful letter. I promise to write a happier one next time.

I think of you every day & pray for you, & now—the baby! Please pray for me, as I will for you. May the angels watch o'er you, dear sister—

Sending Love & Affection
Josie

Josephine took to bringing in stray odds and ends to decorate the schoolroom. The small frame building doubled as the church house, but Bishop Jack Severn, the presiding leader of the settlement, hadn't objected to her ornaments, so she continued to place driftwood and Indian arrowheads and hawk feathers along the window ledges, and even sewed curtains for the front window with scraps from two of Bertie's threadbare aprons.

Each morning the children filed in and sat along the plank benches, boys on one side and girls on the other. Josephine noticed, with consternation, that the girls' side was always sparse on Mondays, when they helped out at home with the wash. The only ones who never missed were the Dodd girls. Bertie wrestled with the scalding water and wet, heavy clothing by herself so her children wouldn't miss a day.

"I can't for the life of me see how a mother can put washing clothes over school," Josephine complained as she sat in front of the fire with Sister Dodd, unraveling yarn from worn-out sweaters.

"Don't be too harsh on them," said Bertie. "Sometimes it's all a mother can do to keep things together, and the girls can make their lessons up later."

Josephine frowned. She guessed that Sister Dodd knew the children wouldn't make up their lessons later, and already the biggest problem was that her pupils were on so many different levels. Some sang multiplication tables and others just hummed along, having not yet memorized the figures. When Josephine passed around the classroom copy of *McGuffey's Reader*, only half the children could read its stories. Unfortunately, the schoolroom had only a handful of slates and a meager supply of chalk, so she was forced to take the other half outside to inscribe letters in the dirt. They laughed as they watched their breath curl in the cold air, but after a few rounds of the ABC's they were impatient to get back inside to the wood stove. Twice a day, Josephine rotated their seats so those far from the stove, their limbs stiff with cold, could move closer and thaw out.

At lunchtime they piled back outside, where Brother Dodd's oldest boy, Emmanuel, led the boys in foot races, while the girls jumped rope or made playhouses out of rocks and sticks. Only one child refused to join in. Rebecca sat on the step, watching the scene with a detached expression, holding the rag doll she had taken from a child's grave.

The little girl didn't talk much, and when she did, it was to whimper to herself that she wanted to go home to her pa. It was no wonder she wanted her father, Josephine thought. Sister Lydia Ashdown had wandered away into another world, one far removed from her own child. Now Josephine couldn't look at Rebecca without remorse, and so she kept her attention on the other children. She told herself the girl's silence was the result of the weary trek, her separation from her father, the vague distance of her mother—and nothing to do with an angry outburst over a dead bird.

All the way down Emigration Canyon, Rebecca had responded in one-syllable sentences when asked a direct question, but otherwise, she was almost completely silent. And now here it was, October, and she was still mute.

Even Brigham Young himself couldn't draw a response from her.

The handcart party had reached Brigham's Promised Land several days after leaving the summit of Big Mountain. They had picked their way down Emigration Canyon, handcart wheels grinding against rock, carts slipping and banging down ravines. Several broke apart, spilling clothing and water barrels and kettles down the steep slopes. Sister Maisey slipped, too, as she negotiated the trail, which was slick with soggy leaves.

As they descended a rise above the valley, the view suddenly opened up. Josephine had walked thirteen hundred miles, but when she took in the bleak settlement and briny lake in the distance, she knew that if she could, she would walk a thousand more miles rather than remain.

Even Peart was affected. "Where are the trees?" she asked, without her usual good cheer. "We came all the way for this?"

The converts from the British Isles stared at the treeless landscape, looking bewildered. The arid plain stretched to the north and south as far as they could see and was hemmed in on the east by towering mountains so sharp they sliced the sky. Below, adobe houses and log shanties and vacant lots squatted along squared-off dirt streets, each street bordered by an irrigation ditch. The canals, flowing down from the canyon, seemed to be doing their best to keep hopeful rows of fruit trees alive, but otherwise, everything was desert.

Peart stomped insects off her shoes and said dryly, "Pshaw! I see the grasshoppers have made us a warm welcome."

Josephine stopped at the outskirts of the city to wash her face in a ditch and re-braid her hair, and then she pulled her handcart with all her earthly belongings down the main street along with the others. Her boots were nearly shredded and her skirt was in tatters, the hem crusted with dried mud, but she was too exhausted to be embarrassed. And to be certain, she wasn't the only one with little to her name. Even some who were already settled in the valley looked poor. Josephine walked past tents and canvas-topped wagon boxes—the wheels removed after the trek—that served as homes. Worn, freshly washed clothing hung on ropes stretched across yards and children played barefoot in the dirt.

She passed a noisy blacksmith shop, and then mercantile shops with false fronts and displays of second-hand goods—homespun skirts and worn poke bonnets. Farther down the street came elegant shops with displays of velvet cape-jackets and satin gowns, feathered and flowered bonnets. And then came the temple grounds, where the new house of the Lord was being erected. Across the street from the grounds, behind an eight-foot wall, were the homes and stables and barns of the prophet.

Suddenly Josephine heard a brass band and saw a procession of Saints coming to welcome them, carrying cakes and melons. Many apologized they didn't have more to offer; the past two summers had brought too little rain and too many grasshoppers, they said.

Josephine was herded, along with the rest, to the tithing yard. Rumors were that the building brimmed with the goods of the kingdom; Mormons brought one-tenth of their crops or livestock here to be given to the Lord.

That's when she saw the church president for the first time, the "Lion of the Lord," his people called him. The thick-set man, cloaked in a green cape and top hat, rode toward them in a carriage. He was seated with three women in silk dresses.

So it's true.

Josephine looked at Brigham Young's wives, noting that the prettiest one sat beside him, her hand tucked in his arm. She wondered if there were more wives at home, hidden behind the wall.

The prophet ascended a platform and took his seat in the middle of a row of dignitaries, all of them solemn in black broadcloth and beards, and after the newcomers had gathered and quieted, he stood and proclaimed, "Welcome to Zion! You have arrived on consecrated soil." He waved a hand sympathetically across the crowd of upturned faces. "I see from your weary countenances that your journey has not been easy."

Josephine felt a lump grow in her throat, and fixed her eyes on the stringy hair and plaid shawl of the woman in front of her.

"Rest for a day or two," Brother Brigham counseled. "Don't bother much about your religious duties. Your first duty will be to learn how to dig an irrigation ditch and grow a cabbage and pluck a chicken."

Josephine studied the prophet's wives. Two were grave looking, dressed in no-nonsense black. The other one was young enough to have been his daughter. Jewels dangled from her earlobes and her throat was rimmed with lace, and she seemed self-assured to the point of pride. Josephine wondered what kind of bargain each wife had made with herself.

"You have been chosen from the world by God," President Young said. "He has planted his people in a place that is not desired by the wicked. Here in our mountain fortress, we are protected from our enemies. You may rest easy that they have no power here."

Josephine looked hungrily at the ears of corn heaped on the steps of the tithing office. Would the prophet allow the immigrants to take a portion? But Brigham Young didn't mention the corn on display behind him. The Saints, he said, were short on food this year.

"You may think your sacrifices are behind you, but God sends trials in order that he might shape you to his will. The famine is testing his people even now, but in the end, you will obtain the gifts and exaltation you have been promised."

Peart stared at the prophet with a befuddled expression, and Josephine guessed she was trying to accommodate herself to the fact that there would be no fat of the ram.

Brother Brigham concluded his remarks with a prayer and eased himself down from the platform. That's when Rebecca came face to face with the man Sister Ashdown had said was her second father—the father of all the Mormons. He glanced at the child, whose eyes were so enormous they seemed to have swallowed her face, and broke away from the circle of elders that surrounded him.

"And what have we here?" the prophet said, bending down. His stern lips broke into an affable smile and the keen intelligence in his eyes softened into mirth.

Sister Ashdown lost her faraway expression and nudged her daughter forward. "This is my Rebecca," she said. The child clutched her doll to her thin chest and fixed her gaze on the prophet's feet. "She carried this doll all the way across the mountains. Isn't that so, Rebecca?"

"You did now, did you?" Brigham Young asked.

Although the bear-like man looked pleasant enough, the little girl seemed frightened.

"She's oftentimes shy," Lydia apologized, patting her daughter on the shoulders as if to prod her into remembering her manners.

The church president persisted, perhaps not accustomed to being rebuffed. "You walked all the way to Zion?"

Rebecca shook her head yes before running to Brother Hans Larsen, who stood nearby.

And then the great sorting out began. President Young said each person would be assigned temporarily to a family, and assigned in a more permanent manner to an occupation. Church elders asked the new arrivals about their former occupations, and right then and there called men to earn their daily bread in Great Salt Lake City or in outlying settlements. Some colonies were in need of surveyors and others in need of shoemakers or masons or bricklayers. The girl overheard Brother Larsen being called to Cedar City, ten days south of the valley, where he would set up machinery for a grist mill. Gavin Sayers would stay on in the valley, where he would play violin with the orchestra at Brigham Young's playhouse, but Josephine was too concerned about her own fate to be interested in his. She watched him limp off, his face betraying his nervousness. Married women were instructed to continue labors long familiar to them, as homemakers and cooks for husbands and children. Single women were called as seamstresses or domestics.

What will they make of me?

She thought of her occupations. A merchant's daughter, she had been groomed to marry and preside over a home, but in the end, she had been forced to make a bad match with the Dorsett & Company Woolen Mill, where her talents were directed toward wrestling dung and burrs from sheep's fleece. Would seven weeks of teaching English and arithmetic on board ship suffice as a profession? Her lesson plans hadn't always been well organized, she knew, and classroom control on the noisy deck had left something to be desired.

Wives stood alongside husbands as first one family and then another stepped forward to receive their calling. Widows were called, and spinsters and bachelors. Occupation after occupation was named, location after location assigned, until the crowd of new arrivals began to thin. Josephine felt her lungs squeezed by a desperate loneliness.

Father in Heaven.

She remembered the orphans in the alleyways near their old flat and realized she had never been forced to look after herself before.

Please, please.

Sister Maisey edged close, until her shoulder touched Josephine's. She hadn't been assigned either. "I hate to think we trudged all this way to be in the comp'ny of the Saints, and now there ain't no comp'ny," she said, looking uncharacteristically worried. "'Specially since there ain't no fat of the ram neither," she added.

Brother Hans Larsen stood nearby, as if waiting to see that Elizabeth's daughter was taken care of. "This lass is a school teacher," he volunteered. "Perhaps Cedar City needs a teacher?"

"My brother Heber complains of it all the time," said one of the brethren. "Brother Brigham moved the settlers there more than a year ago and there's no teacher as of yet. His children are growing up without learning."

"Yes!" Josephine cried. "I can do that! I can teach."

"My brother might could take you in," the man said. He offered his hand. "Ruben Dodd." His face was scarred with pockmarks and his rough boots were caked with mud, but he looked like salvation to the girl. She knew school teachers were housed in a rotating manner with local families, but it would be a home, even if it shifted every few months.

"Sister Peart Maisey needs a place too," Josephine said. "Perhaps there would be something in Cedar City?"

Sister Maisey smiled hopefully, sucking in her generous waist as if to appear fit for any job that might come her way.

"Could this woman stay with your brother?" a church elder asked Ruben Dodd.

"Heber may not take a liking to caring for two." Ruben looked skeptically at Peart. "He's got plenty enough with his own brood."

But the elder pressed. "I know Heber Dodd from his days in Salt Lake, and he's an upright man. He'll see the way of the Lord in this. Famine or no, he can surely put up two for a while."

But Ruben had another idea. "There's a boarding house down that way that needs a cook," he said. "The Lone Tree." He turned to Peart. "Can you cook?" Josephine cringed, remembering porridge stuck to the pot and blackened griddle cakes.

"That I can!" Peart cried with delight. "I can cook as well's the next one. I come from a long line of cooks, fancy ones they was, too." Working up a burst of imagination, she exclaimed, "Cooked for barons, they did."

Josephine stared, open-mouthed. Mercy—a cook? Barons? But she suddenly found herself smiling and saying, "Yes, I can vouch for Sister Maisey! A good cook she is. There's none better."

"It's agreed then," said the elder, making notes. "Josephine Bell to teach and Sister Peart Maisey to cook. Sister Maisey, I reckon you can put up at the boarding house."

"I'm headed to Cedar City tomorrow," Ruben said. "To my brother's. I suppose both of you can come along with me." He turned to Josephine. "Bertie Dodd can fix you up right nice. She runs a tidy household."

Sister Ashdown was assigned last. She would go to Cedar City, where she would work as a domestic. Josephine's hopes rose. Perhaps she would have a chance to coax forgiveness from Rebecca, and words too. If not, she would have a long penance ahead.

18

WE HAVE ASSEMBLED here to have music and dancing. The world have had very strange ideas concerning these things. They have supposed it was a very wicked thing for a Christian to dance or hear music. Many preachers of the day have said that fiddling and music came from Hell, but I say that there is no fiddling or music in Hell. … Music and dancing is for the benefit of the Holy Ones and if those that come here tonight are not holy and righteous and feel to worship and praise God, they have no business here.

—Remarks given by President Brigham Young at a dance at the Social Hall in Great Salt Lake City

November 30, 1856

Dearest Meaghan—

Each day I hope for a letter from you with news of home, but have not received word since I arrived in Cedar City. I know it is a long way from England to what seems like the end of the World, but please don't forget me—

As for my part, I wish I had more time to put my thoughts in order & write a proper letter. The chores consume every minute of the day. Any one who is lazy should never think of coming to the Utah Teritory! I have also been helping Sister Dodd with midwifing as we are short on Midwives here. Birthing is still a bit of a mystery to me but I am learning my herbs & soon I will learn the instruments.

Teaching school is my joy—The children are often disobedient, but

how I love the little ones with their expectent faces & eager smiles.

Thanksgiving was no sooner o'er than the Sisters held a frolic as a break from the chores. I danced with the iron misionaries. They have come on Brigham Young's behest to mine for iron ore. I wore my green satin slippers, the ones I carried here all the way from England!

The Saints here are kind. If one neighbor has flour & the other none, they are sure to help out. Food is not plentiful, but what they have they share.

May Heaven send it's blessing upon your dear self. Give my love to Edward & William. Please write—

Love,
Josie

Bertie Dodd didn't begin her midwifery profession with any particular set of skills, other than orderliness, cleanliness, and a calm set of nerves, along with a few choice opportunities.

She told Josephine, "The midwife didn't get to the neighbor's in time so I delivered a baby in Missouri, back when we first joined the church. And then another baby in a covered wagon when Heber and I came west. And two more right after we arrived in Salt Lake. That's when I decided to start midwifing for serious."

Now Sister Dodd delivered infants in exchange for salt pork or ground wheat or molasses—whatever a family could spare. She was the only midwife within a ten-mile radius of Cedar City, and busier than she wanted to be, what with raising children and a full load of chores. Once Josephine arrived, Bertie began passing on her skills.

"We need more than one midwife here," she told the girl. "And besides, teaching school likely won't last past your marriage. You're bound to get hitched up before long."

They were on their way to deliver the baby of Emalee Severn, the fourth wife of Bishop Jack Severn. His first wife died in childbirth just after Thanksgiving. Bertie attended to the birth and then, sadly, the death, and Brother Dodd constructed the coffin. In return, the bishop offered them enough hay to last Flicker and Jake until the new year.

"Sometimes families can't pay," said Bertie as she clucked to the horses. "But the babies still need delivering whether families can pay or not. Thankfully, Bishop Severn is always good for his word, and he usually pays in beef." The farm wagon lurched over a rut in the road and Josephine steadied Sister Dodd's medical satchel.

"How many of his babies have you delivered?" Josephine asked. She was still astounded that the presiding elder in the settlement could father so many children, and astounded that any woman in her right mind would agree to a polygamous marriage.

"Oh, let's see. Last year there was Patience and Aaron. Two years ago, Ada, and a baby on Christmas day. If I had gotten there in time she might be with us yet. A blizzard hit just as I left home, and I barely made it there alive myself."

"Sister Dodd, do you think polygamy is … right?" Even as Josephine asked the question, she knew the devout woman wouldn't own up to any discomfort with the practice.

"God has commanded it, so it must be right. Thankfully, my Heber would never get such an idea in his head." She laughed. "For one thing, he's too shy. He barely said a word the whole time we courted."

They sat up all night with Emalee, giving her strong doses of brandy in an attempt to quell the pain, but nothing helped. The fifteen-year-old, giving birth for the first time, alternated between moans and screams. Sister Dodd didn't say much, but her even temper took the edge off the fear in the room. Her words seemed to calm Emalee, just as they had calmed Josephine, who had been anxious about childbirth ever since witnessing Sister Ashdown deliver her baby on board the ship.

At dawn, a squirming tangle of arms and legs slipped out, his ear-splitting squeal announcing his arrival to the entire household. Bertie steeped yarrow tea to stanch the bleeding and gathered the bloody rags while Josephine sponged the infant with warm water, laid the newborn on his mother's breast, and placed a cool cloth on her forehead.

Josephine suspected Bishop Severn's fourth wife was his favorite. Emalee was the youngest. Although her skin was milky, her cheeks were the color of cherry blossoms. Her hair was so light it had a silver sheen, and her hands were small and delicate.

Jack Severn, who had been pacing outside the door, stepped in and beamed down at the girl. "My little bride," he said. "And what have we here?" He took the infant from her arms and nuzzled his clean-shaven chin against its silky head. Although the bishop had a full mustache, he was one of the few men in the settlement without a beard.

"A boy," his child bride said. "What you hoped for." Emalee closed her eyes in exhaustion while the baby gurgled and wheezed, as if trying to understand the concept of air.

"I'll leave some dried valerian root for your wife," Sister Dodd said to Bishop Severn.

Even in the dark room, lit only by a small lantern, Josephine could see the bishop's black irises set against his pale blue eyes. He was a handsome man, and the only sign of weakness in his bearing was a broken nose; it had assumed the shape of a hawk's beak. He looked as if he had taken a beating at some point in his life.

"If she shows signs of nerves or restlessness, just give her a dose in some tea," Bertie said. "It should settle her quick."

The bishop handed the newborn back to the mother with a "There, there," and called for his second wife. "Give the valerian to Lyssa," he told Sister Dodd. "She can fix Emalee up with your tea."

The next labor pains in the colony began at an unfortunate time, at least as far as Josephine was concerned. The sisters had organized a frolic to bring some cheer into what was otherwise a dreary winter. The famine had left children hungry, and the brethren were hard put to eke out a living, what with no crops to trade. And so the good sisters gathered cedar branches to hang on the walls of the schoolhouse. They baked cakes with the little bit of flour and molasses they could spare, and issued an invitation.

The night of the frolic Josephine pulled out her satin slippers. There was no mirror, but she knew the green complimented her eyes. They were almost too small. She squeezed first one foot, and then the other, into the tiny slippers and stood up to walk unsteadily around the room. She unraveled her braid and tamed her feisty cinnamon hair into side ringlets and a chignon, and Bertie tied one of her own ribbons around the arrangement.

"You look pretty as a peach," Sister Dodd said.

"I wish I *had* a peach!" Josephine laughed. At the thought of a frolic, she suddenly felt carefree. At church, she had spotted a few older boys, "iron missionaries" who had come south at the request of the prophet to work the iron ore foundry outside Cedar City. Although they joked that the foundry hadn't yet produced enough iron to shoe a horse, they didn't seem dispirited by their task, and their liveliness at frolics was infectious. Bishop Severn had chastised some of them for exhibiting a little too much cheer; he suspected their high spirits were enhanced by colony wine, but even the bishop admitted that, by and large, they were simply well-meaning farm boys.

Josephine wished her apple-green gingham wasn't quite so faded, and she knew her worn dress and elegant slippers were mismatched, but this was the best she could do. She twisted Bertie's ribbon into place again and pinched her cheeks until they hurt, hoping for a rosy blush.

Just as Heber Dodd pulled the farm wagon around to the front of the cabin, she heard a span of horses gallop down the road at a frantic clip, and then a "Hello? Hello!" A man jumped down from his wagon and called for Sister Dodd. His wife, he told her, had been in hard labor for the better part of a day.

"Our oldest girl greased her with lard," he said, his face red with embarrassment, "and I gave her a priesthood blessing. But she still screamed to heaven, and now she's barely breathing."

Bertie quickly changed into a serviceable frock and apron. She gathered her tools and cloak and called for her assistant. Josephine was already there, standing in the doorway in slippers so tight they hurt. The girl blinked back tears.

"Yes, Sister Dodd," she said. "I just need to change my shoes."

Bertie looked at her hopeful face and then smiled, as if remembering her own frolics when she was a girl. She said, "You go on to the dance. I'll take care of this one."

"But—"

"It's all right, Josephine. You're only young this once, and we know that passes all too fast. So you go on now, have a good time. There'll be plenty more births to practice on."

Josephine stood still for another moment, and then ran to the wagon before Bertie could change her mind. She clambered into the back and settled into the circle of Dodd children, smiling to herself.

It's funny how ideas of beauty can change, Josephine thought, as she entered the schoolhouse. Once, just as she was turning fifteen, she had attended a formal ball in a flounced gown, and the ballroom had been lit by grand chandeliers and decked with tapestries and fresh flowers in imported vases. Now, as she looked around, she saw a humble room warmed by lanterns, its split-log floor polished to an uneven shine. Benches were pushed back against the walls, which were draped with ribbons and garlands of cedar. The dancers—young and old—were dressed in homespun, and some already gave off the sour aroma of sweat, but they were laughing and they looked happy, and Josephine gave herself over to the gaiety. The place was beautiful.

The smallest children hung around the dessert table, helping themselves to cookies and slices of cake, delighted by their good fortune. Everyone else, aside from the musicians, was dancing, even the older men and women, and even Emmanuel, who was bashful to the point of blushing whenever he looked at a girl.

"Excuse me, miss, but I wondered if you might care to dance," a young man said to Josephine.

"Well, I just might, at that," she laughed, and accompanied him to the middle of the room. She danced the quadrille with him and the Virginia reel with the next young man, and the one after that partnered her through a waltz. The first unruly tendrils escaped her chignon, and then the entire arrangement fell apart and her hair cascaded over her shoulders.

She noticed that Bishop Jack Severn conscientiously danced with each of his wives in turn, and finally settled in with Emalee. Other polygamists, even as they spun their wives around the floor, were eyeing the single girls.

"Some men act just like a bull in a pasture," Sister Peart Maisey said when Josephine stopped dancing long enough for a drink of water.

"Sister Maisey!" Josephine exclaimed, pretending shock, but she was too gay to be scandalized by Peart's barnyard talk.

Peart frowned and looked back at the dance floor. "Even if they's already got a houseful of wives to their name and they's the oldest rag in the rag pile, they's on the lookout for one more. The most comely."

Josephine followed Sister Maisey's gaze. She fingered her ringlets into place and took a sip of irrigation water, trying not to think about "celestial marriage," as the prophet called it. She had been trying to push the notion to the farthest recesses of her mind since the day she arrived.

Well, she decided, her worry would have to wait for another day. Right now her feet were restless and the music was calling.

Her thoughts were interrupted by Heber Dodd. Without Bertie there, he had been forced to cast aside his shyness if he wanted to dance, and like everyone else, he seemed to want to take a whirl. The merriment was hard to resist.

He cleared his throat and glanced at Josephine, and then politely asked Sister Maisey, "Will you have a turn with me?"

"That I will!" Peart grinned, curtsying as she took his hand.

Josephine was next. After the break, Brother Dodd approached her hesitantly. Bertie had trimmed his hair in order to "spruce him up for the frolic." Now, the few strands that normally lay flat across his pate stuck up. They were, Josephine thought, the only rebellious thing about him.

"Will you dance?" he asked. And then, as if to clarify, "With me." His thumbs were tucked in the top of his trousers as if he didn't know what else to do with them, and his breath smelled faintly of onions.

Josephine barely came to his chest, and so she had to reach to put her hand on his shoulder. She expected him to be clumsy, but he seemed as if he were another person on the dance floor, nimble as the younger men. She was glad the music was too loud for talking; she wouldn't have known what to say. Her slippers began to pinch her toes something fierce, and she wished she could sit down, but the music only sped up.

As the brass band played faster, the dancing kept pace. Skirts swirled higher and petticoats flashed. Couples slipped into corners or out the door. Soon Josephine smelled tobacco wafting in from outside. She suspected it was the iron missionaries even before she heard some of them whooping in the front yard, sounding as if they had broken open a jug of whiskey.

"I see the devil has found a home here!" Bishop Severn's voice suddenly broke into the music. The cornet stopped mid-blow and the room fell silent. Josephine let go of Brother Dodd's hand, which had begun to perspire.

"Some of our iron missionaries are no missionaries at all, just a bunch of ruffians taking pleasure in sin. I believe we've had enough cavorting for one night."

Emalee's face tensed as if she were embarrassed, and glancing at her, Bishop Severn softened a bit. "I reckon most of our iron boys are good chaps. I know most of their fathers from up north. But the Lord has been invited to our dance here tonight, and he sees everything we do, holy or unholy."

He pulled his gold watch from his vest. "In any event, it's near midnight. The Sabbath is almost upon us."

Some couples pouted but the married women obediently gathered their children and cloaks, and the older men pushed the benches back into position for the Sunday meeting, converting the schoolhouse dance hall back into a church. The Saints filed out, talking in hushed tones as they piled into farm wagons, and the few couples who were still laughing shushed each other giddily. Josephine clambered up into Brother Dodd's wagon, taking care to step clear of her skirt, while Emmanuel helped the younger children. Bundled under a fur, she watched the iron missionaries mount their horses and head west toward the miners' camp.

As Heber Dodd pulled out onto the road, Josephine heard the clear strains of a hymn. She looked back and was startled to see Sister Ashdown, gripping Rebecca's hand and standing in the middle of the churchyard singing "The Spirit of God Like a Fire Is Burning." The hymn was Lydia's favorite, one she brought out for all occasions—even the shutting down of a winter frolic, apparently.

Rebecca stared at the ground as Sister Ashdown sang joyously about the visions of old returning and angels coming to visit the Earth. People looked back at the odd woman, confused at the misplaced song. Josephine winced for Rebecca's sake. The child looked so small, standing there in the biting wind. Josephine wondered how the little girl had ever walked halfway across a continent. How had Sister Ashdown, for that matter? These days the woman seemed more distant than ever.

But Brother Dodd ignored Lydia. He seemed distracted. He flicked at the reins and clucked at the horses. "Get along," he said in a queer voice. He looked back to survey his brood, and his eyes caught Josephine's. She quickly glanced away.

"We'll sing and we'll shout with the armies of heaven! Hosanna, hosanna to God and the Lamb!" Sister Ashdown's thin voice followed them as the horses picked up a trot.

The night seemed darker than usual, and Josephine wondered if Sister Dodd had made it back from her delivery. For some sudden reason, she remembered lying next to Momma on board ship, her body tense as she listened to the panting and suppressed moans from the married section. She saw again the image of Jack Severn's hand on Emalee's hip as he swung her around the dance floor, and remembered Emalee's screams as she had given birth.

As the last strains of the hymn faded in the distance, Josephine remembered Heber Dodd's onion breath and his sweaty hands, holding hers.

19

A SUCCESSFUL POLYGAMOUS wife must regard her husband with indifference, and with no other feeling than that of reverence, for love we regard as a false sentiment; a feeling which should have no existence in polygamy.

—Zina Diantha Huntington Young, midwife, teacher, president of the Mormon women's Relief Society, and plural wife of Joseph Smith and Brigham Young

December 8, 1856

Dearest Meaghan—

I received a stack of your letters!—they come all at once or none at all—the mail is inconsistent. Still, it always lifts my spirits to hear from you.

As I read the words I think of you, faraway, writing them. I imagine you are preparing for the arrival of your little one.

All is as well here as could be expected. Pres. Brigham Young has announced a Reformation—to put our hearts right he says. Those who have acted improperly have been re-baptized.

I made 3 pounds of butter today & did 4 loads of clothes & swept out the hen coop.

There is hardly a night I go to bed but that I don't think of my old home, all though that life seems far in the past.

I hope you are well.

Please don't forget me—

Love,
Josie

In the morning Josephine was out, as usual, pitching hay. She didn't need to call Flicker; he was waiting for her at the rail. While Jake snorted and kicked up dust on the far side of the corral, the girl pulled a crate next to Flicker, climbed up, and stroked his ears.

"Flicker." She held out bunchgrass and he whinnied softly. "Good morning."

From the small rise, the girl could see the rest of the town. Near the public square, prosperous-looking adobe homes—one belonging to Bishop Severn and his wives—stood in neat rows, but many outlying cabins looked as if they had been hastily built, perhaps in time for winter snows. The settlement was fairly new, but barns already seemed to sag and hen houses had weathered. Skins hung over the windows of the poorest cabins and Josephine knew several families still lived in wagons. A few families even crowded into dugouts up against the scrub-brown hills and red cliffs. The place had a discouraged look about it.

But the view was softened by tidy fruit orchards and berry patches. Tall cottonwoods lined the creek and gold stubble glinted in cornfields. Water murmured pleasantly along the irrigation ditches. Brother Dodd joked that the place was a one-horse town, but it wasn't; horses waited patiently for the plow in front of almost every home.

And the sun-bleached desert didn't seem so harsh anymore. Lofty mountains stretched along the sides of the endless valley, and the sky was even more expansive than the land. The girl often watched clouds move across the landscape in great quiet shadows, turning the sage silvery-blue. She remembered the dirty clouds that hung over Liverpool; here, clouds soared to enormous heights and drifted as if they had no destination at all. When she had arrived, the vast scale of the place had been overwhelming. Now she took odd comfort from its wildness.

In spite of Josephine's growing comfort with the landscape, Bishop Jack Severn liked to dwell on its barrenness.

"This was a land unfit for habitation when we arrived," he preached. "It was an unwanted land, claimed only by the red man and coyotes and rattlesnakes. Now we are called to make the desert bloom as the rose, to build the kingdom of God in this lonely desert."

He stood erect at the pulpit, his starched collar as upright as his posture. His coal-black hair was parted and slicked back above his broad forehead, but frost had settled on his neatly trimmed mustache. One of the sisters who had heard Joseph Smith preach back in Nauvoo claimed the bishop's eyes were as blue and penetrating as the prophet's. Sometimes Josephine felt those eyes studying her, which made her sit up straighter on the bench, but she noticed he studied everyone else, too. His gaze didn't seem uncaring or intrusive; he seemed as if he were simply trying to size up his flock.

"The Millennium will soon be upon us, when the dividing line between the righteous and the wicked will be drawn," he said. "And I tell you now, God Almighty will draw the line at drunkenness. At coarse laughter such as we heard last night. At even the merest hint of fornication." He let his gaze settle on the iron missionaries.

Josephine had heard about the imminent return of the Lord since she had arrived, and the need to prepare. President Young informed his people that the grasshopper plague and drought, and the resulting famine, were the result of sin, and a fervent Reformation was underway, with leaders from Salt Lake speaking in every settlement, intent on driving out the backsliders and apostates. In accordance with the prophet's request, Bishop Severn had appointed brethren to go door to door, instructing the Saints to search their souls for hidden iniquities.

The prophet, he said, warned that some of those sins were so grievous they even required the shedding of blood by the brethren in order to be forgiven. Blood atonement, Brigham Young called it, saying Christ's atonement was not sufficient for forgiveness. But Josephine was sure Bishop Severn had misinterpreted what the prophet meant. Salt Lake was a long way off, and messages would most likely get muddled in transit.

Josephine had arrived in Cedar City too late for the scene at the irrigation ditch, where the congregation was re-baptized after admitting to a host of sins. She heard that men had repented of taking the Lord's name in vain, not paying a full tithe, or grumbling against the apostles. Gossip had it that several even admitted to lusting. Women repented of envy and complaining, and many had shown anger toward their husbands.

The girl missed the baptism ceremony, but she was not too late to attend the special meeting for women, where the sisters were instructed about dress that was unbecoming to the Lord. Several wives of Brigham Young himself arrived in silk dresses to warn the women against extravagant clothing, but when Josephine looked around the room, all she could see were faded linsey-woolsey dresses and cracked shoes.

Walking out from the meeting Sister Maisey smirked, "What do they want us to retrench from, the homespun or the straw hats?"

But Josephine's thoughts about baptism and silk dresses were pushed aside as Bishop Severn got to the heart of his sermon. "The Reformation demands a higher law of us," he said, and then began to expound on the sacred practice of plural marriage. Brother Brigham had given the word: Those who refused the call to plurality of wives would be damned. Josephine noticed that women whose gaze had drifted out the window and men who had dozed off suddenly sat at attention.

"The world pronounces polygamy a curse," Bishop Severn said. "They say it's a shameful offense against the tender hearts of women. Well, let them call it what they may! It is the most sublime law God has revealed to men. There are those who say it breeds jealousy and resentment. As proof of that falsehood, look at my own wives!"

He gestured to the front row. Lyssa, his second wife, sat with her hands folded primly in her lap, looking at him with a watery smile. His third wife was clearly the recipient of a marriage offered in sympathy. The elderly woman's head shook with palsy, and she seemed half blind; her sister wives always held her hand as they led her into the church house. His fourth wife, fifteen-year-old Emalee, didn't return her husband's look. Instead, she tucked the corners of her paisley shawl about her newborn and rocked him back and forth in a monotonous rhythm, her eyes on her lap. Josephine wondered what Emalee thought about plural marriage—and what she thought of Bishop Severn. She was younger than his oldest daughter.

And what of the others? Josephine shifted on the bench. Was she the only one who felt uneasy about Brigham Young's dictate? Her gaze traveled over the congregation. Sister Ashdown's face was clear to read. She smiled beatifically; Josephine wondered if she was lonely and hoping for marriage at any cost, even if she already had a husband in England and even if a husband in Utah would be shared. On the back row, Sister Peart Maisey fidgeted.

Although Brother Hans Larsen couldn't have been more unlike Bishop Severn in demeanor, the bishop had called him as second counselor. Now Brother Larsen sat on the dais; his expression, usually so transparent, was inscrutable. Josephine wondered if he was remembering his wife and child who had died before coming to Utah, or thinking of Momma.

"I say this, plural marriage breeds virtue," the bishop said, gripping the pulpit. "No woman will be tempted into sin for lack of a husband. No woman will be without a husband who can lead her to her eternal glory. Our way of celestial marriage lifts the human race. It lifts womanhood. Anyone who says otherwise is a liar."

That night for the first time, Josephine heard Heber Dodd use the words "plural marriage." She was sitting in front of the fireplace sewing a calico dress for Rebecca's doll. Whether the child would accept it or not was another matter, but Josephine was troubled by her continued silence, and her distance. She played out different scenarios in her mind. She would approach Rebecca after school one day, and present the dress. Or perhaps she would simply lay it beside the little girl at church. She tussled over the right approach as she sewed, almost missing the conversation in the adjoining room, which was barely discernible.

"Mother, the bishop called me back after church today," Heber said to Bertie.

"Have you been given a calling?"

"Yes. Well, yes." He cleared his throat.

A long pause. Josephine berated herself for her impertinence but strained to listen anyway.

His voice low, he said, "He would like me to take up the practice of plural marriage."

And then their voices became inaudible. When Bertie finally emerged from the room she walked stiffly, pushing stray hairs behind her ears in an unsteady manner. Josephine pretended to concentrate on the tiny stitches.

Brother Dodd followed his wife out. "Now Alberta." He stood for a moment, and then absentmindedly pulled a knife from the cutting board and a loaf of bread from the pie cupboard.

"What, are you taking the children's supper now?" Bertie asked, an edge to her voice.

"No, no. No, I'll wait." Heber put the bread back and picked up the bucket, heading for the ditch out front. "I'm sorry, Mother. I said no to the bishop. There's no need to worry."

"And I am not fretting, Husband," she said crisply. "You'll do as you wish."

Josephine heard no more, and thought the matter was dropped, but she couldn't help but notice that Heber Dodd's eyes began to follow her. His eyes met hers across the breakfast table. When she went to feed the horses, he followed her outside and chopped wood by the back door until she returned. It seemed there was nowhere she could escape. He would nod and smile, and sometimes try a line of conversation.

"How is the hay supply holding out?" he asked, when she well knew he was checking it every week.

Or, "Looks like rain in the west."

Once he complimented her on her baked beans, and another day, on her cobbler, even though she knew Bertie's was better. One afternoon she saw him coming home across the fields with his rifle and a grouse hen, and she slipped down the cellar steps, out of sight, before he could spot her.

On Brother Dodd's fifty-fourth birthday, Josephine was alone in the cabin kneading dough when she felt someone behind her. She heard the familiar cough and felt a tentative hand on her shoulder. She shrank.

"Josephine," he said.

A dull noise hummed in her ears.

"I can give you a home. You'll never want for anything."

Was he asking … *that?* "You have a wife!" Her hands instinctively covered her breasts, leaving circles of flour.

"I believe Alberta will give permission for me to take you to wife." Josephine couldn't help but notice that he used his wife's formal name.

Will he ask me to leave his home if I refuse? Where will I go?

She tried to recall the faces of each family in the settlement. Who would take her in? Who would house her if she disobeyed a commandment from the prophet?

"The bishop said it is of the Lord. That it's required for salvation."

"The Lord has said no such thing to me," she said coldly.

God didn't speak to Josephine, but Bishop Severn did. The following Sunday he asked to see her alone after the service. She stood in the churchyard, grinding a toe in the dirt and wondering why she didn't run as he said his farewells to each member of the flock. He shook the hands of the sisters and clapped the brothers on the back. He paused to help his third wife, her head shaking with palsy, down the step, and tipped his hat to a straggler. Finally, he approached her, his *Book of Mormon* tucked under his arm.

"Josephine, I know it's been difficult for you." He stroked his mustache, watching her intently.

You know nothing about me!

"The Lord has a plan for you."

Josephine remembered waltzing with the iron missionaries, the way the room had whirled in a happy blur of color and laughter.

The bishop seemed to read her thoughts. "Most of the boys at the miners' camp are a rough lot. They can't provide a real home for a refined young lady like yourself. You don't want to be here on your own without someone to protect you. You should be grateful that Brother Dodd is taking you in. He'll give you a permanent home and a name."

"I already have a name!" she sputtered, louder than she meant to. "Josephine Bell!"

He sighed, as if impatient at how far the conversation had missed its mark. "Just think about it. That's all I ask. And pray. The Lord will direct you aright."

Josephine did think about it; she could think of nothing else as she walked to and from school and went about her chores. She rehearsed her refusals as she beat dust from rugs. She asked God for deliverance as she boiled pig fat with lye and stirred the slimy mess into soap. The hardest chore of all was getting out of bed in the morning.

Mostly, her emotions ran to confusion, her mind becoming so snarled she couldn't settle into sleep until long past the time she heard Brother Dodd's snore start up from the other room. Which brought to mind the first, most shameful question: Where would she sleep? Before the fire with the girls like now?

With Brother Dodd?

The following Sunday she heard Bishop Severn ask Sister Dodd to walk with him after church. When Bertie came home she was silent, and after the noon meal took to her bed, an unheard-of occurrence. The next morning she was still sick, and she stayed in bed all week as Josephine taught school, tended children, and shouldered all the chores that now fell to her. Saturday, the laundry still sat, and so Josephine boiled the water and began to sort floury aprons and homespun frocks.

Bertie suddenly appeared beside her. "I will sew your wedding dress," she said in a low voice. She lifted dirty diaper rags into the tub, and then a pair of trousers heavy with mud and manure.

Josephine stared at her. Had it been settled? And was she to have no say? "Sister Dodd—" she began.

"Heber has already purchased the cloth," Bertie said.

"I have not made up my mind. I've not said yes."

"Bishop Severn said ..." Bertie faltered. "The prophet said God requires it." Her shoulders sagged.

"I won't." Josephine struggled to breathe.

Can I make my way to Salt Lake on my own? And where will I go from there?

She remembered her journey from Great Salt Lake City. It had taken almost a fortnight, with a rough road all the way. And Salt Lake was no different from Cedar City; hundreds of miles of wilderness pressed in on all sides.

Bertie knelt over the side of the steaming tub, beating diapers against the washboard until it seemed she would wear holes in the cloth. Her hands were red and raw with the scalding water. A weight settled on Josephine. She knelt beside the older woman and scrubbed, their tears falling into the soapy mess.

Nothing was spoken, but Bertie began to sew the wedding dress— rosebuds-on-ivory calico. She never measured Josephine; it seemed she was guessing at the girl's small size. Heber Dodd told his customers, with an apologetic manner, that their bedsteads and cupboards and baby cribs would have to wait until he finished building a lean-to bedroom on the back of the cabin.

He read the *Book of Mormon* to the family at night as his bride-to-be knitted and his wife pushed her needle through the seams of the wedding dress, and he spoke of becoming clay in the hands of God, molded toward his glory. The family ended each evening with a rendition of "Love at Home"—it had always been Bertie's favorite hymn. Now her voice was muted. Heber offered a prayer, blessing the prophet and his apostles and the sick and afflicted, and then the boys climbed to the loft; the girls bedded down near the hearth. The children seemed confused by the air of careful politeness in the house.

At supper Josephine took up her old practice. She tucked small crusts of bread into her apron. In the dark, lying next to Sarah and Agnes, she sucked until the bread turned to dough on her tongue, and then sucked some more, as if it would dissolve the ache inside. As the embers faded in the fireplace, the wind howled at the door like a wild animal.

One morning, after a sleepless night, she rose even earlier than Sister Dodd. She stirred the ashes to life and built up the fire until its flames spit sparks high up the chimney. She rummaged through the bundle tucked in the corner of the cabin until she found the green slippers. She placed one, and then the other, into the blaze.

Bertie appeared in the doorway with a puzzled expression, wiping her eyes awake with the sleeve of her nightgown. The woman didn't say a word, but she didn't turn to leave either. Together they watched the flames lick the toes, and then the heels, finally consuming the slippers whole.

Josephine put the kettle on. "They were too small anyway," she said.

20

I LOATHE the unclean thing with all the strength of my nature, but Sister, I have suffered all that a woman can endure. I am old and helpless, and would rather stand up anywhere, and say anything commanded of me, than to be turned out of my home in my old age which I should be most assuredly if I refused to obey counsel.

—Phoebe Woodruff, first wife of Wilford Woodruff, speaking about plural marriage. Wilford Woodruff, who served as fourth president of the Church of Jesus Christ of Latter-day Saints, married at least eight additional wives, one of them fifteen years old.

The day they left Heber placed a basket of apples and thick slabs of Bertie's cornbread in the back of the farm wagon; he tucked a quilt around Josephine for warmth. As they pulled out, the girl tried not to look at Sister Dodd, who stood in the doorway, letting winter's chill into the cabin. Bertie's face was a mask held in place so tightly it looked as if it might crack.

At first Josephine heard the crisp *clop-clop* of the horses and the steady creak of the wheels, but soon they were dragging through mud. They headed north under the leaden sky, following the blue shoulders of mountains, their gaunt rock spires staring into the silence of the long, bleak valley. The immensity of the place, something that usually filled the girl with awe, made her feel small. She cried much of the way, and for the first few days it was, "There, there, don't cry," and a touch at her elbow, until he too lapsed into silence.

Sister Dodd, left home with the children, wasn't the only one struggling with the marriage plans. "Why, you's just a child!" Sister Maisey had exclaimed the week before. "And Brother Dodd old 'nough to be your grandpa." Peart had been so agitated she spilled tea on Josephine's sleeve as she poured a cup. "Achh, he's taking from the cradle, that one is. And look at you. You's a rose among the weeds. You can have any man you want." She set down the kettle a little too hard.

"Bishop Severn says God commanded it." Josephine's throat ached.

"Oh tosh! The Lord don't ask young lasses to play second fiddle for rusty old buckets. If Heber Dodd's so all-fired to get married, let him find someone his own age."

"They say it's settled." Josephine dug her nails into her palms. "Sister Dodd has already sewn my wedding dress."

The calico wedding dress, oddly enough, was the first new frock the girl had owned since Momma sold her dresses to pay Papa's debts. It fit perfectly, its bodice snug against her small breasts. Now it was packed in Sister Dodd's valise, which had been wedged under her feet. A fitting place, Josephine thought bitterly.

All the way to Great Salt Lake City—thirteen days of hard travel—she numbly stared at the passing scenery: isolated canyons, red hills covered with scrubby junipers, sparsely settled towns, each a lonely bead on the prophet's string of colonies. She thought about the journey home, and then about the lean-to bedroom Brother Dodd had built on the back of the cabin.

Heber patted her elbow again and again, as if to reassure himself of his luck: She was still there beside him.

Before Brother Dodd touched her in a more intimate way, she was touched by a stranger in the Endowment House in Salt Lake. There, before the wedding vows got underway, the girl was taken to a small room and asked to take off her dress. Then her chemise and stay. Her petticoat. Finally, her drawers.

Too confused to protest, Josephine hugged herself and clutched her shoulders as she felt the cold air on her naked body. Her legs trembled as the woman's hands touched her—here, and here—consecrating her body for procreation. The woman anointed her with oil. Her head, her eyes, her nose and neck. Her shoulders and arms, her breasts. The woman's hands slipped lower, blessing her secret place, washing away sin.

As Josephine felt the cold oil drip down her body, she pretended she was in the corral with Flicker. He was making soft blowing sounds, the sounds horses make when they are happy to see someone. He looked at her with his moist eyes as if he understood her as no one else did. And then they were cantering up the trail toward the canyon, away from the arid plain that had become her life.

The stranger helped Josephine into her new sacred undergarment. The unbleached muslin extended to her wrists and ankles; it represented the covering God gave to Eve to hide her nakedness.

"Wear this at all times, even during coupling," the woman instructed. "It will protect you from your enemies."

My enemies?

Josephine felt as if the nearest approximation of an enemy was the person standing in front of her. The girl locked her hands across her stomach, trying to calm the churning.

Before the wedding vows came the initiation rites, beginning with a reenactment of the story of Adam and Eve. One of the brethren recited the ancient Bible tragedy: The Lord created the Earth, and he created a garden, through which a river ran.

And then the Fall—all for the sake of an apple!

Adam and Eve were cast out of their home, the gates locked behind them. Josephine drew back in terror as God's angel, in the form of a black-bearded man, unsheathed a sword and sliced the air with its sharp blade. The sword would guard the gates of Eden, he warned. There would be no return.

Adam's performance was lusty and full of vigor, but Josephine's gaze was fixed on the woman. The actress looked uncertain in her role, and seemed frightened as she was condemned to wander in exile. She would be ruled by her husband, would bear children in pain. She would learn of good and evil.

Josephine was taught the mysteries of the kingdom—the signs and passwords and handclasps the angels would require before she could enter the highest level of heaven. But when she was asked to pledge an Oath of Vengeance, she looked at the official in confusion. Sweat gathered on her upper lip.

"For a wedding?" Josephine asked helplessly. Her voice was small, sounding like it was coming from far away. She wanted to run but her feet felt like lead.

"God requires it of you." The official repeated the words of the oath, enunciating each syllable for her, as if the problem was one of her not hearing.

"I will pray, and never cease to pray, and never cease to importune high heaven to avenge the blood of the prophets on this nation, and I will teach this to my children, and my children's children unto the third and fourth generations."

Josephine looked in panic at the door.

What if I run? Will they let me out?

Where would she go? Back to the States? How would she get there, across half a continent of wilderness? And what would be there for her?

She thought of the words Meaghan had recited at her wedding. "… to love and to cherish."

The man waited, and the weight of his silence pressed on Josephine's chest like a hot iron. "I would like to leave," she said.

No one moved.

"I want to leave." She felt like she was drowning. She couldn't get enough air.

"This oath is just a formality," the man reassured her. "The sisters won't have to avenge the prophet's murderers. The brethren will take care of it."

Josephine looked from one face to the next, all of them implacable except Brother Dodd's. He gave up a timid cough and looked squeamish.

"I've changed my mind," she said, summoning courage. She would not be here if Momma were alive, she knew.

"I'm sorry. You are required to go through the ceremony if you want to be married."

"But I don't want to be—" She glanced at Brother Dodd, who was staring at the wall and drumming his thighs nervously. "Married." She shook her head.

"You would have done well to think of that before you came here." More silence. Then, "We are waiting the ceremony on you."

It's just words, Josephine thought. This will all be over soon. I'll figure out what to do after that.

Still, she couldn't repeat the passages. No matter, the man lifted her arm in affirmation. He anointed her to be strong in defending Zion and avenging crimes against the prophets.

She tried to repress memories of Meaghan proceeding down the aisle wearing her borrowed gossamer veil, memories of sitting in the ancient cathedral listening to Reverend Phillips preach about the sacred covenant of marriage. That seemed so long ago.

Momma can't see me now.

Meaghan can't see me.

The church official told the assembled group that the initiation ritual was to be kept secret. If anyone revealed the mysteries of the Endowment House, they would pay with their life. Josephine dumbly repeated the required motions: the methods of execution; it was easier that way. She felt light-headed as she pretended to slash her throat from ear to ear. She pretended to tear her tongue from her mouth. She gashed her chest open with an imaginary knife and ripped out her heart and bowels.

And then the wedding vows. She knelt across the altar from Heber Dodd, her new undergarment bunched at the waist beneath her dress. She knew he was trying to meet her eyes, but she wouldn't look at him. He coughed nervously and clasped her fingers so tightly the veins of his hands stood out. Words were said. She was absent. She was listening to Flicker's hooves on rock as they climbed higher, ascending the bluff until the settlement was just a speck of insignificance in the valley below.

By the time Josephine walked out of the Endowment House,

she had been stripped naked, threatened with disembowelment, and sealed to Heber Dodd as his priestess and queen for all eternity.

After the ceremony, her new husband bought her a plaid woolen shawl. "So you'll stay warm on the trip south," he said, gently patting her wrist. "Imagine, I've married a handcart maiden!"

And then he hooked up Flicker and Jake and turned the wagon home. At times she could feel his eyes on her, but she looked straight ahead, dully watching the backs of the horses as they plodded along. Once they passed Salt Creek, a bitter wind stabbed Josephine's cheeks. They slept in the homes of people he had known from the Salt Lake Valley—Brother Dodd in one room and his bride in another. In several places, the quilt seemed to be too small for the bed, as if the quilter had run out of ambition midway through the project. By the time they reached Fillmore, snow was falling deep and hard. They slept on the floor in a lean-to, on separate sides of the room. She never heard Brother Dodd snore; perhaps he had lain awake like she had. All night she heard the branches of winter-stripped trees rattle against each other. In the morning icicles hung from the rooftop, almost touching the frozen ground.

"It's not the honeymoon I wish I could give you," Heber said.

Brother Dodd went hunting, hoping to shoot a deer for the wedding lunch, and finally returned, the fresh carcass packed across Flicker's broad back. Bertie baked cornbread, and the sisters brought pickles and fresh preserves and pies to the church house. The bishop's second wife, Lyssa, baked the wedding cake.

But the most difficult meal for Josephine was the first supper with the family after she returned from her trip north. She tried to keep her face blank and her eyes averted. She furtively glanced at Sister Dodd's hands; the woman twisted her wedding ring between bites. The girl crossed her legs tightly. She looked at Brother Dodd's hands, gnarled from decades of plowing and chopping wood and scything. She saw the scars from his woodworking. The children were mute. Agnes pushed her beans back and forth nervously.

Emmanuel shoveled food into his mouth, keeping his eyes on his plate. Josephine excused herself early from the table, not waiting for the ritual of the scriptures and hymn and prayer, and went to her room. She tried to make her footsteps as quiet as possible, as if she could make herself invisible.

Even though she couldn't stand up straight at the far edge of the lean-to, she was the only one with her own room. After Brother Dodd had stripped cottonwood logs and built the addition to the back of the cabin, he built a bed for his new bride. One of Bertie's quilts lay across the top; he must have placed it there.

Josephine slipped into her nightgown, her feet cold on the floor. She leaned her head against the window frame and listened to the bark of coyotes and Flicker's answering whinny.

How much can I sacrifice? When is it ever enough?

She curled into a ball on the bed, listening for his footsteps. But he didn't come to her bed that night. Nor the next.

The third night she heard him at the doorway, and then felt him ease his lanky body under the quilt. Although he had bathed, his armpits still smelled sour, and she could smell another odor too, something she couldn't identify. They lay there without moving, until suddenly she felt his hands on her breasts. She felt something hard move against her thighs. She shut her eyes and pressed her tongue against her teeth as if trying to steel herself against attack. In her mind, she suddenly saw the vulgar rutting of sheep in English pastures. Brother Dodd began to breathe rapidly, and then to groan. Josephine tried to block out the sound, thinking of Sister Dodd. Was she lying awake? Could she hear her husband through the thin wall? Josephine gasped as a snake—what felt like a stiff snake—pushed its way between her legs and forced its way into her private place. Heber grunted and jerked. His thrusts became more violent, and the girl clenched her jaw against the force as pain broke open inside her.

After that, the rhythm was established. Each day the family patriarch nodded awkwardly to her as she returned from school. Each evening he read two chapters from the *Book of Mormon* while his first wife braided a rag rug and his second wife mended clothing. The family sang a hymn and knelt in a circle while he offered a prayer. After he snuffed out the lantern he came to Josephine's room, where he blundered on night after night, groping in the dark with the girl frozen to the bed. Aside from a stiff peck the day of their wedding, he never kissed her. She turned away each time, until he stopped trying. And so he simply deposited his seed in her, or on her. Sometimes she heard muffled sobbing from the other room.

On Sundays, she could feel the stares of the women, and cringed as she saw several of the older ones impulsively grip their husbands' hands as Josephine—a plural wife with the freshness of youth—walked up the church aisle.

Do they know?

Do they know what happens in the dark in our house?

Josephine remembered the scandal in the parish back in Liverpool when a man from Reverend Phillip's congregation had an affair with a younger woman who worked in his shop. The congregants shunned him and his wife left. For Josephine, there was no leaving.

Heber Dodd still walked home from church arm in arm with Bertie, with his second wife trailing behind, but at night, after family prayers were said, Josephine always came first.

"I feel like an old fool with you," he said.

Bishop Severn said plural marriage was sacred, but to Josephine, it felt sordid. She couldn't wash the smell of it from her body, even though she tried. She heated water and sat in the tin tub, scrubbing her arms, her breasts, her stomach. When the water cooled and she rose, she tied her hair back as tightly as she could, trying to hide her femininity.

The thoughts came unbidden, even as she tried to repress them: Momma, urging her to keep her bonnet on, to keep the sun from her face in hopes of attracting a beau. Reminding her that a young man doesn't want a girl whose petals have been plucked prematurely.

Josephine's husband asked her to stop teaching school now that she was married, but she ignored his request, picking up her *McGuffey's Reader* and walking out the door each morning, her back straight. She wouldn't give him that.

When she arrived home, she often caught Sister Dodd standing motionless with a broom; aside from a short afternoon tea break, she had never seen Bertie put down her chores in the middle of the day. But her sister wife always greeted Josephine with a polite smile. She was trying, the girl knew.

What Josephine also knew was that it was more difficult for the older woman to forgive her husband. When Heber Dodd said "Good morning, Mother," Bertie smoothed her apron and stared out the window.

She reproached him for tracking mud into the house. "What, do you think I have all day to clean up after you? It's enough with the children." And when he offered to hitch up the horses for midwifery calls, she said thank you, she could handle it herself.

Sister Dodd also stopped asking Josephine to accompany her to help with childbirth, but she did begin asking the girl to deliver herbs and remedies to sick people. The girl headed out in all kinds of winter weather. When rain fell, she didn't pull her cloak over her head, and when hail blistered her cheeks, she felt an odd kind of relief, rather than distress.

Sometimes as she rode she thought about the actress in the Endowment House. She remembered Eve's sunken eyes, her thin neck. The woman looked as if the famine had given her a permanently hungry look. Josephine had heard the story all her life: Eve's downfall, the banishment. Exile. As the weeks went by she decided, and not without anger: The story is absurd.

All this? For eating an apple?

Perhaps the woman was simply hungry.

Josephine herself dreamed of apples. By late February, her bleeding stopped and her breasts began to fill out. She ate hog hooves and dug sego lily roots to supplement the Dodd's famine-stricken table.

She was famished.

21

I AM WATCHING you. Do you know I have my threads strung all through the Territory that I may know what individuals do? … If you do not pursue a righteous course, we will separate you from the Church.

—Brigham Young, as quoted in the *Deseret News*

April 19, 1857

Dear Meaghan—
  I have been rather tired lately & so have not gotten to writing for a long time.
  I see from your last letter that you are well—Harold rising in the bank & your baby on the way. It must bring you happiness
  Here—there are so many chores I some times despare, Sister Dodd is often sick & the work falls to me. I am sorry to complain again—There is much I have to be thankful for, I know. Brother Larsen says our aflictions are but a moment but some days I feel I could break down.
  May God watch o'er you & Harold & the little one to come.
    I miss you.

Love,
Josie

The fires of the Reformation continued to burn brightly in Cedar City, lighting up Bishop Jack Severn's sermons. Most of the congregants seemed to listen intently, although some looked a little uncomfortable with what they were hearing. Josephine, sitting between Sister Dodd and a row of younger Dodds, wondered if their discomfort stemmed from guilt, or perhaps from growing unease with the tone.

The prophet had issued the call, his apostles brought it south, and Bishop Severn picked up the hue and cry. "Brother Brigham says we have grown drowsy in our faith," he said. "From the highest to the lowest, people are on the road to hell."

The bishop's broken nose was a mystery. When Josephine wanted to remove herself from the fiery rhetoric, she imagined scenarios. Perhaps a fight. Did someone get the better of him? Was it a dispute over a fence line? Or something worse?

The girl had overheard men at the blacksmith shop heatedly talking about a place called Haun's Mill, where Missouri mobs had hunted down Mormons as if they were animals. Josephine heard other rumors too, so far-fetched they seemed difficult to believe. Men had hounded the Saints from Ohio to Missouri, where the governor issued an extermination order for them. They were driven from Illinois to Iowa and Nebraska, starving and freezing and dying along the way. If the rumors were true, perhaps Jack Severn had been driven along with the rest. Perhaps he had fought back.

The bishop's voice raised a notch. "Brother Brigham wants the stubble and dross rooted out! The devil himself will impale the apostates on the tynes of his pitchfork. The profaners and card players will beg for their salvation."

Josephine remembered Papa and his friends, good-naturedly cussing, intent on their game of whist; their activities hardly seemed like sins. And her own card games with Meaghan. On the velvet settee upstairs, their lapdog at their feet, they would shuffle the cards, play their hands. Wins and losses, of course, were determined in part by the random order of chance.

Josephine wondered: Was one's own fate as serendipitous?

Meaghan was hanging wallpaper in her baby's room while Josephine was sitting on a church bench near her ... the girl couldn't bear to think of Heber as her husband. She didn't hate him, she knew; that was too strong of a word. The emotion was more complicated, involving guilt and resentment and lost opportunities. Most of all, she thought, *I dread him.*

She dreaded his footfall at the divider, a red calico curtain that separated her drafty room from the rest of the cabin. And now, like Meaghan, she was to give birth. Perhaps, as her belly grew larger, the nightly visits would cease.

"President Young has advised those who are unwilling to sacrifice their all—to leave the territory," the bishop exhorted.

Josephine often lost track of the lines of his sermons—sentences twisting in a dissonant circle while her thoughts moved in their own, even more dissonant, orbit. The girl tried to map out the direction of her life, the where and the why and the future, but she always got stuck at the unwanted memory of Brother Dodd's body on top of hers, his thin legs straddling her thighs.

The handcart pioneers had arrived too late for the Reformation's door-to-door questioning, and so Bishop Severn instigated another round, charging his second counselor, Brother Hans Larsen, with uncovering the last of the unacknowledged sins and ferreting out the last of the grumblers and blasphemers.

"I want no wolves in sheep's clothing among this flock," the bishop said.

Josephine was outdoors chopping ice in the horse trough—Heber would have put a stop to the chore, saying something about her delicate condition, had he not been away picking up a load of grain—when she saw Brother Larsen walking down the road with his slight limp, his duck's head cane in one hand and papers in the other. She assumed he was asking about sins, but his chats with farmers over split-rail fences seemed far too amiable for an inquisition. He joked and laughed and patted them on the shoulder. She saw him stop to talk with a mother who held a baby in her arms. The woman looked as if she were crying. She wiped her eyes, and Brother Larsen took the infant from her and handed her his handkerchief. At last he reached the Dodd home. Flicker neighed a welcome as Hans approached, and Josephine stood and arched her back.

"God-ay Josephine. I'm here to see about your sins," Brother Larsen said. "For the bishop's report."

"My sins?" The girl laid her ax across the trough.

"Ya. Do you have any?" He rubbed his beard.

"Any sins." She tiredly pushed hair from her eyes and wiped her damp hands on the front of her cloak.

"Lying, gossiping, sloth?"

"Not sloth!" Josephine exclaimed. Her shoulders ached from bending over. She had felt more tired lately, and her body was moving slowly this morning.

"Murmuring against the brethren?" Brother Larsen scanned his list perfunctorily. "Taking another's irrigation turn? Complaining?"

"I complain only to myself," Josephine said. She bit her lip. "Often too much, I think."

She noticed Brother Larsen glance at her small mound of belly and quickly look away. She moved her hand to her stomach, embarrassed.

"Lass, I'm sure a little complaining never hurt anyone," he said gently, with emphasis. "I'll just mark the report as to your being without any noteworthy sin."

"I …" She looked down. She could feel the blood swim in her ears. "I doubt," she said quietly.

Brother Larsen drew in a breath and let it out slowly. He took off his straw hat and wiped his forehead. At last he said, "You're a long way from home, lass."

She gave him a searching look, noticing how gray his beard had become. Even his bushy eyebrows seemed to have gathered ashes. "Brother Larsen? … Do you think of Momma?"

"Ah, that. I had hoped—" He broke off.

The girl was suddenly abashed at her impertinence.

He set his hat back on his head. "Josephine? I will write that you have no sins to report at this time."

"Thank you," she said.

On Sabbath afternoons, when most of the Saints rested, Josephine walked. She circled the edge of the settlement, watching brown smoke curl from chimneys. Cottonwoods stood in single file along the irrigation ditches, and even though they had shed the last of their gold leaves, leaving naked branches, she took comfort in their presence.

She also took to visiting Sister Maisey, at the Lone Tree Boarding House on the north edge of town. Even the boarders had to settle for cold porridge on the Sabbath, and so Peart was relieved of her cooking duties for one day each week. Josephine found an odd wisdom in the woman's talk, as if her impoverished upbringing and lack of education had polished the dishonesty and social proprieties out of her, and left something purer. The girl could talk to Peart as a confidante in spite of their age, and class, difference. Now the winter day was warm, and they sat companionably on the wide front porch, listening to the squeal of a pig in a nearby yard.

"Sister Maisey, did you report your sins yet?"

"Ah." Peart grinned. "I reported so many Brother Larsen had a diff'cult time getting them all down." The woman took a hearty slurp of scalding tea. She didn't seem to know how to do anything in small increments.

"What did you say?"

"He asked if I murmur against the brethren. I says most every day, more or less." She chuckled. "Gossip? Aye, there's one of my fav'rite sins, I says. Glutt'ny, he asks. What can you es'peck, I says? I put out dessert for the boarders most every day. Does the good Lord es'peck I'll pass up molasses cookies or apple dumplings?"

Sister Maisey's cheek never ceased to astonish the girl, but she continued to direct the conversation along its intended track. "Will you be re-baptized?"

"If you's asking about 'mersion in the ditch, I's too old for that biz'niss." Sister Maisey swatted at a molasses stain on her bosom. "If a sprinkle won't clean my sins, I'll just have to live with them."

Josephine laughed.

"I can't 'magine you had any sins to report."

"I did report—" Josephine fidgeted with the handle of her tea-cup. "I said … I doubt. Do you ever doubt?"

"'Most every day," Peart said cheerfully. "'Specially when I hear Bishop Severn preach. That man's tongue is greased with sour butter. But that don't mean I got to eat it."

"And you don't worry about doubting?"

"Mercy, no! The Lord ain't going to care about a wee bit of doubt. He cares more about if we's kind to each other."

Josephine thought about this for a few minutes while she slowly sipped her tea. "Sister Maisey, are you happy?"

"Happy." The woman seemed to roll the word around on her tongue as if experimenting with the sound of it. After a pause she said, "That I am. I grew up on a empty belly. Always wanting. Not much ma and pa to speak of." She rocked back and forth. "Now I fine'ly have family. I's looked after. The brethren gave me a job, and a good one."

"You like cooking now?" Josephine blurted out, surprised.

"Aye, three meals a day is getting me proper fit to the task. And the boarders is coming to fancy me flapjacks and potato fritters and jam cake. Money's tight but I even scared up a wee bit of cinn'mon. I give them cakes a sprinkle now and then and none's the wiser for it."

Her rocker creaked with an uneven rhythm. "I don't know if this Joseph Smith tale and all that goes with it is God's truth or made up, but I's found a home here. We walked all the way here for it and I aim to be content."

Peart studied the girl with kind eyes. "You ain't happy, I see."

Josephine bowed her head, tears starting in her eyes.

"Child, what goes on 'tween you and Mr. Dodd ain't none of my biz'niss, but it ain't your fault if you ain't happy with it."

"I don't want it," Josephine said, so softly she could hardly be heard. She fingered the top of her slightly swollen belly. "I don't want *this*."

"No one ever said you had to want it. It's certain not every ma wants her own baby."

Peart patted Josephine's hand. "You'll find your own way, love," she said. "I's sure the good Lord don't aim for us to be in the ground pushing up daisies afore we find a wee bit of joy. Old Bishop Bellows can say what he wants, but heaven ain't a thing just for the hereafter. I's sure the Lord means it for the here and now. I reckon he's got some bit of mercy waiting for you somewhere."

The following Sunday a long succession of public confessions held the rapt attention of the congregation. After the confessions, the second round of re-baptisms took place, and in quick order; the icy water had a bite. Brother Larsen performed the ceremonies at a wide spot in the irrigation ditch, laying his hands, first, on Lydia Ashdown's head. He baptized her in the name of the Father, the Son, and the Holy Ghost, immersing her backward. She came up sputtering, hanging tightly to his hands, wiping water from her face, and when she had squished her way out of the ditch, another Saint waded in.

After Brother Larsen had concluded most of the baptisms and was stamping water from his boots, Josephine saw Rebecca ease up behind him, and heard her request.

"Buv-ver Larsen, can I be baptized?"

"Ah. You're not old enough yet, Rebecca. You must be eight. That time will come soon enough."

She persisted, in her most formal voice. "My doll—her name is Hanna—she's eight. Can she be baptized?"

"Does your doll have sins to account for?"

Rebecca thought for a moment, and then, so softly she could hardly be heard, she said, "She doesn't like my mum."

Brother Larsen leaned back, momentarily startled. He quickly caught himself. "I reckon we should have a talk about this with Hanna. I'll need to warm up first."

"Can she be baptized first?"

Brother Larsen glanced across the yard at Bishop Severn, who was distracted by a conversation with some of the elders.

"Right," he whispered. "Perhaps a small baptism wouldn't hurt."

He submersed the rag doll carefully under the water, omitted the ceremonial words, and handed her back to Rebecca. "Ya, she's proper clean now," he said, patting the girl on the head. "Make sure she gets a good drying, and don't forget to say your prayers with her."

Josephine came last. Although Brother Larsen had reported no sins for her, the bishop thought it best she go into the ditch along with the rest. She was baptized by her husband, who dipped her into the water, washed away her unreported sins, and drew her up. Her wet gown clung to her breasts and belly. He held her so gently it seemed as if he thought she might break.

22

... MY WIVES are wives that are given to me by the Almighty God through the proper source; and it is so with every other man. ... Send 2,500 troops here, our brethren, to make a desolation of this people! God Almighty helping me, I will fight until there is not a drop of blood in my veins. Good God! I have wives enough to whip out the United States; for they will whip themselves.

—Excerpt from a sermon delivered by Apostle Heber Kimball in Great Salt Lake City, *Journal of Discourses* 5:89, 95

June 29, 1857

Dear Meaghan—

It cheered my heart to receive your letters—they come in bundles, or none at all. I can picture your little Samuel just as you wrote, clenching your finger with his tiny fist & cooing as babies do—

Here, there is a rumor that federal troops are coming to put in a new Governer. The news was brought by a mail carrier & as for more details, I know only what I heard in Church—We get little news, as we are so far from Great Salt Lake City. I am trying not to worry, hoping that distance from Salt Lake will keep us out of harms way—

It has been hot but the corn is holding up, & the potatos & lettuce are producing. There is always work & now that school is out for the summer, I am busy with out-door chores too. My hands are as rough as a boys.

I think of you each day & pray for the little one—May God hold all of us in his care.

With Love,
Josie

Josephine's belly was not the only thing growing that spring. Bishop Jack Severn's agitation grew as well, and was on display from the pulpit every Sunday. No less than the United States government was railing against the practice of plural marriage, and along with President Young and the apostles, the bishop was preparing for a fight.

"Congress has passed no law against polygamy," the bishop said. "And even if they do, we shall follow a higher law."

Amidst concerns about polygamy and Brigham Young's refusal to bow to Washington, the federal government had sent judges to impose federal laws. The smooth-faced blackguards were run out, Jack Severn bragged, and the Saints made good work of their ungodly court verdicts, throwing the documents down the hole of an outhouse and setting it on fire.

Officials in Washington didn't roll over; instead, they began looking for a political appointee to replace Brother Brigham as governor of the Utah Territory.

"We'll send that snake crawling back to Washington too," Bishop Severn promised, each word sounding like a bullet hitting its mark. "The political hacks sent to rule this territory suppose we're so few in number that we'll submit to their trampling of our rights," he cried. "But they'll find we are not so tame. We will give as good as we get, even if we have to do it from the barrel of a rifle."

The first clue they might have to get out their rifles came in late June, with the arrival of Levi Tasker, a convert from Vermont. Levi was only twenty years old, but he had seen a lot as a mail carrier on the Oregon Trail, and he had heard a lot too, including rumors that President James Buchanan was sending not only a new governor but enough soldiers to put the Mormons in their place.

"A trader at Fort Laramie says they're sending twenty-five hundred troops," Levi told the congregation.

President Buchanan had canceled the territory's mail contract, which meant Levi's courier job had been terminated. Now he had been called to Cedar City as an iron missionary; his broad shoulders and strong back would be put to use cutting and hauling timber for the ironworks. All the way back to Utah, he said, he heard talk of the U.S. Army coming for a face-off with Brigham Young.

Throughout the Sunday service, from her bench in the second row, Josephine stole covert glimpses at Levi Tasker. His chiseled cheeks and full lips set off straightforward dark eyes, and he had the look of an artist rather than a rough-hewn mail carrier. The day was hot, and his muslin sleeves were rolled high, revealing taut muscles along his upper arms. They reminded Josephine of naked statues she had seen in an art museum in London. For some inexplicable reason, she thought of the high-pitched sighs she had heard in the night on board ship, and felt her face grow warm.

Perhaps Levi saw her sneaking glances at him, for he returned the look, although his was not furtive. His glance lasted only a few moments, but its frankness startled her. During the closing song, Josephine held the hymn book high, but she couldn't resist peering around its edge at the new visitor. When she suddenly sensed Brother Dodd watching her, she panicked and lost her place in the lyrics.

After the service, several young women crowded around the door as Levi left the chapel, smiling and offering their hand. Brother Dodd usually took Bertie's arm as they walked home, but today he reached for his second wife's elbow, which caused Josephine to suddenly feel tired. Her back was sore. Her legs were stiff.

She often felt flutters of movement and would slide her hands over the place where she felt life. It was hard to imagine an infant growing right here under her skin. She remembered the babies she and Sister Dodd had delivered, and the way mothers screamed in pain before the baby finally slid forth, taking up the bellowing where the mother left off. Josephine feared the worst, and often wondered about her own mother. Had Momma wailed when she gave birth to her four children?

As Josephine's breasts pushed outward against her bodice and her stomach rounded, her husband became more protective. He protested when Bertie wanted to send Josephine with herbal remedies for the sick, but his first wife pointed out that she herself had ridden out to deliver herbs—and babies—right up until her own labor pains set in. Josephine simply ignored her husband's protests. And without asking, she donned a pair of boys' pants—a pair ample enough to cover her still-small but swelling belly—so she could ride astride.

"A young girl doesn't sit like a man!" said Heber, scandalized, but Josephine pointed out the obvious safety considerations of the position, and he relented.

She tucked valerian root and comfrey and rosemary into the saddlebags and pulled a crate close enough to slip a bridle over Flicker's big head, and even as Heber fretted and gruffed about, she swung up onto the horse's broad back, issued a clucking noise, and trotted out.

Josephine knew how much work waited back at home, so she never told Bertie how often she delayed her return. Sometimes she headed west, out across the desert. Other times she followed a dry gulch toward the sun-bleached canyon east of town, studying the way pinyons dotted the low hills and red cliffs. High blue-green mountains guarded the valley, and at their feet, sandstone bluffs flamed so brightly they sometimes tinged the clouds pink.

One day she came across a copse of cottonwoods near the creek. Dismounting, she took off her bonnet and lay down in the tall grasses, trying to tamp down guilt at being away so long. She watched hawks soar on updrafts and clouds drift from one shape into another. The horse flicked his tail at flies and nickered when he saw jackrabbits, but never let his gentle obsidian eyes stray too far from the girl. Sometimes he leaned down to nuzzle her hair.

Suddenly she heard the low whinny of an approaching horse. Flicker perked up his ears and Josephine sat up quickly, brushing a spider web from her hair. When she saw Levi Tasker ride into view, she was startled. She straightened her back and pulled her trouser legs down to her ankles.

"You're here alone?" he asked.

She was embarrassed. Everyone knew a young woman had better things to do than lie in the grass on a summer afternoon—this was madness—and besides being lazy, the activity was distinctly unladylike. And the trousers! She hadn't worried about manners since Momma had died, and now it was too late.

"I guess I am. Was. Alone." Her stomach fluttered.

"Not that it's a bad idea," he said, doffing his broad-brimmed hat and running his hands through his dark hair.

"I'm not sure I—not sure I should be … Here." Josephine waved her hand at the circle of grass, and started to say, "My husband—" but caught herself. "Sister Dodd would probably not approve."

"She's a good woman, Sister Dodd."

"Yes. I am all too aware of that," Josephine said. Bertie had come down with a prolonged cough, and recently had been plagued with a series of crippling headaches. In spite of her poor health, Sister Dodd was unfailingly kind to her sister wife, but her good cheer seemed forced, and Josephine often wished she herself could disappear. When Bertie stewed preserves inside, the girl would quietly pick up the hoe and weed outside. If Bertie were outside hanging clothing, Josephine would knead bread—inside. She had approached Sister Dodd countless times to confide her guilt and shame, but the words faded away when she saw the older woman's pinched face. One cheek was slightly sunken where two teeth had fallen out, but the hollowness seemed to extend to her eyes, too.

As Levi dismounted, he suddenly noticed the boys' trousers, and grinned. "I'm Levi Tasker."

"Josephine." She smiled weakly.

He held out his hand as she sheepishly started to rise to her feet, and she reached for it, but quickly thought better of the idea and pulled back. "I need to be on my way," she said.

What if someone sees me? What if Heber sees me?

"I understand. You have a husband to get home to."

Josephine flushed. She fidgeted with her cuffs.

His keen eyes searched her face the way an artist might study a vase of flowers, preparing to paint a picture. He hesitated before he said, "You deserve better."

"Yes," she said. "No—" She was flustered. What was it she had meant to say? "The bishop told Brother Dodd … the bishop told me …" She faltered.

"Bishop Severn told you to marry a man old enough to be your father?"

She looked down. Why was he humiliating her? And he had made a mistake: Brother Dodd was old enough to be her grandfather.

Levi seemed to catch himself. "I'm sorry. I see I've misspoken. My mother tried to train the habit out of me, but I'm sometimes not good at—well, she said I was too straightforward." He awkwardly donned his hat. "I'll let you be on your way. It's just that—"

But he didn't finish his sentence. Instead, he held her horse for her, and when she came forward he helped guide her foot into the stirrup. She swung onto the dusty, familiar back and took the reins from him.

She stalled. "I don't usually come out here by myself," she explained, although it was her second time that week. "It's not proper. I mean—"

"I like it out here too." He smiled. "The cottonwoods. The creek." Now *he* seemed to be stalling. "I don't usually trouble ladies who are alone in the wilderness."

She laughed. One part of her felt frightened; another part felt daring. She guessed Meaghan wouldn't have thought it fitting to spend time in a hidden grove of trees with a stranger, and that didn't even take into account the fact that she was married.

But now Josephine didn't know what else to say, and in spite of his self-proclaimed outspokenness, Levi didn't seem to know either, and so she finally said, "Well, goodbye then. Thank you."

"Thank you?"

"For—for helping me up."

Just before she turned her horse to go, he slowly brushed her hand. The lightest caress. And yet it felt as if she had been touched by soft lightning, so strong was the current that shot through her.

"Goodbye." She paused for a moment, and then pressed her heels against Flicker's flanks and trotted the horse unsteadily down the trail without looking back. She wondered if he was watching her, and held the reins too tightly. Her baby jerked its little feet and her heart made wild thudding motions.

As she came to the outskirts of Brother Dodd's land, she saw a deer browsing in a draw, and spotted her husband stalking across the pasture with a gun, intent on harvesting supper. Perhaps dreaming of her own escape, she cried, "Shoo, shoo! Run!" and the animal bounded up and across the field.

Once in sight of the cabin, Josephine saw Bertie going down the steps of the root cellar, on a hunt for spiders. The children had been frightened all week after they saw one crawling across a sack of wheat, and Sister Dodd was comforting them as she began to search. Josephine left Flicker untied at the entrance of the cellar and stepped down into the cool darkness, rolling up her sleeves.

"I just scared away our supper," she confessed. "Deer. Heber had his gun pointed at one."

Bertie straightened up and gave her a long look. Finally she said, "Good."

23

... THE BOSOM of the Almighty burns with anger towards those scoundrels; and they shall be consumed, in the name of Israel's God. We have borne enough of their oppression and hellish abuse, and we will not bear any more of it ... Come on with your thousands of illegally-ordered troops, and I will promise you, in the name of Israel's God, that you shall melt away as the snow before a July sun.

—Excerpt from a sermon delivered in Great Salt Lake City by President Brigham Young, *Journal of Discourses* 5:227, 230

August 4, 1857

Dear Meaghan—
    Thank you for your letter—finally arrived. It is good to know William is to be married & that Edward has secured a position with the new railway.
    The weather is still hot. I am told it won't cool until September or October. The community helped raise a cabin on Saturday. I worked with the women on a Rose of Sharon quilt for Sister Wilmer, who is soon to be delivered—& then a picnic & dance was held—
    There is much work here. I often think of Home Sweet Home

                Love,
                Josie

Josephine heard the news in bits and pieces—in worried conversations at a quilting bee, in men's blustery gossip in the churchyard, in Bishop Severn's swaggering indignation at the pulpit.

Uncle Sam's army was on the march toward Great Salt Lake City, escorting a new jowly-faced territorial governor, but Brigham Young was having none of it. He declared himself in defiance of all governments, especially the U.S. government, and his words traveled quickly throughout the territory. "I will fight them all and I will fight all hell!" he said. His Mormon militia would give as good as they got.

President Young ramped up the manufacture of revolvers and called for the militia to step up their drills, directing men as old as Brother Dodd and as young as Emmanuel to report for duty. Soon the ragtag Iron County Brigade was marching up and down the dusty roads of Cedar City, rifles at the ready, gearing up to help take on the largest military force on the continent.

Bertie looked on with worry every time Emmanuel and Heber left the cabin to join the military drills, but before she had a chance to voice her fears, her husband—uncharacteristically—silenced her. "Brother Brigham is the only rightful lawgiver on Earth," he said. "And the Saints have been chased out of every place we've ever settled. I will not be run off my land again."

Heber said the brigade may soon have fresh recruits, for the prophet had called home missionaries from back East and from Europe, ordering them to bring all the ammunition they could muster. Men were needed not only in Zion; the church leader was sending a greeting party of Mormon vigilantes to meet the federal troops. They were to stampede stock and fell trees across the road and set fire to wagons—indeed, to burn the entire countryside before their enemies if necessary.

As the troops advanced on Utah, Brigham Young urged his people to fast and pray, and he sent Apostle George Albert Smith to the southern settlements to prepare them for invasion by a hostile force.

Josephine watched the apostle as he leaned his great bulk over the pulpit, clasping it with his meaty hands. The church leader advised the congregation to plant fruit trees on the public square. "When we've sent the infidels to hell, their bones will remain to make good fertilizer," he said.

Apostle Smith relayed the news: Brother Brigham was warning emigrant wagon trains to stay away from the territory, and the Saints were forbidden from selling supplies to parties heading west to Oregon and California.

We should consider passing emigrants as enemies, the portly apostle reported. "I say damn the man who feeds them. Damn the man who sympathizes with them."

Josephine noticed that even the rough-and-ready iron missionaries were on edge. Now when they bore testimony of the Lord's true church, they talked of Haun's Mill, where Mormon men had been gunned down—one was even hacked to death with a corn cutter. Women had been violated, they said. A child's head had been blown to bits with a musket. Houses were ransacked, wagons stolen, horses and cattle driven off. The survivors slid the dead bodies of their loved ones down a wooden plank into a well and fled for their lives.

And at last Josephine learned the mystery of Bishop Severn's broken nose. He had been laying straw in the chicken coop when his attackers came, he told the congregation.

"My boy hid in the cornfield. My wife—" His voice broke. "One by one, they ..." He stood silent, sucking his lips as if trying to regain composure.

After they finished with his wife, the leader of the mob beat Jack Severn's face with a rifle butt and left him half dead among his chickens.

The bishop's voice grew in strength as he warned that the butchers and plunderers who had hunted down the Saints back East were coming to Utah to finish the foul deed.

"Brothers and sisters," he said, "the time has come to rise as one and trample our enemies beneath our feet. They'll cry from the grave, wishing they had never heard the name 'Mormon.' I'll take my vengeance, and God himself will be my right arm."

"Why were we persecuted so violently?" Josephine asked at supper. She knew the Dodds had joined the church back in Missouri.

Heber wiped his mouth with the back of his hand. "Outsiders didn't understand the principle of—they might have heard word of …" He looked to Bertie for help.

"Polygamy," she said with a stiff expression.

"But surely that can't account for killing children! And for violat—" Josephine blushed. "For harming women."

"God led the Prophet Joseph to claim lands to build his kingdom," Heber said. "And I suspect the people in those towns didn't like our buying up plots and voting as one body. They reckoned there were not enough of them and too many of us."

Heber finished off a slice of pie. "We should have taken our enemies back then. In Illinois our military was almost as large as the U.S. Army," he said, with a touch of pride. "We were five thousand strong. If Joseph had lifted his smallest finger as a signal, we would have taken down the federal government."

Now the brethren kept their eyes on the approach to Cedar City. The iron mission was shut down and the miners retreated into town. Instead of mining, they concentrated on storing supplies and ratcheting up military drills.

The Iron County Brigade gathered on the town square, where they loaded firearms, practiced sharp shooting, and marched to the tune of a military band. They intended to be, in the colonel's words, "Fighting fit."

That summer the heat rose like a fever. Many days it seared the skin, and sweat ran down Josephine's face as she weeded and cleaned and cooked. Other times the hot spells were broken by purple clouds that hung low and then broke into fierce rain. The girl could hear lightning bolts lash the top of the crimson bluffs. When thunder ricocheted across the heavens it sounded like gunfire, and horses in pastures turned skittish, their ears forward, their eyes wild.

Heber and Emmanuel would trudge home with red mud sloshing from their boots. Emmanuel took off his shoes at the door, but although Bertie asked her husband to do the same, the older man didn't. Instead, he would say, "Hullo Mother," and slump into the rocker, exhausted.

The family began to stock up for the assault. The children picked buckets of apples. Josephine put away beans and smoked ham in the root cellar. Sister Dodd ground sausage and pickled cucumbers, and Heber spent entire days swinging the scythe through the scratchy hay fields.

All the women in the settlement seemed to be frightened, with the exception of Sister Peart Maisey. She said, "The brethren's worked up a head of steam and there ain't no getting ahead of it," and went about her business, slapping griddle cakes on the skillet and frying side pork, cooking three meals a day for travelers, all of them Mormon.

"Ain't no non-Mormons allowed at the boarding house now," she told Josephine. "Where's the good Lord's charity in that?"

But like the other sisters, she had no recourse. "We's in a pickle and the brethren's making it more sour by the day. But there's nothing to be done for it then, is it."

When Brother and Sister Pederson sent an invitation for a cabin-raising, the settlers were quick to accept. Although tensions were growing, people seemed relieved to have a distraction.

Brother Pederson and his sons had felled cottonwoods and hauled the logs, and now they sat on his assigned lot, next to the wagon that had carried them across the plains and served as the family home since arriving. Soon summer would be waning and frost would be on the way, and Brother Pederson was in a hurry to get their cabin up.

The Dodds arrived at daybreak, Heber toting an ax and Bertie carrying a jam cake, their youngsters scampering around them, seeing who could jump the highest.

While the men fitted logs into place, the sisters quilted and swapped recipes and worried aloud about children. When talk turned to complaints about husbands, Josephine and Bertie kept silent, as did the other polygamous wives, including the bishop's wife, Emalee.

Young people eyed each other, and Josephine noticed that when Levi Tasker was asked to stir up daub to chink the cabin walls, three young women immediately volunteered to help, even though the mixture contained fresh manure.

One time he looked up, his arms covered with mud and straw, and his eyes met Josephine's. As he smiled, she quickly looked away.

Was he staring? Was I staring?

Had Bertie seen? Had the others?

Her breath felt as if it had lost its rhythm, the air trapped in the front of her throat. In her belly, she felt the soft weight of a baby. In her chest, she felt the sharp weight of guilt.

But after the cabin walls were up and chinked, after the quilt was taken off its frame and the picnic eaten, after the fiddler struck up a tune, Levi—Levi!—asked her to dance, and she forgot about her husband and her baby and even her guilt.

She and Levi skipped forward and backward and sideways. They joined arms and circled each other. He swung her under his shoulders. All the while she smiled and smiled, but she didn't once look at his face, and she couldn't think of a single thing to say. He didn't talk either. When their dance was finished, he escorted her back to the side. She noticed that several young women who followed her wore lace collars and one even had slippers with bows. They curtsied and flirted and laughed at his talk. Why hadn't she thought to curtsy?

Josephine stood woodenly on the sidelines, watching girls swirl in Levi's arms. They don't have a baby swelling their belly, she thought.

They're free.

She retied the hair ribbons that had come loose and put her bonnet back on. She was seventeen now, only a year older than when she had boarded the ship to America, and yet she felt as old as the sisters who had born ten children. Now some of those same sisters sat with babies on their laps, watching the young people dance while they fanned away flies.

"Sister Dodd?" she said. "I think I'll walk home. I'm feeling a bit tired."

That night at supper Heber was withdrawn. His voice had an edge when he asked Josephine for the buttermilk. He addressed his first wife as "Alberta," the name reserved for disagreements and unpleasantness, but after prayers he went in to her. Josephine heard them in the next room, Heber moaning for all he was worth and even Bertie letting forth a gasp. One of the children on the floor at the foot of the bed mewled softly in her sleep.

When the sighs faded, Josephine pushed back her quilt, quietly rose, and stood at the back door. The silver moon cast a blue light over the desert and she could feel a breeze coming down from the canyon. Wearing just a nightgown, she tiptoed out and made her way barefoot to the corral.

Flicker was waiting. He nosed her hair.

"It'll be okay, Flicker," she said. "Don't worry. It'll be okay."

24

A FRAGMENT

Many a bright picture that gladdens the sky,
Grows faint in the distance as time passes by.
There's many a picture in memory's halls,
And many a castle with crumbling walls.
There is many a tower with ivy grown o'er
That will echo to music and laughter no more.
There is many a joy that lies buried so deep,
That the footsteps of time cannot waken its sleep;
There is many a heart whose brightness has fled,
Its day-dreams departed, its happiness dead.
There is many a hope that was cherished in vain,
And visions of beauty that come not again.

—Mary Jane Tanner, writer and polygamist wife in Utah

August 20, 1857

Dear Meaghan—
 How I wish I was there with you—I feel so lonely to night.
 You haven't mentioned—did you move to your new home yet?
 Supper is past & I just finished attending to the hog & hens. All afternoon I churned butter & dug potatos. The weather has been hot & the ground is hard—This has truly been the longest & most dreary month of my life.

Please pray for me, as I will for you—

Josie

When it happened, Heber was up the canyon, caching a load of flour in preparation for the coming of federal troops, and Bertie was in the garden pulling carrots. Josephine was at the spinning wheel, running fleece through her fingers. She was still unsteady at the job; she lost the rhythm again and again, the yarn twisting into uneven strands. Bertie had been teaching her, but the lessons dropped off after Heber had taken the girl to wife.

Josephine's back had ached all morning, and now her stomach throbbed with hot cramps. Sweat covered her face. Her hands grew clammy, and then began to shake, breaking the string of yarn. Spasms suddenly broke in waves; muscles twisted and pulled until her groin burned with pain. She instinctively pushed, and then pushed again and again, trying to hold back screams as her breath took on a panicky rhythm. Suddenly a gush of something wet and warm slid down her legs, under her petticoat. She looked in horror at the bloody mass lying at her feet, staining the fleece red. A misshapen head. Tiny arms and legs. Fingers.

"Sister Dodd, Sister Dodd!" Her heart beat frantically. She wrung her hands and bent over, clutching her knees as if for safety.

Bertie came running, calling, "Josephine! Stay right there! I'm coming." She took one look, and then built up the fire and put on a kettle of water. She grabbed her medical satchel and some rags, and lifted her sister wife's skirt. The two youngest boys came running, but Bertie shooed them outside. "You go on now," she said crisply. "This is women's business." Josephine looked up to see one staring through the window, looking frightened.

"I stained the wool," Josephine said, trying to fixate on something she could understand. The slimy fetus on the cabin floor was incomprehensible. "I stained the yarn, Sister Dodd."

She woke later in her own bed, with Bertie bending over her. The girl felt the touch of the older woman's hand on her shoulder.

"You've had a fright," Bertie said. "We'll get you all fixed up. You rest now."

Josephine saw a jar filled with sunflowers, placed on a crate near her bed. Candlelight flickered over the log walls. "What happened?" Her head felt heavy and her body felt anchored to the bed.

Sister Dodd daubed the girl's forehead with warm water. "Josephine? ... You lost your little one."

"I did?" Josephine strained to think what the woman was referring to.

"Your baby."

"Oh." She turned over and stared at the wall until she fell asleep.

When the girl woke, she overheard Bertie telling Sister Maisey, "She's had a bit of a shock. I don't think she can take much of a visit." And then, "Peart is here to see you."

"You's had a time of it, hasn't you," Peart said as she unwrapped a cloth package. "Don't tell Alberta, she gets partic'lar and this may not agree with her. But I got a wee bit of shortcake for you. To get your strength back."

Josephine tried to lift her head. "I ruined the wool."

"Bertie says you's fixed on that wool. That don't matter, love. Them sheep'll give more."

The next time she woke, Heber was sitting by her side. As she stirred, he took her fingers in his. "My little handcart maiden." He coughed and cleared his throat. "Our child is in God's tender care." He enunciated each word as if he were choosing them with care.

When Josephine corrected him, more sharply than she had intended, he stared at her in confusion. "I would hardly call that tender," she snapped.

Bertie wrapped the tiny half-formed body and Heber buried it at the far edge of the yard. He pounded a wooden marker into place and brought desert marigolds from the hillside, but Josephine avoided the spot. Bertie roasted quail with sage leaves for her. She baked pumpkin pie. She told the girl to rest as long as she needed. But Josephine went back to weeding and cooking and cleaning within two days.

Strangely, she felt nothing beyond exhaustion. Not sad. Not relieved. At night in her bed, she ran her hands over her belly and wondered what was wrong with her. Why didn't she feel anything? Finally, she settled on an emotion she could understand: guilt. She remembered the brethren telling the women each baby was a special gift from God. Well, she hadn't wanted her gift.

She licked her dry lips and tried praying, but no words came. What could she say to God?

I didn't want my baby, so you took him.

She remembered the way Levi had helped her onto her horse. The way his hand touched hers, just for a moment. And his look. Was she being punished for … what? Wanting to love? Wanting to flee? Wanting to go back and choose her path again?

At the end of August, Sister Dodd led the children's pet out behind the barn and shot it through the forehead. Josephine had never grown used to the butchering of farm animals and looked away in horror as Bertie slit the hog's throat. But before they could begin washing the carcass, Josephine saw the older woman stumble into the barn and sink down on a bale of hay. By the time she caught up, tears were running down her sister wife's cheeks.

"All that blood," Bertie whispered.

"You've done this before," Josephine said helpfully. "For years."

Sister Dodd didn't look at her. She was quiet for a few moments before she said, "I lost a baby. Like you."

"Like me?"

"He came too soon." She wiped her eyes with a corner of her apron.

"A mob in Missouri," she said. "Heber and I were engaged to be married. My father had ten acres, good land, outside the city. It was green. Not like here." She waved a weak hand toward the scrubby hills. "The Prophet Joseph said we should buy up as much land as we could, from anyone who would sell. Christ was going to come there at the Millennium. But the mobs got there first."

Sister Dodd knit her fingers together and stared at the barn wall. "The men who burned our cabin, I think they were from Arkansas, because they were boasting how they used to tear it up at taverns in Little Rock. They burned our cabin to the ground. They burned our barn. They set fire to Father's fields and smashed out some of his teeth. And then they came after my sister and me. They were yelling, 'Let's have us a Mormon girl.'" Bertie covered her face with her hands.

"Heber didn't even know. He married me not knowing I had already been taken." Her shoulders slumped. She looked defeated. "What I lost—it wasn't a baby, really. Just a bloody … a bloody clump. My family fled town. We slept up in the bluffs above some slave shacks all winter. I married Heber in the spring."

"Oh, Sister Dodd. Bertie." Josephine had never used her first name, not wanting to appear presumptuous with her elder. Now she opened her arms to her sister wife. "I'm sorry. I never knew."

"Whether it's right or wrong, I was glad I lost it."

"Bertie? You did nothing wrong. And you weren't … taken. Next to my mother, you are the kindest and most virtuous person I know. Brother Dodd got more than he …" She was about to say "deserved," but thought better of it, and left the sentence unfinished.

Sister Dodd suddenly seemed embarrassed by the attention, and her loss of composure, and she sat up straight. "That's all in the past, isn't it," she said, her voice regaining its briskness. "I guess we should cut up this hog. Maybe you can take a shoulder to the tithing office, with some melons too. I'll take care of the rest."

As Josephine helped lift the carcass into the tub, her own words to Bertie played in her head. "You did nothing wrong." She thought of the coupling of men and women, forced and unforced—the act of taking and the act of giving.

Am I absolved too?

For two weeks Josephine pleaded sickness on Sunday, but she finally returned to church. The sermons had grown increasingly shrill, but the hymns were comforting. Although Levi seemed to avoid her, the church sisters welcomed her with smiles and embraces. And someone else smiled at her.

Rebecca.

After the service the little girl trailed Josephine through the churchyard and when she caught up, she reached out her hand. "Miss Josie?"

"'Becca!" Josephine knelt.

"Miss Josie. You lost your baby?"

Josephine was momentarily startled. Although several sisters had brought stews and fresh bread and even flowers, no one in the community had mentioned her miscarriage to her. "How did you know?" she asked.

"Mum told me. But I'm not supposed to know. That's for grown women to know, she says." Rebecca puffed out her pint-sized chest, as if she had grown some herself.

"That's okay, 'Becca. I don't mind."

"My doll—her name is Hanna—she lost her mum." The child clarified in a solemn voice, "Not her baby."

"She lost her mum? But you're her mum!"

"No. I just take care of her."

"But ... who's her real mother?"

Rebecca sighed, as if explaining a matter that required great patience. "The girl who died on the Or'gun Trail. She didn't carry Hanna all the way to Zion. She went to heaven instead, Mum says. So I 'dopted Hanna. You said it's not wicked to take her doll. It's not, is it?"

"No! No, you did the right thing. I'm sure her doll wanted to come with you."

"I named her Hanna 'cause I like the name. I don't know what her real name was."

"I think Hanna is real enough. ... 'Becca?"

"Yes, Miss Josie."

"I have a dress for Hanna. Do you want me to bring it next Sunday?"

The following week as Heber's wagon pulled into the churchyard, Rebecca came running, and Josephine climbed down and unwrapped the handkerchief that contained the doll dress. The little girl studied the tiny decorative stitches down the front and carefully ran her hands over the folds of the skirt. She turned her blue eyes to Josephine with a quizzical look, as if about to ask if it was really hers, and then she hugged the gift to herself and danced around the yard.

She came close and wrapped her arms around Josephine's legs and pressed her elfin face against her belly. Right where the baby had been. Josephine smiled.

25

THEY DROVE US out to starve. When we pled for mercy, Haun's Mill was our answer, and when we asked for bread they gave us a stone. We left the confines of civilization and came far into the wilderness where we could worship God according to the dictates of our conscience without annoyance to our neighbors. ... But the Gentiles will not leave us alone. They have followed us and hounded us. They come among us asking us to trade with them, and in the name of humanity to feed them.

... I am prepared to feed to the Gentiles the same bread they fed to us. God being my helper I will give the last ounce of strength and if need be my last drop of blood in defense of Zion.

—Excerpt from a sermon by Isaac Haight, president of the Cedar City Stake of Zion, given two days after the Fancher emigrant party passed through Cedar City, headed for Mountain Meadows

September 6, 1857

Dear Meaghan—
There is not much to write. We are busy putting food by. The federal troops are still on the march toward Utah & Pres. Young has asked us to store up in case of attack. Brother Dodd—of the family I stay with—is searching for a safe hiding place in the mountains. The brethren say the soldiers may make it this far South.
A large wagon train of imigrants are headed toward Cedar City &
I fear some of the Iron Co. Brigade are confusing them for the enemy.

I am weary of hearing about enemies.

School begins as soon as the harvest is in, if indeed there are classes at all this year—everything seems to be in a state of chaos.

I hope all is well with you—I miss you & my old life more than words can express—

Love,

Josie

September arrived, and the fragrance of wood smoke and winey apples filled the air. The two-year famine had ended; Bishop Severn attributed the abundant harvest to the Reformation and the thousands of re-baptisms throughout the territory. He also credited the rise in plural marriage, which the Almighty required for salvation.

Brother Dodd began sleeping with his two wives in turn, rather than haphazardly. One welcomed his advances; the other dreaded them. Josephine knew the cost of her marriage. She watched as Bertie burned an entire batch of biscuits and accidentally dropped eggs while carrying them from the coop. Sister Dodd cut herself with the kitchen knife, leaving a long gash along her thumb. Josephine tried to stanch the bleeding, but Bertie took the rag from the girl's hands and went to the front step, where she pressed the cloth against the wound and stared at the garden. Bertie's cough grew more brittle, even though Josephine administered onion syrup every day, and the girl couldn't let go of the knowledge that she had a part in the woman's suffering.

But Josephine determined to make the best of her lot. What else could she do? She rolled her frayed sleeves above her elbows and went about her chores humming the English ballads she and Meaghan had sung as children. Seeking freedom under the wide sky, no matter what the weather was, she volunteered for every trip to Griffiths Mercantile in Parowan or to the new two-story stone tithing office, and Flicker whinnied every time he saw her coming with the bridle. She visited Sister Maisey as often as she could get away, and she continued to walk in the hills on Sunday afternoons in spite of Heber's disapproval. Josephine settled into a fragile, intentional state of acceptance.

Her husband, on the other hand, was agitated. Like almost everyone else in Cedar City, he had lost cows to the drought the year before and was trying to rebuild his small herd. This year the rains came, and the winter pasture at Mountain Meadows was lush and green. Watered by a spring, it was a rare oasis in the desert, and Heber and the other men were looking forward to fattening up their herds.

But their cattle weren't the only ones headed to the meadow. A wagon train was rolling that direction with hundreds of cows and oxen, looking to find their last forage before they crossed the desert on the way to California. Heber came home in a temper from a conversation at Brother Griffiths' store.

"That Tasker boy is going to take all the cattle over to Mountain Meadows and I hope there's something left by the time he gets there," Heber groused at supper.

Josephine became alert at the mention of Levi's name.

"That party's got eight hundred head, is what I hear." He reached for a second slice of bread. "Charlie Packer up in Beaver went against the prophet and sold one of their men a load of grain. I hear two of the brethren gave him a little what-for out behind his barn." He chuckled. "Brother Brigham doesn't want us aiding the enemy."

"Are they enemies?" Josephine asked. "Aren't they just passing through?"

"They're from Arkansas. The brethren say for all we know, they're the same men who killed Parley."

Josephine had heard the tale in church. In answer to Brigham's call, Apostle Parley Pratt had left all—his home, his wives, his children—to embark on a proselytizing mission back East. His preaching was cut short when he was shot and stabbed by the bitter husband of his twelfth wife, who had abandoned her spouse in favor of Pratt. The apostle had died a martyr's death, Bishop Severn said.

"And then there's Mother," Heber said. "Her family was run off their farm by a pack of Arkansas jackals. They burned it to sticks."

Josephine could hear Bertie's foot begin a nervous dance under the table. "Heber, we don't need to talk about this at the supper table," she said.

"I would have whipped them," one of the Dodd boys said bravely.

"What are Arkansas jackals?" his younger sister asked.

"Mother, it's long ago that it happened," Heber said.

"Not long enough, Husband," Bertie said with pinched lips, as if to settle the matter.

Heber was away the day the Fancher emigrant party passed through Cedar City.

"The bishop has called me," he had told his family several days earlier. "He set me apart and gave me a blessing." Josephine thought she detected a touch of pride in his voice. "I'm to join a search party. Bishop Severn says we're to look for the best places to hide. In case the brigade can't hold off the army and all hell kicks loose. We'll hide in the mountains to wait for the last days to be ushered in."

"But the army's not coming here!" Josephine exclaimed, and added weakly, "Is it?"

"They just might, when they don't find anything in Salt Lake but ashes. If it looks like Uncle Sam's boys are going to reach the valley, the Saints will put a match to their homes. Brother Brigham even told them to burn their fields and orchards down to stubble. They'll leave the place a desert, just as they found it. All the Salt Lake families will head south, maybe as far as Cedar City."

"We are to feed them?" Bertie said with alarm. "It's been a good harvest this year, but we can't be expected … We don't have enough food stored by as it is!"

"The Lord fed five thousand with two fish and five loaves of bread," Heber reminded her. "I'm surprised at you, Mother. You're usually the first to sign up for the Lord's call."

Sister Dodd ignored him. "And we are to leave our homes? How far will this go?" She folded her arms.

"As far as the Lord asks of us," Heber replied staunchly. He usually deferred to Bertie, but Josephine had detected a shift in the last month. Perhaps, she thought, his new assertiveness had something to do with toting a rifle around the town square with the Iron County Brigade, gearing up to be "fighting fit."

On the morning of her husband's departure, Bertie, chastened, offered her support. She wrapped bacon and cornbread for her husband. Jake spooked as he saw Heber coming, and cantered to the far side of the corral where he bucked up dust and switched his tail. The dirty-colored horse looked as if he'd rather trot to hell than give Heber a ride up the canyon.

"You're taking Jake?" Bertie asked.

"He's more ready for a fight than Flicker ever was," Heber said as he strode across the corral to face down the stubborn horse. Jake's nostrils flared and he snorted in agitation, but Heber heaved the saddle over the horse's back, and soon was headed toward the rendezvous with the scouting party. And that's how he missed the spectacle.

At the approach of the Fancher wagon train, Josephine left the butter in the churn, swung the youngest Dodd child onto her hip, and ran to the main street. The militia ceased its endless drilling on the square and marched to the edge of town where they waited warily, firearms at the ready.

The first thing Josephine saw was the dust, great clouds of it rising on either side of the long procession. Soon the throng of beasts lumbered into view, longhorns and oxen and mules bellowing as hired hands bullwhipped them into line. The girl noticed that some of their ribs showed through their hides.

"It looks like those cows haven't had much to eat," Josephine said to Bertie, who had caught up with her.

"Yes, and it's a wonder they've had anything at all, considering no one's sold them a single stalk of hay since they came to Utah."

Josephine was surprised. She had never heard Bertie speak ill of the Saints or their actions.

The wagons were strung tightly together, as if trying for safety. Peering out from the canvas wagon bows were women and children, their eyes fearful.

"It looks like there are more women and children than men," Josephine said.

She noticed the church sisters standing on the sidelines in their pitiful homespun, many with bare feet. They gazed hungrily at the emigrant women, whose bonnets were still trim in spite of their journey. Their dresses were dusty, but not worn to rags. Watching the men in their sturdy leather boots, Josephine remembered her own trek across the West, walking in worn, and then half-shredded, boots. This party had a wagon for every family, while many Cedar City families had pushed their meager belongings in handcarts.

Josephine saw a tall, well-groomed man dismount and approach one of the brethren. She didn't hear what he said, but she watched the church elder gesticulate angrily. Suddenly Brother Larsen strode forward. He ushered the man off to the side of the road and talked with him for a few minutes, and Josephine saw them shake hands. When Brother Larsen rode away, he was followed by three Arkansans and a supply wagon.

But it wasn't that easy. The second counselor was made to pay. That Sunday in church Hans Larsen was castigated from the pulpit.

"The troops are marching on Utah, and who's to say the Fancher party is not the advance guard?" Bishop Severn railed, the tendons on his neck standing out. "I have been driven from my home for the last time, and God being my helper, I will fight to the death to defend Zion.

"But now, brethren, we see a man who supposes he knows more than the church leaders. 'Our mill is open,' Brother Larsen says. 'Bring your grain here.' Yes, feed the enemy! When we pled for our lives, our enemies gave us vengeance. Now we stand at the edge of destruction, and he grinds their flour. Who is to say these emigrants are not the butchers who killed Apostle Parley Pratt? Or even the

Prophet Joseph Smith?"

Brother Larsen stood. "You're only guessing at that. There's more to the State of Arkansas than one wagon train of farmers. And are the women and children the enemy as well?"

"Your flour may not carry the emigrants as far as you think," the bishop warned. "The Paiutes may have at them."

Less than a week later Heber attended a hastily called meeting of the brigade.

When he came home, Josephine was alone in the house. His breath was sour and his jaw was set. He didn't acknowledge her, or speak at all. His movements as he packed his saddlebags were jumpy. Thunderheads were gathering in force along the ridge top as he cinched up the horses and called for Emmanuel.

"Heber, where are you going?" Bertie came running from the fields, her skirt flapping in the wind.

"The militia has been called up," he said. "The Paiutes have had a go at the wagon train and we're needed to bury the dead. Emmanuel! Where are you, son?"

"You're not taking that boy!" Bertie cried.

"He's a member of the militia in good standing, and he will go with me."

Emmanuel had overheard the argument and came running from the barn, shovel in hand. Heber stared at him for a moment, looking confused. Finally he said, "Put that shovel away, son."

Now it was Emmanuel's turn to look confused, but Heber said, "Bring your rifle." Still looking perplexed, the boy hung up the shovel in the barn and went for his gun.

"Goodbye Ma," he said as he followed his father, gun slung over his shoulder.

The sky glowered with a strange yellow-violet cast, and far out on the horizon lightning flashed. Thunder rolled across the bruised sky, and the hair on Josephine's arms stood at attention. As she heard the clop of horse hooves fade in the distance, she remembered something Bishop Severn had said. "Some of the brethren still have a few ounces of lead in their bodies from the attack at Haun's Mill, and we will pay it back with usury."

Sister Dodd stared at her retreating husband and son, and then she stared at nothing, holding her arms tight around her waist.

Josephine felt a knot of fear rise in her throat, but she patted her sister wife's elbow and said—as if she were asking someone to pass the potatoes—"I guess it's back to the chores then. Come on, Bertie. They'll be back soon enough."

26

WE WOULD NOT kill a man, of course, unless we killed him to save him. … We have those amongst us that are full of all manner of abominations, those who need to have their blood shed, for water will not do, their sins are of too deep a dye.

—Excerpts from sermons by Apostle Jedediah Grant

October 24, 1857

Dear Meaghan—
    I have not heard word from you for some time. I hope you have not forgotten me, even though my letters must sound dull—There is little to write—
    School classes began after harvesting. Some pupils graduated last year & have moved north to Salt Lake—others are new this year. They are learning Scriptures—& stories & poems from McGuffeys as it is all I have to teach from.
    I am busy with the chores which seem endless. There is little time to pick out the tangles in my mind & arrange my thoughts properly. All though I make a brave effort at cheerfullness my spirits are low. I hope all is well with you—please don't forget me because I am so far away
    Give my love to Harold and your little one. I miss you

        Josie

Brother Dodd returned home Sunday afternoon with Emmanuel trailing behind, the boy's face sullen and hard. He hurled his rifle across the yard and brushed by his siblings, climbing the ladder to the loft. His father stood outside at the washbasin and scrubbed for a long time. Finally, Heber stepped inside, leaving his boots on the doorstep. They were scabbed over with dried blood. When he hung up his jacket, it was blood-stained too. Josephine, sorting beans at the table, noticed dark paint behind his ears. It was as if he had washed his face, but missed some spots.

When Bertie saw him, she wiped her apron and then stood stock still before turning away. She put her lips together until they were a thin line, and walked to the back room.

"Where have you been?" Josephine asked. Her heart beat fast and her legs felt shaky. "Why are you …? The blood."

"Emmanuel!" Heber shouted. "I told you twice to put Jake and Flicker away." He was pale and his voice scratched like a saw across a dry log.

"Do it yourself, Pa!" His son appeared at the edge of the loft, his fists balled. "If you want it done, do it yourself. That's what men do when they want something done. Right? If others don't do it, they do it themselves."

"I'll have no more of this! Get outside and put those horses away."

When Emmanuel refused to move, Brother Dodd went out to the corral himself. Josephine saw him lean over and vomit into the horse manure.

"Did you bury the dead?" Bertie asked hesitantly at supper. Josephine noticed that her hand had crept over her heart.

Heber munched his green beans noisily. Finally he said, "There were too many."

His son stared at him, then got up and walked out, and Heber let him go. After that, all Josephine could hear was the sound of the man chewing. His children had grown quiet.

That night Brother Dodd slept with neither wife. Josephine woke several times to the howls of coyotes, and each time she looked out the window he was still there, hunched on a stump near the woodpile. In the morning, the half-moons under his eyes looked like bruises, and he limped, haggard and old, out to the fields.

"Emmanuel, help me with the scything," he called, but his son kicked at a stone and said, "I'll help Ma in the garden," and knelt by his mother's side. Together, they worked their way up and down the rows while Josephine kept an eye on the younger children and beat rag rugs against the rail fence, pounding them so forcibly her shoulders felt as if they would shatter.

"Josephine, you'll split those rugs into pieces," Bertie said. But her expression said she didn't care one way or the other.

That night Heber came in to Josephine. Before he blew out the candle, she could see his eyes, glassy and red. His breath smelled of whiskey, and although Josephine had never before seen him touch a drop of liquor, she knew he had been into Bertie's medical supplies. He leaned in so close she could feel his unshaven chin, and when he pulled his member from inside his sacred garment and reached for her, she recoiled like always.

How did this become my life?

Suddenly, acting on an instinct deeper than propriety or obedience, she shoved him away with a roughness she didn't know she possessed. "I don't have to do this anymore," she said, realizing, for the first time, that she didn't. She would take the consequences, no matter what the cost.

He seemed oblivious to her refusal. "Josephine. My little handcart maiden."

"You're drunk," she said, yanking down her nightgown sleeves until they covered her hands. "You smell like the gutter."

"My queen for all eternity." He pressed himself into her back, but the whiskey had done its job; she felt his manhood deflate.

"Not for eternity. Not for another wretched day!" Josephine grabbed the quilt from the bed, leaving Heber uncovered, and went and laid down on the pallet in front of the fireplace beside the Dodd girls.

"You're sleeping here tonight?" Agnes asked in surprise.

"Every night," Josephine said. As she pulled the quilt over her shoulders she felt a small opening inside, something jarring free, and although she was exhausted, nerve endings all over her body were awake. She thought she heard Bertie stir in the other room, and upstairs in the loft, a boy mumbled in his sleep. The girl studied the bundles of dried lavender and yarrow hanging from the rafters and wondered how much longer she would carry herbal remedies for Sister Dodd—how much longer she would be living at the Dodd home. And then she watched the embers glow until they settled into darkness, and she fell into a deep and restful slumber.

The following Sunday, Apostle George Smith was nowhere to be found—he had headed back to Salt Lake—and Bishop Severn seemed subdued and uneasy, his face gaunt and the bombast gone from his voice. He paused several times during the announcements to wipe his forehead with a handkerchief.

The first order of business was to sustain a new second counselor. Brother Hans Larsen had stepped down, Bishop Severn said. From the back Josephine heard a man say, "And good riddance." Another man shushed him. Brother Larsen himself was absent, and as Josephine looked around the room, she noticed that Levi Tasker was not in his usual place either. The bishop's first wife wore a new lilac bonnet trimmed with silk flowers, but his fourth wife, Emalee, wore her usual paisley shawl. She rocked her infant back and forth with an absentminded rhythm, her eyes dull.

Josephine saw five new children in the congregation, one with a mangled arm that hung limply below her elbow. They sat next to some of the sisters, their little bodies rigid, their eyes wide with terror as they looked blindly from one person to the next, as if searching for someone. A few women stared but most studiously looked away, as if something outside the window was drawing their attention.

On the way out, one of the new girls suddenly seemed to catch sight of the bishop's second wife, Lyssa, and began to run after her screaming, "That's my Ma's bonnet! That's my Ma's."

Bishop Severn caught the child and clapped a hand over her mouth. "You are not to say that. You are never to say that," he said gruffly, but he seemed unnerved.

Josephine, walking behind, heard Lyssa hiss under her breath, "Jack." Her voice sounded like breaking ice. "You liar." She hurriedly untied the bonnet, as if it would scorch her hands, and threw it in the red dirt. She ground the delicate lavender flowers with the heel of her shoes, which also looked new. "You godforsaken liar."

When Josephine arrived home, she locked herself in the outhouse and stood near the foul-smelling hole while hot tears ran down her cheeks, and then down the front of her blouse.

When she dropped off potatoes at the stone tithing office, the church official abruptly nudged her back out the door, but not before she saw the stacks of shoes. Women's. Men's. Children's. She saw heaps of blood-stained clothing, and the room stank, giving off an odor like the rotting carcasses left at the side of the Oregon Trail. She was suddenly more frightened than she had ever felt in her life. She backed out so quickly she stumbled down the top step.

Out in the yard she stuttered, "Potatoes. I've brought potatoes. I don't need to bring them inside." Her eyes were trained on the elder's receding chin, the yellow-gray stubble of his whiskers. Josephine couldn't bring herself to meet his eyes.

She threw the sack on the ground and clambered into her wagon, turned it around and clucked the horses into a run. She flailed helplessly with the reins but Flicker seemed to know what to do. He galloped along the back roads, the wagon jouncing, Jake trying to match his stride. When they passed the corral of Jack Severn, and then the pastures of his first counselor, and those of the colonel of the Iron County Brigade, Josephine noticed their herds had swelled with Texas longhorns, and she prodded her horses faster.

She thought of the blood on Heber's jacket when he came home from Mountain Meadows, of how he stood at the basin soaping and scraping, unable to erase the stain no matter how hard he tried. The stain was given over to Bertie, who knelt at the washtub, pounding and scrubbing until the jacket looked almost clean again, even though both his wives knew it would always be tainted.

The girl wondered how many men had come home with blood, and why some men had longhorns to show for it, and others just had a haunted look.

Things changed around the house. Emmanuel avoided his father, and Brother Dodd didn't go into his carpentry shop, even though Sister Dodd asked him repeatedly how they were to support themselves without his earnings. How would she trade for molasses if not for his cabinets and chairs? How would they get their wheat ground? But Heber had become a hollow presence.

In his absence, Bertie took over. She organized the boys' chores, directing them to repair the irrigation ditch and bundle the wheat, even though, *Yes*, she acknowledged, their father wasn't helping any. She even took over reading the *Book of Mormon* each night and offered prayers while Heber stooped in the shadows. His eyes were red-rimmed. He rarely spoke.

Josephine threw herself into the chores, which had taken on a frantic pace as the federal soldiers advanced on Utah. But after supper she put away her darning and knitting and took down *McGuffey's Reader* from the mantle. She prepared lessons. As soon as the crops were gathered—if things got back to normal, whatever normal now was—school would begin.

The first day of classes, several new children came in late. Josephine had seen them in church and heard they were orphans from the Fancher emigrant party, which had been attacked by Indians. They sat on the back row, and even though the day was cold, they didn't move closer to the stove.

At the noon break, Josephine's pupils exploded out the door, except for Rebecca and the new children, who hung back, looking lost. As Josephine sat at her desk, she saw Rebecca cautiously approach the smallest girl.

"You're new," Rebecca said, but there was no reply. "You can play with me. And Hanna." She carefully held out the rag doll to the girl. "My name is Rebecca. But they call me 'Becca. What's yours?"

The girl ignored the doll and stared at Rebecca as if she didn't comprehend the words. Finally she replied, in a voice so soft she could hardly be heard. "Hope."

"That's a pretty name." Rebecca gently patted Hope's hand. At her touch, the girl began to cry with a dog-like whimper. Rebecca pulled back her hand with a worried look, looking at Josephine for direction. She seemed confused about how to proceed. And then she gave it another try.

"Miss Josie is our teacher. You'll like her." Rebecca sucked at the gap in her front teeth.

"Do you have a momma?" Hope asked through her tears.

"My mum is Sister Lydia Ashdown. But she doesn't talk. She just hums all the time." Rebecca patted her doll. "Hanna—she lost her mum—I'm her mum now."

"Oh."

Rebecca eyed the girl's arm, which dangled at an odd angle. "What happened to your arm?" she asked, but Hope just looked at the ground without speaking.

"Hmm. I know, let's go play outside." Rebecca held out her hand. "There's a bird's nest. I'll show you."

Bishop Severn's flock was growing smaller by the week. Wagons, loaded until they were desperately top-heavy, left Cedar City every week. By early November, in spite of winter snows, a good number of people throughout the settlement had abandoned cabins and dugouts and even hard-won adobe houses. Josephine noticed that many who left were handcart pioneers. Some were even pushing their handcarts. Bent over their loads, they looked frightened and weary.

She knew Sister Maisey heard rumors over the table at the Lone Tree Boarding House, and asked her if she knew anything about the "backouts," as they were called.

"People are afeared," said Peart as she poured a cup of elderberry tea for Josephine. The woman settled into her rocking chair with a sigh. "Some handcart families is going to Salt Lake, but some's pulling their carts right back to where we come from. Back East. And a few's headed to Cal'fornia or Or'gun."

Josephine paused, running her thumb back and forth across the rim of her teacup. "Sister Maisey, what happened to the Fancher train? Brother Dodd says it was the Paiutes."

"Some boarders are reg'lar church bells with their talk, that's for sure. 'Specially when they's had enough colony wine they can't see a hole in a ladder." Peart seemed to be avoiding the question. She briskly rolled an entire pan of chicken legs in buttermilk and flour before she said, "I just cook and mind my biz'niss. You can't believe everything you hear."

Peart went on to the chicken breasts, dipping each one in breading. She heated the lard until it sizzled in the skillet. She seemed to be weighing how much to tell the girl, and finally ventured, "There's Indians, and there's Indians. Rumors say some of them look frightfully like men from the settlements around here. 'Specially when the men's wearing war paint."

"But—"

Peart seemed not to have heard her. "I hear the elders got them Lamanites all hell-fired to use up them em'grants. But the plan went off plot. The Paiutes took too many bullets and decided it was foolishness. They didn't do the job."

Even though it was November, Josephine felt sweat run down her back. The tea suddenly tasted like vinegar. Surely Sister Maisey had gotten things dreadfully wrong. Sometimes the woman was confused. Surely the brethren couldn't have—

Josephine remembered the blood on Heber's jacket and the paint behind his ears. She remembered Emmanuel shouting at his father.

If you want it done, do it yourself. That's what men do when they want something done. If others don't do it, they do it themselves.

"Some of the brethren say them em'grants was outlaws, full

of sin." Sister Maisey looked worn down. "That their women was painted ladies and a danger to the church. They say the em'grants murdered the prophet and had to be blood atoned for their sins." Peart shuddered, but once she started confiding, she couldn't seem to stop. She unburdened herself, even as her words burdened Josephine.

"The brethren butchered each one like they was killing a back-yard hog. More'n a hundred poor souls. All I pray is that the Lord'll have mercy on them little ones what's left. Seventeen without their ma and pa, spread 'round the settlements."

A chill ran down Josephine's spine as she remembered the Oath of Vengeance, the one she had refused to repeat during her marriage ceremony. Even the prophet preached that some sins are so grievous the sinners can only be washed clean through blood atonement.

"Brother Brigham commands us to spill the blood of the wicked so they can be saved," Apostle Smith had thundered at the pulpit.

"The brethren took a vow of silence after the deed was done but now some can't stop talking," Peart said. "The busy mouths sit there over my chicken fixings and run their mouths like I's not there." She shook her head in disgust. "Some got the devil sitting on their shoulder, keeping them awake at night thinking 'bout hell's fires."

Josephine thought of the close-lipped men who carried pistols or rifles on errands about the settlement. She had known, and yet not known. She hadn't wanted to know, and unlike Sister Maisey, she herself hadn't heard any busy mouths. All she had heard since September was silence, and that silence was deafening. In church, people bore testimony of the truth of the gospel, and women traded gossip at canning parties, and when Josephine went to the dry goods store she caught snatches of conversation among the brethren, mostly about the crops and the weather, but she heard no one talk about the blood stains or the terrified orphans. The town was silent on the subject of the sudden appearance of hundreds of cattle, each with a newly stamped church brand. No one seemed to notice the row of new covered wagons parked outside the church house on Sundays. There was no acknowledgment of new Colt revolvers, burnished to a shine, or gold watches in vest pockets and cameo brooches at the necks of store-bought dresses. And Bishop Severn wore his new high-topped silk hat as if it had been fitted out just for him.

"I hate this place," Josephine said. And then louder, "I hate this place. Everyone can go to blazes."

"And I reckon blazes is where some'll go." The grease spattered as Sister Maisey turned the chicken breasts. "Not every Saint is a saint, lass. There's frightful doings in this world. But there's lots of goodness too. A lot of the brethren went to the meadow, but even more stayed home. And there's the sisters. Bringing fresh-baked bread and flowers when you was sick. And people like Sister Bertie. If someone asked, she'd give half an arm."

Or half a husband, Josephine thought sourly.

"And Brother Larsen. The kindest man God ever smiled on."

Sister Maisey was right about Brother Larsen. Josephine had seen him repair fences and cut hay for polygamous wives whose husbands, overwhelmed with multiple families, had left them to their own resources. She thought of the man with the long white beard who lived down the road. Every week she saw him hauling water for widows. And the women with their community-stitched quilts for new mothers, and the stews they brought when someone passed away.

"I reckon some's acting twice as kind so's to wash the place clean of the sins of others. And I reckon some's trying to get back to the gospel we was first preached. Praying. Tending to others."

"Some days it's hard to remember that gospel," Josephine said.

Peart took the skillet off the fire. "Pshaw! And no wonder." She wet a rag and scrubbed a stain on her dress. "But I reckon the Lord's still up there in the sky, ain't he. Looking down and worrying about his flock. You're in his sights too, lass. He's slow with the blessings but he's set some aside for you. I's sure of it."

And with that, Peart slid the chicken onto the serving platter and rang the supper bell.

27

LEAD, KINDLY LIGHT

Lead, kindly Light, amid th'encircling gloom;
Lead Thou me on!
The night is dark, and I am far from home;
Lead Thou me on!
Keep thou my feet; I do not ask to see
The distant scene—one step enough for me.

—Excerpt from a hymn sung by Mormon pioneers, words by English priest and theologian John Henry Newman, music by John Dykes

December 16, 1857

Dearest Meaghan—
  Still, no word from you.
  There is a hymn I have been singing. Perhaps you know it? Written by an English Priest who was a long way from Home & longing to return
  —The night is dark & I am far from Home—lead Thou me on. It has become my prayer.
  I miss you Meaghan—

  With Love & Affection,
  Josie

Josephine pretended sickness so she could have the morning to herself, and after the others rode off to church she sat alone in the small cabin. Pale winter sunlight pooled on the floor as if making a half-hearted attempt at warming the drafty room, and she pulled her shawl more tightly about her shoulders. It was the Sabbath; no chores called, and so she simply tended the fire and gazed out the window at the fields of golden stubble.

She tried to remember. First, there were the missionaries—standing on their crates in front of the Cork and Barrel, calling the crowd to gather to the Rocky Mountains. And the crowd? They were the castoffs of Liverpool. Road sweepers and washerwomen and fishmongers. The destitute on their way home from sweatshops. Beggars and even streetwalkers with rouged cheeks.

What was it the missionaries had promised?

The blessings of heaven. And long before one reached heaven, an earthly kingdom, a place that would supply all their wants. "A feast of the fat of the land," they had said.

Josephine took stock. When she arrived, she found not feast but famine. Wheat was scarce and hunger had driven even the children to help Bertie dig for roots.

As for the kingdom? Utah was a kingdom of sorts: She had been sealed as a queen to Brother Dodd. And as far as her wants being supplied? She had wants so deep they sometimes seemed to suffocate her.

And Bertie. Josephine could only guess at her wants. Sister Dodd's eyes were vacant and her face had taken on a gray cast. She walked with a new heaviness, even as she welcomed Josephine to her table each day. For it *was* her table. Josephine was an interloper.

And Brother Dodd. Was he an evil man? Or just unforgivably weak? He was a man, Josephine knew, who had been caught up in the temptations of the flesh and the dictates of a bishop and the promise of celestial glory. And later, when the call for troops had been issued, a man who had obeyed. Now he was haunted, just like scores of men. She tried to hate him, but she couldn't.

She pictured his son Emmanuel, slight and gangly. In his profile, he looked like his father, but he wasn't anything like Heber. He hadn't spoken to Brother Dodd since mid-September, and Josephine once caught him ripping pages out of the *Book of Mormon* and mixing them in daub, chinking the cabin walls with them. She smiled at the thought of it: the stories of Lamanites and Nephites keeping out the cold.

Josephine poured another cup of tea and blew across its surface. She wondered: Was the Lord still up there in the sky, as Sister Maisey asserted? Her own God was more complicated than Peart Maisey's—that she knew.

She remembered the God of her youth. The Church of England's deity was properly dignified and yet unfathomable, and in spite of being preached at every Sunday, Josephine never had concerned herself with his doings. The table had been filled with roast beef on Sunday, her wardrobe was filled with flounces and frills, Papa and Momma indulged her. As for her wants? She and Meaghan had complained prettily of the trivial necessities of being ladylike— needlework and manners and corsets. Their vision had extended only as far as what to wear to afternoon teas.

And what of the dark, unheated mill where she and Momma watched children work to the crack of a whip? Or the streets of Liverpool, where starving urchins clutched at hope as tightly as they clutched at tossed coins? There seemed to be no God there.

And here, in the Promised Land, people bore testimony of a Mormon God. They spoke of his glory. They spoke with tears in their eyes; they spoke in tongues. Their God had sent, first, his Only Begotten Son, and then his prophet to cleanse the Earth, and he required washings and anointings and vows. He avenged enemies, which even now were marching toward Zion.

Perhaps we see in God what we want to see, Josephine thought. She stirred the fire and watched sparks flick up the chimney. She knelt on the cold floor, her knees stiff.

Heavenly Father ... Are you there?

She had bargained. She had obeyed. She had pulled a handcart across the country, left her mother in a shallow trench, married a man who didn't belong to her, carried what would have been his baby. She had followed the road on a map someone else had drawn, looking for … what? Heaven? Security? A stomach that didn't ache with hunger? Now, what she feared most was the future.

Since her wedding, she had studied the women around her. In church, where they shushed children and sang hymns. At funerals, where they presided over tables of casseroles and cobblers. At Griffiths Mercantile, where they bartered for bolts of calico and cast iron pots. She watched as they hung the wash in their yards and met in prayer circles. Were they happy?

Can you hear me? Father?

Who are *you?*

She spoke the words aloud. Her throat felt dry. If she prayed hard enough, could she pry open heaven?

I'm only talking to myself, she thought.

After the family arrived home from church, Josephine wrapped herself in her cloak and stepped out the door.

"Where are you going?" Sister Dodd asked. "Should you be out when you have a cold?"

"I don't have a cold," Josephine said. "I'm not sick."

Mud collected on her boots as she walked to the corral. She saddled Flicker and turned toward the hills. She held the reins, but she didn't guide him. She just let the horse lead the way, taking her where he wanted to go.

Clouds, high and pure and white, drifted across the heavens with a wild sort of abandon as Flicker followed a faint trace up through the scrub oak toward the canyon. A jackrabbit loped across their path, and once she saw a mule deer lift its head. The creek was low and the path along its banks was strewn with leaves, fading and rotting into the earth; the trunks of trees were barren and black. At the top of the ridge, she pulled the horse alongside a boulder and climbed down. She knelt on the red sand and looked up at the winter sky.

Are you there?

Silence. No sign, no still small voice. ... Nothing.

And yet—there was something.

A red-tailed hawk circled above, and the Earth was so hushed she could hear the *shhh-shhh* of air beneath its wings. She ran her hands along the gnarled trunk of a juniper and felt its hardness and softness. The wind tangled a loose strand of her hair.

And then she felt it. Flooding her, releasing her.

There is an edge—the yielding, unlikely edge where sorrow spills over into revelation, where silence is deeper than sound. The sky felt moist, or was it tears?

The desert is a place, she knew, where life and death meet easily, every day. A place where the air, once the dust settles, has a certain clarity. In front of her, rabbitbrush appeared to be growing right out of rock. It lifted its scaly branches upward, as if the most natural thing in the world is to survive.

.

PART FOUR

Eden

28

I WAS OBEDIENT but not wise. I married a girl but she did it more of fright than of love; for that reason it could not last long …

—Excerpt from the journal of Peter Madsen, Utah pioneer whose plural wife divorced him in 1858 after nine months of marriage

February 27, 1858

Dearest Meaghan—
    I hope you are well. Much is happening here—
    I went sleying last Saturday & the air was so crisp it stung my cheeks. The snow hangs on all the trees & glistens. Afterward some of us made molasses candy and gathered in the parlour.
    We sang I Gave My Love A Cherry—how it reminded me of you! Do you remember that swing that hung from the cherry tree down in the meadow, by the stream—where Middleton Street ended? I remember we sang that lullaby as we swang back & forth. Momma used to worry about our skirts flying up—with good reason!

In my free time, which I admit is precious little, I have joined the sisters knitting & sewing clothes for the poorest amongst us.

I imagine your little Samuel is growing fast.

How is Harold? Do you hear from Edward & William?

I hope to receive a letter from you soon—In the meantime, I am sending all my love.

With Affection,
Your Josie

Emalee Severn, the bishop's youngest wife, was the first to ask for a bill of divorce.

Josephine heard about it from Sister Maisey, who thought it long overdue. The rumor was that her sister wives hadn't made it easy for her when she joined the family.

"And no blame to them!" Peart said. "In all my born days, I's never seen such wifely suff'ring. No matter if you's the first wife or the last. Them men know how to pile on the misery."

The winter day was warm enough to sit under the wide awning on the front porch of the Lone Tree. Peart had sliced cheese and sausage and arranged it on flowered plates, chuckling over the sausage as she plumped herself down into the rocker. "Bags of mystery. No one knows what's in 'em but their maker. And I ain't telling."

Sister Maisey seemed amused by her own cleverness, but Josephine didn't join her laughter. The girl's thoughts were elsewhere. Emalee Severn, she knew, had been left out of family sleigh rides and picnics, and bullied into washing clothes for the entire household. Josephine thought about Bertie, who had treated her with unfailing kindness. And then she thought of Heber. He had gone back to his carpentry work, but his slow gait and disheveled hair betrayed the state of his soul. He was broken, and Josephine didn't know if Sister Dodd or God would be able to put him back together again. She had decided to approach Emalee, to ask how a girl went about acquiring a divorce.

As if Sister Maisey could read her thoughts, she said, "You don't have to stay with that man, you know." She popped a slice of sausage in her mouth. "A lot of sisters taken up as plural wives reckon they want to be single after all."

The table at the boarding house seemed to serve as the regional newspaper, and Sister Maisey, bustling in and out with gravy and cornbread, delighted in hearing every bit of gossip she could get her hands on. Now she told Josephine that Apostle Jedediah Grant, up in Salt Lake, was pushing even harder for plural marriage, and calling for the sword for women who divorced.

"But they say Brother Brigham's tired of the complaining. He says he'll write the whole lot a divorce. Wash his hands of them."

"He will?" Josephine was startled. "Anyone?"

"Wives of drunks, deserters, murd'rers. Wife beaters. Men not doing their duty in bed." Peart smirked. "There's one other. The one to hang your hat on." The woman wrinkled her brow as if trying to recall the phrase. "In—com … Incompat—"

"Incompatibility?"

"Aye, that's it!"

It couldn't be that easy, could it? And there was Brother Dodd to think of, too.

"Do you think Heber would make it difficult?"

"I reckon that old bean's too worried about meeting his Maker to worry about a wife that's run off."

Josephine laughed, and then became serious. "I've been wondering how I … where I could live. How I can support myself. I'm not sure if people will still have me as a teacher if I'm …"

"Divorced? Why lass, they's so strapped for a teacher they'd hire the devil if they got to. Why don't you come live with me? At the boarding house. Aye, you shan't go hungry here neither. Now that them grasshoppers left us some crop this year, we got plenty to share." She sawed off another slice of sausage and handed it to Josephine.

The girl looked at Peart hopefully. "You have room?"

"For you, love, more than 'nough."

Josephine lifted her chin and took a deep breath. "I'll move here tomorrow then!" As the idea settled in, she clapped her hands in excitement. "I'm guessing Sister Dodd will have no problem letting me take the wagon to bring my things. Not that they wouldn't almost fit on the back of a horse.

"Sister Maisey, I'm not sure how I would have managed without you. Ever since …" Josephine remembered the woman's kindness after Momma died. "Thank you."

Peart broke off a slice of cheese and chewed it in a contented manner. "Just what we women do for each other, ain't it."

On the way home, Josephine remembered that "tomorrow" was the Sabbath, but she would just have to ignore the day of rest; she was too eager to move. As soon as she arrived home from church, she loaded her small bundle of belongings into the wagon. As she drove out of the yard, Heber stood at the railing in his straw hat, clearing his throat as if he were going to say something, but she flicked the reins, hardly noticing the forlorn figure.

Instead, she thought about Bishop Jack Severn. The bishop had not preached the law of celestial marriage since the attack at Mountain Meadows, and not one man in the settlement had brought home a new plural wife. To Josephine, it seemed as if the community had relaxed their fierce attachment to polygamy. They even seemed to withhold judgment for young plural wives who left the old men they had been persuaded to marry, and when the former brides turned up on the arms of young men at dances, many Saints seemed to look the other direction.

Josephine also noticed that the bishop's sermons included a touch here and there of Christ's teachings of charity and forgiveness. It seemed as if a new humility had taken hold, and his once-fiery Reformation talk had sputtered down into admonitions against chewing tobacco, and if men must chew, they weren't to spit on the sisters' clean floors. "Take it outside," Bishop Severn said.

"The Reformation was strong coffee," Sister Maisey said.

"I reckon the brethren got tired of drinking it straight."

Before her divorce was even formalized, Josephine began to attend the Saturday night taffy pulls and sing-alongs with young people. She noticed other young polygamist wives there as well, and once she moved out of the Dodd house, she could almost pretend she wasn't married. The conversations at the gatherings were different from those of the older Saints. There was no talk about when to plant or the dear price of sugar or where to graze sheep, no complaints about misbehaving children and untalkative spouses. Instead, there was a lot of laughter—and flirting. Josephine grew wistful as she watched couples slip out early. Later, she would see their initials carved in the fence poles out front.

She attended a dance in Parowan, twenty miles down the road, and danced with every iron missionary there, but in spite of her best intentions for a gay time, she felt a sense of detachment, and an odd unease. She wondered which missionary had gone to the meadow, who had painted their face, who had joined the attack. And she was still waiting for her bill of divorce.

Emalee Severn attended the gatherings as well, while her infant was tended by one of the sisters. She planned to return to her family in Virginia, although she wasn't sure how she was going to get there.

"I'll figure it out," she told Josephine. "I'll walk if I have to." She even planned to approach the sisters' Relief Society for help with travel supplies, although Josephine thought her request sounded hopeless.

The Relief Society in Cedar City originally had formed to sew dresses and shirts for the Paiutes. Now they had turned their zeal toward helping their own, braiding rag rugs and collecting food for the poor. Emalee would qualify as poor the moment she left Bishop Severn's household, but Josephine wasn't sure if a new divorcée would still be considered "one of our own." At any rate, Emalee was determined to ask for their help.

In February, Josephine received a letter postmarked Oregon City,

Territory of Oregon. Her eyes slid down to the familiar handwriting on the envelope: *Meaghan Baker.*

Her heart quickened; her hands began to shake. Oregon …? How could that be? She hadn't heard from Meaghan for … how long had it been? She tried to remember. Months and months, she was sure.

She held the letter carefully in her hand, not sure whether to open it immediately or save it for later. In the end, she slipped it into her apron pocket and waited until after supper, rushing through the side pork and gravy. She lit a lantern, climbed the stairs to the small room she shared with Sister Maisey, and perched on the edge of the bed, staring at the envelope. It was crinkled and showed wear, as if it had been a long time in transit. Josephine slowly slit it open with a knife from the kitchen, took out the thin paper, and unfolded its creases. Lantern light flickered across the words, and she narrowed her eyes to read the neat handwriting.

> *Dearest Josie,*
>
> *You must have wondered why you haven't heard from me for so long.*
>
> *Harold and myself and the baby have been enroute to the Oregon Territory. We had to go as far as around Cape Horn!—and then up the Coast—past San Francisco north to Oregon City. I thought of you often, and your travails aboard ship, for we had our own.*
>
> *Once, I feared our ship would founder on the rocks and we would perish at Sea. But at last we arrived!*
>
> *I must tell you how we came to be here. The Liverpool Mail carried an account of Oregon City that caught Harold's imagination. My husband has dreams that he could not persue in the Old Country—and he has come here for opportunity. Oregon City lies at the end of the Oregon Trail, and more people are arriving every year, for land can be had for very little in this Territory. Harold says the new imigrants see farms, but he sees farmers who need plows and harnesses and feed—and he plans to open a dry goods store with his savings. This place is a regular little city now, with mills and schools and churchs.*
>
> *We have heard that the Winter rains are enough to drown frogs,*

but the Valley is lush and green, with oak trees and prairies filled with flowers, and a large river runs through it. Mountains border the Valley to the East & West both, their hillsides abundant with timber and streams with fish.

My Samuel, my dear little one, is growing fast and has already taken his first steps! His first word was Momma. You would think it funny to see me so settled. You and I weren't much for "shoulds", were we?—the lace strings loose on our corsets, and giggling through Rev. Philips sermons. But now I am a lady—married to a husband coming into his own. He jokes that I must behave now that I am to be the wife of a merchant.

Edward and William send their love. They have regretted their harsh words a 100 times, and wish they could take them back. I will write a long letter as soon as we are settled in, and tell you all the news. For now, I am sending all my love. I know the Oregon Territory is still a long way from Utah but I dream of meeting again, for now we are a little closer. Please write and tell me you are well. I think of you every day.

With affection for your Dear Self,
Meaghan

Tears filled Josephine's eyes. She read the letter again, and then again, so quickly she could scarcely take in the words. She ran downstairs and grabbed Sister Maisey's hands and danced her around the kitchen, tipping the butter churn and sending a rolling pin clattering to the floor. She was too excited to sleep that night and so she sat for several hours on the stairs, chin in her hands, smiling, remembering long afternoons in the room she and Meaghan shared at the top of the stairs on Middleton Street. Stitching the dreaded samplers, or standing behind gauze curtains gossiping about passersby on the street below. Trying to best each other in cribbage, not caring who won, and imitating Papa's pompous guests after they had departed, or even when they still sat in the parlor with their tobacco smoke wafting up the staircase.

In the morning she rose early and walked with a determined

step to the Dodd cabin.

"Bertie?"

"Why Josephine, what are you doing here? You haven't decided to—" Sister Dodd's face tensed. "You are still asking for divorce?" The woman was standing at the woodpile, a stack of split logs at her feet, and although her hands suddenly clutched the ax more tightly, Josephine hardly noticed her distress.

"Bertie, my handcart. Is it still in the barn?"

"I suppose so. That's where we last put it. Behind the stall."

"Can I see it?"

Josephine had left her handcart at the tithing yard in Salt Lake after Heber's brother offered her a ride south, but the Holt family quickly claimed it, loading its bed with their belongings and pulling it to Cedar City after they, too, were assigned to the outpost. Their own cart had slipped as they picked their way down Emigration Canyon to the Salt Lake Valley, rolling down a steep slope and breaking apart in the ravine below. Now Josephine's handcart was sitting abandoned in the Dodd barn.

Bertie put down the ax and led the way to the barn. She slid open the door and waited while Josephine inspected the wheel rims. Looking at them, the girl's heart sank. She thought with a touch of anger about Brigham Young's handcart design—no metal rims. The cart looked as if it wouldn't stand another trip. And yet … the girl bit her lip, her hands on her hips, not taking her eyes from the weathered wooden contraption. She remembered pushing and pulling it up mountains, holding back its weight as it slipped down steep slopes, tarring its sides and dragging it through rivers. She remembered the graves they passed, and the heaviness she felt when she picked up the crossbar and pulled out of Mormon Flat, leaving her mother buried in that lonely wilderness.

"May I take it?"

"It's yours, Josephine. Although for the life of me I can't see why you would want it."

Josephine didn't mention her plans to Bertie as they pushed aside sacks of feed. They rolled the wheels back and forth through the straw scattered about the floor, finally heaving the cart free.

"How will you get it all the way to the boarding house?" Sister Dodd asked.

Although Josephine had been wondering the same thing, she couldn't help but laugh. "I pulled it thirteen hundred miles, Bertie. I suppose I can pull it up the road a bit."

The sides and bottom were splintered and dry, and the cart was heavier than she remembered, even without a load. She picked up the crossbar and awkwardly strained forward, slowly pulling the handcart across the yard and out onto the road, and then she hauled it north, stubbornly fighting ruts and a wobbly wheel all the way to the Lone Tree. She arrived just as Sister Maisey came out on the porch, wiping floury hands on her apron.

Peart's eyebrows went up, but she didn't ask, and somehow, she didn't seem too surprised. She just looked at Josephine as if she were sizing her up in a new way.

"Aye, there's that."

29

WELCOME TO SPRING

O, gentle spring; thy presence everywhere,
Renews the life-pulse, e'en in earth's cold heart,
And from its bosom, buds and blossoms fair,
In rich profusion, all spontaneous start. ...
And hope springs up afresh in saddened lives;
Dark clouds disperse and heaven again is clear;
The tenderest trust and confidence revives,
For spring has come and beautified the year.

—Excerpt from a poem by Emmeline Blanche Wells, poet, president of the Mormon women's Relief Society, women's rights advocate, and polygamous wife

March 5, 1858

Dearest Meaghan—

I received your letter at long last! How happy I am to know you are in Oregon Teritory! & happy to know you survived the Ocean journey around the Cape. I can only imagine the beautiful Valley you speak of. Harold is smart as a whip & I am sure he will make a go of it with a dry goods store—& to think you will be the wife of a Merchant!

I can not tell you how much it meant to hear that Edward & William send their love. How often I have despared of the way we parted. I have

not written them but will henceforth send a letter in the next dispatch.

Here, Spring is on the way & all the World beginning to awaken, glad of the warmth. The stars at night shine with a peculiar intensity— like the constelations themselves are alive. When I look at them I try to imagine they are guiding me as they did explorers of old. There is much I long for & the future is uncertain but I pray that I will find the place where I belong—

As you say, the Oregon Teritory is far from Utah but I am hopeful that we shall meet again—perhaps before to many years roll away. I am holding you in my thoughts each day.

All my Love & Affection,
Your Josie

The first thing Josephine always noticed when she entered the cool darkness of Griffiths Mercantile was the smell, an odd but not unpleasant blend of cheese, kerosene, pickles, and leather. She didn't see Brother Griffiths as she idled at the counter studying the soaps and candies. After a few moments, she knocked on the door in the back.

"Brother Griffiths?" she called hesitantly.

He came out so fast he almost tripped over her. "Just filling the vinegar barrel," he apologized, wiping the sour liquid from his hands. "Oh. Josephine. I suppose you're looking for a letter? It seems like you just got one last week. I should think that sister of yours has more to do than write every day." He chuckled.

But Josephine was intent on her mission and didn't seem to hear him. "Brother Griffiths, do you have a map I can look at?" She sheepishly confessed that she couldn't afford to buy it. She just wanted to look.

"You planning a trip?" he asked, looking her up and down. "You look awful young to be doing the planning."

"I haven't worked out the details yet," she admitted.

The details—those were the problem! They included supplies, handcart repairs, a party to travel with. Most of all, they revolved around how to pay for everything. She had no money. Like all the laborers in the area, she had been paid with goods rather than cash. Her school lessons so far had brought in chickens and milk, a quarter barrel of sauerkraut, potatoes, and corn, and enough bushel baskets of beans to make her tired of them long before they ran out. She also had received a brass bucket, a straw hat, and a used quilt. She set aside the hat; everything else she dutifully handed over to the Dodd family.

Now she thanked Brother Griffiths and took his map out to the front porch. She unfolded its creases, laid it out across the bench, and traced her finger along the Oregon Trail. Great Salt Lake City to Fort Hall, and then along the winding Snake River, over the Blue Mountains, over the Cascades. After she studied the map for half an hour, trying to memorize the forts and mountain ranges and rivers, she walked back inside and handed it to Brother Griffiths. She slowly wandered to the back of the store, bypassing harnesses and buggy whips and plows, until she found what she was looking for.

"How much do you want for a water barrel?" she called. "Would you take eggs and butter?" She turned back to study the barrels, looking for cracks between the ribs. They looked watertight, but there was no way she could afford one, and certainly no way to carry that much weight.

Don't despair, don't despair, she thought. Hundreds of impoverished Saints had made the trek from Iowa City. There must be a way to outfit herself and find an emigrant party going the rest of the way to Oregon.

Josephine heard someone come in the front door. "Morning, Mr. Griffiths."

"And a good morning back to you," Brother Griffiths said. "What brings you here?"

"I'm looking for a yoke. Sturdy enough for a trek."

The voice was oddly familiar, but by then Josephine was absorbed in the weight of water barrels.

"Josephine?"

She turned, and started as she saw Levi Tasker.

"I—I thought you were gone," she blurted, and admitted, "I didn't see you in church lately."

He lowered his voice so Brother Griffiths wouldn't hear. "I started going jackrabbit hunting on Sunday mornings. No need for Mr. Griffiths to know and start the gossips going. It's more peaceful this way."

Josephine hadn't seen Levi since the wagon train attack back in September and wondered if he had left the area, but of course, she couldn't ask anyone. Before then, she had stolen glances at him in church and had surreptitiously watched him drilling in the square, marching along with the rest of the men, his firearm at his side. But he couldn't have participated ... Could he? What did she really know about him? He had an honest face, and had seemed kind enough when they met unexpectedly in the canyon, but what did anyone know about anyone in Cedar City? It seemed as if there were a lot of secrets.

While she lived with Brother Dodd, she hadn't admitted to herself how often she thought of Levi, but since coming to live at the Lone Tree, she couldn't count the number of nights she had sat on the porch watching the patterns in the stars, listening to the rustle of small creatures in the grass and letting her thoughts about Levi shape themselves into a walk under the stars, his arm around her shoulders.

Once, at the supper table, a man in a rough leather jacket, just passing through, said, "Yeah, that Tasker fellow went to check the meadow. Supposed to take the cattle there for the winter. Thought he would see if there was a blade of grass left after the Fanchers drove their herds through. He came back in a hurry." The man laughed in a crude manner.

"Did he leave the area?" Josephine had asked, as casually as she could. She felt her face grow warm.

"Well hell, that's what all the girls are wanting to know." The man roared and slapped his thigh as if he had just topped everyone in the "amusing" department.

"I didn't ... I don't care—" Josephine took a hurried spoonful of Sister Maisey's soup. She still burned with embarrassment when she remembered the conversation.

Now Levi asked, "A water barrel? Are you planning a trip?"

"Well ..." She straightened her shoulders. "Yes."

"The Dodds are leaving? Heaven knows enough people are."

"The Dodds?"

"Your husband." Levi looked away, fingering an ox yoke with sudden concentration.

"Oh." Josephine winced. "He isn't my husband. I mean, he *is* my husband. Now. But not much longer."

Levi ran his hand the length of the curved wood, as if he was contemplating the news, and then seemed to remember the drift of the conversation. "So you are taking a trip."

"Probably not this year. ... I'm planning—looking at what I'll need. I'm hoping to go next year. I—I'm going to pull my handcart."

Levi took his hand from the yoke and stared at her with an incredulous—and admiring—expression. "Where are you thinking of heading?"

"Oregon City." She hoped he wouldn't laugh, but instead he said, "That's a lot of pluck. Do you know how far that is?"

"I just looked at a map."

"There's the Columbia River. You have to float down the falls."

"I haven't worked out the details," she confessed, for the second time that morning.

"With a handcart."

"I pulled it here."

He suddenly became serious. "I hear more than two hundred people died on those handcart treks last year."

She chewed her lip. Her plan was ludicrous. She could see that now. And yet, what choice did she have?

"I didn't know it was that many. Brother Brigham said most people made it through in good stead."

"Yes, well, Brother Brigham sometimes embellishes the truth." He seemed angry, and then lowered his voice and said more gently, "You're leaving Heber?"

"I asked for a bill of divorce," she said stubbornly. "I'm expecting it any day now." She couldn't read Levi's expression.

"Where are you living?"

"The Lone Tree."

A pause. "May I come by?"

Yes, yes, yes!

She whispered, "Yes," and then louder, "Yes."

"Saturday evening?"

"Saturday. Supper?" A giddy feeling rose in her throat and she tried to steady her voice.

"Supper."

Walking home, she felt an odd sensation in her stomach, of freedom and fear. She was still married. But she had heard that other plural wives, the youngest and last acquired, had moved back in with their parents, and she remembered their newfound gaiety at the schoolhouse dances. And Josephine decided Sister Maisey was right after all. "What the good Lord and the law of the land didn't join together, 'tain't a marriage at all."

Levi arrived smelling of wood smoke, his broad-brimmed hat tucked under his arm.

That afternoon she had hauled the wash tub into the room she shared with Sister Maisey and rinsed her hair with yucca root to bring out the shine. She soaked until the water cooled, and afterward dressed carefully in her apple-green gingham. The dress had been repaired so many times there was little to recommend it, but it was the best she could do, and she hoped the green ribbon in her hair would bring out the highlights in her eyes. She twisted ringlets at each side of her face, pinched her cheeks to bring up a blush, and finished off with a dab of Sister Maisey's homemade rose water on her wrists. Peart was as worked up over the young man calling as Josephine was, and the girl was fairly certain the older woman wouldn't mind her using the rose water without asking.

All throughout the meal Josephine had trouble following the conversation. A husband and wife, just down from Salt Lake, talked about the latest play at the Social Hall while Sister Maisey bustled in and out with potatoes and meatloaf. Two men, headed to St. George, boasted about their stallions; a prim woman in a high collar pursed her lips when they mentioned breeding. Josephine took note of Levi's fingers, long and slender, and noticed he was quieter than the others. Once, his thigh accidentally touched hers, and her heart caught.

After supper they stood at the doorway of the parlor. Lodgers were coming and going, but most looked as if they were entrenched for the evening. The St. George men were still gloating over their horses, a freight hauler put up his feet by the fire and snored, three children ran laughing up and down the stairs, and the prim woman read scriptures in the corner. Josephine wished they all would take their activities elsewhere, but of course, the boarding house offered nowhere else to go.

"I'm sorry. It's noisy."

"A little noise never hurt anyone." Levi smiled at her.

Josephine looked around, distressed. There was nowhere to sit. Every couch and chair was taken, except a small space at the end of a worn velveteen couch. "Will you sit down?" she asked, feeling awkward at the lack of options.

Is it too forward to sit that close?

"That's hardly one seat, let alone two!" he laughed. "Would you like to walk?"

After they left the noisy banter of the boarding house, the night was so quiet all Josephine could hear was the rustle of cottonwood leaves and the soft bleat of sheep settling in for the night. The full moon cast silver-blue light across the dirt road. With each step she felt her old life drop away.

She didn't quite come to his shoulders, but in spite of his longer legs, he matched his pace to hers. They walked in silence. In spite of hundreds of imaginary conversations Josephine had shared with

Levi, now that they were here together she couldn't think of a single thing to say. When he didn't speak either, she began to feel a panicky sensation. She desperately tried to remember what Meaghan had said about her courtship conversations with Harold, but not a single thought dropped into her head.

"I like it when the moon is full," she said weakly. She could almost hear her own heartbeat.

"When I was a boy, my momma and us kids would sit on the porch at night and watch the moon rise," Levi said. "I guess that's what you do when you don't have much money." He laughed.

And then—although she should have asked him about his mother, and their home, and his sisters and brothers—she grew tongue-tied and lapsed into shyness. They walked up one street and down another, with only the breeze-ruffled leaves breaking the silence.

By the time they arrived back at the Lone Tree, Josephine was heartbroken at her lost opportunity. He must think her dull, she was sure of it. But as he walked her up the steps of the wide front porch, he asked if he could come by the following Saturday night.

"Yes!" That was more than she had said for three blocks.

His face brightened. "It's settled then."

He escorted her to a footrace between the Mormon and Paiute boys, and a dance at the schoolhouse. They went to a taffy pull at the Kelley home. Young women curtsied when Levi came in, acting as if he weren't already taken—Josephine was still married, after all—and all evening they directed dainty comments his way, but Levi seemed oblivious. After the taffy was sampled and the custard pie served and it was polite to leave, he asked if she would like to slip out.

They slowly found their way to conversation. She told him about her home on Middleton Street, and then about living in the crowded tenement, and about the textile mill where she and Momma had picked at burrs. She told him about the trek to Utah, about Meaghan, and Meaghan's settling in Oregon City.

He told her about growing up poor on a Vermont farm—only

half an acre to support a family of ten. His father was a carefree sort; he preferred teasing folk tunes from a harmonica to shoring up the crumbling stone walls of their home. His mother was dreamy, out gathering dogwood blossoms when she should have been tending the garden. Levi tried to make up the difference. When both parents died before he turned sixteen, he signed on to deliver mail on the Oregon Trail. The mail companies, he told Josephine, looked for able-bodied orphans, young men without ties who could commit themselves to the trail until they got too old for its rigors. Levi had ties—he sent his wages home to his younger siblings—but otherwise, he fit the bill.

He had been gone too often for romance. And before he met a pair of Mormon missionaries and switched over to Brigham Young's mail courier company last year, his trail companions liked to get liquored up to the point of disorderliness, and so Levi sat alone and sketched trail scenes to amuse himself. Buffalo, rock formations, birds. He liked the stability of belonging to a church, but since he rarely saw any Mormons, he found companionship in books, hungrily reading novels left behind by overloaded pioneers, and he devoured Oregon Trail guidebooks and old newspapers at the forts. When the feds punished Brigham Young's insubordination by canceling his mail service contract, Levi came to Cedar City to cut and haul logs for the iron operation.

They often walked. Along the road under the line of cottonwoods, and then farther afield—out through the fields, along the gully east of town, toward the canyon, all the places where young couples shouldn't walk. She knew people probably were talking, but she tried not to care. She kept reminding herself that she wasn't the first young woman to flee plural marriage.

They didn't kiss on their first outing, or their second. On their third meeting, as he reached for her hand, helping her over a boulder, he suddenly caught her waist and pulled her close. She held her breath as she felt his arms close around her.

"I've never been held. Like this." She was nervous and not nervous.

"Your momma must have held you when you were born." He brought his hand to her neck and ran his fingers along its length. He touched his lips to her cheek. His lips dropped lower and brushed hers. He hesitated, and then all hesitation disappeared.

She opened her mouth and felt the curious softness of his tongue. She had never let Heber Dodd kiss her. No one had ever kissed her. She remembered everything she had been taught. The cautionary tales of fallen young women. The admonitions from Momma. The warnings from Bishop Severn. But now those memories seemed like echoes from another life. This was so wrong, and yet it didn't feel wrong. For hadn't the rules already been rearranged? What was virtue? She had lain with a stranger, a man she didn't love, a man who belonged to someone else. She had carried his child. What could rules possibly mean now?

Suddenly he pulled away. "I'm sorry."

She felt confused and shy. "You don't need to be." She already had been taken—by Brother Dodd. And yet, she hadn't been taken.

They found places where they could be alone, where she would sit and he would sketch. She pulled her skirt up past her ankles, and then to her calves, and he drew the curves of her legs. She rolled her sleeves up, and he drew her arms and her neck and the tangle of her cinnamon hair. He traced her arm with his pencil.

All my life I have lived at the edges, she thought. She had experienced seventeen springtimes, and never one where she felt so alive.

And yet. Through it all, there was an air of reserve about Levi. His unexplained detachment continued even as she relayed the news that her divorce had been granted.

"Sometimes you're—" She stopped. He was what? She tried to keep her voice even. "It's as if there's a hidden place in you."

He was quiet for so long she thought he hadn't heard her, or chose to overlook her words. They were sitting on a log at the side of the river, and all she could hear was the thrum of water against pebbles. She felt the air—not cool, not warm. Spring. The March sky was alive with clouds and sun, and tiny, hopeful buds were forming on trees. The cottonwoods had put forth catkins and the scent of fresh-turned earth rose from the fields.

He picked up a twig and bent it double until it broke. He fingered the twisted wood fibers as if he was stalling for time. "I was hauling a load of grain," he finally said. "I ran into the Fancher party just outside Parowan." He studied her face as if he was wondering how much to confide.

She stiffened, flooded with a sudden sense of dread. Was he going to tell her about being at the meadow? He had drilled with the brigade. He knew how to fire a rifle as well as the rest of them. Was he there when it had happened?

She and Levi had talked about books, about families. They had laughed over church gossip. He had sketched her with her hair undone, tangled up in curls. They had embraced, probably too often. But she suddenly realized how little she knew him. They had barely met.

"They were going to Cedar City before they headed out over the desert," Levi said. "Captain Fancher was a stockman too. Alexander—that was his name. The same name as my grandpa. He seemed like a man with common sense."

In front of them, a hawk dived. "He planned to restock in Utah, but no one would sell them anything. Nothing. All the way through the territory." The hawk lifted into the air, a mouse in its talons.

"That poor party was mostly women and children. They were terrified." He stopped, sucked in his breath. "This isn't a story for a lady."

He tried to look away, but in spite of her light-headedness, Josephine held his gaze. "Tell me."

"Hell, those who were there aren't supposed to talk. And those who weren't—they aren't supposed to know about it." He jammed the heel of his boot into the sand.

"But you weren't there when—" she said, the knot in her chest growing tighter. She could feel sweat gather on her lip.

He went on as if he hadn't heard her, as if he were in a trance. "I went out to scout. I was supposed to take the herd to winter pasture.

There's no other place, really. The other meadows around here are too dry.

"I could smell the meadow before I saw it. I had to hold my kerchief over my nose it was so bad. There were bodies everywhere, more than a hundred. All rotted. Lying in the grass. Stripped of their clothing, even the children." He rushed through the words as if they had been piling up in his head for months.

"There were skulls smashed in. Scraps of dresses. I saw girls' bonnets, and long hair tangled up in sagebrush. The wolves had eaten some of the faces away and eaten out their—" he broke off.

"I wake up almost every night with that scene," he said through a clenched jaw. He picked up a pine cone and began to rip out the scales, one by one.

"A hundred men from the settlements around here—that's what I hear. A hundred *Saints*"—he spat out the word—"rode out and bludgeoned and shot a bunch of strangers. They slit the necks of the women. They killed all but the youngest children. Blood atonement, that's what some are saying now. Shedding their blood so they can be forgiven of their sins." His voice was thick.

"Oh, Levi." Josephine reached for his hand.

At last he said, "And so, no. I don't go to church anymore. You asked once. You said you didn't see me there. ... But you go. You'll probably want to mar—" he broke off, and then began again, choosing his words more carefully. "Be with a Mormon."

It was true—Josephine had kept going, in a way that felt more like drifting than intention. Each Sunday she occupied a bench and silently argued with almost every point of Bishop Severn's sermon. To his discredit, he had regained some of his swagger. But everyone she loved went. Sister Maisey. Sister Dodd and the children. Brother Larsen. Rebecca. They were family.

They had each made their reconciliation. Brother Larsen was planning on moving up to Provo for a fresh start. In a moment of candor, he had told Josephine that he wasn't leaving the territory with the backouts. "Ya, too much evil happened here. Now the place seems cursed, so I want to leave like the rest. But I'm not ready to go too far away, or to give up on the Saints. I can't help but feel that this is my people, and if the Lord'll have me in the leadership again—my flock.

"For every man who went to Mountain Meadows, a man chose not to go," Brother Larsen said. "For every blood atoner, there's a good man who goes out to his fields and works hard and prays to his God, and treats others with charity. And I've never seen such kindness as the sisters have. They do right by each other. Tend to the needs of those who are carrying a grief around."

And Peart. She had chosen to settle in, to ignore the events that happened back in September. "Thing is, I's plain too tired to move again," she told Josephine. "These old drumsticks won't take another trek. And besides, I've a home here. This is the first real home I's had. I's treated good. And taken a fancy to cooking. And I like the gossip at the table." And then she chuckled and began to relay a rumor about Opal Haslam's mother-in-law.

Only Sister Ashdown seemed unaffected by events—or perhaps in her madness, she was more affected than the rest. She stood proudly in testimony meeting, rolling and unrolling her hands while she spoke in tongues. Before Bishop Severn rose to cut her off, she recounted visions. She had seen God the Father and his Son out by her woodpile. She was to bring forth a great work.

Sister Ashdown's work apparently didn't include caring for her daughter, for Rebecca usually came to school late, her hair uncombed and her smock dirty. Josephine brought extra lunch, for Rebecca often had none.

"My mum saw Hea'nly Father," Rebecca reported to her teacher. "She had a rel—what's that word? Hmm ... Rel-levation! She just stays in her room and hums. ... Sister Josie, did you ever see Hea'nly Father?"

Now Josephine and Levi sat, their hands locked, their knees touching. The river thrummed, cliff swallows flitted down from the rock outcropping in the canyon. She replayed his words in her mind: "You'll probably want to be with a Mormon."

"Levi?" she said hesitantly. She tried to keep her voice light. "About me being with a Mormon …" She waited for him to finish the conversation he had started, but he was silent, watching the swallows. "I want—"

She wasn't used to saying what she wanted anymore. She paused. She picked up the pine cone he had dropped. "You said you go jackrabbit hunting on Sunday mornings. Instead of church." She rolled the cone back and forth in her fingers. "Maybe I could go with you. Or—well, just for a walk."

She remembered meeting him in the aisle of Brother Griffiths' store. She had put away thoughts of leaving now that she was seeing him. Her dreams had shifted from Oregon City back to Cedar City. But she knew he was restless. In the dry goods store, she had been so distracted by the sight of him she lost track of the conversation. She tried to recall: Had he said something about a trek?

"You were looking at an ox yoke in Brother Griffiths' store," she said, her voice low.

"A yoke …"

"Yes." She curled a strand of hair around one finger and pretended keen interest in the swallows.

"Back when I was delivering mail, I saw a newspaper at Fort Laramie. An ad for the Willamette Valley, in the Oregon Territory. They were calling it an earthly paradise. The gates of Eden. But I already had a home, in Utah, so I put the place out of my mind. Until last month. I was at Mr. Griffiths' store that day, thinking about it."

She waited, looking at him without speaking.

"Land is so cheap there it's almost free, Josie. To people who will settle. They say the soil is so fertile you can get two crops of wheat a summer. And you can raise almost anything. There's timber in the mountains. And salmon so thick in the rivers they say—" He laughed. "The Indians say you can walk across the rivers without touching the water.

"I've put money away," he said. "From my days on the trail. I had been thinking of forming a wagon party."

Her heart beat faster. What was he saying? And this—this valley he was talking about. "Levi, is this Willah—how do you say it?"

"Willamette Valley."

"Is it near Oregon City?"

"The Oregon Trail ends there. In the Willamette Valley."

"My sister—" Her words trailed off. "Meaghan." Something joyous was rising within her.

"In Oregon City. You said." His smile started in his eyes and spread from there. "You were looking at a water barrel."

"Yes, a water barrel."

He traced the top of her hand with his thumb. "You know, Josie, riding in a wagon would be a lot easier than pushing a handcart."

They both laughed. It was that simple. It was decided.

30

PROVIDENCE ... has made Oregon the most favoured spot of His beneficence. ... the forests are heavy and extensive; and the trees are of vast dimensions; and vegetation, generally, is luxuriant to a degree unknown in any other part of America ... The section of the country ... is remarkable for a mild climate, a clear sky, a serene atmosphere, and a soft and brilliant sunshine. The nights, when the moon is near full, and the hemisphere studded over with stars, are indescribably beautiful.

—Excerpts from *A Geographical Sketch of That Part of North America, Called Oregon* and *A General Circular to All Persons of Good Character, Who Wish to Emigrate to the Oregon Territory*, written by Hall Kelley

May 19, 1858

My dearest, dearest Meaghan—
  Just a few words, as I am off to the Oregon Teritory in the morning!
  So much has happened I can scarcely tell it all in one telling. I have met someone—Levi Tasker—& given him my heart & hand. We are heading West on the Oregon Trail, & this, dear sister, is my best news. We are to settle in the Wilamete Valley! I will see you again—& watch your little one grow up, & become better aquainted with your husband. Perhaps we will even purchase farm tools from him!
  We are coming in haste & plan to make good time, so eager are we to arrive—I hope to see you by summers end. May kind Providence

smile upon both of us.
I will write more soon—

With Affection & Love & all the
Blessings under dear Heaven,
Your Josie

The women brought old rags and pails to scrub down the church house, and even Sister Maisey abandoned her kitchen to help. The mothers of Josephine's pupils worked the hardest, polishing the benches until they shone, and Bertie, who supervised the effort, arranged spring blossoms in jars along the front. When the sisters were finished, they stood back and surveyed their work. The mid-morning sun had begun to flood the room, and they pronounced everything beautiful.

Josephine, standing there by the dais, remembered her talk with Bishop Severn. He had gotten wind of the upcoming nuptials and waylaid her after church, advising her to wait, to be properly sealed in the Endowment House in Salt Lake.

"No!" Josephine blurted, forgetting her manners. She remembered the touching of secret places, the oath of vengeance. She remembered the raised sword at the gates of Eden, barring entry.

"And besides," she said, "hasn't the Endowment House been shut down?"

Sealings in the building might be on hold, she knew. Sister Maisey had heard the rumor: Great Salt Lake City was emptying out. The prophet was determined to hold on to his position as governor, and as the federal troops—escorting the newly appointed governor from the States—continued their march toward Zion, President Young warned the soldiers that they would find an abandoned city upon arrival. He had begun the removal of his people— tens of thousands of them—south to Provo. Windows were nailed shut, doors were locked, and the Saints loaded their wagons and handcarts, gathered their sheep and cows and pigs, and began the long march to Provo, where they would live in tents, wagons, and dugouts. A small band of men would be left behind to torch homes and barns should the enemy arrive in the valley; even the orchards would be set afire.

"Our necks shall not be given to the noose," the prophet had proclaimed. The Saints could worship in one place as well as another. Now the road south was crowded with his people—women, children, men, hauling their worldly goods in a long, weary procession.

"I'm not sure the Endowment House is closed yet," the bishop persisted.

"No," Josephine repeated. "No Endowment House."

She and Levi had already bypassed the bishop and asked Brother Hans Larsen to perform the marriage ceremony. The couple was firm on this point: no washings, no anointings, no pretended disembowelments.

"A simple 'Do you take this man for your wedded husband?' will do," Josephine said.

They didn't wait long, only a few weeks; they didn't want to get a late start on the Oregon Trail. Josephine wore wildflowers trailing through her hair and joined hands with Levi as Brother Larsen proclaimed them husband and wife and the community looked on. Babies cried throughout the ceremony, and afterward, during the wedding lunch, boys ran around the dessert table so rambunctiously they tipped it over; the pies and the frosted cake went flying into the dust.

"Let's not take that as an omen," Josephine said to Levi, laughing as they retrieved what they could.

After supper, Peart made it up to them with Levi's favorite, hot doughnuts, and when it came time to retire, she gave up her room and bedded down on the velveteen couch in the parlor.

Upstairs, Levi slipped off his shirt and trousers and blew out the candle. Josephine hesitated before untying the drawstring of her chemise. She could feel her belly tense as she lay down beside him.

Her mind raced. She remembered Brother Dodd's unwashed body pressing against her, and Emalee's screams as she gave birth. She remembered the moans and sighs aboard ship; they had been moans of pleasure, she knew, but the idea was a mystery to her.

Levi was gentle. At first he seemed unsure of himself. There in the darkness he ran his hand along her cheek, and then along her shoulder, exploring a new landscape. He touched his lips to her throat.

"We promised to cherish each other," he whispered.

"We did at that." Her voice sounded different to herself—lower, huskier—as if it belonged to someone she didn't yet know. She was frightened, but this felt like a different act than the one she had known before.

That night they kept their promise. They cherished each other, and afterward lay together in wonder at what they had done.

The morning before their departure, Josephine found Sister Maisey in the kitchen. The woman looked tired. "It's good we're leaving," Josephine said contritely. She suspected Peart wanted her bed back. For two long nights, since the wedding, she had slept on the couch.

"Aye, that's for certain. One more night of the couch and I'll not stand up straight again."

Josephine flushed, embarrassed about her nighttime activities, and then said, "I made you something."

She handed the woman a carefully stitched sampler. Peart looked up, surprised. Obviously, she wasn't used to gifts; she immediately forgot her fatigue and swelled her bosom at the momentous occasion.

"Lass, what's all this then?" she said, beaming as she unfolded the sampler ceremoniously.

> *Roses will fade and violets wither*
> *Friendship's flowers will bloom forever.*

Peart tried to pick out the words, but simple literacy was beyond her. When Josephine read the message, the woman's eyes filled with tears. Finally, she managed, "In all my born days, no one's given me a gift. And all those alph'bet letters! With you not caring the wee-est bit for stitching."

"I don't care for it. Unfortunately. But there are things a pioneer has to get used to."

Then Josephine cut through orchards to the Dodd home, smiling as pink-white petals drifted down onto her shoulders and a meadowlark called. She noticed green shoots already pushing up in gardens.

"Why, Josephine, what's this?" Sister Dodd fingered the sampler carefully. "And to think that you don't care for needlework."

"Does everyone need to remind me of the fact?" Josephine groaned theatrically. "I can carry off needlework when it's absolutely necessary."

"I'm afraid it will continue to be necessary."

"Sister Dodd … Bertie, thank you. You gave me a place at your table, and it wasn't easy for you. I'm sorry." At last Josephine said the words she had wanted to say for more than a year.

"I know." The woman averted her face and busily smoothed her apron, as if the conversation had become too intimate. Josephine guessed that Sister Dodd was more than happy to have her husband to herself again, even if he was just a shell of his former self.

Out in the corral, Flicker stood swishing his tail at flies. When he saw Josephine, he nickered softly and came running.

"Flicker." She caressed his dusty forehead, remembering rides into the canyon, and resting in the grass watching the clouds, her friend steady and calm at her side. She pulled a handful of bunchgrass: her going-away gift.

"Flicker. I'm going away. All right?" He nudged his big head against her shoulder and looked at her with gentle, long-lashed eyes. She listened to the familiar rhythm of his munching. "I'll never forget you," she said.

Will someone love you after I'm gone?

She stood stroking his ears until she saw Heber emerge from the back door with an ax, headed for the woodpile. Josephine slipped away the other direction.

She had delivered her gifts, but the newlyweds received presents as well, including apple seeds from Brother Larsen.

"I saved them from last year's crop," he said. "You can take some to Oregon for your orchard. I hear apples grow so thick in the trees there's no room for the birds."

Levi pressed the seeds into Josephine's hand and later he kissed her out behind the chicken coop and mischievously said, "Perhaps we'll plant more than apple seeds."

The next morning as he pulled on his shirt, Josephine said, "Levi?" She watched him bend over the wash basin as she brushed her hair. "About seeds." Her face reddened, thinking of their bodies together in the bed. She took another stroke, pretending to be absorbed in a tangle.

He stopped washing his face. "Josie? Are you all right?"

"About children." She tried for a casual tone. "What do you think about little girls?"

"Well, considering we might have one, I should think they're rather nice."

"What would you think about having one sooner rather than later?" She took a deep breath. "Rebecca Ashdown."

He looked surprised. "I know you feel close to her. But … she's not our child." He wiped his face.

"I don't think Lydia Ashdown remembers she has a child." Josephine's eyes pleaded.

Levi carefully hung the towel on a hook and slowly buttoned his shirt. He seemed to be stalling for enough time to roll the idea around in his head. "Sister Ashdown is sure to say no."

"I'm not so certain of that," Josephine said.

He gave her a long look, which slowly transformed from befuddlement to admiration. Then he chuckled and said, "Josie, I have a feeling you're going to be getting your way a lot."

When Josephine approached the Ashdown cabin, Rebecca was

playing alone in the yard and came running. "Miss Josie!" But Josephine was too nervous to offer much of a greeting. She knocked and poked her head in the open door.

"Is that you, Jesus?" Lydia called. "I'm here!"

"It's Josephine. Not Jesus."

"I've been waiting for your return." The woman balled her hands into fists and stretched her fingers wide, and then clenched her hands again.

"Sister Ashdown, I want to take Rebecca. Is that all right? I want to take your daughter."

"I have fought the good fight, O Lord. I have kept the faith."

"To go west, Sister Ashdown."

Lydia began to hum an aimless tune. She stared blankly out the window.

Josephine touched Rebecca's shoulder. "Where are your things?" she said in an urgent whisper. "Your dresses. Your doll. Do you want to come with me?"

"Where you going, Miss Josie?"

"We're going to a place where you can chase butterflies and pick wildflowers. All day long if you want. And there will be enough to eat, and someone to love you."

"Enough to eat?"

"Yes." Josephine thought of Levi's description: a lush, grassy valley with a great river running through it. Orchards loaded down with fruit, streams teeming with salmon.

"Who will love me?"

"Me. I'll love you, 'Becca."

"Okay."

Josephine picked up the small bundle of Rebecca's belongings and cautiously backed out of the cabin. Once outside, she grabbed the child's hand and ran.

Now the day of departure had arrived. The sun spilled over the mountain east of town, and up and down the street roosters crowed and dogs barked. Cottonwood trees put forth their sweet, musky scent. Josephine and Levi packed carefully. Water barrel on the side, flour and salt pork and cornmeal in the wagon, a worn flowered quilt on the makeshift bed. Levi tied a butter churn to the back.

The oxen pulled the heavy wagons into a line, with cattle and sheep strung out along the main road. Josephine smiled and waved as she saw Emalee Severn, heading west, instead of east as she had planned. She and her infant had been taken in by a family traveling to the Oregon Territory, like Josephine and Levi, to claim a plot of land.

"You write now, you hear?" Peart said, huffing up to the wagon. "As soon as you get to Or'gun." She still couldn't pronounce the name, and Josephine knew Sister Maisey couldn't read either, but she also knew the woman would codger a nice young lodger, preferably male, to read letters to her, and pictured them sitting on the front porch after supper. "You'll be missing my good cooking by tomorrow," Peart said.

Josephine remembered the long trail west from Iowa City, and the cornmeal pancakes that fell apart and the baked beans still hard in their skins. She remembered the way Sister Maisey had fibbed about her ancestors cooking for barons in England so she could land a cook's job. Now Peart bragged that the man who ran the boarding house said he wouldn't let her go for all the gold in California.

"Yes, I'll miss your cooking." Josephine laughed, but she knew she *would* miss the woman's cooking. Sister Maisey had perfected her potato fritters and Swedish jam cake and buttermilk doughnuts sprinkled with cinnamon. "I think your family must have cooked for barons, after all."

She suddenly spotted Hope, the Fancher train orphan, standing timidly at the edge of the public square. Rebecca saw her and began to run, calling, "Hope! Hope! I have something for you! I asked Miss Josie and she said it was all right."

Rebecca slowed in front of the girl and handed her a well-worn doll, cradling it as carefully as one might hold a newborn. "Miss Josie says you're going back to the States—that someone's coming to get you. Do you want to take Hanna? She doesn't cry much."

Hope clutched the doll but before she could reply, Rebecca fidgeted and said, "I have to go now!" She turned and sprinted for the wagon, as if she were afraid of being left behind.

Josephine thought back to her last day of teaching. The Fancher boy had read the Bible passage. "To every thing there is a season, and a time to every purpose under the heaven." He pronounced each word with care. "A time to be born, and a time to die. A time to plant—"

"Miss Josephine!" Brother Haslam's boy, the one with buck teeth, shouted from the back. "I planted last year! I helped Pa in the fields."

"Yes, you did. And next week all of you will start in the fields again."

"—And a time to pluck up that which is planted," the Fancher boy plodded along patiently. He was used to interruptions. After three more children cut in, he finished the Bible passage. Finally came the moment for Josephine's farewell speech. She had memorized it, but she was cut off by pupils eager for freedom.

"Goodbye, goodbye!" they yelled as they bolted for the door. A few held back, tearing up at the separation, and Hope approached slowly.

"You'll be back next year?" the orphan asked shyly.

"I'm leaving for Oregon," Josephine said. She had dreaded breaking the news, but she had some good news, too. She crouched down to Hope's level and took her hand. "I hear your relatives may be coming for you. You hold on, all right? They'll take you back to the States."

After the last child left, Josephine ran her hands along the railing and then over the cover of *McGuffey's Reader*, and stood, gazing at the classroom. Although it served as both church house and school, she knew she would remember it as the latter. She suddenly heard someone in the doorway.

"A time to break down, and a time to build up." Levi stepped over the threshold, carrying a bouquet of dandelions. "I came to walk you home on your last day." He pushed back the brim of his hat.

"A time to weep, and a time to laugh," he said. "A time to mourn … I know the words by heart. My mother recited them to me when I was a boy."

Josephine held out her hands for the humble flowers. "Elegant," she said, teasing him. "You robbed them from some bee, didn't you?"

"She didn't sting me, so she must have approved."

Levi put one hand on Josephine's shoulder and the other around her waist, and led her. "A time to dance," he recited. One step back, one step to the side. Back. Side. Back. Side. Around the room in a waltz so slow there was no rhythm, or perhaps there was a deeper rhythm than dance.

"A time to embrace," she said, pulling him close.

"A time to love," he said. She laid her cheek against his chest, feeling the scratch of his linsey-woolsey shirt. He ran his fingers along the ridge of her shoulder. "Josie."

"A time of peace," she whispered.

For all her praying, Josephine had never really heard God speak. But she remembered kneeling near a gnarled juniper on a winter day, watching a red-tailed hawk feather the sky. The desert had poured into her like a sacrament—the scent of sun on old wood, cliffs fired crimson, silence. High solemn clouds moved over the landscape, painting the sage with blue shadows.

Now she ran her hands over the metal rims of the wagon wheels. She checked the seams of the water barrel and straightened her bonnet. She climbed onto the wagon seat and took a last long look around.

Perhaps God speaks in his own time and his own way, she thought. Perhaps he doesn't speak through sermons, but perhaps, more often, through the voices of the people you love. Perhaps one feels his presence in the fragrance of rain on the hard red earth after a long drought, and in the downy seeds that float—free—from cottonwood trees in spring. Perhaps one learns to believe by falling in love, or by watching the moon begin its age-old ascent in rhythm with the sun. Each night that moon cast its silver light on a lonely cluster of cabins at the far edge of a desert kingdom, and in its constancy, it touched her mother's grave, too, and then wandered west across the heavens, to cast its spell over the apple orchards of Oregon.

Josephine knew thousands of people would go on speculating whether God was the province of Joseph Smith. Others would claim God was in residence at Saint Nicholas Church, shepherding the flock of Reverend Phillips. And more than a few would spend their lives condemning the indifferent being who looked down on the dirty streets of Liverpool, saw the hungry children, and did nothing.

But perhaps, Josephine thought, she would sort out all of this another time, for right now Levi was flicking the reins, the oxen were heaving forward, and a stout woman with a molasses stain on her apron was calling out, "Cheerio! Cheerio then!"

It was more than enough.

Author's Note

This story is based on the letters, journals, and family accounts of several hundred Mormon pioneers who lived in the mid-19th century. The narrative also drew extensively from the sermons and writings of early church leaders and the scholarship of later historians, Mormon and non-Mormon alike.

Although it may not seem so to my extended family, many of them devout Latter-day Saints, this book is a work of love. I am awed by the courage of my ancestors, who abandoned their roots in Europe and embarked on a journey of faith across a treacherous ocean and into a remote wilderness.

The story of Josephine Bell was initially inspired by the account of my great-great-grandmother, Mary Ann Barton Allen. Her family joined the Mormon Church—now officially titled The Church of Jesus Christ of Latter-day Saints—and emigrated from Lancashire, England, to the Utah Territory in 1856. At the time, factory workers in the newly industrialized cities of Great Britain were suffering from hunger and severe poverty; thousands were drawn by the missionaries' promises of a "land flowing with milk and honey." In 1856, the year Mary Ann sailed to America, work was particularly scarce and prices were inflated, and desperate converts viewed the promise of Zion with great hope.

Many converts died on board the immigrant ships, and those who arrived safely were the objects of curiosity, jeers and even violence as they made their way by rail from the East Coast to the "jumping-off" town of Iowa City.

The five handcart companies of 1856, the first year of the handcart experiment, lost more than two hundred people to starvation, exposure, exhaustion, accidents, and disease. One woman recounted that "my sister and I used to pray we could die to get out of our misery." Another survivor described wolves coming down to the camp, waiting for the Saints to leave so they could devour the bodies of the dead. Many who did survive lost toes or fingers, or entire hands and feet.

Mary Ann, fourteen years old at the time, was one of those stranded in the Wyoming Territory by winter storms and bitter cold. For her handcart party, the journey turned into a death march. She ate the hides and feet of cattle to survive, and the four men in her tent, including her father, died. He wasn't buried, but wrapped in a blanket and laid under a tree on the frozen ground. When rescuers from Salt Lake finally arrived, Mary Ann was passed over with the comment, "Well, here is another dead girl." When she opened her eyes, her rescuer was startled; he freed her by chopping her hair from the ice.

Wallace Stegner wrote of the handcart companies:

Perhaps their suffering seems less dramatic because they bore it meekly, praising God, instead of fighting for life with the ferocity of animals and eating their dead to keep their own life beating, as both the Fremont and Donner parties did. … But, if courage and endurance make a story, if human kindness and helpfulness and brotherly love in the midst of raw horror are worth recording, this half-forgotten episode of the Mormon migration is one of the great tales of the West and of America.

The survivors of Mary Ann's party straggled into the Salt Lake Valley in late November, and she reported, "We were waiting on the streets for people to ask us home with them." In the shuffle for a home and security, the girl soon ended up as the plural wife of a man almost four decades older than herself, old enough to be her grandfather.

The practice of polygamy was instituted by Joseph Smith, founder of the Mormon religion. Smith testified he had received a visit from God the Father and his Son Jesus Christ, who warned him he would be damned if he didn't take additional wives.

Polygamy's adherents included one of my great-great-grandfathers, who fathered nearly sixty children, and a great-great-great-grandmother, Mary Elizabeth Rollins Lightner, who received a lock of hair from Joseph Smith when she was a girl and wed him as a young woman, despite the fact that she was married to another man at the time. The prophet persuaded Mary Elizabeth, telling her an angel with a drawn sword had threatened his life should he not obey the command to marry her. She wrote, "Joseph said I was his before I came here and all the Devils in Hell should never get me from him."

Beginning in 1852, polygamy was publicly promoted and openly practiced in the Utah Territory. Thousands of women and girls, some as young as fourteen years old, were persuaded to enter polygamous marriages. Plural wives struggled with jealousy, bitterness, loneliness, and often, poverty, and their accounts are heartbreaking. Under pressure from the federal government, the Mormon Church renounced the practice in 1890. It now excommunicates members who practice polygamy, although multiple women are still "sealed" to one man in Mormon temple ceremonies. These plural marriages are slated to take effect in the hereafter.

Brigham Young directed thousands of pioneers to colonize remote settlements throughout the territory, where they built homes and churches, dug ditches, and planted orchards. When Mary Ann's family was called to southern Utah to help build up the kingdom, they obeyed.

According to her account, they moved to Parowan, near Cedar City, five years after the Mountain Meadows Massacre had occurred. At one point Mary Ann lived on a farm outside the nearby settlement of Summit, where she made a life for herself and her children. According to her granddaughter, she "had to depend a lot on her own resources."

She kept the garden weeded and the wood chopped, and she rose early to make pies before the heat set in. When a band of Indians entered her house uninvited, she was so frightened she gave them food sorely needed by her own family. She also took her husband into her bed when he visited from Parowan, where he lived with his first wife.

In Mary Ann's memoir of several pages, she recounts how one New Year's Day she walked five miles to that town, a four-day-old infant in her arms, to take in a washing. In spite of her best efforts, her ten—twelve by one account—children went barefoot from April to November.

Mary Ann kept the faith, although it couldn't have been easy. The year she arrived, the Utah Territory was racked by drought, famine, and insect plagues of Biblical proportions; hunger drove people to beg on the streets and dig wild roots. In response, Brigham Young attributed their hardships to sinful behavior and instituted a fierce Reformation, which led to door-to-door questioning, public confessions and widespread rebaptisms, and—at the president's decree—a sharp upsurge in polygamy.

The territory also saw growing xenophobia, in part a reaction to federal troops marching on Great Salt Lake City; they had been sent to rein in the renegade governor, eradicate polygamy, and enforce federal laws. In the wake of their advance, Brigham Young directed thirty thousand Saints to abandon their Salt Lake homes and move south. A handful of men were left behind to torch the place should the soldiers make it to the borders. President Young ordered the destruction of his city rather than allowing his theocracy to be governed by a federal appointee.

Spiritual devotion, for some, became religious zealotry, and the violent rhetoric culminated in the brutal massacre perpetrated by Mormon men on a passing wagon train. The Fancher party of more than 120 emigrants was composed primarily of women and children, many of them practicing Christians. At least one hundred Latter-day Saints participated, bludgeoning and shooting fathers, mothers, and all but the youngest children. Many participants had been forged in a crucible of mob violence; they responded with violence.

Afterward, standing in a field strewn with corpses and realizing—with horror—the enormity of their crime, the men took a vow of silence. As the months passed, and then the years, that silence only grew more deafening; most of the men couldn't quiet their own consciences, and many were haunted until their deaths.

Existing records, at least those available to the public, don't allow us to determine whether Brigham Young condoned the killings, but it is certain the president's inflammatory language and teachings of blood atonement contributed to the buildup of violence. Blood atonement dictates that some sins are so heinous that Christ's atonement won't suffice; sinners can be saved only by the shedding of their blood.

In 1990, members of the Mormon Church and descendants of the Fancher wagon train dedicated a monument at the massacre site. At a memorial service, descendants of both those who were slain and those who carried out the murders stood side by side, and embraced.

Mary Ann often sang "The Handcart Song" to her children and grandchildren, and related the story of her harrowing pioneer journey, but her granddaughter said that "in later years she would not talk of these things." She passed away in Utah at age 72, a devoted Latter-day Saint until her death.

My last tangible link to my great-great-grandmother was a small pioneer home in Summit. I made the pilgrimage there each time I visited southern Utah. The house belonged to her daughter and son-in-law, and sat abandoned at the edge of the town, which itself is almost abandoned. The only inhabitants were the swallows that flew in and out of the windows. The trees had withered and the irrigation ditch had long since dried up. A neighbor told me that sometime around 2012 the home was struck by lightning, and in the midst of a ferocious storm, burned to the ground.

But the last time I was there, I noticed something I hadn't seen before. In the deserted lot behind the blackened ruin, out beyond the tumbled-down rock cellar and weather-beaten barn, I could see a scattering of gnarled logs, and the decaying corner of a pioneer structure, sinking into the earth. Looking at the scene, I wondered where Mary Ann's dwelling once had stood, and even wondered if these logs were the bones of her old home.

The structure has almost disappeared, but the hills at its backside remain. In that place, fragrances are so rich you can almost taste them: sharp pinyon pine, musky cottonwood trees, rain. Hawks circle overhead, and each night the crickets, the scourge

of early settlers, serenade the handful of locals. In a paradox of
fate, the southern Utah landscape—so harsh it tested the faith of
every pioneer, so parched it was unclaimed by white settlers until
the Mormons came along—now attracts visitors from around the
world. They are drawn by its indescribable beauty. In spite of the
influx, much of the area is still wilderness.

Individuals are confined by their circumstances; novelists are free to
give them different endings. I took many liberties with the account of
Mary Ann's life, until it became its own narrative. Perhaps I wanted
to rescue her from grasshopper plagues and the unceasing loneliness
of a polygamous marriage. Although my great-great-grandmother
didn't settle in southern Utah until five years after the massacre, and
although her husband didn't participate, she lived in a society so
psychologically scarred it would be decades before Mormons could
acknowledge what had happened at Mountain Meadows; I wanted
to rescue her from that, too. In short, I wanted to write a different
sort of story.

In a scrapbook photo, Mary Ann gazes forthrightly at the cam-
era. She doesn't look like a stern woman, as some pioneers do. Instead, her round face appears childlike, and there is a sense of wanting to trust. Her eyes slant downward at the outer corners; to me,
they appear sad. She wanted to secure a place in the kingdom of
heaven, I know, but perhaps she also wanted a bit more heaven
on Earth.

In the mid-19th century, the Mormon community in Utah was
tightly interwoven, and the Saints provided support for each other,
and friendship. They affirmed each other's faith. But not all believers
retained their once-fervent testimonies. Disentangling oneself from
the insular, theocratic community was difficult, and leaving the remote area entirely was even more challenging, especially for women
and those without means. In spite of obstacles, many did manage to
begin new lives elsewhere.

In an odd twist of fate, I was born in Utah exactly one hundred
years after Mary Ann first arrived. I was raised in the faith, and I

was one of those who left the fold. But in a sense, the Mormon pioneers are still my tribe. Contemporary Latter-day Saints include some of the kindest and most-well intentioned people I know. These modern-day Saints still carry the weight of their history, including polygamy, blood atonement, and a brutal, unprovoked massacre. In part because of their history, Mormons have the legacy of being viewed as a "peculiar people." This story seemed to write itself because, for me, there is no historical movement as colorful, unusual and utterly fascinating as the early Mormon Church—the religion established by a fourteen-year-old boy who went to the woods to pray and came back with visions of God.

THANKS for reading *The Gates of Eden*! If you liked the book and have a moment to spare, I would really appreciate a short online review as this helps future readers find my book.

Book Club Discussion Guide

1. Who was your favorite character and why? Who was your least favorite?
2. Were Elizabeth's baptism and journey to Utah rooted in belief, or in the desire to secure a better life for her daughter?
3. What similarities did the 19th-century European immigrants, making the journey to Utah, have in common with today's refugees?
4. In 1859 the writer Charles Dickens wrote about the aptitude for organization, steadiness of purpose, and orderliness of the Mormons aboard an immigrant ship. What do you think accounted for their social cohesion?
5. The Mormon Church focuses on the courage and sacrifice of the handcart pioneers, while some historians focus on the organizational mismanagement of the handcart plan, and the human cost. The plan enabled thousands of European converts to escape lives of poverty and degradation. Do you think the Mormon handcart experiment was a success?
6. Would you consider Heber's consummation of his plural marriage to be a form of sexual assault, or love? What were his motivations for marriage to Josephine? Did he love her?
7. The Mormon prophet, Joseph Smith, initiated polygamy and married a fourteen-year-old girl, as well as women who were already married to living husbands. Do you think an act can be moral in one social or historical context and immoral in another?
8. Do you think plural marriage would be more difficult for the first wife, or the second? What circumstances would make it more, or less, so?
9. Are there differences between Mormon pioneer polygamy and contemporary polygamy among fundamentalists?
10. Polygamy is illegal in every state in the U.S. but it is quietly tolerated due to the difficulty of prosecution. Instead, officials target sexual assault and rape involving underage girls living in polygamous communities. Should polygamy be legal? What

should be the age of consent for marriage?

11. The book began as a story about an innocent young girl coming of age. Did the violence she encountered surprise you? What were her coping strategies?

12. What were the motivations of those who participated in the Mountain Meadows Massacre? Do you think the book is sympathetic to or judgmental of 19th-century Mormons in southern Utah?

13. The novel, set more than 150 years ago, touches on themes of religious violence. How are these themes still relevant? Do you see religious extremism, divisive rhetoric, and xenophobia at work in contemporary religions?

14. Religious history is often "sanitized" by religious leaders. This has become more difficult in the age of the Internet. Is it more advantageous for religious leaders to be upfront about human failings in their historical past, or attempt to suppress information?

15. Josephine matured over the course of the story. She began as a merchant's daughter whose greatest burden seemed to be the strictures of Victorian etiquette. How did her experience change her?

16. If one is unhappy with the tenets or practices of one's religion, is it better to stay and work for change from within, as Brother Hans Larsen planned to do, or leave, as some pioneer dissidents did?

17. For centuries, philosophers have debated this question: How can God allow the suffering of innocent people? In the last scene of the book, Josephine recounts this dilemma. Is there a way she might eventually reconcile this question?

18. Did Josephine experience both faith and doubt at the same time? In the final scene, do you think Josephine found peace from religious confusion?

19. What, if any, is the difference between religion and spirituality? Did Josephine experience both? What role did nature play?

20. What would you like to see happen to Josephine? Where would you like to see her in five years?

Gratitude

Historical fiction is not written in isolation. In my case, *The Gates of Eden* was nurtured along by a wide circle of generous and talented individuals.

I am profoundly grateful to Jane Parnell for her encouragement and astute editorial talents, and to friends who provided support along the way. I am indebted to Oregon Book Award winner Joyce Cherry Cresswell for her thorough edit and to Jo Hockenhull, Emerita Professor at Washington State University, for her enthusiastic cheerleading and suggestions. Readers Susie Allen, Karen Bartlett, Katherine Daniels, Phyllis Hall, Mady Kimmich, Barbara Curtin Miles, Sue Sanborn, Robyn Shelby, and Jan Taylor were instrumental in correcting numerous mistakes and helping shape the narrative, plot, and characters. I also am indebted to members of my writing group: Jodi Kilcup, Jan Bear, Tara Robinson, and Kate McWiggins, whose suggestions helped me gain a foothold as a writer of fiction. The kind and gentle Lucy McIver, an elder woman of Choctaw descent, helped me gain clarity about how to portray the virulent racism that was common in the 19th century. Sue Armitage, Emerita Professor of History and Women's Studies at Washington State University and co-editor of three collections about women on the Western frontier, reviewed the manuscript and generously offered her expertise about the westward migration. I give each of you my heartfelt thanks.

My immense appreciation goes to Jennifer Quinlan at Historical Fiction Book Covers, for the evocative cover design. I also appreciate her associate, Anna Bennett, for offering editorial suggestions on the first chapter. The background photo was provided by Bashkatov and the boots photo by Nicola Hanney.

I am deeply grateful for the assistance of knowledgeable archivists, library researchers, and museum docents. In Oregon, researchers Claire Bolyard and Jey Wann at the Oregon State Library and archivist Susan Wallace Masse with the Marion County Historical Society were especially helpful. I appreciate the enthusiasm of docents Holly Miles and Bill Perin at the Willamette Heritage Center, along with docents at the Old Aurora Colony Museum and the Polk County Historical Society, all in Oregon. An enthusiastic thank-you goes to volunteers with the Oregon Coast Scenic Railroad, who provided a delightful ride aboard a historic train, and to Sue Sanborn, who talked "horses" with me and allowed me to ride her horse, Flicker. I am indebted to staff and volunteers at This is the Place Heritage Park and the Daughters of Utah Pioneers Museum, both located in Salt Lake City, Utah.

Numerous authors and scholars have devoted themselves to keeping alive the history of the Mormon pioneers. *The Gates of Eden* was informed and guided by their work. These individuals include Laurel Thatcher Ulrich, who authored the groundbreaking book, *A House Full of Females: Plural Marriage and Women's Rights in Early Mormonism, 1835-1870*; Paula Kelly Harline, who wrote *The Polygamous Wives Writing Club*; and Jolene Allphin, whose *Tell My Story, Too* collection sheds a poignant light on the trials and joys of the 1856 handcart pioneers. Will Bagley's *Blood of the Prophets: Brigham Young and the Massacre at Mountain Meadows*; Juanita Brooks' *The Mountain Meadows Massacre*; and Leonard Arrington's *Brigham Young: American Moses* were invaluable. I appreciated hearing the voices of pioneer women in Kenneth Holmes' *Covered Wagon Women: Diaries and Letters from the Western Trails, 1854-1860*; and Susan Butruille's *Women's Voices from the Oregon Trail*. The encyclopedic *History of Utah: 1540-1886*, written by Hubert Hugh Bancroft and published in 1889, was a key resource. Important insights were provided by early Church publications, including the *Journal of Discourses*, *The Latter-day Saints' Millennial Star*, and *A Collection of Sacred Hymns for the Church of the Latter Day Saints*, compiled by Emma Smith, wife of Joseph Smith.

Additional resources included *Devil's Gate: Brigham Young and the Great Mormon Handcart Tragedy*, by David Roberts; *Recollections of a Handcart Pioneer of 1860*, by Mary Ann Hafen; *Great Basin Kingdom: Economic History of the Latter-Day Saints, 1830-1900*, by Leonard J. Arrington; *The Gathering of Zion: The Story of the Mormon*

Trail, by Wallace Stegner; *Mormon Country*, also by Stegner; *Mormon Polygamy: A History*, by Richard Van Wagoner; *Women's Voices from the Western Frontier*, also by Susan Butruille; and *Women's Diaries of the Westward Journal*, by Lillian Schlissel.

I am grateful for the extensive digital resources provided by the Harold B. Lee Library at Brigham Young University and the J. Willard Marriott Digital Library at the University of Utah. Invaluable research materials also were made available by the online Google Books, which has undertaken the enormous task of preserving thousands of historically significant books that may otherwise fade into obscurity. Original news editions found at NewspaperArchive provided fascinating glimpses into the past. All historical errors are mine.

I appreciate the many volunteers with the Willamette Writers in Oregon and the Historical Novel Society, who provided inspiration and support along the way.

Most of all, I am grateful to my husband, Richard Yates. When I gave him the first draft of my first chapter, he urged me to look deeper, to probe my characters and their backstories more fully, and to strengthen the personal story that lay atop a confusing mass of historical detail. He then offered quiet space and encouragement each day, and at the end, read the manuscript with care, offering helpful suggestions. His affirmation and love guided every step.

Bibliography for Chapter Quotations

Chapter 1
Young, Brigham; Kimball, Heber C.; and Richards, Willard.
"Seventh General Epistle of the Presidency of the Church of Jesus
Christ of Latter-day Saints," *The Latter-day Saints' Millennial Star*,
No. 21, Volume XIV. Liverpool, England: S. W. Richards,
15, Wilton Street, July 17, 1852.

Chapter 2

Anonymous ("An American Lady"). *True Politeness: A Hand-Book
of Etiquette for Ladies*. New York: Leavitt and Allen, 1847.

Chapter 3

Smith, Joseph, Jr. *The Book of Mormon: An Account Written by
the Hand of Mormon, Upon Plates Taken from the Plates of Nephi*,
Moroni 10:4. Palmyra, New York: E. B. Grandin, 1830.

Chapter 4
Young, Brigham. Correspondence to Joseph Smith, May 7, 1840.
The Joseph Smith Papers.

Chapter 5
Phelps, William W. "The Gallant Ship is Under Way," *A Collection
of Sacred Hymns for the Church of the Latter Day Saints*. Kirkland,
Ohio: F. G. Williams & Co., 1835.

Chapter 6
Dickens, Charles. "Bound for the Great Salt Lake, The
Uncommercial Traveller," *All the Year Round. A Weekly Journal*.
London, England: Chapman & Hall, 1863.

Chapter 7

Roberts, B. H., editor. From a discourse delivered by Joseph Smith at the funeral of two-year-old Marian Lyon on March 20, 1842 in Nauvoo, Illinois; reported by Wilford Woodruff. *History of the Church of Jesus Christ of Latter-day Saints*, 4:553–54. Salt Lake City, Utah: Deseret Book, 1902-12.

Chapter 8

Davenport Daily Gazette, June 3, 1856.

Chapter 9

The New-York Times, April 27, 1858.

Chapter 10

McAllister, John Daniel Thompson. "The Handcart Song," circa 1856.

Chapter 11

"Very Late from Utah," *The Latter-day Saints' Millennial Star*, No. 41, Volume XIX. Liverpool, England: Orson Pratt, 42, Islington, October 10, 1857. (The article purports to be reprinted from a *New-York Daily Times* article dated September 12, 1857, but is almost completely fabricated.)

Chapter 12

First Presidency in Zion. "The General Epistle," *The Latter-day Saints' Millennial Star*, No. 4, XVIII. Liverpool, England: F. D. Richards, 42, Islington, January 26, 1856.

Chapter 13

Young, Brigham. Correspondence to John Taylor, July 28, 1856. Young Letterbooks, Church Archives.

Chapter 14

Clayton, William (lyrics). "Come, Come Ye Saints." Traditional English tune. 1846.

Chapter 15

Young, Brigham; Kimball, Heber C.; and Richards, Willard. "Sixth General Epistle of the Presidency of the Church of Jesus Christ of Latter-day Saints," *The Latter-day Saints' Millennial Star*, No. 2, Volume XIV. Liverpool, England: F. D. Richards, 15, Wilton Street, January 15, 1852.

Chapter 16

Peterson, Hannah Mary Bouvier. *The National Cook Book: By a lady of Philadelphia. A practical housewife; and author of the "Family save-all."* Philadelphia: T. B. Peterson & Brothers, circa 1866.

Chapter 17

Snow, Eliza Roxcy. "Think Not When You Gather to Zion," *Sacred Hymns and Spiritual Songs, for the Church of Jesus Christ of Latter-Day Saints* (14th ed.), Hymn 327. Salt Lake City, Utah: George Q. Cannon, 1871.

Chapter 18

Young, Brigham. Remarks given at a dance at the Social Hall, Great Salt Lake City, January 2, 1854. Wilford Woodruff journals, 4:239-240.

Chapter 19
Young, Zina Diantha Huntington. Interview, *New York World*, November 17, 1869.

Chapter 20
Anti-Polygamy Standard, April 1882.

Chapter 21
Young, Brigham. *Deseret News*, November 28, 1855.

Chapter 22
Kimball, Heber C. Excerpt from sermon delivered in Great Salt Lake City on July 26, 1857. *Journal of Discourses* 5:89, 95.

Chapter 23
Young, Brigham. Excerpt from a sermon delivered in Great Salt Lake City, September 13, 1857. *Journal of Discourses* 5:227, 230.

Chapter 24
Tanner, Mary Jane (1837-1890). "A Fragment." *Visions of Beauty: Pioneer Poetry and Art*, p. 36, International Society Daughters of Utah Pioneers Collection. Salt Lake City, Utah: Wasatch Marketing, 2005.

Chapter 25
Haight, Isaac C., (president of the Cedar City Stake of Zion). Excerpt from a sermon delivered September 6, 1857, recorded in the Cedar City Ward Records. Haight's sermon, inciting the Saints to violence, was given two days after the Fancher emigrant party

passed through Cedar City, headed for Mountain Meadows.

Chapter 26

Sessions, Gene A. Excerpts from sermons delivered by Jedediah M. Grant on March 12, 1854, and September 21, 1856. *Mormon Thunder: A Documentary History of Jedediah Morgan Grant.* Urbana: University of Illinois Press, 1982.

Chapter 27

Newman, John Henry (lyrics) and Dykes, John (music). "Light, Kindly Light." 1833 (lyrics) and 1865 (music).

Chapter 28

Madsen, Peter. *Peter Madsen Autobiography*, 28. J. Willard Marriott Digital Library, University of Utah.

Chapter 29

Wells, Emmeline Blanche (1828-1921). "Welcome to Spring," p. 54, *Musings and Memories*, 2nd edition. Salt Lake City, Utah: *The Deseret News*, 1915.

Chapter 30

Kelley, Hall J. *A Geographical Sketch of That Part of North America, Called Oregon*, 1830; and *A General Circular to All Persons of Good Character, Who Wish to Emigrate to the Oregon Territory*, 1831.

Nadene LeCheminant has degrees in history and art from Utah State University. As a university writer and magazine editor, she has been recognized with eight top-tier CASE writing awards, and as a public speaker she has provided communications strategies to national and regional nonprofit organizations.

Her love of the southern Utah desert—the backdrop for much of *The Gates of Eden*—was nurtured on a bare-bones survival trip, during which she walked several hundred miles across the Utah wilderness without a sleeping bag or tent.

LeCheminant lives in Salem, Oregon. This is her first novel.

For historical images and more information about the book,
visit www.NadeneLeCheminant.com.

CPSIA information can be obtained
at www.ICGtesting.com
Printed in the USA
FFHW021930270219
50708360-56112FF

9 780960 021505